THEIR VIRGIN SECRETARY

THEIR VIRGIN SECRETARY
Masters of Ménage, Book 6
Shayla Black and Lexi Blake

Published by Shayla Black and Lexi Blake
Copyright 2014 Black Oak Books LLC
Edited by Chloe Vale and Shayla Black
eBook ISBN: 978-1-939673-05-3

This is a work of fiction. Names, places, characters and incidents are the product of the author's imagination and are fictitious. Any resemblance to actual persons, living or dead, events or establishments is solely coincidental.

THEIR VIRGIN SECRETARY

Masters of Ménage
Book 6

Shayla Black and Lexi Blake

Bonus material and excerpts at the conclusion of this book.

Chapter One

Annabelle Wright sipped champagne and glanced at her best friend as she prepared for the "big day," a deep sense of déjà vu settling over her. "Haven't we done this before?"

At the last wedding Kinley Kohl had planned, she'd been kidnapped and whisked away to Alaska by three super-hot men. Luckily, they'd saved Kinley from her asshole of a fiancé who, it turned out, made his money by fencing blood diamonds and running other profitable scams while giving the FBI the finger. He also hadn't minded a little murder just for fun. The trio of guys who had taken Kinley before her nuptials had eventually made her their own, so being abducted had worked out well for her.

Kinley grinned as she fluffed out the veil she'd selected. "Oh, we've been here before. Hopefully, this wedding won't have the same drama as the last. Just in case, I tried to convince Dominic we needed extra security but he gave me *that* stare. You know, the Dom Dom stare."

Belle couldn't help but laugh. Dominic Anthony was part owner of Anthony Anders, one of the top security firms in the country. He was also a Dom in the D/s community. And yes, she'd seen that particular glare, the one meant to convey that Kinley better do what the Dom wanted—and quickly. Belle frequently glimpsed a very similar expression from Kellan Kent. When he turned his blue eyes on her, she ached to fall to her knees and fulfill his every demand. Unfortunately, *that* stare of Kellan's usually wasn't directed at her. "I think we're safe this time."

"Probably so," Kinley agreed with a peaceful sigh. "Everyone who hates me is enjoying a nice long stay in prison. I heard Becks got shanked. She still managed to live though. Oh, well, maybe next time."

Nearly being killed by her former fiancé and her sister had made Kinley a bit bloodthirsty. Belle couldn't blame her. She'd wanted their blood and misery, too, after she'd learned just how close they'd come to ending her best friend. Months later, the thought still made her shiver. But before the happy ending, Belle's first instinct had been to rush to Kinley's side and help in any way she could. Kellan had forbidden her.

You're not going anywhere, Belle. If you try, I'll tie you up and spank your ass so hard you'll never forget the feel of my hand on your skin. Eric, Tate, and I will handle this.

Even months later, his edict didn't make sense. Unlike Eric and Tate, Kell almost never took her to lunch or showed more than a passing interest in her.

When she'd asked why she couldn't help save her best friend from three abductors, he had frowned and turned away, heading for his computer. *Because I won't have you hurt, Belle. I'll protect you. Even from myself.*

She'd only thought she heard the last part since it had been muttered under his breath, but that moment had been a turning point. While Kellan thought that threatening her with a spanking was the worst thing he could do, Belle had been forced to face the truth: she didn't want to spend her whole life not knowing what it felt like to have Kellan's hands on her. Or Eric's. Or Tate's. But now it seemed like she would.

She forced the maudlin thoughts aside.

"Dallas has been good to you." A bit of sorrow crept into her voice. Since Kinley had moved in with Dominic and the Anders brothers, Law and Riley, she hadn't had a ton of time for her bestie. And now Kinley was pregnant. Though she wasn't showing yet, Belle knew Kinley would soon be engrossed in all things baby. It didn't help that she lived in Chicago and her position as Girl Friday at Baxter, Cohen, and Kent consumed all her time. Lately, she'd been thinking about changing that. She couldn't imagine not being around for Kinley's child.

Belle had simply thought she'd have one of her own by now. Or at least be planning to start her own family. But she wasn't even close.

"I miss you," Kinley said, pulling her in for a hug.

"I miss you, too," Belle admitted, teary-eyed. She really couldn't remember a time Kinley hadn't been her best friend. Even when they had attended different colleges and began their careers a few hundred miles apart, they'd always had each other. Now everything between them was...different. "I'm getting tired of missing you. Maybe I should move closer."

Kinley pulled back with a shake of her blond hair, her brows forming a concerned *V*. "Away from Chicago? Away from your men?"

Belle took another long sip of her cocktail and forced herself to swallow the bitter truth. "They aren't mine, Kinley. They never will be."

Kellan Kent, Eric Cohen, and Tate Baxter were gorgeous lawyers, but she worked for them. They were her bosses, not her lovers. Just because she harbored fantasies of them didn't mean they'd ever feel the same. In fact, after a solid year of working together, not one of them had made a pass. Belle doubted now they ever would. Apparently, her place was behind a desk, not in their arms.

She would have been happy with any one of them. Then she'd discovered they preferred to share women. That knowledge had given her libido one hell of a boost. Yes, she'd been shocked at first, but after some consideration, it had made an odd kind of sense. The three of them had become an unusual sort of family, each relying on the others for balance. She couldn't imagine one of them without the other two.

Sadly, while they shared women, they just didn't seem inclined to share her. Or even to touch her. The ache that terrible truth caused had become too much to bear. Tonight was her last-ditch attempt. She didn't know how to look better than this. If they weren't attracted to her tonight, then it was definitely over.

Kinley frowned. "I don't know about that. I see the way they watch you."

She'd seen it, too. Or rather she thought she'd seen it. When Kinley had been in danger and they'd feared she would get pulled into it, all three men had gone into über-protective caveman mode. She'd felt their eyes on her. That had given her hope. But as soon as the trouble had blown over, they'd gone back to treating her like a coworker. Clearly, they didn't want to lose a really efficient office assistant.

"You're reading too much into it," Belle insisted. "They're lazy. They don't want to have to hire someone else. You should see the intern they brought in. He's some judge's kid. He constantly says 'dude' and he likes his...ahem, herbal refreshments. I have no idea how that kid is going to get through law school."

"Don't change the subject. And stop fooling yourself." Kinley crossed back over to the small veil, fluffing it out again. "Why don't you talk to them and tell them what you need? Doms can't read your mind."

"I'm not in the lifestyle."

Kinley submitted to her three Doms in the bedroom. Since starting down the path, she'd become very vocal about the communication aspect of D/s.

"Besides, that isn't normal in vanilla dating. I should be able to pout like every other woman, then eat ice cream and play angry-girl music when I don't get my way."

"Brat." Kinley winked at her. "But I see through your

sarcasm. You're completely interested in their dominance. And I know you like them."

Like? She was pretty sure she was in love with them.

Kellan was the alpha male, all power and protection. He had everything under control and he always made her feel safe. Eric was the charmer, fit and funny and just really enjoyable to be around. She went to lunch or dinner with him often, and they talked about movies, sports, current events, and life. He was a sexy mix of athleticism and charisma. And then there was Tate. He believed he was the social outcast of the bunch, but Belle saw him as the brilliant nerd who'd turned into a smoking hottie. Half the time, she giggled at the outrageous things that came out of his mouth because he had no filter whatsoever. That also meant he tended to be the most honest. When he told her she looked beautiful, she believed him. The other half of the time she spent with him, he often floored her with his astonishing intelligence. His mind fascinated her as much as his body.

Apparently, all her feelings were one-sided.

"I don't think that's such a good idea, Kinley. They've had opportunities and passed them over. None of them are shy. If they were interested...I'd know it. Instead, I watch them date other women. It hurts." She would only admit that to her best friend. The ache in her chest had become a real, physical thing. "I don't think I can do it anymore. Seeing you so happy, knowing what life could be, I can't stay here in limbo, hoping and waiting. I need to move on."

Kinley took her hand, her fingers tangling with Belle's. "Do you want me to throw mud pies at them? It worked on Tommy Harte."

Belle laughed, remembering how Kinley had taken down the boy who'd made fun of her in fourth grade. But they weren't children anymore, and revenge wouldn't make those three lawyers love her. "It's a sweet offer, but like I said, I'm thinking it's time to move on. I'm not getting any younger."

She was twenty-six and had barely been kissed.

Kinley squeezed her hand, her eyes widening. "Are you still…?"

"A virgin?" Belle frowned, trying not to be embarrassed. She told herself she had no reason to be. Maybe it was weird to others. Most twenty-six year olds had a couple of lovers under their belt, but Belle was picky about everything. She'd once spent three months deciding on the right curtains to put over the tiny window in her bathroom. She wasn't about to take a lover just to keep others from laughing at her. That part of her life—or lack thereof—wasn't anyone's business.

"Don't you think I would have told you if I'd done the deed?" Belle asked. "Although I didn't get a phone call from you until weeks after you'd slept with your guys."

"I lost my virginity during a kidnapping. They took my phone or I swear I would have called you immediately." Kinley made a cooing call. "Come on, Gigi."

Kinley's Yorkie yipped a little and jumped from her comfy spot in Kinley's Prada tote. The dog tended to travel in whatever designer bag Kinley carried. The very pampered pooch stretched and yawned before jumping onto the ottoman and settling herself down. She didn't make a move as Kinley placed the tiny veil on her head.

That was one well-trained dog.

The sound of yipping floated through the door as it opened and Dominic Anthony walked in. He looked urbane with his artfully mussed inky hair and perfectly tailored tux, but the effect was somewhat ruined by the three wriggling puppies in his arms.

"Kinley, sweetheart, you know I love you and I want you to have a great day, but I'm going to kill the puppies now. I'll make it quick. They won't feel a thing."

"No, you won't! Those sweet babies are proof of Gigi and Butch's love."

"They're proof we should have gotten our damn dogs fixed. Number two pooped in my shoes. Three chewed up the curtains in the groom's room, so we're paying for that. And One ate a bar of soap, then yakked all over the place. Promise me our kids aren't going to be this destructive." He put the pups down and they immediately started darting all over the room, looking for mischief.

"No promises," Kinley said with a saucy smile. "You've got about seven months before the chaos begins. I can promise you I won't be having a litter, though. Just one for now. And I'll make sure he doesn't poop in your shoes. You know, it's really a sign of affection. They like your smell."

"Yeah? I don't like theirs," Dominic groused. "Now that they're weaned, it's time to find them happy homes." Placing a gentle hand on Kinley's stomach, he kissed her, then sighed. "And now I have to go clean my shoes. Damn it. Do not eat the flipping curtains again, Three. They're expensive."

As the puppy barked, Dominic shook his head and left.

Kinley and Gigi seemed utterly inured to the chaos around them. Belle watched as the pups continued exploring the room, nose first. "One, Two, and Three?"

"The guys won't let me name them because they think I'll want to keep them." She petted her dog softly. "Gigi's been fixed now so there won't be any more little four-legged surprises. But I'm going to find these three the best homes ever."

Belle hoped Kinley could work miracles. The poor little things wouldn't find anyone willing to take them on looks alone. They were a weird mix of Yorkie and whatever the hell Dominic's huge dog Butch was. In short, those were some fugly little pups.

But she had something in common with them. She was looking for a new home, too. Despite the fact that she'd settled into her Chicago apartment, somehow it just had never felt like home.

She thought again about the letter she'd received a month before. She'd been putting off addressing the issue because they'd had big cases to tackle at the firm. She couldn't leave her bosses in a lurch. Then she'd been too tired, too battered by recent rains, too afraid to give up today when they might come around tomorrow. She'd found just about every excuse to not rock the boat.

But watching Kinley with her husbands made Belle certain this boat needed to be rocked. She'd tried to drop anchor in Chicago…but clearly it was time to float elsewhere.

"Doesn't she make a beautiful bride?" Kinley held Gigi up and stared at her angular little canine face. The damn dog wore a wedding dress.

Belle loved Kinley, but sometimes, her bestie was completely insane. "Yep. Let's get this show on the road. There's an open bar at the other end of this wedding, right?"

Hopefully the reception wasn't all kibble.

"Of course." Kinley laughed. "I know a dog wedding is silly, but Dominic, Law, and Riley insisted on a quickie Vegas ceremony for us. They thought they could get out of a big party. Ha! I might be making an honest woman out of my Yorkie, but that reception is going to be all me. We've got a full bar, and those men will be dancing."

Belle had to hand it to her friend. Kinley knew how to get her way. "Well, I'll be there beside you."

They finished getting ready and gathered the dogs. Belle couldn't help but think that even the dog was getting married before her.

It was definitely time for a change.

* * * *

"We're at a damn dog wedding. We flew down from Chicago to see two freaking canines bark out their vows. Please tell me someone else sees how illogical this is." Tate Baxter shook his head as he looked at the happy "couple."

Gigi and Butch were seated in places of honor at the

elaborate reception, silver bowls in front of them. He often marveled at the crazy things people did for their pets. He'd never had one. Didn't see the rationale. When he wanted company, he walked into Eric's room. That had caused a few uncomfortable situations because he'd never seen any particular reason to knock first.

"It is," Eric agreed.

Tate sat back in his chair at the table he shared with his two friends, still shaking his head. "I put off prepping for an important case tonight to come to this event."

Well...sort of. The case was on his laptop, so he could just as easily do it on the plane ride home tomorrow, but that wasn't the point. He certainly hadn't come because he had any grand desire to see two dogs get hitched.

"Not exactly," Eric corrected. "You came for the same reason I did. We want to be wherever the hell Belle is. But hey, it ended up being the most entertaining wedding I can remember. The groom tried to hump the bride in the middle of the ceremony. And right in front of their three illegitimate kids," he joked. "And did you see that one of the puppies peed on the minister?"

Kellan set his beer on the pristine white tablecloth in front of him, shaking his head. "Don't fool yourself. This shindig wasn't about the dogs. Kinley is topping from the bottom in a big way. She wanted her grand wedding and this is how she got it. I would say she's earned one hell of a spanking, but Dominic's gone soft."

Tate fought hard not to roll his eyes. Kellan was a hard-ass. He took the whole Dom thing way too seriously, if anyone asked him. Which they didn't. And that was a mistake because he'd been smart enough to figure out that he liked to dominate a female sexually, but he needed a woman who took charge of him when he missed social cues or forgot to put on matching shoes—stuff like that. "Ease up. She's pregnant. They're being indulgent."

Law Anders was out on the dance floor with his wife,

swaying to the music and wearing a big smile as he rubbed himself against Kinley. Dance had been a mystery to Tate for years, until Eric had explained that it was really just an excuse for a guy to rub his penis all over a girl and not get slapped in the face. After that, Tate had totally seen the logic and understood why men bothered with dance. He really enjoyed it now.

As he glanced around, Tate looked for Belle, hoping for an opportunity to rub his penis all over her. Inside her would even be better. Whatever she'd allow.

One year, two months, and four days. Four hundred thirty days all totaled, but he hated to calculate their time together that way. It depressed him. Ten thousand three hundred twenty hours wasn't much better, considering that was how long he'd gone without sex. Because that was how long it had been since he'd first laid eyes on Annabelle Wright. She'd walked into his office with her resume in hand, and he'd just stared, dumbstruck. He didn't believe in love at first sight, but he'd found lust in that single glance. Oh, yeah. He'd taken one look at the goddess applying for a job and known exactly why he'd gone to the gym five times a week since he'd turned seventeen.

But love? He'd taken a whole week of consideration before deciding that he had fallen in love with Belle. After all, he was a careful man. He liked to think things through.

"Indulgence leads to chaos. Dominic is going to rue the day he let that sub run wild." Kellan frowned at Kinley.

Tate just swiveled his gaze toward the dance floor. "Who is that?"

Kellan's gaze shot straight to the dance floor and he scowled.

Belle danced with some overgrown ape whose smile seemed way too friendly. She looked gorgeous in her emerald cocktail dress. Its *V* neck and body-fitting lines showed off her every curve. She wasn't a tall woman, but those crazy-sexy black shoes she wore made her legs look deliciously long. Tate had no idea how women maintained their balance on those high, thin heels. He was pretty sure, however, they would look great wrapped around his neck.

The only thing he didn't like about the way Belle looked was the animated expression she turned up at the lug hanging on her. Then she laughed—a sound that always did strange things to his insides.

Eric slapped a big hand across his back. "Chill, buddy. That's Cole Lennox. He's a PI here in Dallas. We've used his company before. He's happily married. I don't think he's trying to mack on our girl."

Tate still didn't like it. "Why isn't he dancing with his own wife?"

He was rational enough to know that jealousy was a completely illogical response in this situation. Technically, Belle wasn't his. She'd never even gone on a real date with him. They'd had lunch exactly fifty-two times over the last year, but they'd mostly talked about work. He'd taken her to happy hour fifteen times, where she always ordered vodka tonics, Cîroc or Grey Goose with a half a twist of lime. They'd still talked about work. And the weather. None of that counted, though, because she'd treated him like a colleague, not a boyfriend. He hadn't kissed her or made his intentions clear, so he had no right to be jealous that Belle danced with another man. For once, he didn't care if he made less-than-perfect sense.

Kellan pointed to the other end of the floor. "He can't. His brother is dancing with her. They're twins and I've heard they share."

"Really?" Tate sat up and sent a challenging glance to Kell and Eric. "I'm seeing a pattern here. The Lennox twins married the same girl. Those three oil tycoons over there have one wife, and we all saw the trio of royal princes walk in with their bride. Hell, the whole board of Anthony Anders decided to marry the same woman. But it can't work for us? Explain that."

That was the argument Tate had heard from Eric and especially Kellan for the past year, ever since the night they'd sat around the office and each admitted they were crazy about their new secretary. Administrative Assistant. Office Manager. Belle had changed her title more than once. She took exception to the term secretary, but Tate thought it was kind of hot.

Kellan sighed, turning toward him. "Just because it works for other people doesn't mean it would work for the two of you."

"The two of us? Really? You're still going to play it that way?" Eric challenged. "Tell me you don't want her, too."

Kellan's eyes hooded. Tate had made an almost scientific study of his friends in an attempt to really understand them. Kellan had four major expressions that he used like masks. This particular one Tate had named "stubborn asshole." Kellan used it a lot.

"Of course I want her. I've never denied that. She's a beautiful woman, not to mention lovely, kind, and very smart. If I was interested in getting married again, I would be all over her. But I'm not, and I doubt she's the type of woman to have no-strings-attached sex."

"I want strings." Tate needed to make that brutally clear because his partners seemed to constantly forget. They should take notes during their conversations the way he often did. But again, no one asked his opinion. "I want to be tangled up in all her strings. She's the one. I get that what we want is unusual, though it really doesn't seem that way today. I swear the two dogs are the only non-ménage relationship here. Belle might be surprised that we all want her, but she's not going to be shocked. She's fine with Kinley's marriage."

Eric sighed. "Maybe, but we need to be careful. She hasn't dated anyone since she started working with us."

Tate knew that very well since he'd been keeping an eye on her. Hopefully she never knew the extent of his observation because what he'd done was somewhat illegal.

And possibly a little stalkerish.

"There's some reason for that," Eric went on.

Didn't they get it? "Because she's waiting for us to make a move."

"Or she's just working hard and isn't ready to settle down," Kellan pointed out. "She's young, man."

"It's not like we're old."

At least Tate didn't feel old. He was thirty-two. Given that the average life expectancy of an American male was seventy-six, that didn't sound old. Then he did the math and realized that he was forty-two percent of the way through his accepted life expectancy. Forty-two percent—closing in on half. When he looked at it that way, he did feel old. He refused to waste another second.

"That's it." Tate stood and straightened his tie. "I'm going in."

God, he hoped he looked halfway decent because he often got rumpled and didn't notice. He would probably still be wearing pocket protectors if he hadn't become good friends with Eric in high school.

He'd tutored the jock through Algebra II, and Eric had taught him that jeans weren't supposed to hit above the ankles. They'd been a weird duo, the jock and the nerd. But their relationship meant more to him than any other. His parents were cold intellectuals who had told him he'd failed by not going into academic pursuits—because yeah, Harvard law had been a breeze. His brothers cared more about their experiments than family. So Tate and Eric had stuck together like blood, and Kellan had joined them after college to form the tight-knit trio.

But Tate realized now that he needed more. He needed Belle. So did they, but if they had their heads too far up their asses… Well, she had to come first. "I'm going to do it. I'm going to offer her my penis."

Eric's head hit the table and he groaned. "Dude, how do you ever get laid?"

So he wasn't smooth. At least he was honest. "She already has my heart. I would like for her to take my penis, too. Is that so much to ask?"

"If you ask her like that, she'll smack you," Kellan pointed out.

Frustration welled. He sat back down. "Damn it, that's why we need to go after her as a pack. I'm not good at the smooth stuff."

"By smooth stuff, he means any type of actual communication with a woman." Eric rolled his eyes.

They were totally missing the point. "I communicate fine. She'll know what I want and how I want it."

"Which is precisely why she'll know where she wants to slap you next." Kellan shook his head. "This might be a bad idea, but it couldn't hurt for you to dance with her. Can you do that without asking her to take your penis in marriage?"

He wasn't completely sure. His cock had a mind of its own. "I'll try to handle it."

"Good. Go on, then. I'll talk to Eric." Kell sighed. "I guess we really do need to figure out how to handle her. I can't stand the thought of another uncomfortable plane trip back. She didn't talk to me the whole flight down. The hands-off approach isn't working. I get the feeling she's just about ready to throw in the towel and leave us all." Kellan's eyes narrowed suddenly. "And that asshole isn't married. Go. Make sure he doesn't get his hands on Belle."

Tate's stare zipped to her. Sure enough, a guy was cutting in on Lennox. He leered down at Annabelle, then stared directly at her boobs.

Those boobs were his, damn it. At least he fully intended for those boobs to belong to him. Well, a third of them anyway. "You two work it out because I'm making a move by the end of the night, and if you leave this up to me, it could all go to hell."

He knew he was the social idiot of the group, but he was the only one completely honest with himself. Belle was the one for all three of them. She made him feel like the best version of himself, encouraged him to actually give a damn what other people thought, helped him put someone else above himself, and gave him no choice but to love her. Sure, the real world would think he, Eric, and Kell were freaks for loving the same woman, but the real world sucked. According to them, he'd been a freak most of his life. So what? They'd have their circle of friends, all of whom had a similar relationship with their own wives, to make them feel normal.

Either way, he wasn't going to let Belle slip through his fingers. He had a genius-level IQ, but he'd figured out something his parents and brothers hadn't: His intellect meant nothing if he didn't have people to care about, those who truly loved him in return. A Nobel Prize wouldn't keep him warm at night, wouldn't give him something to really live for.

But she could.

Tate stared at her for a moment, loving the way the light played on the coffee color of her skin. She smiled up at her dance partner, her expression lighting up the whole damn world.

She was his, and he was tired of waiting. It was time to really start his life and that meant it was time to claim her.

Fuck, he hoped he didn't step on her feet.

Chapter Two

Kellan watched Tate awkwardly take Belle into his arms, trying to find his rhythm. He couldn't dance for shit, but he sure tried. Belle didn't seem to mind his lumbering moves. She gave him a glowing smile and followed him with the grace of a woman who moved her body easily and well.

She would move that way in bed, reacting to her partner's every touch with sensual grace. She would follow him, letting him lead, allowing her Dom to take control of the situation to bring her maximum pleasure.

He would give just about anything to be that Dom.

"I can't hold him back much longer," Eric said, leaning over the table. "The truth is, I don't want to. I'm with Tate on this. It's time to figure out what's between us."

Kellan was pretty sure something strong connected them and Annabelle Wright. The invisible bond to her that tugged at him, even when he tried to sever the ties, was what he feared most.

He'd never wanted a woman the way he wanted her, not even his own ex-wife. That desire went far beyond the physical. He wanted the right to protect and own her, to be her best friend, lover, confidante, and rock. He wanted to know her inside and out. In short, he wanted to be her everything. Kell sighed. *Dumbass.* He knew his hard limits and marriage was one of them. He couldn't go there again.

The first time had been a disaster. No reason to think he'd gotten any better at it.

Belle deserved someone who could love her without hesitation and trust her with his whole heart. Kell had lost huge chunks of his over the years. She was sweet and brave, smart and funny. And loyal, he admitted. Everything he wanted in a woman. And he would never completely trust her through no fault of her own. She deserved better.

Eric watched his best friend dance. Kellan looked back at the big goof with a shake of his head. Tate towered over Belle by about a foot, his long arms wrapped around her petite frame. His size fourteen feet weren't exactly the most nimble or light, but somehow he and Belle looked good together. They looked right. Kell knew he should be happy for Tate and Eric—and he was—but watching them create their happily ever after was going to hurt.

Still, he loved them, so he'd step aside. Kell owed them that. They'd saved him, after all.

The three of them had gone to law school together. By then, Eric and Tate had already become a team, managing to seduce women left and right.

After graduation, Kell had married and thought he'd found his future. Then it had all come crashing down. Next thing Kellan knew, he fled DC only to find himself sleeping on Eric and Tate's craptastic couch in a bad part of Chicago. It hadn't been long before he'd begun teaching them how to truly run an office, because while they were great lawyers, they'd turned out to be lousy businessmen.

Kell had been relieved that he had something to offer them. In return for their friendship, for being the only people in the world willing to take him in when he'd been down, he gave them his acumen—and his undying loyalty.

Was he really going to watch them settle down with Belle and not join them?

"He thought about claiming her two weeks after she came to work for us, you know." Eric sat back, leaning negligently against his chair as he watched the dance floor. "He would have approached her with good intentions, but probably said something horrifically stupid that would have made her run. The only reason he didn't try? He was worried about you. He knew you liked her too, but he didn't want to do it wrong and embarrass you. He also knew you weren't ready."

"Oh, I doubt he waited for anyone but you." Tate was Eric's other half. Sometimes Kell worried he was just the extra guy, the one who refereed when necessary. Though seemingly opposites, Tate and Eric had an almost psychic connection Kell didn't completely understand.

Eric frowned his way. "Me? I've been ready. And trust me, he didn't put off going after Belle because he worried about embarrassing me. He does that all the time without caring how much I want to strangle him. But he looks up to you. He actually told me you were pretty smart."

Kellan snorted. Tate didn't think anyone was smart. "He was being sarcastic."

"He wasn't. Tate might be an ass sometimes, but he's honest. He knows damn well that you saved us."

Years ago, but Tate was a little like an elephant. He never forgot. "You put too much liquid cash in property. You didn't have a good billing or accounts receivable system in place. I just came in and managed the money better."

"You saved us. We thought we were the shit after we graduated. We were arrogant. You actually knew what to do."

He'd just adjusted a few processes and made some calls to bankers he knew to renegotiate some loans. Then he'd joined their business. "I didn't have a job and I wasn't going to find one in DC. I fixed the business problems as much for myself as the two of you."

"We're a team." Eric put a hand on his arm, a familiar gesture he'd come to view as actual affection. "We worked together then. We'll work together now. I know you probably never thought you'd end up in a ménage relationship, but look around you. It can work. God, man, especially for you."

"Why the fuck do you say that?"

Eric didn't back down. It was one of the reasons they'd stayed friends. Eric saw through his bullshit and didn't allow Kell to shove him away. "Because if you're left alone, you'll die that way. You might have sex but you'll never really let a woman in."

That was nothing he didn't already know. "You guys want Belle. I respect that. But I don't have any interest in settling down."

He'd been there. Done that. Gotten his soul ripped out of his body and pissed on.

"I don't think you'll give any relationship enough time to grow without us. But if Tate and I handle the heavy lifting in the beginning, you might soften up enough to realize that not every woman is like your ex-wife. You don't have to commit now. Tate and I will take care of her until you're ready."

Eric was offering him the keys to the kingdom. Sex with the woman he was crazy about—and without a shred of responsibility so he wouldn't get too close. That way, she couldn't break his heart. What more could he want?

He looked out over the dance floor in time to see her turn his way. She laughed at something Tate said. God, her vibrancy made her the most beautiful woman in the room. Her lips curled up and her eyes sparkled. Her goodness came from within. Everything about her compelled him to watch her. Belle enjoyed life in a way he never had. He might have grown up with every privilege imaginable, but he didn't think he'd ever smiled in sheer joy the way she did.

Tate looked down at her and the fucker beamed. He was a first class, hard-core nerd who dissected every situation and never spared anyone's feelings. But the man practically melted when Belle was near. Since she had walked into their lives, she'd suggested that Tate stop studying everything to death and just enjoy life. The transformation hadn't been overnight, but after a little coaching from Belle and a whole lot of conscious thought, he had relaxed until he'd become almost human.

A year ago, Eric had worked every waking hour. Belle had urged him to jettison his father's mentality that being anything less than number one simply made him a loser. She'd helped him forgive himself for almost failing shortly after he and Tate had opened the practice. After a few months of listening to her, the weight slowly lifted from his shoulders. Now, he even took an occasional vacation day.

They had every reason to love Annabelle.

She said something to Tate that had him laughing. Then he wrapped her hand in his and led her off the dance floor as the music faded. Someone gently tapped a fork against a wine glass to get the crowd's attention.

As the pair approached, Eric leaned over to Kell with a whisper. "All I'm saying is you're welcome to join us. You helped us out when we were in trouble, man. Let us help you. Tate and I will handle everything. We'll move her into our place. All you have to do for now is be kind and show up for sex."

Their place was a big two story that looked ready for kids and a wife and all that suburban shit Kell had given up on long ago. They'd invited him to stay in one of the empty bedrooms, but he needed his own space.

Hell, that was what he'd told himself. The reality was he didn't want to rattle around that big house with all its silent promises mocking him. Backyard barbecues, family dinners, and rug rats playing. Eric and Tate headed toward a destination he couldn't handle. It would benefit everyone if he kept himself apart.

But what if he could have some stolen nights with her? Not alone, of course. He would utterly respect their claim on her. After all, they would take care of her financially, mentally, emotionally. He would just be the one who brought her momentary pleasure.

Belle sank down into the chair next to him. She'd sat at the table of honor during dinner, but as soon as the dancing had begun, she'd returned to them. "Come on, guys. It looks like Kinley is going to play this to the hilt. Pray she doesn't ask me to toast the bride and groom. I have no idea what I'll say."

But she would come up with something. Hell, if Kinley asked her to serenade the dogs, Belle would get up and belt out a tune because she was fearless.

"Before we get to more dancing, I wanted to invite the maid of honor up to say a few words about the bride and groom and their beautiful love for one another." Kinley nodded toward their table.

The bride was asleep, curled up on her chair. The groom was scratching his ear as he looked out over the room.

Belle sighed, but rose to her feet. "All right, then. My friend is insane and I'm going to talk about dog love. Just another day in my off-kilter life."

He watched as Belle crossed the room to Kinley and took the microphone. "Love comes in many forms. Gigi and Butch…"

She continued on, talking about adoration, respect, and commitment.

"Tate is right. I think we should go in." Eric asked. "What do you say?"

"Are you serious?" When he nodded, Tate's eyes widened. "Thank god. I got on the dance floor and we started talking. I couldn't think of anything to say except how much I admired the symmetry of her face. I gave her percentages as proof of how symmetrical her face is because I extrapolated measurements from her pictures. It was either that or offering her my penis."

Eric sighed long and hard. "It will be a miracle if she says yes."

Kell silently agreed. But if she did, he might have a

couple of nights of happiness. His friends would cocoon her in their protection and care. They would make sure he didn't hurt Belle. "All right. If we're going to approach her, we'll need to formulate a game plan soon. No more percentages or numbers, Tate. We play this smooth and easy. She won't know what hit her."

* * * *

Eric stared down at Belle two hours later, wishing they'd had a chance to plot her takedown and wondering why the hell they had wasted so much time. As they swayed to the music, she sighed softly and rested her head on his shoulder. She felt so perfect in his arms.

Of course, he thought everything about her was perfect, so it shouldn't surprise him. What also felt right was the fact that his two best friends were waiting in the wings to continue the seduction. Well, Kellan was. He was pretty sure Tate was still planning on offering her his junk in a weirdly formal speech that would make Eric cringe.

Thankfully, Belle knew Tate well. She would probably just laugh.

"She's trying to get me to take one of those fugly puppies." Wrinkling her nose, Belle glanced back toward the main table.

Eric had seen the aforementioned creatures. Those three little things had been wreaking havoc all evening long. The Anders brothers had been trying desperately to contain and control them, but those puppies had been romping everywhere, yipping and chewing on a disturbing mix of drapes, buffet food, and shoes anyone had kicked off in favor of dancing. "Just tell her no."

Belle frowned. "It's hard to say no to Kinley. And it's not like I have a crazy, full life. Maybe I should think about a pet."

She didn't need to think about anything except that she'd

26

soon have three lovers who would require most of her attention. He fully intended to have her moved into the house he shared with Tate within the week—hopefully minus a rambunctious critter. "Later, maybe. Right now, you need to think about something more important."

Her gorgeous dark eyes widened. "Like what?"

Eric drew in a bracing breath. It was time to see if he could lead the witness where he wanted her to go. "It means you should think about your future, Belle. What do you really want out of life?"

Even as she moved against him, he could see her contemplating his words. "I've been giving this some thought, actually."

That encouraged him. "Yeah?"

"Well, since you've read my resume, you know I went to the Pratt Institute in Brooklyn for interior design. Lately, I've been thinking about using what I know."

Her words threw him for a loop. What did design have to do with her love life? "You're talking about decorating?"

Yes, he'd known from the minute she walked into the offices of Baxter, Cohen, and Kent that she wouldn't be happy as their administrative assistant forever, but he'd thought she would stay a little longer. And he'd definitely thought that tonight, after the wedding—even if it was a doggie union—that she'd have romance on her mind.

"Yes. I've always loved designing homes especially. Even when I was a kid and we were living in a two-bedroom apartment, just my mom and me, I thought about all the ways I could make it pretty. People are happier when their surroundings are efficient and lovely. I really enjoy listening to the client's problems with a space, then making it both more functional and elegant."

He'd known she'd gone to the Pratt Institute and gotten a bachelor of arts, but he'd never asked what her concentration was in. He'd been too busy looking at her boobs to ask. Now that burned him. She was gorgeous and so genuine it hurt sometimes. He should know more about her—wants, past, dreams, and desires. He would bet Tate knew everything down to the last detail. "How old were you when your dad died?"

Her expression didn't change at all. "Eleven. I wish I remembered more about him. My mom was the housekeeper for the Kohl family."

Kinley's parents. He'd known that Annabelle had grown up with the Kohl family in their brownstone on the Upper East Side of Manhattan. She'd seen the good life, but hadn't really been a part of it because she'd lived in the servant quarters. "Is that how you became such good friends?"

It was obvious, but he would ask any question if it kept her in his arms.

She nodded. "We grew up together. Despite her family's money, they sent her to public school, too. We often had the same classes, but no one could keep us apart after school. My mom would make us both snacks while we did our homework together."

She wore such a wistful expression.

"Why did you leave New York?" He frowned.

"I got a job at a design firm here in Chicago, but it went under a month after I hired on. I was stranded without any money. I could barely afford my crap apartment and I had a hundred thousand dollars in college loans to repay. I thought about moving back to Manhattan, but I just couldn't go back a failure. So I started looking for other jobs. I was the assistant to a CEO for a while and learned the administrative function before I had to leave."

Yes, he'd wondered about the very short assignment listed on her resume. He had his suspicions about how it had ended. "Had to leave? Why?"

"My boss decided that my job should be more…intimate."

Was she saying what he thought she was? "Come again."

28

Annabelle sighed. "He chased me around his desk and told me I should do more of my job on my back with my legs spread."

So the asshat had sexually harassed her, just as he'd suspected. *Fuck. Fuck. Fuck.* Anger raged through Eric. Yet wasn't that pretty much what he'd been planning on asking of Belle? Though he hadn't imagined having to chase her. He'd hoped she would simply want to spread her legs for him.

Well, hell. Now what?

"That's a scary look." But Belle didn't appear even a bit afraid as she searched his face. Then her lips curved up in a smile. "Wow, it's always the quiet ones."

Eric recoiled. Had she guessed what he was thinking? "I'm not the quiet one."

Sometimes he was the only guy in the office who would talk. When Tate got obsessive and Kellan started to brood, Eric had to find the right welcoming or soothing words for their clients.

"Sure you are. Oh, you might be talkative and social, but you hide more. Kellan growls at the world, and while the lion won't tell me how he got that thorn in his paw, it's obvious he's wounded. And without any sort of filter, Tate doesn't have the faintest clue how to hide what he's feeling. But you…" She studied him, wearing an almost quizzical expression. "You're the one I can't quite pin down."

Tate was better at hiding his feelings than she gave him credit for since she hadn't yet figured out how crazy he was about her. Eric hoped she didn't before she was in too deep to be freaked out by Tate's personal brand of interest. "I'm an open book, sweetheart."

"Really? Then why did you just go all caveman on me?"

"Caveman? I'm dancing like Astaire. I didn't grunt or growl a word."

"Maybe not, but you looked ready to kill someone. I've never seen you like that. You're usually smooth as silk, even when you're angry."

Because he'd been very careful around her. "I didn't like the thought of some old letch trying to use his position to get you into bed."

Kellan had a million and one reasons of his own and Tate wouldn't know how to verbally seduce even a hooker out of her clothes, but Eric was nervous about the whole "boss" thing. He'd never admitted it, but that was one reason he hadn't made a move, along with the Tate factor…and what she'd likely see as a "ménage surprise." Despite those multitude of reasons not to go after her, Eric saw only one real reason he should—because he couldn't stand the thought of never knowing what it meant to make love to her.

"Well, I found you guys, and now I don't have anything to worry about. You don't need to bang the secretary. You've already worked your way through half of Chicago's female population."

Was that bitterness he detected? She'd had a couple of glasses of wine. Belle was always in control, so polished and smooth.

Eric managed to chuckle. "Certainly, it's not anywhere close to half."

She shrugged with a little roll of her eyes. "It doesn't matter. When did you and Tate start sharing your girlfriends?"

It was the first time she'd acknowledged that she knew they took women together. Maybe the ménage wouldn't be a surprise after all. Had she guessed…or paid attention? Eric wasn't sure. Belle had asked the question without a hint of disdain, sounding simply like one friend asking another about a curiosity.

Hope started to thrum through his system. He was good at reading body language, seeing past simple words to the hidden meaning beneath. Unlike Tate, most human beings didn't just throw themselves out there. They talked their way around a problem. They asked questions—just like Belle did.

"We were in high school."

"Are you serious? Gosh, in high school I was worrying about finals and whether or not I would get asked to the prom."

He wondered if he would have been smart enough to have seen her back then. Probably not. He'd been pretty damn dumb. He hadn't cared past the next game, the next party, the next lay. "Well, I didn't worry enough about finals, which is why I ended up meeting Tate."

"I would have thought you came from different social circles."

"Completely. Tate's mom and dad were both academics, professors at the nearby university. His brothers were all into science. I was a dumb jock. My dad drove a truck. My mom was a waitress. All I wanted was to be a quarterback in the NFL." It seemed funny now. He'd come so far from the narrow path that had once seemed like his only way out of the lower-middle class existence he'd loathed. His dad had coached him to want it more than anything.

She shook her head as though she couldn't imagine it. "What happened?"

"Algebra II. I got benched because I was flunking math the fall semester of my junior year. My mom was actually happy because I'd had my second concussion that season." He could still hear his parents arguing as they'd stood in his hospital room. His mom had insisted that he quit football then and there, and his father asked what the hell else his son was good for.

The point had become moot when his Algebra II grade had dipped below passing and he'd been temporarily benched. In need of a tutor, he'd met Tate, a dweeb of the highest order. For whatever reason, something between them had clicked, and they'd fallen into a friendship that had shaped the rest of his life.

"Did you pass?" She sent a curious little smile his way that almost looked flirty.

He would never forget the way it felt when Mr. Zimmer had passed him that final exam. "Ended up with a B. I went on to take calculus. I switched from the normal track to honors classes and I went to college on a scholarship. I thank Tate for that. He taught me that I was smart."

"And what did you teach him'?"

"That he was more than the sum of his knowledge." He'd been Tate's first real friend. "His parents hate me to this day because they believe I swayed him to the dark side—in other words, girls."

"Did you?" Annabelle looked amused.

"No. Tate was always interested in females. He just didn't think he had a shot. I helped him improve his chances."

"By sharing girls with him?"

"Not at first. To begin, we started working out together after school. I taught him how to dress. I still haven't been able to impart any level of smooth talk to him, but it's cool. I'm not sure I'd know what to do with a Tate who didn't shove his foot in his mouth three times a day."

"I like how honest he is." She swayed as the music changed to a slower beat. "I can always trust what he says because he can't be bothered to lie. Of course it also means that when I ask him if I look fat in a pair of jeans, I get a percentage. He told me I only looked three percent larger and then went on to explain how the cut of the jeans slightly added to the visual footage. I didn't understand his calculation, but I stopped buying boot cut jeans anyway."

That was Tate in a nutshell. "He didn't mean to make you feel bad."

"He didn't. He also said that given my relative dimensions, such a low percentage of change in perceptive body mass did not diminish my attractiveness."

Eric couldn't help but laugh. That was how Tate would tell a woman he thought she was hot.

He caught sight of his friend, who stood just off the

dance floor, obviously watching them and waiting. Would Belle be shocked by what they wanted?

"I'm glad everything worked out for you two. It's just not working as well for me. I think I might go back to design." She said the words so quietly he strained to hear her.

"What do you mean? On the side?" She already worked pretty late hours. If they were in the office, she tended to stay, too. He wasn't sure how she would work in a hobby.

"No. I'm thinking about making a change. I guess I should warn you guys. This just isn't what I wanted to do with my life. It's not that I don't like my job, and you all are great, but I need something more. I watch you, Kell, and Tate. You have purpose. You're doing what feeds your soul. I need to find that something for me."

He had to force himself not to stop in the middle of the dance floor. "You're telling me you're quitting?"

That wasn't supposed to happen. Eric tried not to panic. They needed her close. Nothing would work if they didn't see her daily. Now, he might not see her at all.

How the hell had this happened?

"No, I'm not quitting. I mean, not yet. I need to find the courage to find another design job or go out on my own. Wow, I just realized how mercenary I sounded. I'm not trying to use you. Like I said, I like all three of you. I just need a career I love." She was the one who stopped, her feet seeming to plant on the floor beneath her. Her gorgeous face twisted in regret. "I shouldn't have said anything. This whole wedding has me throwing myself a pity party. Please don't fire me."

He felt like he'd been tossed into the middle of a hurricane. One minute she was quitting, and the next he was going to fire her? He felt his control slip. Crap, he had to get himself together. He couldn't rely on hotheaded Kellan. And Tate wouldn't know the words "emotional control" if they whacked him in the face. Somewhere in the back of his head, Eric knew they were all in trouble if he lost it, but he couldn't seem to help himself.

"Why the hell would I fire you?"

She shook her head and spoke slowly, as though she realized he was struggling to keep up with her. "Because I just told you I'm going to quit eventually. You might think it's a better move to replace me now."

"I have zero interest in replacing you. But I'm shocked we're not making you happy. I thought we were." They took care of her in every way she'd let them. They made sure she got home safely at night. Under the guise of Tate's curiosity about combustion engines, they'd gotten a mechanic to fix everything on her old clunker because they couldn't figure out a way to con her into accepting a new car from them.

"It's not you," she assured softly. "This just isn't what I wanted to do with my life. For a lot of reasons, I just…I don't think I can ever be truly fulfilled in this situation."

Anger began to rattle through his system. They treated her like a freaking queen. She ruled the office. When Belle wanted to replace the coffee maker with a cappuccino machine because she liked an afternoon latte, they'd bought a machine that Starbucks would envy. She hadn't liked the carpet. Yep, two days later it was gone and they were out thousands of dollars on something she'd called Brazilian cherry. They'd even let her pick the floors.

"You think you'll find better bosses elsewhere? You want to take the chance that you'll be hired by another asshole who will chase you around his desk?" He suddenly itched for a fight.

Belle shook her head. "Honey, I wasn't talking about the work situation. I wasn't. You three are wonderful bosses. I couldn't ask for better." She reached out, cupping her fingers around his cheek. "You've got that eye twitch thing going. Take a deep breath and calm down."

When he got really angry, an annoying tic spasmed over his left eye. The fact she could see it only pissed him off more.

Belle soothed the pads of her fingers over it, her voice slowing and calming. "See, everyone thinks Kell is the angry one, but you hold so much inside. You're going to explode one day, Eric. I wish you would just let it out."

Just like that, his anger turned on a dime, morphing into something tender. She understood him. He needed that from her. Hell, he needed *her*. She calmed him. She fucking got him.

He reached up and caught her hand in his. "I don't want you to leave, Belle. I'll do pretty much anything to make you happy so you'll stay with us."

With her this close, he could feel the silky smoothness of her caramel skin, the warmth of her body, and he couldn't hold back.

"It's not just about the job, Eric. Yes, I want to be creative and use my degree, but I also want what you guys have," she admitted, her voice vulnerable. "A little family."

He took her by the shoulders and brought her as close as he dared. "You're a very important part of our family, Belle. We won't function without you."

God, he had spent the last year plotting how to make her the center of their lives, but now he could see how easily she'd already found her way there. If Belle left, they would be gutted.

She shook her head. "I can't be just the secretary, Eric. It hurts too much."

As soon as the words were out, she clasped her hand over her mouth with a gasp.

"What does that mean?" he demanded.

Belle stumbled back, just out of his reach. "Nothing. I've had too much to drink and I should shut up. It's time I go to bed and put this idiocy behind me. We have a meeting in the morning. I'll see you then."

She turned and headed toward the edge of the dance floor. Tate watched with a frown and pushed his way through the crowd.

"What the hell did you do?" Tate demanded, his voice rising. "You're supposed to be the smooth talker, but she was crying."

Kellan, thankfully, hadn't lumbered across the floor like an overgrown bear. Instead, he'd followed Belle.

Eric watched as she race-walked in her stilettos toward the ballroom doors, her hips moving in that assertive sway he knew so well. Fuck, even when she fled from him, she made him hard.

"Let's go." He urged Tate to follow Kellan.

They needed to move this confrontation somewhere private because his dance with Belle had proven it was past time to show her where she belonged. She thought she wasn't a member of this little family? By god, when he was done, Eric vowed she'd understand that she was the center of it. By morning, he'd make damn sure she had no more questions about quitting her job or starting some new family apart from them. If she wanted to go into design, she could damn well do it in their building. They would set up an office for her where she could be close to them all the time. But there was no fucking way he would let her go.

"Explain what just happened." Tate gestured to the hallway down which she'd just disappeared, Kellan following like a wolf stalking a particularly juicy bit of prey.

But they were a pack and they needed to take her down together.

"Come on. I'll fill you in on the way." Eric started toward the doors.

He felt Tate fall in beside him, just like he'd been doing since they were teenagers.

"It's time, isn't it?" A goofy-ass smile spread across his best friend's face.

To start their future with Belle? "Oh, yeah. It's time."

Chapter Three

Belle had to force herself to breathe. God, she'd just made a complete and utter fool of herself. What had she been thinking? She'd blamed the alcohol, but that was a lie. She'd had exactly two glasses of wine all night long. The liquor hadn't muddled her brain or turned her into an emotional mess. No, the wedding had done that. Not the canine vows, but watching Kinley with her men, the Lennox brothers with their shared wife, not to mention the close-knit James gang and the royals doting on their pretty bride. Seeing all the love in the room and realizing that none of it was for her had driven pain into her heart.

Her plan to snare their attention tonight had utterly failed. She'd chosen her clothes so carefully, selecting a dress she hoped played well against her cool skin tone and a cut that hugged her curves. Hoping they'd finally see her as a woman—their woman—she had bought a pair of black-and-white Pradas that set her budget back by months. She'd nearly succumbed to the urge to take Kinley's advice and tell them what she wanted, especially when she had been on the dance floor with Eric…but she'd lost her nerve. If they knew what she wanted, would they simply pity her or laugh outright?

As the evening had dragged on and several single beauties eyed her bosses, Belle hadn't been able to watch. She couldn't stand the thought of seeing them hook up for the night. No, she didn't think they'd noticed any other woman, much less tried to get anyone's attention, but men that hot didn't have to. Before the end of the party, some thin thing would wink their way, and the three of them would probably disappear with her. And Belle knew her heart would break.

She strode down the hall toward her room. She was stuck being something between a little sister and an employee to them. They'd never pretended to want more. They hadn't promised her a thing. She was going to owe Eric an apology in the morning. They were the best bosses anyone would have, but she'd complained. Not surprising that he'd misunderstood. He must think the worst of her, and she couldn't blame him. The thought only made her tears come harder.

"Where do you think you're going?"

Kellan. Even without turning around, she knew it. His voice stopped her in her tracks.

Belle couldn't look at him while she had tears in her eyes. Thank god for waterproof mascara, but he would still be able to tell she was crying. Without a doubt, that would raise questions. He'd bark them, and she didn't have the heart or the energy to answer.

"I'm tired, Kell," she said without facing him. "It's been a long day. I'm going to my room. I'll be ready for the meeting in the morning."

Please let him go away. Please. Please.

No such luck. He moved silently, but she felt the moment he entered her space. "Look at me."

It took everything she had not to obey him and turn around. When he used that voice on her, she wanted to so badly. In fact, when he spoke to her like that, she'd do just about anything to please him. Belle closed her eyes and dredged up the strength to refuse him. "Please, Kell. I just want to go to bed."

"What did Eric say to you? Turn around, look at me, and

tell me what happened so I can fix it."

Crap, he wouldn't go away. She should have known it. If she started down the hall, he would just follow her. He was a dog with a bone, especially when he got his inner Dom rolling. She should be happy she was dealing with him alone and not the whole trio. They were all lawyers and damn good at interrogation.

She took a long breath and prayed she didn't look as bad as she feared. Letting out a breath and trying to hide her defeated expression, she turned. Her heart fell when she saw Eric and Tate storming out of the ballroom in her direction. The doors shut behind them, muffling the music. The hallway fell something too close to silent.

"Tell me now what he said to you." Kellan scowled fiercely. His expression probably should have sent her running for cover, but she knew he would never hurt her physically. Emotionally, he was napalm.

"Nothing. Eric didn't do anything wrong. I'm just tired and cranky." She sighed and hoped she could escape this without fighting the three of them. Or them fighting each other. The guys were so close, but when they threw down, their arguments were legendary. "I'm the one who said something. Can we just let it lie?"

"She's going to quit." Eric took his place on one side of Kellan. Tate stood like a sentry at the other.

Kellan's gloriously blue eyes flared. "Quit?"

Tate shook his head and stepped forward. "Why would you do that? What did we do?"

Annabelle wished she'd never opened her big mouth. "It's nothing any of you did. I want to be an interior designer. It's what I studied in college, but I spoke too soon. I'm not quitting tomorrow. It's something I plan to do down the road. I just thought you all should know."

There. She could try to play it off as something eventual, not pressing. But now that it seemed obvious they were more concerned about her professionally than romantically, she'd have to leave soon.

"If that's the case, why are you crying?" Kellan thrust an arm out, stopping Tate from coming forward.

She wished she was one of those women who could turn her emotions on and off, but she'd never been good at hiding what she was feeling. Right now, that was a profound sadness that they would never be hers. "I just got emotional about the wedding."

"About the dog wedding?" Kellan asked, his voice flat.

"Yes, it was beautiful in its own way," she insisted, hoping he'd leave it be.

Kell held her stare, his eyes narrowing. "That's lie number one. I'll keep track, Belle, and you should expect punishment if you continue."

Punishment? As she sniffled past her surprise, she studied them. They stood around her in a semicircle, Kell in the middle, while Eric and Tate moved closer to flank her. All three men wore stern expressions, and she had a little flash of instinctive fear. Suddenly, she was struck by how alone she was with them and how big they loomed. She wasn't some petite pixie, but at the moment, these men made her feel like a rabbit surrounded by hungry lions.

What the hell was that stare about? She didn't know, but they damn sure weren't looking at her like she was some sort of wayward employee anymore.

She took a step back. "I just had too much to drink. You know how whiny girls can get when they're drunk."

Kellan shook his head. "That's lie number two. I watched you all night. You had exactly two glasses of Chardonnay and you ate all of your dinner. You also had several glasses of water. You're digging yourself a hole, love."

Belle tried to take a step back from the displeased Dom. Suddenly, Tate hovered behind her, cutting off her escape route. The heat of his body blanketed her, sending shivers up her spine. How had he sneaked around her without her noticing?

"That's more than enough in a two-hour period to counter the effects of alcohol," Tate added. "Given your body weight and normal intake of eight ounces a day, you shouldn't be feeling even a light buzz. I'm sure you're below the legal limit, so you're perfectly capable of speaking rationally and making decisions."

She had a glass of wine every night when she got home from work. Just one glass, but that was probably enough to ensure that two in one evening wouldn't have much of an effect on her. "How do you know what my normal intake is?"

He shrugged. "I think you mentioned it once or twice."

Tate never thought—he knew. Her earlier fear that they were indifferent faded, now morphing into confusion. How did Tate know her habits at home?

She turned back to Kellan. "You were too busy to keep tabs on me all night, so you don't really know what I drank."

"Wrong. I'm never too busy to watch you. I also tipped one of the waiters to keep an eye on you," Kellan explained without a bit of shame. "You had one glass with Kinley before the wedding and one during the reception. Everything else has been water."

They could have knocked her over with a feather. "You really did watch me."

"I do it all the time. You just don't notice. But I make sure you stay safe and out of trouble. I'll keep doing it. And you will not be allowed to quit," Kellan insisted.

Not allowed? She glared at Kell, then sent a sharp, questioning glance Eric's way. He alone hadn't given any indication that he spied on her. "And what about you? You been keeping track of who I talk to and dance with, maybe?"

The sexiest smile curled his lips up. "No, honey, that's Tate's thing. I've just been watching your ass. Have I ever told you how much I fucking love your ass? It looks amazing in that dress."

Belle dropped her jaw and couldn't seem to pick it up,

even as heat spiked through her. Had Eric really just said that? What the hell? Maybe she'd had way more to drink than she thought and this was some sort of alcoholic haze. She shook her head, too confused and emotional for this bizarre conversation.

"Every man in the damn room has been watching her ass," Tate complained.

"No, they weren't," she insisted. "None of you are making sense right now. Maybe you're the ones who had too much to drink. Let's just call it a night. I'll see you in the morning."

She turned and ran straight into Tate's massive body. He was right at six foot five, every inch of him pure muscle. She had to strain to look up at him.

"You think we're going to sit down over breakfast and have a company meeting on appropriate protocol when the secretary threatens to run away?" Tate challenged with a biting smile. "Maybe draft a flow chart?"

He looked younger than the other two, though she knew he'd been born just a few months after Eric. Somehow he managed to look both boyishly handsome and sexy as hell in his suit. For the longest time, she'd wondered what he looked like out of those tailored suits.

"Tate…" She sighed. "Can you let me pass?"

As an answer, he grabbed her shoulders to hold her captive. "Or I could write a manual. You know how much I like documentation. One of the first things I would do is prohibit that dress in public. Your breasts look gorgeous, by the way. All the men were looking at those, too. And the chick from the bar who plays for the other team. I know that should piss me off, too, but I find it oddly hot."

Belle rolled her eyes. She wasn't even sure what he was trying to say. "I'm not in the mood to fulfill your girl-on-girl fantasies, Tate. Good night."

She tried to walk past him and head for the elevators. Eric stepped in front of her, blocking her path. "Not quite yet.

The girl-on-girl thing isn't his biggest fantasy. That's taking you to bed, which I totally support if I can join in. But don't let him write a process manual on how to deal with you unless you want him to tell you what to wear. He's insanely possessive. Now me personally, I don't care how many men look at you as long as they don't fucking touch. That should be rule number one in the manual."

"And right under that, I'll make sure there's a section on proper discipline just for you." Kellan brushed against her, murmuring in her ear.

She shivered, totally surrounded by them, trapped. If she moved an inch in any direction, she would be pressing her body against one of them. Damn if that wasn't igniting her libido. "What game are you guys playing?"

She wished the question hadn't come out so breathy and sultry. She'd meant to convey disinterest or at least take the reins on this runaway conversation, but no. Inside, she was melting, her female parts threatening to take over and encouraging her to let her bosses do their worst. Belle tried to remind herself that she wanted a relationship with them, and if she let them simply take her to bed, it would likely only be for one night.

True, but at least then she'd know what it felt like to be in the middle of all that masculine beauty. She would experience for a short time what it meant to be theirs.

"We're done playing games, Belle," Tate vowed solemnly.

"Speak for yourself." Kellan's words rumbled low, his breath hot against her neck. How close was he? "I've got some games to play with her."

Dirty games. Sexy games. She knew what he meant—to dominate her. Again, not for more than a night, but at least she would know how the flat of Master Kellan's hand on her ass stung, the way that dark voice commanded her to do things she'd only ever fantasized about.

"I don't understand." Her mind raced. Her blood

hummed. She wanted this so badly, but she knew exactly what a one-night stand with them would mean. She would be devastated if she woke up in their bed tomorrow morning and they again treated her like a kid sister. After that, she wouldn't be able to work with them. "This has gotten out of hand and gone too far."

"It's going where it should have in the first place." Eric touched her first, just a brush of his hand on her shoulder. Nothing overwhelming, but she shivered at the heat flashing through her. "Straight to you with the three of us. We'll take it slow if you need, Belle. But we want you."

Really? They wanted *her*? After a year of almost no hint of any desire on their part, this revelation blew her mind. Unless seeing wedding guests group off to get it on had an effect on them too… She shook her head again. The alcohol might not have affected her judgment, but the arousal they coaxed from her damn sure had.

"We always have," Kellan said. "But you should know that I'll be a lousy boyfriend. I shudder at the word. I'm not built for the whole commitment thing, but I want you right now. I'll be good to you in bed."

Because some woman had damaged him. She was pretty sure it was his ex-wife, but she hadn't pried.

"Boyfriend?" Didn't they just want to sleep with her tonight?

"I'll be a good boyfriend, but I'll want a lot of sex," Tate said. "The average person has it one hundred three times a year, which is one point nine eight times per week. That's not enough."

"But we don't have to work that out tonight," Eric insisted, glaring at Tate. "Let us take you to bed and show you all the affection and pleasure we can offer you. We'll satisfy you so completely that you won't want to walk away tomorrow."

Belle heard the speech, but it didn't make any sense. "I don't think the question is whether I'll walk away. Isn't that what you usually do the morning after?"

Eric looked stunned. "You think this is just a fuck for us?"

Wasn't it? "I don't know. You tell me."

"We want a relationship." Tate's expression was so earnest, it stunned Annabelle. "The average male is age—"

"No numbers," Kell cut in. "You agreed."

Tate clapped his mouth shut for a moment, then apparently decided he had something else to say. "This is more than sex for me. Way more."

"Exactly," Eric added.

Amazing. She looked at Kell expectantly. If he didn't think he'd be much of a boyfriend, where did he stand on this relationship business?

"You're a remarkable woman," he murmured. "There's no way I could use and discard you."

"I don't understand." They'd kept their distance for over a year. "What changed?"

"In some ways, everything," Eric said. "But in other ways, nothing at all. We don't want to let you go, Belle. We've always wanted you, but what would you have done if we'd asked you out your first day at the office? Or the second? Or even a month after you'd come to work for us?"

She winced. Okay, so she'd been a bit scared of them in the beginning. After the way her last boss had treated her, who could blame her? The thought of working for three big, gorgeous men had terrified her. After they'd offered her the job, she'd thought of turning them down, but she'd desperately needed the income. She had been living paycheck to paycheck. Her mom didn't have extra funds to help her get back on her feet, and Belle refused to be a burden.

"I might have been a little…intimidated at first."

"A little? You wore turtlenecks in August." Tate's face softened. "We all knew you were scared of us, so we did our best to make you feel comfortable. We fell into a pattern of keeping our distance. You should know I wanted to offer you my penis the minute I saw you."

"Tate!" Eric barked at him.

She heard Kellan sigh, but Tate's ridiculous honesty broke the tension. Belle laughed at the mental image those words painted and relaxed into him, leaning on his big body for strength. She imagined Tate wrapping a red bow on his penis and gifting it to her like most men would a dozen roses. She giggled even more.

He bent and curled his thick arms around her tentatively, like he was terrified she would balk. He wasn't lying. The rapid beat of his heart gave his feelings away. This big, gorgeous, unbelievably gifted man wanted her. As he urged her against his body, he nestled close to her in a sweet hug, and she felt every inch of what he planned on offering her brush against her stomach.

Whoa. That was not some small penis. Tate was built on big lines—everywhere.

"I would miss you so much if you left, Belle. I understand you want a career that makes you happier, but please don't leave altogether." He sighed as if a profound worry had just settled on his shoulders.

Belle clutched him both to give him comfort and for her own strength. Despite his facts and percentages and sometimes slightly abrasive nature, he had a big heart. "I don't want to leave you guys. And you're right that I would have run. I was more afraid of my previous boss than I let on. I joke about it now, but he was aggressive."

"We sat down that week you first came to work for us and talked about your skittishness," Eric admitted. "We were all interested in you, but suspected that something or someone had you spooked. On top of that, we worried our lifestyle would be difficult to explain. You wouldn't be the first woman who didn't get it."

She couldn't imagine anyone turning them down. "You can't possibly have a problem finding dates."

Tate shook his head. "Dates, no. Relationships, absolutely. Most women don't want to deal with three men. You would think it's the demanding sex that would give them pause. But no. It's often the laundry. Accordingly, I began doing my own."

"You're determined to be an idiot, aren't you?" Kellan asked, shaking his head.

"He's fine." Belle had to defend Tate all the time. No, he wasn't smooth, but he meant well.

The laundry hadn't really occurred to her. But the sex had. Sex with all three of these men had been the cornerstone of her fantasies for a year. When she tried to picture the reality, however, she shied away. Could she even keep up with them? What would they say if they knew she was a virgin?

"Do you want this?" Eric's mouth descended to her shoulder, where the straps of her dress met warm flesh. Heat flashed through her when he ran his lips across her skin. "Us?"

Belle wanted them more than her next breath, but she felt pretty sure it was a bad idea. How could an office romance between four people really work? Kinley held such a relationship together, but they didn't sign her paychecks and all of her men were committed. In love. Was Kellan just planning on being around for the bedroom stuff? Would he ever want anything from her beyond a screw and some dictation? Was she about to become their favorite booty call?

On the other hand, did any of that matter when her whole body felt lit from the inside out with anticipation? When they were giving her a golden opportunity to have her first experience with the men she loved? She'd never felt this way, never had pure arousal running through her veins like the sweetest wine. Besides, if she turned them down tonight, would this opportunity ever come again? Or would this unprecedented honesty be smothered if they donned the polite, politically correct business masks they'd been wearing for over a year?

"I want this." Her voice shook.

"Then come up to our suite." Kellan stepped to her side and held out his hand, his blue eyes somehow full of pride and hot promises. "I know that took courage. Let us reward you."

A deep breath rattled through Belle's chest and she dredged up the courage to slide her fingers across the masculine heat of his callused palm. Finally they touched not as colleagues, but as lovers.

Belle squeezed his hand. Kellan wasn't a pampered boy who'd never done a lick of hard work in his life, and his hands proved it. They were big hands that could shelter and protect, hands that could offer such pleasure.

As he led her toward the elevator, Tate and Eric flanking them, peace washed through her. This was right. She was ready.

* * * *

Tate dragged in a long breath and briefly wondered if his cock could saw through his pants. Of course, it wouldn't happen. Physics made that outcome impossible, but his cock throbbed against the cotton of his boxers, insisting it wanted out—and inside Belle.

She'd said yes. He stepped into the small, elegantly decorated elevator and turned to watch her enter behind him. Eric put a hand out, making sure the door didn't close on her. Damn it. He should have done that. Sometimes social niceties eluded him, but he vowed to make a study of them because Belle deserved a gentleman.

In fact, she made him want to be a better man. He'd watched his parents push each other to publish more, to excel in their fields. The almost palpable jealousy between them had pervaded their home as though they'd bred competition into the walls. His mother and father had always been rivals of a sort, even taking small delight in the other's failure. They'd trained him to measure himself against his brothers and only be satisfied when he was on top.

Tate didn't want to compete with Belle. He wanted to make her happy and swore he'd do everything possible to make that happen. Still, doubt niggled. He wanted a future with her so badly. But what if he said the wrong thing? What if she didn't care for him the way she did Eric and Kell? Or what if all she wanted from him was sex? It wouldn't be the first time a female had slotted him in the awkward idiot category and shunned him once they climbed out of bed.

God, he hated feeling so vulnerable.

"Hey." Belle's voice brought him out of his thoughts as the elevator doors closed, cocooning the four of them alone.

Tate swallowed hard, nerves getting the best of him. "I'm not smooth, Belle." He couldn't give her what Eric and Kellan could. He stood a better chance at crafting an argument to win over the Supreme Court than being anything beyond a liability at a simple dinner party. He'd learned that his genius didn't buy him love.

She stared up at him, cupping his face in a way that made him feel adored. "I don't need smooth, babe. Will you kiss me? I'm nervous, but I think I'd be much calmer if you kissed me."

A happy shudder went through his body. She wanted him to put his lips on hers. Still, he hesitated. Should he have the first kiss? He'd shared women with his best friends before but nothing with this much gravity, nothing he'd intended to last. But Belle was the one.

Eric nodded his way, which set him at ease.

Kell stepped behind her with a wry smile. "I think we would all be a little less nervous if you kissed her, big guy. Let's see if you can do it without your penis poking out of your pants."

Crap, could everyone see his erection? On the other hand, if Eric and Kell didn't have massive hard-ons, Tate would eat his latest case file.

"I'll try," he joked. "No promises."

Then he turned his attention back to Belle, who looked up at him with both a radiant smile and a silent pleading on her delicate face. She wanted him to kiss her. Eric and Kell were okay with him claiming her lips first. If Tate had his way, they would share thousands of kisses during their lives together. But he still wanted their first to be special.

Cupping her cheeks in his hands, he lowered his mouth to the dusky peach pout of her lips, losing himself in their softness as he poured every ounce of longing he felt into that kiss. The minute his mouth fused to hers, rightness pounded his brain, seared through his body.

Belle responded instantly, both with him and there for him. She kissed with her whole being, giving him a soft little moan and leaning into him like he was a lifeline. His self-consciousness melted away. Suddenly, he didn't feel awkward trying to express his feelings because he didn't have to talk. He could simply show her with his mouth and hands and cock. Yeah, he wasn't awkward with those.

Tate had practiced sex with the same vigor he'd put into his studies. After his first experience, his libido had skyrocketed, sure. But he'd applied himself because he'd been determined to be good in bed. Thanks to his decadent youth, sexual confidence wasn't a problem now. He planned to employ every bit of that knowledge to please Belle, to stroke her warm mocha skin and penetrate her sweet pussy until he gave her so much ecstasy she'd never want to leave. All the women in the past who had used him for sex no longer mattered. Only the woman he planned to spend the rest of his life with did.

He stroked his tongue over that plump bottom lip he loved. In fact, her lush mouth had incited more than one fantasy. Over and over, he'd imagined how she would look on her knees with those sensual lips parted and taking his cock deep. Even the thought incited him to urge her lips apart and demand entry. A spike of pure desire filled Tate's cock. He needed more of her. He'd waited over a year just to touch her. And damn it, if he was already forty-two percent of the way through his life expectancy, he refused to let another moment slip past before he claimed her.

Belle's mouth flowered under his. He breathed a sigh of relief at her utter welcome and kissed her deeper, clutching the back of her dress with his fists and dragging her against him. In turn, she wrapped her arms around his waist and tilted her head back, offering even more of her lips. He plunged back into the sweet heat of her mouth. Her velvet tongue stroked against his. Their dance during the reception had been slightly awkward, but this moment shimmered with sheer perfection.

Where he'd been cautious on the dance floor, he now took full possession. She followed his every move, conforming to him like a leaf in the wind. He repositioned her mouth for optimal penetration, brushing a hand down her spine and settling a palm against the small of her back to meld their hips together.

His cock pressed against her belly, urgent and hot. Tate worried she'd back away, but instead, she held him tighter and caressed her way up his shoulders, as though memorizing his every muscle. Then she found his hair. He wore it too short for her to sink her fingers into, but she curled them against his scalp—a silent plea for him to come even closer.

No way would he turn that down.

The kiss turned carnal. He stopped thinking as heat sizzled through his body and need took over.

With their mouths still crushed together, he lifted her against him. Even in heels, she was comparatively petite. He lifted her up with the ease of a man who worked out hard seven days a week. He backed her against the wall of the elevator and pressed his chest to hers.

"Do you know what I want to do to you?" He whispered the words against her lips as he notched his cock against her hot center.

"I have a good idea." Her voice trembled.

As he stared into the sincerity of her dark eyes, Tate had no doubt she wanted this. By the end of the night, he'd prove that her trust wasn't misplaced and that he would never let her go.

"I want to eat every bit of your pussy while you wrap your beautiful legs around my head. I've dreamed of tasting you so damn long and hard that I won't ever get the flavor of your arousal off my tongue."

She drew in a shocked little gasp, searching his gaze as if seeking the truth. "Y-you want to do *that* to me?"

"More than I want my next breath." He needed to make her understand how gorgeous she was. He'd seen her self-doubt at times. Was she attractive? Was she too curvy? Tate didn't want her to have any doubt that she was perfect.

"I want to do that, too." Eric hovered beside them, closing in, watching with hazel eyes.

Kellan stood at the door as it opened with a ding. "We all want it, Belle. We all want *you*. Pick her up, big guy. I'm worried you'll perform some act of public indecency in the middle of the hall if I don't herd you two into the suite. Control is going to be the word of the night."

Control, huh? Kell was far too in love with the word, but at least tonight he was right. Tate knew he'd need every ounce of it he possessed not to toss her up against a wall and fuck her. He wanted to give her everything he'd promised, all the pleasure he'd learned to bestow over the years.

Eric held the elevator door open as Kellan strode out, his keycard in hand to get the suite open so they could take their princess into the castle.

Tate swept Belle up into his arms, holding her against his chest and carrying her like a bride. He loved the weight of her in his arms and the way she clung to him. From now on, she didn't have to walk anywhere. He'd just carry her.

As they neared the threshold, Tate wanted to get one

thing straight. "Belle, what are you going to do with us tonight?"

He hoped she had the right answer. If not, that would suck because he didn't want her to remember this night for any reason except that it was their first together. But if she answered with "go to bed" or "fuck," Tate knew he'd be forced to stop everything and explain his expectations of their future more clearly, then let the chips fall.

Serenity made her glow as she settled into his arms as though having him carry her delighted her. "Make love."

That was the answer he'd been dying for. "Yes. We're going to make love. You'll see this can work. Everything will fall into place as long as we let it."

They could worry about her career later. He would give her all the encouragement he could as long she stayed close. They could even deal with changing residences if she lived with them. He and Eric had bought their current house with her in mind about six months back, but they could always sell it and find another if that made Belle happy.

He started down the hall, wearing a big smile. Tonight, everything would change. He and his friends would do whatever necessary to erase the memory of every other man from Belle's memory bank. After tonight, she'd have no more room in her head—or her heart—for any men except them.

Kellan held the doors to the suite open as Tate swept her inside. He didn't like the grim lines on Kell's face. Clearly, his pal was still worried, but that would change after this night, too. Belle and her giving nature would melt that sheet of ice around his heart. And he'd help however he could because she deserved the family she wanted.

It would work. It had to because Tate knew he would break if it didn't.

Chapter Four

Belle felt like she was floating in a haze of happiness. Tate carried her as if she weighed next to nothing, and that was so far from the truth. She hadn't been cradled like this since childhood. She reveled in the way he held her close, the embrace so warm and intimate. Maybe other women about to take on three strapping lovers would be worried. Belle wouldn't deny that she was a bit nervous, but they made her feel so safe—yet so desperate. Tate leveled a hot stare in her direction. Her breath caught. Then Eric looked her up and down, his hazel eyes undressing her without a word. Somehow, that stare made Belle feel naked. Her heart drummed. Finally, she cast a shy glance at Kell. His taut expression told her that he plotted to devastate her from head to toe and show absolutely no mercy. Arousal clawed through Annabelle unrelentingly.

"All right, love. Tate's had his turn. Now it's mine." Eric eased her from Tate's arms and into his.

Breath hitching, she settled against his lean strength, drawn as always to his sharply-cut golden hair and glittering hazel eyes, full of sexual promise. When they dropped to her chest and flared, she glanced down to find that her bodice had shifted and her breasts were almost exposed.

"Oh, I need to fix that." She reached for one of her straps.

Eric's hands tightened on her. "Don't you dare. We'll have you out of that dress shortly, so your modesty, while very sweet, is utterly unnecessary with us." And unwelcome from the sound of his voice. "You should be far more focused on all the pleasurably dirty things I plan to do to you. Want me to tell you all about it?"

Belle barely managed a shaky nod.

If he was anything like Tate, the next words out of his mouth would damn near set her on fire. She'd never guessed Tate could talk like that, but she felt as if she'd glimpsed a new side of him, one with a confidence he didn't often display. He'd taken over the minute his lips had touched hers—turning surprisingly commanding—and Belle hadn't wanted to do a thing beyond follow his lead. Now, she ached to know what Eric had in mind.

"Please."

A wicked smile curled his lips. "I want to strip you bare so you have nowhere to hide and I can take in every single inch of your gorgeous flesh. Then I'm going to touch and taste every part of it. I'll caress your shoulders, kiss your nape, run my tongue down your spine, suck your nipples, and lave your clit until you're crying out."

Wow. He and Tate had gone to the same school of seduction. All of that sounded wonderful…and a bit overwhelming since no man had ever done any of that to her. Just the mere suggestion had need bubbling under her skin, her nipples tightening, her clit aching.

"Why don't you start by kissing me?" She responded with a sultry tone of her own. She wasn't sure where it had come from—or the confidence that accompanied it. Maybe she was not only uncovering a new side to them, but they'd sparked one in her with their touch.

"My pleasure." Eric's lips found hers, teasing gently, a brush of heat and softness that left her wanting more.

He seemed to surround her as he kissed her, never pausing or faltering as he slid his fingers through her hair and pressed her body to his own. Belle opened for his onslaught and tasted a hint of the beer he'd had at the reception, along with a spicy, addicting tang. With a little moan, she opened to him and threw herself into the kiss, aroused by Kell's eyes on her, by Tate sidling up behind her to feather his lips up her nape.

God, she was melting.

Before she'd even finished the thought, all her bosses worked together to ease her to the floor. Eric didn't miss a beat. He covered her, steadying himself above her. As he plunged his tongue deep in a silky kiss, he reached under her skirt and brushed one warm palm up her thigh, to her hip. He parted her legs with a nudge of his own and rocked his erection right against that sensitive spot that had her gasping. Heat flashed from her lips all the way to her core.

"You look too pretty not to ravish, Annabelle," Kellan said over the roaring of her heart.

She was wet in a way she'd never imagined. She'd read about passion, knew the basics, but no man had ever taken her there before, ever made her feel so restless and needy and ready to beg.

"In fact, I think I'll start now. It's my turn," Kellan insisted.

As Eric raised his head with a growl, Belle gave a little shiver and glanced at the only one of her bosses who hadn't yet kissed her. Kellan impacted her like a sex bomb exploding all through her system. As unwilling as she was to end the addictive perfection of Eric's kiss, she was dying to know the flavor of Kell's mouth and every dirty desire he wanted to slake on her.

Eric brushed her hair back and planted a final kiss on her lips, his eyes seductive. "Don't be scared of the Dom there. He might want some things that seem strange at first, but they'll bring you pleasure in the end."

He'd mentioned discipline. That meant spanking or flogging or something mysteriously kinky she barely knew about. She risked another glance up at Kell.

He was six foot three inches of pure sin, from his conservatively cut dark hair, all the way to his stylish black Italian loafers. As he crouched beside her now, his shoulders loomed broad, his stare hot with demand. Annabelle swallowed hard. Kellan Kent had a body built for sex.

She noticed that he'd loosened his tie since entering the suite. A sexy five-o'clock shadow graced the sharp line of his jaw. Kellan's face was all planes and angles, making his beauty undeniable but predatory.

"Take off your clothes, Annabelle. Now. I want to see every inch of you. You'll present yourself to me. Do you understand? Is that command spelled out for you in those books you read when you think no one is looking?"

She felt herself flush. He knew what was on her tablet? "That's private."

Kellan's eyes flared, and she realized she'd just challenged the Dom. "Oh, no it's not. That tablet is company property, bought for you with my credit card, and I was beyond excited to find out that you used it to read erotica— and not just any erotica."

She read BDSM and ménage. And judging from the looks on their faces, they all knew it. Could they guess that when she read those books, she imagined that her bosses were the heroes and she was the lucky woman in the middle?

Belle rose unsteadily to her feet with their help. The men she worked for were obviously nosy bastards, and she made a mental note to put a passcode on everything.

"Answer me. Do you understand what I'm asking of you?" Kell barked.

In that moment, she was thankful for her books. "You want me to undress and present my naked body for your pleasure, Sir."

A look of deep satisfaction crossed his face. "That's exactly what I want, and we're going to sit back and watch you take off every stitch of clothing."

They were all watching her now. The three of them stood side by side. Having already ditched his suit coat, Eric worked at the buttons of his shirt, but he'd been an athlete all his life. She already knew how gorgeous he was going to be. Tate had stripped to the waist in the last few minutes and now shocked her as he showed off his jaw-droppingly muscled chest. His slacks rode low on his hips, showing off the notches there. He might have an amazing brain, but he obviously knew his way around a weight room. And Kell...she'd accidentally caught sight of him changing shirts in his office once, so she knew how gorgeous he was. Hell, those three men were practically Greek gods. Annabelle had always felt too big—big butt, big boobs, big dreams. Her mouth was a bit too sassy, her skin a shade too dark. What did they see in her?

"Stop thinking, Belle," Kellan commanded. "Focus on the orders you should obey and the Masters you should please." His voice went low, the very sound of seduction. "You don't have to worry about anything, love. We think you're beautiful."

"Yes," Tate agreed. "Show us."

"Let us see what we've been dreaming about for a year." Eric finally slipped out of his shirt, leaving her gaping at his perfect form—wide shoulders, hard pectorals, tapered waist, ridged abdomen.

They weren't stupid men. They must see her flaws. Shockingly, they didn't seem to care. She forced her fears aside. She'd let them rule her for too long, and that hadn't gotten her anywhere. The only path her anxiety had taken her down was a lonely one.

Belle reached around for the zipper of her dress, trying to grasp it between her fingers. Since she'd needed Kinley's help to get dressed, it shouldn't shock her that she couldn't quite reach.

Kellan slipped behind her. "Allow me."

She stood still, head bowed as he brushed her long hair

over her shoulder, her breath catching as he dragged the zipper down. Cool air caressed her back. A wave of heat seared her when Kellan brushed his palms across her skin, parting the dress, letting it slide from her torso and fall to her waist.

Eric and Tate stared. Their gazes sizzled her flesh, flared her need again. But Kell took his time exploring, his fingertips tracing her spine and down to the small of her back.

He leaned in, his breath playing on her skin. "You're so soft."

A shudder went through her. Belle closed her eyes and drowned in sensation. She felt soft—and vulnerable, yes, but so strong and ready. She let her head drift back to his shoulder, the masculine scent of his aftershave washing over her.

His fingers drifted up her back to play between her shoulder blades, along the curve of her spine. Thank god she'd thought to wear pretty lingerie. Usually she didn't notice or care what went on under her clothes as long as the undergarments were clean, but the lacy white bra she'd worn under her cocktail dress tonight had scalloped edges and demi-cups. Not that it seemed like she would be keeping it on for long.

She'd barely finished the thought before Kellan unhooked her bra with shocking efficiency. Belle caught the cups against her and shielded her breasts.

"Don't," Tate protested. "I want to see them, Belle."

"He'll be the easy one to deal with. I have no problem telling you that if you don't drop your hands, you'll find yourself over my knee," Kellan said.

"I'd pay to see that, baby." Eric shimmied out of his pants and socks, then stood before her in nothing but his boxers. His cock tented the cotton.

Belle tried not to gape—or let on that her mouth practically watered at the sight.

"Oh, you'll see it. She owes me for the lies earlier," Kellan explained. "But it's up to her just how red she wants her ass to be when we take her to bed. What's it going to be, Annabelle?"

She dropped the bra, baring her breasts to their gazes. A low ache simmered deep in her pussy, a new and wholly erotic feeling that made her so very aware that she was a woman.

"Everything else," Kellan commanded as he strode across the lavish suite and gracefully tossed his big body into one of the chairs, then looked back at her expectantly.

A king on his throne, waiting for his lover to reveal her treasures to him. The image was so clear in her head that she couldn't help but comply.

With shaking hands, she pushed the dress over her hips and let it slide to the floor. Her panties were the same gossamer white that had hugged her breasts—so much sexier than the underthings she normally wore. When she'd looked at herself while dressing, she'd liked the way the pale fabric made her skin gleam. She tried to let that memory bolster her confidence so she could stand before them in almost nothing.

"All of it, Belle."

She nearly cursed Kell for pushing her out of her comfort zone so quickly, but she didn't dare say it out loud. Besides, she already knew he wouldn't let her hide behind anything.

Still, Belle bit into her bottom lip and hesitated. No one had seen her naked in years. But what did she have to be ashamed of? She might not be a beauty queen or a movie star, and yes, she might have a few too many curves, but she wasn't atrocious.

The truth was, if she wanted to know what it meant to have their eyes all over her, what it felt like to have these three men pleasure her, then she had to get brave.

Drawing in a bracing breath, Belle eased her thumbs inside the waistband of her panties and pushed them off. As she fought off a quiver, she stood in front of them wearing nothing but her budget-busting shoes and an apprehensive smile.

Silence. Utter, terrifying silence. Well, what had she expected? Applause?

Finally, Eric swallowed thickly and took a step toward her. "God, you're more beautiful than I thought."

"So fucking gorgeous." Tate toed off his shoes and started in on his slacks. "I can't wait."

Only Kellan refrained from tearing off his clothes. Instead, he sat, watching her, dissecting her. "Come to me, love."

Annabelle heard the approval in his voice, saw warmth in his blue eyes, and she breathed a sigh of relief. Maybe this wasn't just a post-wedding hookup. Maybe this really meant something to them.

She cast a questioning glance at Eric and Tate, both of whom gestured her over to Kell. Yeah, she had absolutely no question about who was in charge. Still, she stood rooted.

The reality of the moment, the gravity, made her heart pound until it roared in her ears. Just walk across this suite totally naked in front of men who, up until tonight, had merely been her bosses? At her hesitation, Kellan raised a sharp brow. Guess the answer was yes. Clearly, he wasn't going to let her slide or give her the easy out. He managed to communicate that without a word.

She fidgeted. It would be so much easier for her if they would just pounce on her, but no. Kellan forced her to make the choice to approach him. Her implied yes obviously wouldn't do. Eric and Tate watched her with keen, unblinking stares, obviously on board with his plan.

Talk about being circled by sharks.

Kellan sat up and patted his lap, leaving Annabelle no doubt he meant to spank her. "I won't force this on you. If you prefer, I'll walk out and leave you to them. They'll fuck you senseless and give you pleasure. That might be enough for you, but I think you need something more. I think you crave the dominance I'm wired to give you." He shrugged casually, but Belle sensed he cared very much how she felt. "If you don't want to try, tell me now."

"If I did, you would be disappointed." The thought slipped out.

"Yes. That's perceptive." He nodded. "I think a power exchange would work well between us, but if you choose not to submit to me, I won't treat you any differently than I have for the past fourteen months."

There was only one answer in Belle's mind. She'd fantasized about this a million times. She couldn't imagine making love without all three of them. She hated to disappoint Kell. Despite all the pretty words and implied promises tonight, the future might not work out for the four of them, but they'd have no chance if she didn't give it her all now.

Taking in another fortifying breath, Annabelle crossed the room with a smile.

Something eased in Kell's eyes. "Excellent. I'm proud of your courage. Let's get your punishment out of the way so we can focus on making you feel good for the rest of the night." He sent her a little smirk. "Although I suspect you'll enjoy this, too. Over my lap." He took her hand and urged her down. "If you need to stop me tonight for any reason, just say the word and I will. Later, you'll have a safe word. We'll also have a contract. But tonight, we'll keep it light."

Annabelle frowned. She didn't like the idea of a contract with Kellan. She wanted to share her heart with him, not a legal document. But not only was he a Dom, he was also a lawyer. Both sides of him would insist on spelling out the terms, rights, and conditions of their relationship, including its ending, before it had barely begun. She suspected his ex-wife also had a lot to do with that. Kell would need a crystal-clear agreement between them to feel safe. The realization made her sad.

"Let me help you get in position." Tate raced to her side, his warm hand searing the small of her back. He glanced down at her butt. "God, Belle, look at that ass."

She winced. "I try not to."

As he smoothed his hand down one cheek, his eyes narrowed with desire. "Hmm. I won't be able to get it out of my head." He squeezed the plumpest curve, then stepped back with a sigh of regret. "Get the discipline over with, Kell. I want to put my mouth on her."

Desire pooled between her legs, making her feel shaky and overheated. She pressed a hand to her stomach as if that would calm the butterflies dancing inside. When it didn't, she tangled her fingers with Tate's for support and lowered herself over Kellan's lap.

Trying to perch over his thighs was nothing short of awkward. She shifted and rebalanced, seeking a comfortable position.

Kellan's big hand anchored her at the small of her back. "Stop wiggling."

Belle did her best to comply, stilling and breathing through every heartbeat, trying to clear her head of everything except giving him what he wanted. At least that's what the Doms wanted in the books she read.

When she calmed and stopped squirming, Kell rewarded her with a caress up her spine. Another hand joined his, this one on her outside hip, skating up to cup her ass. She suspected that belonged to Eric. Belle knew she'd guessed right when a third hand planted on her skin, palming her nape before long fingers tangled in her hair. Definitely Tate's.

Desire tore through her. They were all touching her at once, exploring her together. She'd wanted and waited, never imagining for a moment it would happen. But here she was, at their mercy.

She kind of hoped they didn't have much.

"Will you look at that?" Eric's voice broke the thick silence.

"I'm telling you, that is the juiciest ass I've ever seen," Tate said.

"Sustained," Eric quipped as he squeezed one of her cheeks. "This visual is all the evidence I need."

"Ah, do you smell that, gentlemen? Our sweet secretary is aroused." A wealth of satisfaction darkened Kellan's voice.

"Administrative assistant," she piped up, her belly and her breath tight.

She ran that office, damn it. Regardless of the fact she was draped over her boss's lap, her naked ass in the air, that didn't mean she had no professional pride. Her current job might not be her dream, but she did it well.

At that, the hands caressing her, except the one at the small of her back, lifted away. A moment later, she heard a whoosh she couldn't place. A sudden *smack* followed it. Then hot pain blasted across her right cheek and flared over the skin of her ass. Her breath fled. Her heart raced as Kellan held his hand on her.

"In the office, I'll call you whatever you like." His voice turned silky. "Hell, you keep the place functioning most of the time. But in the bedroom, you're our sweet little secretary."

His words revved her up. The independent woman in her said that she shouldn't like what Kell murmured, but no denying that he made her even wetter. Her emotions were all askew, running haywire. And now that the pain had passed, a burning tingle flared just under her skin. No, a deep arousal—hot, wicked, and addictive. "Yes."

Another *smack*. "Just yes? Think carefully."

Sensation blanketed her brain, muffling her thoughts. Belle tried not to lose herself in his touch, in her desire to feel his hand on her ass again. She had to focus. What was it he wanted?

"Sir. Yes, Sir," she blurted as soon as she figured it out.

"Much better." He smoothed his hand over her cheeks, distributing the heat and rewarding her—for the moment.

"Now, let's talk about lying. I don't like it and I won't tolerate it."

"I second that," Eric put in.

"Me, too," Tate added.

"There you go. I'm not talking about social situations. But Belle, we're not merely your friends. You can't blow us off with a polite excuse. We're about to become your lovers. If you lie to us, expect consequences. We need to know how you feel, when you're hurt or sad, scared or worried. You can't just smile away your emotions."

"They belong to us," Eric explained. "Like your body is about to."

"So, for lying to me in the hallway, I'm giving you a count of twenty. If I catch you lying again, I'll give you more. You will always tell us how you feel. Like now." Kell's expectation hung in the air between them.

She didn't even think about withholding or lying. The words just spilled out. The situation was so intimate there didn't seem to be room for anything but honesty. "Hot, achy, the tiniest bit scared."

"Perfect. Thank you for your honesty. We know you're nervous because this is our first time together. We'll make sure that you come to trust us."

"Yes, Sir," she breathed.

Three quick smacks had her moaning when the pain hit. The next two made her writhe as the ache deepened. He clearly meant business with those slaps, but the shocking sting morphed into something she found herself craving even more of.

After another five, they were halfway through the punishment. A haze of desire descended and she slowly lost herself in the rhythm of Kellan's discipline—the whack of his hand and his hard exhalation, followed by Eric's moan, Tate's groan, and her whimpering out the count before it started all over again.

Belle shook, on fire, desperate for more. She gripped his

leg, dug her nails into the wool of Kellan's pants. He drew in an audible breath, dragging in her scent again. She felt the thick line of his erection against her belly harden even more. Disciplining her really did something for him.

"How are you, love?" he asked.

Shaky, shocked, and so, so alive. "Good, Sir."

"Excellent. Keep counting."

"Hurry. As soon as you're done, I'm definitely offering her my penis." Tate sounded so completely earnest that Belle cracked a smile.

"I have no doubt," Eric drawled. "We all are."

Kellan ignored them and peppered five more quick slaps across her cheeks, branding the heat under her skin until she felt helpless and drowning in sensation. Completely needy.

"Can you take five more?" He didn't demand, but everything in his tone told Belle that he really hoped she could.

Happily. "Yes, Sir."

She closed her eyes, wanting to block out everything but the sound of his flesh striking hers, the feel of his hand rubbing the heat into her skin. She counted each time his palm stuck her bare backside. Belle savored each smack, delighting in the sting and the blaze that followed, settling into her pussy.

God, who would have guessed that she'd like it? Descriptions of spankings in books had always made her uncomfortably wet, but the reality... Belle sighed in contentment. The reality of this oddly sharp pleasure went far beyond anything her imagination could have conceived. He dissolved her into a shaking, aching mass.

Before she knew it, Kell delivered the last slap and ended the punishment. He stroked her heated bottom one final time, then eased her off his lap. He urged her to curl up against him for a blissful moment as he cuddled her. Pressing her cheek to his lapel, she reveled in the feel of his strong arms around her, his heartbeat against her ear. She even enjoyed the heat of her naked skin against his designer suit.

All too soon, he tipped her chin in his hand and lifted her face just under his. The masculine splendor of his sculpted lips hovered just over her own. "You did very well. Now that it's over, tell me...Can you handle me, Belle? I need this in a way the other two don't. I'll always want to discipline you. I'll always want to tie you down and have my way, but I promise I'll make it good for you. Did you enjoy that?"

"I did, Sir." Her throbbing backside was a memento of the intimacy they'd shared. But rather than the ache upsetting or angering her, the sensations settled under her skin and calmed her in some way she didn't quite understand.

"I want to know for myself." He dropped his hand on her knee, gently pulling them apart. "I need to feel exactly what I did to you."

That he needed anything from her moved Belle. She willingly parted her legs for him. Kellan was always shut down, so often distant, but in that moment, she felt close to him, shared the sort of bond with him she'd fantasized about.

His big hand slid between her legs, palm covering her pussy gently before his callused fingertips moved in a silky slide down her wet folds. As tingling erupted and her body broke out in goose bumps, Kell dipped to her opening and eased two fingers inside with a low male groan.

Her breath fled as his fingers thrust just inside her slick heat, teasing her with soft friction, taking her by tingling surprise. In seconds, Belle began to gasp and arched to him.

"How wet is she?" Tate dropped to one knee beside her and cupped her breast, skimming her nipple with his thumb and spreading the need.

"Soaking," Kellan replied, sounding mighty pleased. "Do you want to come, love?"

"Of course she does. And I want to watch her." Eric winked, standing over them.

Belle was relieved that Eric saved her the trouble of stating the obvious. She was pretty sure she had never truly climaxed before. She'd had little pleasures by her own hand, but nothing she'd done had ever felt half so good as what Kellan did to her right now.

Then his fingers slid over her clit and rubbed a slow circle. She stared up at him, stunned by the lush desire rolling through her body.

Kellan just smiled. "Let's hear you scream."

"I concur." Tate hovered over them, watching Kell's fingers with rapt, dark eyes.

"Amen, brother," Eric murmured, his hazel eyes glittering.

Kell's mouth descended on hers before she could reply with anything but a moan. She opened automatically. He kissed her hard and deep, possessing her as his tongue slid home in time with his fingers. The pressure built quickly, little lightning bolts of pleasure that jolted her system, making her shudder in his arms.

She tensed, her fever rising. It wasn't long before her skin felt too tight. Her breathing went choppy. She drowned in Kellan's scent and nearness as he drove her up high, where the flames licked her flesh, until the need compelled Belle to spread her legs wider. She tried to break the kiss, toss her head back—but he refused to allow that, instead keeping at her mouth with one hungry kiss after another until she whimpered. Desperation rose right along with sensation. She felt overcome, undone, turned inside out as pleasure converged and unraveled her. No matter how she fought to savor the delicious agony, she couldn't hold back.

As the orgasm burst over her, Kell tore his lips from hers. A long and throaty scream clawed from her chest as euphoric joy drugged her veins and pulsed down her nerve endings. In the aftermath, she panted, utterly dazed.

Yeah, she had been right. She'd never really come until now. They were probably damn proud of themselves for that ear-splitting shriek. No denying she'd loved what they'd given her.

"Beautiful," Kell murmured.

As she lay in his arms afterward, Belle felt that way. Finally, she understood why she'd never truly climaxed before. What he'd given her—with the silent support of Eric and Tate—had been more than pleasure. The sense of pure connection couldn't be pretended when she touched herself. It made everything they shared more beautiful and meaningful. It proved she belonged with them. She'd always been able to be herself around them at the office, but to know without a doubt that extended to even the most intimate situations… God, what a relief.

"I'm so glad I waited," she sighed up at him with a happy grin.

Belle couldn't imagine her first time with anyone except the three of them. Her heart was so full in that moment. They would make it far more meaningful than the simple act of bodies coming together. They would make it a moment that brought them all closer together. Something they would remember their whole lives.

Kellan stiffened. "Waited?"

His word hissed like the crack of a whip. She forced her eyes open. His forbidding frown seized her chest and squeezed hard.

"I'm not glad," Tate argued, gliding his hand down her body until he cupped her thigh. "We wasted a whole year."

"I don't think that's what she meant." Kellan arched a sharp brow her way. "Is it, Annabelle?"

Belle squirmed self-consciously. The sweet haze of desire dissipated, replaced with something cold. Eric looked stunned as he stared, jaw dropped. Tate merely appeared puzzled. He might not understand now, but once he did, he probably wouldn't like the truth any more than the other two.

In that instant, she tried to curl up and cover herself. Her nudity had seemed sexy earlier. Now she was keenly aware of her vulnerability. How had everything changed with one sentence? If they really cared about her and wanted her for more than the night, her virginity wouldn't disappoint them. How had she read the situation so wrong? Or had they misled her for a piece of ass? God, she felt so humiliated.

Tears threatened. Damn it, she had to get out of here.

As she tried to scramble to her feet, tears clouded her eyes. Belle couldn't see, couldn't quite get her balance. Kellan didn't try to hold her down, thank goodness, but she was too unsteady to stand.

"Help me, please," she beseeched Tate.

His arms wound around her and he dragged her to her feet, into his arms. Belle curled against him, shielding as much of her body from Kellan's searing stare as she could. Crap, where had her dress gone?

Tate's concerned gaze sought hers. "What's the matter? Tell me what you meant. If there's a problem, we'll find a logical solution."

Kellan moved beside her, straightening his clothes. His expression hardened again. "I asked you a question."

Belle blinked, knowing her answer would only disappoint Kell. She glanced Eric's way. He still stood unmoving, in mute shock. No help there. Only Tate's arms kept her protected and safe, but even against the warmth of his big body, she shivered. Would he still be her safe harbor once one of the others explained exactly what she'd waited for?

She didn't want to take that chance. Time to get out of here.

But when Belle tried to move, Tate's arms tightened around her. "What's wrong? What is going on here?"

"I need an answer, Belle." Kellan ignored Tate, staring at her with flat demand.

Kellan had asked for honesty. Fine, he would get it. She'd never intended to hold back the truth about her sexual inexperience. Once the clothes had started coming off, she'd known she would have to confess. The perfect, tactful moment simply hadn't appeared before she'd accidentally let the truth slip. Of course, she'd expected them to be a bit surprised, maybe even give her a good-natured ribbing about it. Belle hadn't expected Eric's mute shock or Kellan's terrible coldness.

"You're right. I'm a virgin." *So what?* No way they could miss the subtext in her voice. She did her best to glare right back, but Belle felt decidedly vulnerable wearing absolutely nothing.

Eric's hazel eyes went wide. "You weren't kidding?"

Tate eased back and he gaped at her. "*That's* what you waited for? To have sex? Holy shit!"

Kellan's jaw tightened. "Precisely what I thought you meant."

Eric moved beside her, shaking his head and still looking shocked. "How the hell are you a virgin? You're twenty-six years old."

"I am well aware of the advanced age of my hymen." She twisted, evading Tate's arms, looking for her dress again. It had to be somewhere here on the floor.

Anger started to thrum through her. They sounded almost betrayed by her purity. So much for the guys considering it a gift. Maybe they had expected someone more experienced. Maybe she wasn't worth sleeping with because she wouldn't know what to do. Fine. As soon as she found her clothes, she was out of here. Coming to their suite had been a huge mistake.

Kellan beat her to the punch, grabbing his jacket and heading for the door. "I'm going to go."

Annabelle felt as if he'd slapped her.

"What?" Tate asked his friend, obviously shocked.

Kell didn't answer, just kept gathering his things.

She glanced all around the room, trying not to watch Kellan walk away from her. Finally, she located her dress and all but ran toward it. "I'll go, Kell."

Tate took her arm and stayed her. "Belle, what are you doing?"

"I'm leaving." She yanked from his grip and dashed across the room to grab the emerald fabric.

As she darted toward the bathroom, her humiliation choked her. God, her ass was hanging out. She felt so wretchedly exposed, but she wasn't about to dress in front of them and let them gawk at the dumb little virgin anymore. It was better to leave and save herself the tiniest bit of dignity. She slammed the door behind her and locked it just in case. Barely a second later, she heard them yelling.

Without them staring and judging her now, the mortification of the evening pressed in on Belle, crushing her dreams. She went to her knees and let the tears fall.

* * * *

Kellan's stomach turned as he stared at the bathroom door Belle had just slammed. Fuck, what had he just done? One moment he'd had his hands on her, stroking her and making her come. She'd been the sexiest woman he'd ever touched because he'd wanted her for so long and her pleasure had been so honest. He could still feel her, smell her, so hot and wet and perfect. The moment she'd stripped naked for them, the primal need to carry her to the bed and sink his cock inside her had gnawed at him. He'd leave her body only long enough to see Eric and Tate please her before they started all over again. But that was a fucking fantasy. A joke.

Now, he found his two best friends staring him down. And they looked wildly pissed. He could hear Belle quietly sobbing in the bathroom.

"What the hell is wrong with you? How could you do that to her?" Eric strode across the room, grabbing his slacks with an angry jerk.

Staring at the ceiling, Kell sighed. He should just fucking walk out, like he'd promised. Opening the door and leaving would be the kindest thing he could do because hoping that he could share a woman with his friends had been a horrible mistake. He'd ruined everything, and they would never forgive him. He'd already learned the hard way that a man didn't get second chances.

The door was right there. No one was guarding it. Eric still stumbled his way into his slacks, and Tate stood on the other side of the suite, pressed to the bathroom door, trying to coax Belle out.

None of this nightmare would be happening if he hadn't deluded himself into thinking he could just fuck her without feeling anything or screwing the whole situation up.

Still, Kell couldn't bring himself to go. He owed her an apology at least. "I can't."

Eric walked across the room, face red, teeth gritted. "Can't what?" he snarled. "Act like a human being? Do you know what you just did to her?"

Taken all her sweetly blooming sensuality and crushed it under his loafer? Yeah, he knew he'd done that. "I can't be with a fucking virgin, man. What the hell would I do with her?"

God, that had come out completely wrong. He sounded like the worst kind of asshole douchebag, even to his own ears. But as soon as Belle blurted that she was glad she'd waited, his stomach had done a tailspin. She would need so much more than he could give her—love, attention, devotion. She deserved all that and more. She'd waited for a man who could love her, not just a man who could fuck her all night long.

She needed a man who would move mountains or part the sea for her, fight off demons, and fill her heart—do anything for her.

The realization physically hurt him, but Kell knew he wasn't that man. He never would be.

"You can't be with a virgin? Are you fucking kidding me? What the hell is that supposed to mean?" Eric's cheeks mottled even more. "You treated her like she has some dreaded disease."

"Belle?" Tate knocked on the bathroom door. "Baby, answer me. I can hear you crying. Talk to me. Let me hold you."

At least Tate was preoccupied.

"You knew I wouldn't get serious with her. Hell, you said I didn't have to when you invited me to join this party," Kell pointed out.

He'd told Belle he wouldn't make a good boyfriend—and he'd been right. He had also made it clear to Eric and Tate that he couldn't commit. They knew his past. Yeah, he could have handled his shock about her virginity better. He regretted hurting her. But how could any of them think for a second that Annabelle Wright would—or should—accept what little he could offer? She hadn't waited all these years for a lover who could get her off. No, she'd waited for lace and monogrammed towels. She'd waited for *love*.

Kellan shuddered. He hadn't been enough for his bitch of a wife. She'd walked out and utterly destroyed his world, his family, and his heart. She'd proven that he wasn't enough of a husband for the average woman. Belle was anything but average.

But the idea of never holding her in his arms made something in his chest buckle violently. *Fuck.* He was dying inside and he had no idea what to do. Kell ached to walk to that bathroom door and kick it open, insist that she never lock him out again—but he didn't have that right. He would never have that right with her.

No denying that if he had dreamed up his perfect submissive, Annabelle would fit the bill. She nurtured. She cared. Smart, funny, loyal, sassy… Hell, who was he kidding? Even if she'd slept with a hundred men, she would be far too good for him. But the reverent way she'd said it—*I'm so glad I waited*—had gutted him. He'd spoken without thinking. Now that would cost him not just the woman he wanted above all others, but his two best friends as well.

Tate stormed over, every muscle in his body tight with

fury. "I can't get her to come out or speak. You made this mess. You go talk to her and apologize. You clean up this shit and make it right."

Before his pal even finished speaking, Kell began shaking his head. The minute he saw her again, he just might go down on his knees and beg her to take him back. He might offer her everything he couldn't deliver because he was too weak to walk away. That would lead to a nuclear disaster for Belle's heart. He wouldn't do it to her. Better to find the fucking strength now to walk away.

How the hell was he supposed to even work with her? He couldn't anymore. And if Eric and Tate couldn't coax Belle back to their side, they wouldn't want to share a business with him anyway. Goddamn it, he had to leave and lose another family. This time he wouldn't find a replacement. He would be alone, the way he deserved to be.

"I'm sorry," he said tightly. "But I can't do this. You understand that if you take Belle's virginity, you're responsible for her? She waited twenty-six fucking years. She's not going to be content with a damn one-night stand."

"Good!" Tate hollered back. "I don't want to fuck and run. I want a wife, a family, a future that doesn't include going to a bar and picking up a girl eager for the thrill of banging three guys."

"Good for you. I can't be responsible for Belle. I'll only destroy her."

"You're protecting yourself," Eric growled. "Not her. You're just too fucking afraid to put your little heart out there again."

Tate invaded his space. "You hurt her to save yourself? I have *no* respect for that."

It wasn't logical, but Kell wanted to put the fucker on his ass. "Back off, Tate. Do it now."

"I don't think I want to." Tate kept coming.

Eric moved between them. "Stop it, both of you. This isn't helping a damn thing."

Maybe not, but since Kell had no idea how to put a pretty pink Band-Aid on the situation and make it all better, the thought of taking out his anger on Tate seemed like a damn fine idea. Yeah, he should probably 'fess up to the truth that Tate was a better man and Kell resented him for it, but beating the hell out of him would feel so much better. His gut rolled with rage. Unfulfilled desire warred with a terrible sense of self-loathing that had been constantly weighing him down since his divorce.

Except those moments when Belle had looked at him with her big dark eyes sparkling with trust. She'd been so gorgeous as she placed herself over his lap for her first spanking. In that moment, he hadn't thought of anything but her, the way she smelled of jasmine, how warm her flesh had become as he disciplined her, the undeniable certainty that his spanking had made her wet. She'd responded to his touch with absolute honesty and openness, all but offering him her innocent body.

Kell hated like hell that he couldn't accept it.

"You're a pathetic piece of shit, Kent. You ruined everything." Tate never held back.

Which was good because that meant Kellan didn't have to stifle his words, either. "I didn't see your boy over there getting on his damn knees and thanking her for remaining pure for him. He was just as shocked as I was."

Eric's jaw tightened, his face going stony. "Of course I was shocked."

"Don't stop there. Spit it out. You weren't any happier about her whole virginity thing than I was, you shit. You're going to let me take all the blame though, aren't you?"

It was typical. He always got to be the bad guy. He took the hits for the whole team while Tate and Eric sat back and played the good guys everyone loved. He might have earned it, but he was damn sick of it.

"You're so far off the mark," Eric insisted. "I'm glad that I'll never have to picture Belle letting some random asshole grunt and sweat on top of her. Look, none of us imagined Belle would be a virgin. It was a shocker, but that just means it's time for us to slow it down and talk a little. We sure as hell shouldn't blow the whole thing up. Do you have any idea what you did to her by walking out?"

"I could have handled it better; I'll give you that. But did you stop to think that she misled us a little? Tell me what virgin is ready to just hop in the sack with three men? She either didn't know what she was getting into—and if that's the case, it's a good thing we stopped—or she didn't really intend to be with all of us." Kell couldn't resist a sidelong glance at Tate. Being left in the cold was his buddy's hot button, and if Belle hadn't planned on embracing the big guy...well, better that he found out now before he fell even harder in love.

"She kissed me. That wasn't a good-bye, you asshole." Tate took that moment to curl up his fist and rear it back.

Kellan just stood there. Maybe this hurt would detract from the agony twisting his guts. The impact came, and he was surprised at just how hard Tate, a man who watched way too much science fiction television, could punch. Kell's jaw took the brunt and pain flared through his system.

He saw red. It triggered his aggression. Immediately, he went on the offensive, putting every ounce of his roiling rage into his fists. Before he really knew what he was doing, he had Tate on the ground, pounding into the man who had been his friend for nearly a decade. When Eric tried to get between them, he just decked Eric, too—a hard crack to the chin.

"Stop. Please stop." Belle's shaky pleading broke through the furious haze that filled his head.

The three of them stopped everything, just froze as if someone had hit the off button to stop all motion. Vaguely, he was aware that his body ached. Blood trickled down his lip, but the shame that suddenly overtook him was worse than any physical discomfort.

Belle stood before them looking more stripped of

confidence than he'd ever seen her. With eyes swollen and nose red, she'd obviously been crying. The sight of her tears kicked him in the gut, tearing through him in a way Tate's fists couldn't. Her pretty cocktail gown was wrinkled. Just minutes before, she'd been naked in his arms and she'd practically glowed. Now her light was gone, replaced with a deep grief stamped into her face. His words had done that to her.

"Please stop," she said, her voice beyond weary. "I can't stand the fact that you're fighting, especially about me. Please."

He scrambled to his feet because he couldn't cause her another moment of pain. "I'm sorry, Annabelle."

He took a step toward her, and she flinched back, shaking her head. "Don't."

Tate was on his feet, reaching out for her, but Eric stopped him.

"I'm going to go." Belle looked down, focused on the shoes she held in her hand.

God, she couldn't even look at the three of them. That fact, along with the sight of her bare feet, made him realize just how vulnerable she must feel. He'd made her self-conscious, stripped her bare. He couldn't lie to himself. Eric might have been surprised, but Kell knew that if he hadn't opened his mouth, the guy would have recovered. He and Tate would have not only saved the situation, but treasured her innocence.

Kell should have left her to the two men who would love her always, but he'd blurted out the first thing in his head, not even thinking about the possible outcome. He'd been shocked and bitter that he'd never be good enough for her. He hadn't even realized how badly his words would crush her—more proof that he didn't deserve her.

"Belle, I'm so sorry." For so many things. That he'd upset her, yes. Mostly he was sorry that he was too damaged to show her how much she meant to him.

78

She gave him a shaky nod. "Me, too."

As she headed to the door, Tate called her back. "Belle, let's talk about this."

She clutched the door handle and turned back. "I can't tonight. I'll see you tomorrow morning at the meeting."

And then she was gone, the door closing quietly behind her with terrible finality.

"We can't let her leave like this," Tate said, starting after her.

Eric wedged himself between Tate and the door. "Give her a little time, man. I don't think she's up to talking tonight. Let her have some space. Once she's less fragile and we're less angry, we'll all sit down and work it out, but now, we'll only fight."

"But she was crying." Sometimes Tate was good at pointing out the obvious.

"We need to let her cry, if that's what she wants."

"She shouldn't have to do it alone. She should know how we feel about her," Tate argued.

"I think, deep down, she does. But if you go after her now, you'll be sending her a message," Eric explained. "She wants all of us. Contrary to dumbass's suave speech tonight"—he pointed at Kell—"we all want her. If we're going to make this right, we have to go after her together or not at all. And before we can do that, the three of us have to sit our asses down and hash this out because that was a total cluster fuck."

Kellan looked to Eric, totally shocked that his old friend wasn't shoving him out the door or starting another fight. "I think I should go find another room. This is a conversation for you and Tate. We can talk about how to break up the business later. I won't be there for the meeting in the morning."

Eric's eyes rolled. "God, you're such a dramatic fucker. We're not doing that."

"I still want to beat the fuck out of you." Tate got up and

ambled to the bathroom.

The shower came on, and Kellan figured their fight was over. He turned his attention to Eric, willing him to understand. "I can't stay around, man. She won't ever work with me again, and Tate will blame me for the rest of our lives if Belle walks away."

"We'll come up with a strategy and we won't let her walk away. We'll come up with a plan." Eric sounded resolved as he started righting the furniture they'd nearly wrecked in their fight. "You're lying to yourself if you think you don't want her anymore."

He should be walking out. There was no reason to stay. He'd sealed his fate the minute he'd broken her heart. So why wasn't he packing up and moving down the line the way he always did? Because he owed his friends some honesty.

"I still do."

"All right then, you're lying to yourself if you think you don't love her."

What did he feel for Belle? Kell really wasn't sure. He wanted her so badly, but it went beyond her body, beyond her lovely face. Of course he liked her. In fact, he loved to talk to her, loved to just sit in her presence. He found an odd peace when they were in the same room. They didn't even have to be speaking, just going about their business. She often hummed a little as she worked. He always looked forward to the moment she inevitably turned to ask if he wanted coffee, showing her submissive, nurturing side. He'd loved to fantasize that she might go down on her knees and ask how else she might please him.

The idea of never having those quiet afternoons with her again pierced his heart.

Fuck, did he even know what love was? Would he know if it bit him in the ass?

"I don't know, man. I just know I can't get married again."

Eric regarded him with a serious expression. "When you

weren't thinking at all, you were setting up a D/s relationship with her. You take that seriously. You were more than willing to initiate her into Dominance and submission, but you won't teach her about sex? Look, I was shocked, too. I have no idea how a woman that hot manages to stay a virgin, but I don't care how many lovers she has—or hasn't—had as long I get to be one of them. The last of them. Can you stand the thought of her kneeling for another Master?"

Eric's words made him see red all over again. His pal might not be a good liar, but he was a fucking master of manipulation. He'd known exactly where to strike. "Of course I don't, but I just broke her."

"So help us put her back together."

Eric made it sound so simple, but Kell didn't see how. Belle would never forgive him. Would she?

"I'll see her tomorrow, but only to apologize." He would make sure she understood that her virginity wasn't the problem, just his scarred heart. He would swear to her that if he was half the man he should be, he would give her everything he owned, share every day and night with her. He would love her.

But that was a stupid-ass pipe dream. So even if it killed him, he would leave and let her find the love she deserved.

Chapter Five

Belle looked through the peephole of her hotel room door, praying that she wouldn't see Tate or Eric standing in the hall. Even an hour after she'd been utterly humiliated, she was still shaking a little. A shower had soothed her, but she couldn't seem to stop crying.

She sighed in relief when she saw a blonde with a puppy in her arms, grinning like a loon and waving at the peephole.

It was Kinley's big day. Belle couldn't bring herself to ruin the closest thing her friend would have to a wedding. Wincing, she stepped back. Maybe Kinley would think she wasn't in.

Another knock. "Belle? Belle, I know you're in there. Open up or I'll convince the desk manager that I think you're dead in there and I need to collect your body."

Annabelle groaned and reached for the bolt because Kinley would do it. The woman would march right back here with the manager and persuade him to open the door.

With a sigh, Belle saved her friend the trouble.

Kinley's grin faded as she took in Belle's appearance. "Oh, honey. Who do I kill?"

Belle sniffled as the door shut, but she let Kinley hug her tight as the puppy in her arm used the proximity to lick her cheek. Belle was just about to scold the dog when she really looked at the little thing. Okay, so it wasn't the most

82

attractive canine, but there was a well of sympathy in its dark eyes that had her tears welling again. The puppy stared at her, then rubbed its face against her cheek as though it knew she needed comfort.

Reaching out, Belle gathered the pup into her arms. It looked to be the runt of the litter, possibly the ugliest of the three, but in that moment, the dog seemed so sweet, she couldn't help but cuddle the wiggly little thing against her robe.

"I'm serious, Annabelle." Kinley locked the bolt and followed her into the room. "I want to know who to murder horribly. Well, I want to know who to get Law to murder horribly. He used to be Special Forces. He told me he misses killing rat bastards sometimes, so you would be helping him out."

Annabelle shook her head and sank onto the edge of the bed. Her room wasn't anywhere near as opulent as Eric and Tate's, but it was comfortable. "No murder, Kinley. I'm fine."

She just had to be tough. So, it hadn't worked out. Kell had wanted nothing to do with her. And in the end, Eric hadn't seemed much more enthusiastic. Tate had been kinder, but he'd let her go, too. It was all right—or it would be once she figured out how to mend her broken heart. That might take a long while, but she'd bounce back. Somehow, she always did.

Belle scratched the puppy behind its ears and it immediately settled onto her lap, as if it belonged there.

Kinley sat down beside her. "I saw you leave the ballroom. All three of those lawyers stalked after you. I expected you to stay the night with them, but Jessa Lennox saw you fleeing their suite. I don't guess you're running back here to find some sexy lingerie, huh?"

How did she explain this to her best friend without sounding pathetic? "No. We tried. It didn't work out."

Kinley's eyes narrowed. "What does that mean?"

She let her fingers sink into the puppy's scraggly fur. "It means that we came to the conclusion that a sexual relationship between us wouldn't work."

Kinley's delicate bow mouth dropped open. "That's impossible, sweetie. No guy decides something can't work sexually. Not if they're attracted to you, and those three definitely are. Guys will usually just keep trying to please you so they can coax their way into your panties. Or they buy a ton of little blue pills." She gasped. "Are you saying they...struggled?"

Not in any way, shape, or form. No, those were not men who needed any help—chemical or otherwise—to get hard. They'd all had massive erections...that had deflated the minute they found out she was a virgin. "Kinley, it doesn't matter."

Her bestie was like a dog with a bone. "It does. You're hurt. You've been crying. Do you think I can't tell? I want to know what happened."

Kinley would twist her arm until she confessed. "They wanted someone with more experience."

"More experience doing what exactly? Sex isn't rocket science or brain surgery."

"They just didn't like that I was a virgin." There. She couldn't be freaking plainer.

The puppy's tail thumped along her leg in time to the stroke of her hand petting its back. She found the rhythm soothing, enjoyed her connection to the little furry creature. Besides Kinley, she had no one else anymore.

"Unbelievable." Kinley heaved a deep sigh. "God, sweetie. I'm so sorry. It's inconceivable to me that they would be such assholes. But they're men."

A deep sense of weariness invaded her veins. They weren't assholes, really. They were just men looking for something she didn't have. "It's fine. It was a mistake to think it could work anyway. The problem now is, what to do about the fact that I almost slept with my bosses."

Almost, but not quite. God, she could still feel the heat of their bodies as they'd surrounded her. The pleasure of their touch had almost been too much to take. She'd been a different person when she'd lain across Kellan's lap, offering herself up to all three of them, to their vision, their sensuality, their desire.

In the end, they hadn't wanted what little she had to offer, so now she had to figure out where to go and what to do next.

Kinley stood and paced the room. "I just don't understand."

Of course she didn't. She had three men who were crazy about her, who didn't give a crap about anything except that she loved them. "It doesn't matter. Just…please have my back when I say I can't work there anymore."

Her friend froze, her brows forming a confused *V*. "Of course you can't work there anymore." Her eyes narrowed, and Belle knew from experience that meant her friend was plotting something evil. "Unless you intend to very cleverly kill all three of them off. Again, I—with Law's assistance—will totally help you."

Annabelle couldn't not laugh, and something deep inside her eased. Her best friend wouldn't abandon her, no matter what. "I'll be fine, hon. I'll figure everything out. Shouldn't you be with your husbands for your big 'wedding' night?"

"Not when you need me. They remember how you helped me." Kinley glided across the room and dropped a gentle touch on her shoulder, her face soft with understanding. "Belle, you're part of our family. We love you."

Stupid tears. They were right there on the edge of her eyes again. "I love you all, too."

They had been smart enough to love Kinley, to save her from a potentially murderous marriage. Belle had loathed Greg, Kinley's fiancé. Dominic, Law, and Riley had stepped up to protect Kinley. So when Kellan, Eric, and Tate had formed a shield around Belle at the same time during all the danger, it had given her hope. They hadn't allowed her to see or even talk to her friend while the threat was imminent. Kellan had put his whole career at risk to save Kinley, and it couldn't be because he was such good friends with the Anders brothers and Dominic Anthony. So why had he gone out on such a limb?

God, she was so confused. She only knew one thing: Whatever his reasons, whatever his feelings, she couldn't face those three in the morning. Despite her parting words to them, she just couldn't sit down at that meeting beside them and pretend nothing had changed. Or return to Chicago and watch them work—or date—without her anywhere in the picture. She definitely couldn't stay and see them fight again. They were closer than brothers, and she'd ruined that. No matter how she tried to block the vision, every time she closed her eyes, she could still see Kellan straddling Tate, pummeling his face with punches. She'd caused that, and the guilt was eating her alive.

Kinley took a deep breath and wagged a finger at her. "You're going to stay here in Dallas with me."

Oh, she was so not going to do that. That finger usually said that Kinley meant business, but the only thing worse than going back to Chicago would be staying here with her newlywed friend and becoming the pathetic, can't-get-a-man houseguest. Not happening. "I'm going to New Orleans."

"What? Why would you do that? Mardi Gras is months away."

She snorted. "Like I'd be in the mood to show off my boobs in exchange for some beads? No. Remember, I told you about six weeks ago that my grandma died?"

Kinley nodded. "Yes, I was sorry to hear about it, but I don't remember you being close to her. This was your dad's mom, right?"

"Right. And I barely knew her. Even when Dad was alive, he wasn't close to her—at least from what I recall. I

86

remember Mom and Dad arguing about her once." It was one of her earliest memories. Her mom thought her dad should forgive the woman in New Orleans. She'd said something about her grandmother doing the best she could, but her dad had just shaken his head implacably and vowed that he wouldn't let that life taint his little girl. To this day, Belle had no idea what her father meant. And now that both he and his mother were gone, she'd probably never know.

Funny. She hadn't thought about that day in forever.

"Did you ever meet her?"

"Only once. She came to Dad's funeral." The petite woman had worn beautiful clothes and a heartbreakingly sad smile.

Belle had been a child then—confused and angry that her father was suddenly gone forever. The grandmother she'd never met had hugged her for one brief, mournful moment, exchanged a few words with her daughter-in-law, then she'd been gone again. But not before she'd stood over her son's casket and whispered, "I'm sorry, baby boy."

Belle knew almost nothing about her grandmother. The woman and her past were mysteries. Belle could use some of those to get her mind off her own problems now.

"I remember her. She was the beautiful older lady in the tweed Chanel suit." Only Kinley would remember what someone had worn fifteen years before.

Belle had no idea what the stranger had worn, but she did know the woman had bequeathed her something. "She left me her house in the Quarter."

The package from her grandmother's attorney had been very light on information. When she'd talked to the man on the phone, he'd assumed she would wait until the will finished probate, then he would handle selling the house. Apparently the place needed some repairs before it realized its true market potential, but he'd assured her he could find a buyer.

The will had been finalized two days ago. And Belle

87

realized that she didn't want a buyer; she wanted a challenge.

The plan crystalized in an instant. She needed time to heal and figure out where she was going. She needed a place to stay that was far away from everyone she knew. New Orleans would be perfect.

The puppy in her lap looked up at her, complete adoration in its dark eyes. Oh, she was such a sucker. "Kinley, I'm taking the dog."

Kinley's eyes widened with delight. "Are you serious?"

She pulled the puppy up and checked to see if she was getting a boy or a girl. Fate, she sighed. He was her man now, and he wriggled with excitement as though he knew his little doggie life was changing.

"Yes, I'm taking him with me. And I know just what to call him. Sir." He would be the last man on whom she bestowed that title.

"Oh, honey, you can't call him that. You'll get your ass spanked."

By whom? "Nope. His name is now Sir." She giggled. "I'm going to build this puppy's self-esteem. He's going to be an alpha dog."

Sir wagged his tail.

"I don't think he'll ever be an alpha, but he's lucky to have you." Kinley reached out and grabbed her hand. "How can I help? What do you need?"

Sometimes it was good to have a best friend who had an indulgent, rich husband. "A car."

"Oh, you're plotting. You know I love a good plot." Kinley hopped to her feet and dashed to the desk. "We need to make a list."

Kinley and her lists. There was something soothing about letting Kinley take over. She really did like to plan. Kinley started jotting notes and making calls.

Belle settled back, the sadness of the night washing over her. She would leave notes for her bosses about the meeting, then another that explained why she was leaving. Maybe. Or maybe they wouldn't care. Most likely, they would be relieved not to have to deal with her again.

But Belle feared she would miss them forever.

Chapter Six

Eric straightened his tie and kept his eyes on the hostess station. He checked his phone again. Eight thirty-five. Belle was late. She was never late. In fact, she always arrived early, just in case something went wrong. But he'd walked into the café about twenty minutes ago, hoping for a chance to talk to her alone. He'd scanned the place, fully expecting to find her waiting at a table surrounded by all her notes. Instead, he'd seen no trace of her.

Concern niggled at him—not that she'd fallen victim to foul play. It wasn't impossible, but the odds of Belle being attacked in her hotel room, especially one this nice and full of guests from the wedding, seemed slim. She was much too smart to let a stranger in her room. Operating on the premise that she hadn't been hurt left Eric one major worry: What if she just decided not to show? And what did that mean?

He had to track her down.

He pulled up his contact list on his phone. Belle's number was easy to spot. She was the only one of his hundreds of contacts with a photo attached to her profile. His heart did a weird flip-flop as he stared at her picture. In the still, she sat at her desk, the morning sun illuminating her from behind, making her glow angelically…but she wore a devilish little grin. That was his Belle. God, he hoped she was still his Belle. The alternative was too horrific to contemplate.

His call went straight to voice mail. Damn it. He thought about hanging up, but as her greeting played, he considered that maybe keeping interaction about business on a professional footing would relax her. That would seem normal to her, right? And hopefully, if he played along, she would realize that none of them would pounce on her in front of clients. Then maybe she'd be comfortable enough to join them.

"Belle, the Hughes brothers should be here soon. We need you for the meeting. We're in the hotel café. I snagged us a table in the back. See you in a few. Thanks."

Frowning, he touched the button to end the call.

"She's not here?" Tate scowled as he wandered into the room and searched it as he sat. The lack of sleep showed on his face, just like Eric knew it was reflected in his own.

"Maybe I should go to her room and talk to her." Kellan pulled out a chair, but hovered over it, seemingly perplexed and less confident than Eric could ever remember. "We might have to clear the air before she'll feel comfortable working with me again."

Eric shook his head and gestured for them to sit. "If you go to her room, Tate and I should come along. We all need to talk to her at once and get on the same page. But Oliver and his brothers are due any minute. Damn it!"

"Maybe she'll show up first." Tate sounded hopeful, then he glanced at his phone. "Except...she sent me all her notes about their business dealings at two this morning."

"Well, they're your clients. Belle always sends notes about a meeting to the lead." Eric tried to encourage him— and maybe himself a bit.

Tate scanned her message, his finger brushing up the screen of his phone. Then he frowned. "They're very thorough, far more than normal—everything we could possibly need to conduct the meeting."

"She's not coming." Kell gritted his teeth and gripped

the back of the chair, looking ready to lose it. "Shit."

Eric scrubbed a hand down his face, worried like hell that Kell was right. Still, he looked for any reason to refute his friend. With a cold chill of dread spreading through his body, Eric looked over Kell's shoulder as he took the phone and quickly skimmed the notes.

"I'm right." Kell looked so damn bleak. "Her notes are way more than we'll need for this meeting. Goddamn it, she's left."

Tate frowned. "Belle doesn't have a car, and she's booked on the same flight we are. She can't have gone far, right?"

"Right," Eric assured absently. "Maybe she's just with Kinley."

She'd had a rough evening. Maybe she'd needed some girl time. Or maybe she'd overslept. He wouldn't blame her if she showed up at the very last minute to avoid any chance for personal talk, then attempted to leave the minute the clients did so she could be assured there'd be no confrontation. They couldn't allow that. They needed to have a very in-depth chat with her—one that ended up with her right back in bed where she should have been last night.

The three of them had stayed up damn near all night discussing how to deal with Belle. They'd made progress, though he still didn't think Kell saw the big picture. Right now, they all had to put their energy into a little groveling and begging, but Belle was a reasonable woman. She wouldn't be any different in this situation. He hoped.

Kell shook his head. "Belle doesn't pout. I don't see her skipping a meeting to cry to her best friend. Whatever's wrong is bigger." He put a fist to his lips as if trying to hold in another curse. "This isn't good."

Eric looked for a logical way to refute him, but he couldn't find one. Kell was right. He wanted so badly to run back to Belle's room and see if she was there, if she would talk to him.

But an approaching man in an impeccable navy suit and severely short blond hair approached, flanked by two men who looked very much like him—minus the severe expression.

"Good morning."

Oliver Thurston-Hughes had gained back some of the weight he'd lost after his wife's death, but there was no way to mistake the grim look in his eyes. Yasmin had been a cousin to the ruling family of Bezakistan, but she'd also turned out to be a murderous traitor. She'd sold her cousin, Alea, into slavery. When the poor girl had figured out that her own flesh and blood had nearly ruined her life, Yasmin had attempted to kill her. She hadn't cared that Oliver got caught in the crossfire. The incident had turned the once happy-go-lucky aristocrat bitter.

"Thank you for meeting us," his brother Rory, the youngest of the three, greeted them in his equally upper-crust British accent.

The last of the Hughes brothers simply nodded behind a pair of aviators. There were already whispers going through the café about *the* Callum Thurston-Hughes. The man had the kind of face that lent itself to posters and print ads, and he'd made a very nice fortune smiling for a camera. Currently, however, he was on a farewell tour with his professional soccer team. If the man could hear his thoughts, Eric had no doubt Callum would roll those famous eyes of his and remind him the correct term was football.

Rory slid into his chair with a smile. "Let's get this over with. I met a girl last night at a bar, after the reception. I've been in America for four days and I haven't gotten any action yet."

His brothers both groaned as they sat. After ordering coffee, the group immediately dove into conversation about their American businesses and all the objectives they hoped to accomplish with this trip. The dog wedding had been a nice—if painful—reason for Oliver to see his late-wife's family, with whom he'd maintained ties...and maybe get some closure.

Eric lost himself in the complex conversation. Their group had several legal tangles to unravel before they could buy more property in the States and proceed with their planned endeavors. Eric spoke with the confidence of someone who knew this area of the law well, while Kellan offered his expertise when needed. Tate cited specific facts and precedence, jotting notes along the way, as he often did. Everything should have felt much the same, but nothing did without Belle's smiling face or efficient manner.

Thirty minutes turned into an hour, and before Eric knew it, they were paying the check. The Hughes brothers stood and offered their hands.

"Until our follow-up meeting next month." Callum nodded.

And the truth punched Eric in the gut. Belle hadn't shown up. Discreetly, he double-checked his phone. Nothing. She'd never once skipped a meeting the whole time she'd been with them. She'd never even taken a sick day in fourteen months. Now she hadn't even called to let them know she wasn't going to be there. It was so unlike her.

Rory smiled as he shook Eric's hand. "Tell Belle we're sorry we missed her."

Eric might just let Kellan deal with this one. Yes, they'd been assholes, but she was still a part of their business and he'd never dreamed that she would shirk responsibility because she was sulking. "I'm sure she's sorry to have missed you as well. She's not feeling well."

Though the clients wouldn't care, he felt the urge to cover for her. Or maybe that's what he wanted to believe because it was easier than contemplating a scarier possibility.

Oliver's brows rose over his sharp blue eyes. "She looked perfectly fit this morning."

So someone had seen her today. She was still here. Eric breathed a silent sigh of relief.

Tate leaned in. "Where is she?"

Eric exchanged a glance with Kellan. They had to teach Tate how to adopt a halfway decent poker face.

"I don't know. It actually wasn't morning when we saw her, more like the middle of the night." Callum chuckled. "We went out drinking a bit after the reception. It was three a.m. when we returned. I was surprised she would leave at such an odd hour."

"Leave?" Tate demanded.

"We presumed she was," Rory said, pushing his chair in. "She rolled her baggage out. That's an ugly dog, by the way."

Eric gaped, realizing that he wasn't doing a good job of hanging onto his own poker face. "She left with her suitcase at three a.m.?"

"She had a dog?" Tate looked really perplexed.

Kell elbowed Tate. "Did she say anything?"

"Not a lot, simply that she planned to start a new business." Oliver shrugged. "I'm sad to see her go. She was always efficient and quite kind. But it looks as if she's making out all right. That Mercedes was a beauty of a car. Brilliant."

Rory sighed. "There's something terribly wrong when you notice the car before a woman as beautiful as Belle. I sincerely hope, for everyone's sake, that your libido makes a reappearance soon."

Callum took a swipe at the back of his little brother's head. "Stop being a barmy fuck."

Oliver's expression turned even colder. Eric could barely remember the Oliver he'd first met—the life of every party, the first with a joke or a smile.

Now, the man simply nodded their way. "Thank you for breakfast. I'll be on my way. Gentlemen."

As he walked away, Callum and Rory sighed.

"Sorry about that. He's still not himself. I'd hoped coming on this American tour with me would revive his spirits. It's been over a year since Yasmin's death." Callum watched his older brother go, concern etched all over his famous face.

Eric knew more about the story than most. Not only had Yasmin tried to kill her husband, she'd aborted several of his children, all the while calling them miscarriages and using her "grief" to extort money from her mourning husband.

Yeah, Oliver might never trust a woman again.

Rory leaned in, obviously not one to let a little tragedy keep him down. "Hey, when you hire your next secretary, make sure she's at least as hot as Belle. Gorgeous girl, but she took that rule about not dating clients far too seriously." He shook his head. "I tried. More than once. Shame."

After a good-bye Eric barely heard, the Brits walked away. And he felt a nasty hollow gnaw at the pit of his stomach. Anger threatened to take over.

"She went back to Chicago without us?" Kellan's jaw formed a tight line. He was obviously as furious as Eric felt.

Tate was already on his phone, but he hung up quickly. "It's going straight to voice mail."

The other two looked to him. What the hell should they do? Giving Belle time to herself hadn't done anything but allow her to run. Worry started to shove aside the anger and guilt. She'd gotten on the road at three in the morning? By herself? She couldn't have had any sleep. She shouldn't be driving on lonely highways while exhausted. "We don't know that she went back to Chicago. That's a long drive to make by herself."

"Well, apparently she has a dog with her." Tate's fingers tapped against the desk, a nervous habit Eric recognized from their high school days. "Why would she run?"

"Because she wants to teach us a lesson." Kellan cursed and his mouth turned down, his eyes softening with regret. "Because I hurt her last night. Damn it. I need to see her. Even if this doesn't work out, I need to apologize. She should know why I can't commit to anyone."

A sudden thought hit Eric. "Doesn't Kinley drive a Benz?"

Kellan sighed in clear relief. "She's probably gone to Kinley's. Thank god. They only live about thirty minutes from here. We'll find her in less than an hour. Let's go."

As they turned to leave, a familiar blonde strode into the café with Jessa Lennox and the oil tycoons' wife, Hannah James. The ladies smiled and laughed, but the minute Kinley saw them, her pretty face morphed into a mask of contempt. She turned on her heels and directed the other women to a different section of the café.

"Well, we're persona non grata," Tate said with a frown. "I guess we won't get invited to the baby shower. Thank god."

Eric didn't give a shit about that, only that Belle clearly hadn't left with her best friend. Still, Kinley must know damn well where Belle had gone. He felt his eyes narrow as she sat down, putting her back to them as she leaned to whisper something. Then the other two women were turning up their little noses at them, too. Oh, hell. Women. He would never understand them. He lived with Tate, and they didn't spend their time "bonding" by sharing their feelings or whatever. But clearly Belle had marched away from what had probably been the most humiliating evening of her life and immediately told the tale to her friends. *Perfect.*

Okay, she was pissed, but that was much better than sad. Pissed he could work with...once she calmed down enough to have a rational conversation.

Eric stood. It was time for him to take charge. "I think we need to go see Dominic and have a chat with him."

Tate followed. "Why Dominic? Can't we talk to Riley? He and I speak the same language."

But Kellan seemed to follow his line of thought. "Oh, no, we're talking to Dominic because his sub is keeping us from ours. Yeah, I like the way you think, Cohen. Let's have a nice talk, Dom to Dom."

Kellan strode forward, taking the lead now. This was why Eric couldn't give up. They worked in tandem, and he liked it that way. He couldn't give up on his best friends, his partners.

And he damn straight wasn't about to give up on the woman they would call their wife.

* * * *

Belle held Sir in one arm, looking up at the three-story Spanish-Colonial house. It looked unassuming from the front. Pinkish plaster walls that needed repair and blue shutters that framed what looked to be original windows. The upper levels would have a bird's-eye view overlooking the lively, eclectic street. The walls butted up to the brick-paved sidewalk. The house oozed charm.

She'd managed to park down the street, then lug her bags through the throng of tourists who walked up and down the Quarter, even in the middle of the brisk fall morning. As she stopped before the house, she stared, letting reality soak in. This would be home now.

Coming closer, Belle decided she liked the overall vibe of the place. The air of the house looked a little sad and neglected now, but she'd change that. Since her best friend knew how to plan an escape, Kinley had already arranged for a moving service to pack up her Chicago apartment. Once her things arrived, she'd move in, spruce it up, and start a new life.

"Annabelle Wright?" A distinguished older man in a pinstripe suit strolled up the sidewalk.

She nodded, fighting back a yawn. She'd driven straight through the night from Dallas to New Orleans. Managing eight hours on largely empty roads with no sleep hadn't been easy, but she'd had her will to keep her going.

After she'd forwarded the notes to Tate and sent her resignation letter to the office via fax, which should be monitored by the intern, she'd loaded up Kinley's car and driven through the darkness with Sir, trying not to think about the fact that she could still feel her former bosses' hands on her. She probably always would, but now she had a new future to focus on, one that didn't include them.

"Yes, I'm Annabelle Wright. Are you my grandmother's lawyer?"

The man looked to be roughly fifty, given his silvery sideburns, but otherwise in good shape. He nodded and carried his briefcase up the walk. "I'm Malcolm Gates. I've been handling your grandmother's legal issues for the last twenty years. She was with my father before that. Welcome to New Orleans."

He had a lyrical, flowing accent. *N'awlins*, he'd said.

Her father had grown up in the city, but she didn't remember him with such a thick accent. She'd had family here for years, but had never visited. The way she'd heard it, this city was almost an alien world. Her drive in had confirmed that fact in some ways, but been an amazing revelation in others. She found it beautiful, odd, and more than a tad mysterious. She had a feeling she was going to like the city and spend a lot of time learning its heartbeat.

She could definitely make a fresh start in New Orleans.

He did the gentleman thing and took her suitcase, then led her through a wrought iron gate.

"Where are we going? Isn't the front door that blue one?" She pointed to the entry facing the street at the front of the house, complete with a ratty old screen door.

"No, that was for servants and leads to the butler's pantry and kitchen. The entry would have been more private and built before air conditioning with maximum shade in mind. It's this way." He wended his way into an amazing atrium-style courtyard.

Fountains and old brick, a lovely terrace with lush foliage everywhere made her drop her jaw. This was an amazing oasis in the heart of the city.

"If you don't mind me saying so, you look an awful lot like your grandmother. Even at her advanced age, she was still one of the loveliest women in New Orleans. When the mood struck her, she would set up a table in the Square and read palms all afternoon. I think the men came to her because she was so beautiful."

Belle reared back. "My grandmother was a palm reader?"

Was that the "tainted" life her father had objected to?

A little smile played at the corner of his lips as he ushered her forward. "She was a psychic, one of the best. I never could understand how she handled living here, but she loved it." As they stepped onto a wide flagstone patio with a quaint white table and chairs, surrounded by a lush Eden of color, he placed a fatherly hand on her shoulder. "You know, the house has been vacant for some time. It will be dirty. I can have it cleaned before you take possession."

Right now, she just wanted inside so she could cry in private and sleep. She'd find the ice cream to drown her sorrows later.

"I'll take care of that myself." Later. "But thank you."

"Well, then… I have some good news for you. I've lined up a buyer for the place. One point two million, no repairs required. He'll take the property as is. I think you'll agree that's a very good deal."

She didn't know exactly what the place was worth, but just a glance at the wide house with its expansive grounds, the adjacent guest house, and the property's prime location on Dauphin Street told her it had to be worth far more. The square footage must be four thousand feet. True, she didn't know how much repair the place needed, but she wasn't looking for an easy sale. She wanted to fix something up and make it her own. This old home could be a showcase once she'd used her knowledge and creativity. It had great bones.

Belle cocked her head at Mr. Gates. "The will just finished probate. Has this buyer even seen the property? Has it been appraised recently? This is really sudden."

"I understand it's a lot to take in at once, especially after your loss. However, this buyer, a judge and a pillar of the community, is very eager. He's had his eye on this place for years. And yes, he's seen the home. He was a particular friend of your grandmother's. He tried to persuade her to sell for a long time, and with Marie now gone, he's eager to restore the property to its historic charm. I can have that money in your account by the end of the day, if you'll send me your bank routing information. You don't even have to spend the night here. I'll find you a suite somewhere tonight and you can return to your life in Chicago tomorrow."

She was a designer, not an idiot. She glanced around at the property with its southern elegance and felt herself falling in love. It wasn't in perfect condition by any stretch, but underneath that layer of dust, small cracks, and a need for paint, Belle sensed something extraordinary.

"I'm sorry, Mr. Gates. I'm not interested in selling right now, especially before I go through my grandmother's personal effects. So I'd like to see the inside now. I'm assuming you have a key?" She sent him a tight, expectant smile.

The lawyer frowned and produced a key from his suit coat. He led her around another side of the building, up the bricked walkway, past the lovely yard, to a pair of massive double doors with an arched brow window over the top and two levels of balconies overlooking the gardens.

Seeing the house from this angle, it was official. Belle was definitely in love.

The door creaked when he opened it, and a faint musty odor greeted her, tinged by a lingering hint of perfume. But windows could be opened, fans turned on. The smell wouldn't last, but this architecture would.

Gaping at the lovely foyer, Belle wandered inside, visually drinking in everything around her. In an instant, she envisioned the place all restored to its former glory.

Mentally, she pictured the entrance with a grand, classic palate—white marble and rich floors, gray walls, crystal chandeliers, along with a pop of something bright, like red or peacock—something as bold as New Orleans. She'd drape coordinating fabric to frame the graceful windows and let light in. The area rugs would have to be replaced and the hardwoods refinished with a rich, dark stain, but the raw goods were there. No one made beautiful, solid wide planks like this anymore.

Wow.

Smiling to herself, Belle turned to Gates, ready to tell him that she had no intention of leaving. She noticed then that he hadn't followed her inside.

He stood just beyond the threshold, his briefcase twitching at his side. "You don't want to do this, miss. I understand that you think the place is worth more. Maybe it is, but you should take the easy money and leave this house."

"Thank you for the advice, but I'll be fixing it up."

Sir's head came up, and he started barking at an empty room.

She tried to settle him down. "Hush, now."

Malcolm wouldn't step a foot in the house as he pointed at Sir, who squirmed to be let down. "See, you should listen to your dog. He knows this place is bad news. Everyone who lives in the Quarter knows its…unfortunate nature," the lawyer said with a little shudder.

"But the judge, the pillar of the community, doesn't? Why would he want to buy this house if it's so terrible?" God, she'd been working with lawyers too long.

"I've advised him against it. He's not listening." Gates looked somewhere between uncomfortable and spooked. "Sell it now, miss. With the exception of your grandmother, women fare poorly in this house."

Was that some sort of veiled threat? It didn't really sound that way, but Belle couldn't decide exactly what that note in his voice was. "What does that mean?"

He cleared his throat. "Two women hung themselves here. *Young* women. Rumor is, the place is haunted. Now, whether you believe that or not..."

What she was more inclined to believe was that Gates meant to scare her away. He probably made money if he persuaded her to sell the house to this judge. Too bad.

"I don't like the thought of you living here all alone," he went on.

Sir's whole body began wriggling, so Belle set him down since he seemed determined to run. He immediately found a spot in the middle of the room and started barking, but this was a happy sound. His tail wagged, and he did a little dance as though he was excited to see someone.

Except no one at all was there.

So the place was beautiful...and had an interesting energy. She hadn't even seen the rest of the huge house, and she could already imagine that being here by herself at night could be a tiny bit creepy. What else had she expected out of a New Orleans mansion?

Exhaustion weighed on her. It had been a terrible couple of days, but she'd take dealing with a supposed ghost over returning to Chicago and facing her former bosses any day of the week. Decision made, Belle dug her heels in. She wasn't letting some old stories push her out of her rightful inheritance. Her grandmother had wanted her to have this place. Belle sought to learn as much about the woman and her undoubtedly colorful past as she could, and living in her home seemed like a good way to start. Her family had a whole secret history that she longed to discover. Besides, it might take her mind off of Eric, Tate, and Kellan for more than thirty seconds.

"Thank you for your concern, but I'm not selling. I can handle anything this house throws at me. So let's get the legalities out of the way. What do I need to sign in the way of probate papers so the key is mine? I really need a nap."

Sir pranced around the place like he owned it. At least he

seemed to have calmed down. He yipped occasionally and sat back on his haunches, staring up at the air with a little growl.

The lawyer dug into his briefcase and extended the papers to her through the open door. He handed her a pen a moment later. Gates could be superstitious if he wanted. If her grandmother had lived here alone for all these years without incident, Belle figured she'd be fine, too.

"There are more papers for you to sign at my office. I'll have them finalized and get all the property details and reports to you. Your grandmother also left you a little money in an account. I think it's roughly thirty grand. I'll send you all the details shortly."

Thank god. Thirty thousand wouldn't be a lot compared to all the work the house would need, but it might be enough to finish off a room or two. She would start with an office she could use and turn it into her showplace.

This spur-of-the-moment plan might just work.

Gates frowned and shook his head. "I really wish you'd reconsider."

Belle merely smiled and shook her head. With a sigh, he left. The door closed, and she was finally alone. Well, hopefully.

"All right, Grandma." She looked around the parlor as a sense of responsibility engulfed her. "I'm going to make this place shine again and call it my home."

Weariness swamped Belle, and she yawned. It had been such a long night, and she still needed to check out the house and unpack. So much to do—right after her nap.

She lay across a slightly dusty rose-velvet settee and rested her head against the back. She wouldn't sleep long, just long enough to rest her eyes. But as she drifted off, visions of Eric, Tate, and Kellan haunted her.

Chapter Seven

"Please join us, love."

It took everything Kellan had not to laugh at the nervous look on Kinley's face as her husband ushered her inside the living area of their suite. Her eyes widened briefly when she caught sight of the five other men waiting for her. He, Eric, and Tate had joined Kinley's other spouses, the Anders brothers, in their suite's living area. After a brief meeting with Dominic during which they'd laid out the chaos his wife had aided, Dominic had agreed to allow a polite interrogation of his wife. He'd also vowed she would feel the sting of his hand later.

Even Butch sat with the men while Gigi's little head poked out of Kinley's Prada tote. The minute she put the bag down, the dog hopped out, running through the suite to hide behind the drapes as if Gigi knew trouble was coming.

Kinley wasn't given that option.

"Why don't you have a seat?" Kellan said to the blonde, taking over the conversation now. "We have some questions for you."

He had to give her credit. After her initial apprehension, she steadied and sank into the chair they'd left for her in the middle of the room. She held her head high as she looked them over, like a queen gazing down at her subjects. Oh, Dominic so needed to whack that ass.

"Is this an interrogation or can I have a cup of coffee? I didn't get one since I was pulled away from breakfast."

Law Anders rose. "I'll get us all something. I get the feeling we're going to need it. You've been a bad girl, baby." He softened the assertion by winking her way.

"I love it when you cause trouble, sweetheart." Riley leaned in eagerly, as though he was getting ready for a show. His smile couldn't quite hide his excitement.

No wonder Kinley was running rampant. Kellan tried not to roll his eyes.

Dominic frowned. "Hey, you two need to take this seriously. Do you know what she did?"

The Anders brothers shook their heads. Law made his way to the coffeepot in the room, but upon hearing Dominic's displeasure, he sent a sidelong glance to Kinley.

She looked at her hands, folded in her lap.

"Start talking about Annabelle," Dominic demanded.

Her head popped up and her smile illuminated the room. "Of course, Master. I could talk about my best friend all day. Where to start? The beginning, then. Belle was born on a crisp autumn morning…"

Dominic growled her way. "That is not what I meant. You're digging yourself a hole. Consider this your first and last warning."

That was one more than Kellan would have given Kinley. If she was going to be difficult…well, Kellan had dealt with hostile witnesses before. "Where is Belle now?"

"I'm not exactly sure."

"Kinley…" Dominic barked.

"Yes, Master? I'm telling you the truth. I don't know *exactly* where she is." Kinley tried to appear cooperative, even contrite.

Kellan wasn't buying it.

"But you have a very good idea, don't you?" Dominic drawled.

She pursed her bow mouth, obviously unwilling to

answer.

In the face of her mute response, he scowled. "That's ten. Answer the question, Kinley. This is important."

"To you, Master?"

"To Kellan, Eric, and Tate. Disappointing them will be disappointing me. Tell Belle's lovers everything you know about her whereabouts."

Kinley's whole face went stormy and stubborn, her eyes narrowing. "Belle's never had any lovers. She's a virgin. She was waiting for the right men to come along." She sent them an acid glare. "I guess she hasn't found them yet."

Tate wilted like a fucking hothouse flower. "We're so sorry about that, Kinley. Honestly, I loved knowing that she'd waited. I kind of wished I'd waited, too, but then our experience together would probably be horrible for her because it takes a man some time to build up stamina. I blew my load in three point seven seconds the first time."

"Really?" Eric stared at his best friend, rolling his eyes.

"Dude, you were there. And you, like, came in her hand. Belle deserves better." He turned to Kinley. "Please. We want to apologize and ask her for a second chance. You have to tell us where she went."

"I like him. He can live," Kinley pronounced.

Kellan would use whatever she gave him to hunt Belle down. "Excellent, then tell him where to find her."

"I really don't know exactly. I was shocked to discover she'd left." The little brat's mock surprise crawled all over Kellan.

"She left in your car," he pointed out. "You gave her the keys."

"She needed them."

"But you're surprised that she left?"

Kinley squirmed in her seat. "She didn't say why she needed the keys."

Kell sent an angry glare to Dominic, who crossed his arms over his chest and speared her with a dark glare. "That's ten more, love. We're up to twenty. Want to make it thirty? I can arrange that."

"Come on, Kinley." Riley sent her a glance that suggested she be reasonable.

Law watched the entire event unfold, a smile playing at his lips, as if his wife's little defiance amused him.

"You gave her the keys to your car without asking where she was going?" Kell raised a brow.

"She's my friend. I trust her because she's got a lovely heart. She'll return the car to me when she no longer needs it. I just wonder about that male she was with. She called him Sir." Kinley shook her head as if the situation was so, so sad. "Guess you guys lost out. Sorry."

"What?" He bit the word out violently. Belle had found another fucking Dom in a few short hours? That was incomprehensible. Impossible. Although given who Dominic's friends were, it was possible an unattached Dom might have been around the hotel last night after the wedding. At this point, what surprised Kell more was that the guy hadn't come with two or three friends.

Or maybe that's who Belle was driving to meet. The thought stopped Kell cold. On the other hand, Oliver and his brothers hadn't mentioned Belle being with another man. He scowled. Something was fishy here…

"She wouldn't leave with a man she'd just met and she certainly wouldn't be calling him Sir," Eric said, shaking his head. "I'm going to call her again."

"You snooze, you lose," Kinley said in a little sing-song voice.

"For your disrespect, that's yet another ten." Dominic's foot tapped against the floor as he glared at her. "Your ass is going to be red after thirty."

Kinley ignored him, then her purse began ringing. She put a hand over her mouth, blinking as if she was utterly surprised. "Oh, my gosh. Belle's phone must have fallen into my bag."

So Belle had gone somewhere in Kinley's car in the middle of the night without a phone. And possibly with another man. Kellan's palm itched fiercely.

"Kinley, you had to have seen which direction Belle drove off," Riley prompted. "Help the guys a little. They seem genuinely eager to have her back."

"I only saw that my friend was crying and heartbroken because the men she's longed for turned out to be complete douchebags who refused to touch or collar her. They made her feel inferior simply because she hadn't slept with a man yet."

"That isn't what happened," Kellan insisted, trying to gather his patience. "And if she was crying and heartbroken over us, why would she be with another man?"

"Well, of course he was going to console her," Kinley shot back.

Kell was amazed Dominic didn't take his wife over his knee now. But since he didn't seem inclined to, it was time to point certain truths out to Kinley and watch her carefully. Every witness had tells. As cool as Kinley was behaving, she would still react to his questions. "You allowed her to drive off without her phone. What if her flight gets canceled?"

Nothing. Not a drop of emotion crossed those pretty features. "She'll be fine. She has my car."

"I'll go to the airport right now and find her," Tate offered.

"Sit down, Tate." Eric understood that Tate sometimes needed a handler. Or maybe a leash…

So, based on Kinley's reply, Kell guessed that Belle hadn't gone to the airport. He changed tactics. "Do you know how dangerous the highway could be in the middle of the night? If she's driving any distance, she could break down. Without a phone, she'd have no way to contact you or roadside assistance."

A flicker of worry crossed Kinley's delicate face, underscored by the way she shifted in her seat before she shook her head. "The car is in perfect condition."

"But tires go flat, don't they? Belle doesn't know how to change one."

"She doesn't," Tate put in with a nod. "She called me a few months ago when her beater got a flat."

"It's a new car, so the tires are new, too," Kinley defended.

"That doesn't help if she accidentally runs over glass or nails. She could be all alone, stranded on a highway right now, and you'd never know."

Kinley fidgeted, looking to a corner of the room, not meeting anyone's gaze.

"And there are a lot of drunks on the road at three in the morning. What if something happened to her? How long would it take for us to know?"

Kinley bit her lip, then sighed. "She's fine, okay. She's already where she needs to be, so you can stop worrying. We bought her another phone and I've already talked to her. Don't expect me to give you the number. She doesn't want to talk to you. And she wasn't alone because she had Sir."

Kellan had his doubts about Sir. "Tell me about this guy. Where did she meet him?"

"I introduced them. All he wants is her happiness. When he kissed her and she put her arms around him, I left them alone. I knew they'd be fine together." Her eyes slid off and to the right again.

Maybe Kinley wasn't coughing up the whole truth, he decided, but she wasn't totally lying, either. Had she packed a blow-up doll in Belle's bags as a joke? Or maybe they'd taken to naming their vibrators, but then why say they were kissing and hugging? Kell wasn't sure about that, but he doubted highly that Belle had run off with some guy she'd just met. She hadn't saved herself all these years only to give her innocence to the first prick Kinley introduced her to.

Unless she was so hurt and angry that she decided to do away with her hymen to spite them. That didn't sound like the Belle he knew. But he also hadn't imagined she would skip this morning's meeting without a word. She was definitely hurt and making decisions that could affect all their futures.

All the more reason to find her.

But Kinley hadn't cracked so far.

Tate leaned closer to Kinley, his whole face pleading. "Please just tell us where she is. I can't stand that she's out there hurting and thinking we don't care."

Kinley's face softened from rage to regret. "Belle asked me not to. I'm sorry, but I won't betray her confidence. And Dom Dom here can spank me all day long." She hooked out a thumb in Dominic's direction. "I'm not talking."

Dominic stood and held a hand out to his wife. "I'll add that to the list, too. After this child is born, you should know there's one hell of a hurricane waiting to hit your backside, love."

She put her hand in her husband's. "I accept that. I'll do anything to protect Belle."

With a sigh, Dominic tucked Kinley against him and turned to Kellan. "I'm afraid she's done. She and Belle are like sisters. I can't say I don't understand. I wouldn't break a brother's trust myself. The truth is, Belle isn't your submissive since she hasn't accepted your collar." He shrugged. "If there's anything I or the company can do to help you, I'll arrange that, but I won't expect Kinley to divide her loyalties anymore."

"We'll hire you." Eric stood, looking incredibly resolved.

Kellan shook his head at his friend. They had a resource they hadn't yet used because he'd hoped said resource was no longer behaving like a damn stalker. "Hold up on that request. I think we should talk to Tate first. He knows about Belle in a way we don't."

Tate flushed.

Bingo. Even a lawyer had tells.

"Let's go pack up while Tate tells us everything he knows about our girl." Kellan gave Tate his best big-brother look. "I mean *everything*."

* * * *

Tate let the door to their suite shut behind him, wondering if he would get punched once he told Eric and Kell the truth. He was pretty sure they were about to ask him a bunch of questions he didn't really want to answer. But there would be no pleading the fifth.

Eric turned on him the minute the door shut. "Dude, you told me you'd stopped the stalker stuff."

He rolled his eyes. "You make it sound like I'm lurking outside her bedroom window, snapping pictures of her while she's undressing."

"You wanted to," Eric pointed out.

Of course. He wanted to even more now that he'd seen her naked. Still, even he knew there were boundaries that, once crossed, got a man slapped with a restraining order.

"But I didn't. So let's stop lecturing me and find Belle. I don't care what Kinley says. She shouldn't be out there alone. Anything could happen to her."

He hated not knowing where she was and if she was truly all right.

Kellan ran a hand through his hair, looking tired and wrung out, before he dropped onto the sofa. "We'll find her faster than Anthony Anders, even without Kinley's help, because you've obsessively memorized everything about her. Haven't you?"

Frustration welled. "I'm not stalking her. I only followed her home to make sure she was safe."

"Yeah," Eric drawled. "You keep telling yourself that, buddy. Let's dig through that treasure trove of trivia in your head about Belle and figure out where she's gone."

She was his whole world, so yeah, Eric's implication

was a safe one. He didn't see why that made him a stalker. He'd followed her home at night because there had been a rash of rapes in her neighborhood. Imagining what could happen to her if he didn't see her in safely made him sick. He'd feel better after they installed a security system in her place. Or better yet, after they moved her into their house, into their bed.

And so what if he checked out her Facebook page more often than necessary? They were friends. She'd accepted his request, giving him permission to look at everything on her timeline.

"Think, Tate. If she's already reached her destination, then it's within a ten-hour drive from here. She's likely in Texas, Louisiana, maybe Oklahoma, or even as far as Kansas. Has she talked about having friends in any of those places?"

"She has Kinley here, but most of her friends are in New York or Chicago." Tate sighed, trying to get his brain to work. Usually he was perfectly clear, but now he understood why his father had warned him that emotion was deadly to logic. All Tate could think about now was the fact that Belle was alone and upset, that she probably hated him…and was planning to spend her life without him. That there was even a remote chance this guy she called Sir had already taken their place.

"I don't think Kinley has stashed her somewhere," Eric said. "I watched her face while Kellan questioned her. She lent Belle the car, but I don't think she helped our girl get to wherever she was going in any other way. They're in touch, but if Belle got a new phone before she headed out and gave Kinley the number, then I don't believe she's staying with or near Kinley. Belle wouldn't want to disrupt her friend's life that way."

"Since Kinley is a newlywed, Belle would refuse to be a hindrance or burden," Kell agreed.

Tate shook his head. Kell could say he wasn't interested

in anything long term all he liked, but any man who'd studied a woman that closely was definitely interested, even if he was a completely damaged fuck-up and behaving like a pussy.

Hmm, maybe he hadn't completely forgiven Kellan for last night.

"Right," Tate agreed. "She doesn't have a ton of family. Her dad died when she was a kid. No brothers or sisters. Her mom lives too far away. She just lost a grandmother, but Belle didn't know the woman." In fact, she'd brought him a copy of her grandmother's will a few weeks back to look through.

"So she probably hasn't gone to family." Eric paced by the windows, staring out as if he hoped she would show up at any moment and open her arms to them.

Tate hoped she would too, but he knew better. What he didn't know? Where the hell she'd gone.

"Even if we find her, what are we going to say?" Tate asked. "We talked for hours last night about shit between us, but what could we say to persuade her to give us another chance? Belle can be stubborn."

He couldn't stand the thought of her shutting them out. He'd tried so hard to get behind her walls, but Belle, while friendly, could be shy and very private. After a year of working with her and watching her more closely than he should admit to, Tate still found her a mystery. Belle possessed layers and layers he might never delve. That realization choked him up.

He'd been her friend because the others hadn't been ready to be her lover. He'd gotten as close to her as she'd allowed. At this moment, that friendship didn't seem to be helping him.

"Doesn't she have a college friend who moved to Oklahoma City?" Kellan asked. "She mentioned something about being shocked that her very urbane friend had fallen in love with the Midwest."

Yes, but Belle wouldn't go there. She was hurt. She wasn't the sort who'd seek a shoulder to cry on. No, Belle suffered in silence. She would go deep into herself. For that, she would want privacy. If she'd taken off somewhere in the middle of the night and abandoned her job before a meeting, that meant Belle sought to start over.

God, she was leaving them and if he couldn't find her, he might never see her again. Every single second she was gone, she drifted further and further away. The longer they let her stew in her own anger, the less chance they'd have to get her back.

And that dude she called Sir? Tate had to believe that was some exaggeration on Kinley's part. The Belle he knew wouldn't turn to someone else now. She would mourn. She would shut down.

"Hey, didn't she have a cousin who married a guy from Houston?" Eric had pulled out his laptop and started browsing the firm's vacation calendar. "Yeah, here it is. She went to the wedding six months ago. Maybe we should contact her cousin."

Belle's family was few and far between, so she held every member dear, she'd explained to him once. Her father's death when she'd been so young had been a tragic blow. He remembered the moment she'd told him about that terrible winter vividly. The sun gleamed across her blue-black hair and illuminated the tear on her cheek she'd tried to hold back. She'd fingered the picture she kept framed of him on her desk, looking at it so wistfully. Right then, Tate had ached to tell her that he, Eric, and Kell would be her family. But she hadn't been ready to hear that any more than she'd been ready to know that he wanted to make a family with her.

Now, Tate paced the suite, trying to shove out the panic that threatened to scatter his logic. Belle liked to feel close to friends and family, but she wouldn't burden them with her troubles. So that ruled out New York or Chicago. She couldn't have driven there in ten hours or less anyway. So where would she go? What money did she have without a job? Sure, she had a little saved in her bank account, but nothing that would last long without a paycheck. She'd need a roof over her head.

Jangling the change in his pocket, Tate crossed to the other side of the room, turning all the possibilities over in his head. Somewhere in Texas, Oklahoma, Louisiana—

Tate's head snapped up. That was it. Her late grandmother had left her a house in the French Quarter. Belle hadn't known the woman, but when he'd looked over the will, she'd admitted that she wished she had. It was a free roof in a new town. Somewhere she could start over. According to the documents he'd seen, the house was older and needed both repairs and updating. Belle would probably love to get her hands on the place. She could throw herself into that project. It would take her mind off the fact that her heart had been ripped out by three dumbass men who couldn't get their act together.

"She's in New Orleans. Give me two minutes and I'll tell you where exactly." He needed his laptop. He'd scanned in the files she'd given him because he'd served as her lawyer in this matter.

Kellan moved in behind him and stared over his shoulder as he started hunting down the file. "Why do you think that?"

"Because her grandmother left her a house," he explained as he located the document on his hard drive that had been prepared by a Malcolm Gates, esquire. At the time, the man had advised Belle that the will would take a while to go through the probate system.

"How did I not hear about this?" Eric looked over his other shoulder.

"She needed someone to look at the will and the transfer documents. By the time she received them, her grandmother had already been buried. I think she was sad that she'd never get to know the woman. Apparently, she only met her grandmother once. I guess her father and his mother had a falling out and they never repaired it. When we talked about the house, Belle didn't know what to do. She wondered if she should donate the house to the city as a historical site because she didn't have the money to fix it."

"She still doesn't, does she?"

"No, but if she gets a new job there or fixes it up herself..." Tate shrugged. "You know how she can be when she's determined."

"Yeah." Kellan glanced down at the address on Tate's screen and whistled. "Shit. That's right in the middle of the Quarter. That's a multimillion dollar property. Fixing it up would make it worth a few months of Ramen noodles and bologna sandwiches."

Tate frowned. He hadn't known that. "I never saw any documentation about the value. If they sent anything like that to Belle, she didn't forward it to me. She just said the place needed a lot of work."

"She's going to go there and sink herself into refurbishing that property, isn't she?" Eric asked.

The challenge would call out to her. "I'm almost certain of it."

"How can we be sure?" Kellan said. "I don't want to waste time on a wild goose chase."

"If we rent a car and drive to New Orleans, it's roughly eight hours," Tate pointed out. "Even if we were able to catch the next flight, by the time we factor in check-in and wait times, it might not be much shorter."

"She would have to get into contact with the lawyer to make sure it's out of probate. If it was, someone would need to let her into the house, get her keys, and have her sign some paperwork to transfer the ownership."

Eric groaned. "So she called him. Awesome. She bought a burner phone that we can't trace and she's going to use it for all her business."

"Not necessarily." Kellan grinned. "Do you remember

how we tried to teach Belle to put contacts into her phone and she still wouldn't do it?"

She kind of hated technology, Tate recalled. "Yeah. She would have to get the attorney's number from an e-mail. She might dump her phone, but she won't change e-mail accounts."

Belle wouldn't even know how. Thank god for that.

"Still, her e-mail is password protected," Eric pointed out.

Tate felt himself flush. Shit. Yeah, this might be the stuff he didn't want to admit to.

"You know her passwords, don't you, you magnificently perverse asshole?" Kellan slapped him on the back.

He pulled up her e-mails because there was just no comeback except that he was *her* perverse asshole. He sifted through her messages and found what he needed. He also read that, according to the lawyer, the house Belle was very likely settling into at that moment was notoriously haunted.

Lucky for him, he didn't believe in ghosts.

"Let's get packed." He closed the laptop. They were headed to the Big Easy.

Chapter Eight

"I think you're wrong about them, hon." Kinley's voice sounded through the speaker of her new phone.

Buying a new phone and changing her number had been Belle's idea because she'd suspected her former bosses would call, at least to settle any items related to their business. She couldn't stomach the thought of talking to them in cold, business-like terms. She'd left her office passwords and the statuses of her most important tasks with the intern— whom she hoped would remember all the information. He said dude a lot and often reeked of herbs that were illegal in most states.

She dusted off the gorgeous Queen Anne desk she'd found in what seemed to be her grandmother's office. The heavy cherry-wood antique anchored the room now with its elaborate moldings, scroll work, and mahogany inlays. After vacuuming the dupioni silk drapes, Belle had scrubbed the stained glass windows, and now sunlight poured through. She wasn't completely sure, but she thought that might be actual Tiffany glass. The huge chandelier in the dining room certainly was. In fact, everything in the house, while old and dusty, was classic, well made, and worth a small fortune. Her grandmother had possessed amazing taste. Who knew palm reading was so lucrative?

Now soft afternoon light illuminated the whole room,

and Belle surveyed all her hard work with pride. Thankfully, that hard work had prevented her from dwelling too much on her former bosses—at least until Kinley's call.

"I don't want to talk about them," she said to her bestie. "I just want to forget them and move on."

"Do you really think it's that easy?"

No, but that didn't mean she wasn't going to try.

"Sir is doing really well. I think he likes it here. He's napping in the window seat." His little puppy chest rose and fell with each breath. His paws moved as though he was running in his sleep. Puppy dreams. Belle smiled faintly.

She didn't want to think about what she would dream of tonight. She knew. The minute she'd closed her eyes, she'd been right back in their arms, feeling their hands stroke her body, their lips claiming hers, their fingers on her nipples and in her aching pussy.

"Don't change the subject. They were genuinely worried. And they put me through a serious interrogation."

Damn it. Belle hadn't meant to get Kinley in trouble. "I'm so sorry."

"Don't be. It was fun. I rarely get the chance to be so bratty anymore. Dominic tied me up, and I swear I was begging him, Law, and Riley after about ten minutes of torture. Luckily, Law is a cuddle bear."

"You mean he took pity on you?"

"Yep." She giggled. "I cried a lot, and he gave me an amazing orgasm."

Wow, that was a lot of personal information. "I'm glad that worked out for you."

Kinley cleared her throat as if realizing that she'd just spilled way too much information. "So Sir is adapting?"

Suddenly, he raised his head and twisted, his ears perking up as he stared out the window intently with a low growl. He began barking his little heart out.

"He was. But every once in a while, he's just loud." She moved, trying to see what had the dog's attention. "It's weird. He barks when I see absolutely nothing to bark at."

She could almost picture Kinley's shrug. "Animals are more sensitive to their surroundings than humans. I'm sure he'll settle in. Belle, I really wish you'd listen to me about your men."

They aren't my men. "Sir will be fine eventually, though he isn't exactly housebroken yet," Belle sidestepped Kinley's comment. "But I guess that will take time. Got any good tips?"

Kinley huffed. "Stop trying to change the subject. They're worried about you. Tate was practically crying. He's weirdly hot, you know. He's got that soulful geek thing. He's longing, Belle. Pining. All for you."

She closed her eyes, trying not to imagine that look on his face. She was sure Tate would be on her doorstep if she hadn't made herself scarce…though he was smart enough to track her down. If he wanted her, he would find her. She hoped she had the strength to turn him away.

"It wouldn't work with just me and Tate." He must know that, too. And it would be cruel to tear him away from his buddies when she knew their pairing couldn't last. "I care about him, Kin. I really do, but he needs Eric and Kellan. They understand his quirks and forgive him when he says the wrong thing. Without them, he'd just retreat into his shell. And they need him because he's logical and honest. I can't get in the middle of that. It would be like separating brothers."

"Of course you can't do that, honey," Kinley's voice was soothing even from five hundred miles away. "They're a set. Besides, you need something from each of them and you wouldn't be happy with just one."

It seemed wrong. So many women out there couldn't find one man, and Belle was insisting on three. Maybe she wasn't the right woman for any of them. "It doesn't matter."

"Does lying to yourself really help?"

Belle sighed. "I just don't think it's meant to be."

"I think you're giving up awfully easily." Kinley paused. "Kellan was leading the charge to find you."

That shocked Belle. "He must feel very guilty."

"Or he realizes he made a terrible choice." Her long sigh sounded over the line. "You know, you might be expecting Shangri-la between the three of you too quickly. Riley fought his feelings for me at first. He had things to work through. We talked. We argued. He had a lot of hesitation and second thoughts, but eventually he came around. Maybe Kellan needs more time and you need more patience. Men take their time in coming to conclusions that women just instinctively know. They fight their feelings, especially when they have baggage. Kellan has a whole boatload of it from what I can tell."

She thought so, too. Still, what she'd overheard from the bathroom in their suite had been very clear. He didn't want responsibility. He didn't want permanence.

"I don't think it's that simple."

"Nothing worthwhile is. A relationship like this isn't easy, and if you're expecting it to be, you're setting yourself up for failure. It takes a lot of work and honest talk. You three aren't communicating."

Maybe Kinley was right, but honestly, what else was there to say? She couldn't make Kell want her for more than a night.

Suddenly, Sir's whole body went on full alert and the barking began anew. Belle frowned as she moved to the window. From here, she had a great view of the courtyard that now swayed with the wind as the weather turned a bit chilly. A pretty orange and yellow tabby cat pranced across the bricks and turned her smug feline face toward the dog, looking deeply entertained by the dog's irritation.

Belle pulled Sir up into her arms and dropped the shade over the window, hoping the cat would be out of sight and out of mind. It wasn't working for her when it came to Kell, Tate, and Eric. Weariness set in. "Kinley, hon, I've got to go.

I still have to get the bedroom ready for tonight and find some kibble for the little beast."

She hoped she could find a store nearby. It would get dark soon.

"All right. I love you. Promise me you'll think about calling them, at least to let them know you're all right."

Belle bit her lip. In some ways, hearing their voices would be so tempting, but what would it accomplish? What she wanted hadn't changed. "They're probably on their flight home to Chicago." Then something occurred to her. If Kellan was spearheading some effort to find her, then... "They did catch their flight, right?"

"I don't know. They checked out of the hotel and caught a cab. You know what I know."

"But if you had to guess?"

Kinley hesitated. "I don't think they're folding up their tent and going home."

The answer filled Belle with both dread and an insidious thrill. "Thanks."

The phone clicked, and she was alone again. Belle had a feeling the night would be long.

A loud bang shot through the room. She started and let loose a little shriek. Sir scurried to huddle against her breast and buried his face.

What was that?

Dead silence followed. The roof didn't cave in. No murderous fiend jumped into the room. Nothing.

About thirty seconds passed before Belle let out a breath. A nervous laugh shook her chest. She would have to get used to the sounds this old house made. Maybe the furnace had kicked in.

"Some guard dog you are," she teased Sir.

When she turned back toward the desk, she noticed a piece of molding hanging from the bottom, just under the alcove where she'd tuck her knees when she sat. Belle frowned. Weird. She hadn't noticed it when she'd been dusting or sat there earlier.

With a puzzled frown, she knelt and tried to fit the piece back in place. Belle hoped this wasn't a sign the desk was falling apart and would need replacing. That would be a huge shame. Her grandmother's antique was a stunning, one-of-a-kind treasure.

As Belle fiddled with the molding, her fingers found a hidden niche the wood had concealed. It was deep under the desk. She set Sir down and crawled under, the Persian carpet a soft cushion for her knees. Though the space under the desk was too dark to see, she could feel the open compartment with her fingers. As she reached into the little space cautiously, she immediately encountered two items tucked inside. With a wince and a ginger tug, she pulled them out and crawled back.

Two old, pocket-size journals, one slightly more faded than the other. Belle frowned. This was her grandmother's office and her grandmother's desk. She flipped open the cover of one and glimpsed the handwriting. Decidedly feminine.

"Looks like Grandma wrote her memoirs. Or hid some secrets," she said absently to Sir as she sat on the rug.

Sir plopped himself down on her lap and immediately went back to sleep. She opened the other volume, the smaller of the two, and rifled through it a bit.

Belle frowned at the slightly yellow pages. Maybe her grandma had been on the crazy side because all she'd written in this journal was a list of long, random numbers that corresponded to even more random words, like "sunny," "backdoor," "raincoat," and "canceled." None of it made a lick of sense. What did 10056 00099873 have to do with "pink" and "fuzzy?"

Even more strangely, the latter half of the book had been written by a different hand. Same sorts of odd codes, but different penmanship for sure.

Frowning, she laid that one aside. Maybe the odd entries

in this book had something to do with her grandmother's psychic business, though Belle had no idea how. Maybe the code protected her clients' anonymity? The second book was bigger, and Belle knew what it was the minute she skimmed the first page.

Grandma's diary.

Belle's heart skipped a beat.

September 27th, 1955. Her father's birthday.

Oh, my baby boy. How I love you.

Tears pierced her eyes as she realized she was reading her grandmother's uncensored thoughts—those of a stranger related to her by blood about the birth of her own father. Belle thumbed through the pages, her wonder growing. She'd wanted to figure out who her grandmother had been. Well, this would probably be a good start. In fact, after skimming ahead a few pages, it seemed the whole volume was a book of letters written from mother to son.

Her grandmother hadn't been heartless or indifferent. She'd loved him very much, based on just the first page or two alone. So what had happened? Why the rift?

Belle was willing to bet the answers lay in this book. She slid the one filled with gibberish back in its hiding place and jimmied with the molding until she felt a little groove slide back into a seemingly corresponding tongue. It locked in place easily, as if made for just that purpose.

As she stood to head to the bedroom, she wondered how the strip of decorative wood had come loose like that. It seemed so secure now. And where had the loud bang come from? When she really thought about it, the noise had seemed too close to be the furnace. She'd have to solve that mystery when she wasn't utterly exhausted.

Sir followed her from the room with a sleepy yawn, and she shrugged away her questions. Since nothing terrible or tragic had happened, did it matter now? She had some reading to do. But not until she washed the sheets on the bed and made sure the house's many doors and windows were all locked.

As she looked around once more, Belle shook her head. An inch-thick layer of dust, the ancient hot water heater, the peeling wallpaper. Being the owner of a home with so much history and recent neglect was hard work…but at least it might keep her mind off her broken heart.

* * * *

Eric finally managed to get that fucking intern Belle had hired to pick up his phone just as they turned down the narrow, busy street that should lead them to her new home.

Her temporary home.

"Yeah?" Warrington Dash III had an upper-crust name and three judges in his family, which was good for him because Eric was pretty sure the kid had a lot of pot in his system. Without such familial influence, he'd probably be behind bars.

"Sequoia, we've been calling you for hours. Why haven't you been answering the damn phone?"

The kid was all of twenty but had already decided not to go by Warrington, the family name he'd been given. Instead, he'd chosen the name Sequoia in honor of trees or some shit. He was studying to become an environmental lawyer, and that made Eric weep for the planet.

"Dude, I was doing yoga. No phones. It blocks the process. Hey, I could get you in sometime. You three could use some serious introspection."

They'd have better "process" with another intern. "I need you to handle the calls at the office for a bit. Something's come up on this trip, and we're going to be away a few more days."

Kellan pulled into a parking space and gestured up the street, letting him know they weren't far from her address. Tate bounded out of the car in an instant.

Eric put a hand over the phone. "Catch him. He'll run

down the street, screaming her name like some *Streetcar Named Desire* impersonation." Eric turned his attention back to his call the minute Kell closed the car door. "So I need you to go back to the office and grab the calendar on Belle's desk."

"Dude, Belle and I already had this conversation. I've already done all of the stuff she told me to do. It's a total bummer she quit."

"She did *what*?"

"Yeah, she called a couple of hours ago and said she wasn't coming back. Oh, and she faxed her resignation, too. I'm supposed to tell you guys that she found a new home and stuff. Do you think she's going to want the yogurt in the fridge? I could use that tomorrow because work makes me hungry and it's the only vegan thing in the office. You guys eat a lot of animal flesh. Do you really think that's good for you?"

She'd quit—and she'd done it by telling the goddamn intern. She hadn't even had the courtesy to call them and tender her resignation. "Don't touch her yogurt. No matter what she told you, she's coming back."

He stabbed at his phone to end the call, then hopped out of the car, his heart pounding in his chest. Anger simmered in his veins, mixing with cold panic and encroaching dread.

He jogged up the street, his dress shoes slapping against the concrete, heading for the other two. Kellan had managed to contain Tate, and the two of them stood in front of a three-story house set right against the street with a blue door. In the dark, he thought it might be connected to the little house around the corner, but he couldn't be sure.

"Belle quit. She called Sequoia and told that pot-smoking fucker she wasn't coming back," Eric grated out.

Kellan cursed. "That's not a good sign. I really expected her to tell me off, then give me the cold shoulder until I groveled."

And just like this "move," the fact that she hadn't more

than suggested she really didn't intend to come back. This wasn't just a snit. They were about to launch a battle to bring her back...but for the first time, Eric wondered if the war was unwinnable.

Eric stared at the pale stucco house with its bent screen door. It might look a little rundown, but once it had a coat of paint and a few repairs, the place would shine and look like the mansion Belle's paperwork suggested she'd inherited. In fact, in both location and historical significance, he was looking at pure New Orleans splendor.

Restoring the house would be Belle's dream project.

"Shit." Tate stood beside him, shaking his head as he studied the place in the streetlamp lit evening. "She's never going to want to leave here. We have three bedrooms that she says need paint with 'personality,' whatever that means, and a game room she refers to as the man cave. She holds her nose when she walks in there. Do you think that means something?"

"It means you should pick up your damn socks," Eric groused.

"I'd even be grateful for that," Kell put in. "But you've heard her diatribe about your kitchen. Even if this house needs a lot of work, she's going to be far more interested in redoing a historic charmer in New Orleans than some suburban abode in Chicago."

"We're fucked. Our only saving grace might be that she can't live here forever. This place is way too big for one person. I looked around for the front door. That guest house behind it is attached, but I didn't find the main entrance. This isn't it." Tate pointed at the little blue door.

Usually, Eric liked to be aware of the problems he faced. This time, the entire conversation just unnerved him.

Kellan studied what they could see of the place. "The taxes will be a killer. I don't think Belle has a ton of cash, unless that was part of her inheritance."

"Her grandmother left her some money," Tate said. "But

the amount wasn't specified in the documents I saw. Those were about the house, but if her grandmother had a lot of money, would the place be in disrepair? Even if Belle sinks her whole bank account into the house, I doubt it will be enough."

"Before we can worry about the house or her intentions, we need to remember that she ran. Will she even let us in the door, presuming this is it?" Eric hoped there was a hotel nearby with rooms available. Even this late at night, tourists walked up and down the street. They all had to sleep somewhere. He and the guys did too, though he sincerely hoped it would be with Belle.

He scanned the exterior of Belle's new house, assessing the modest but colorful door flanked by shutters. The rusted screen door flapped a bit in the breeze. He didn't see any light from the inside coming through the windows. Was she still awake or had she gone to sleep, blissful that she hadn't had to talk to them all day?

He'd played through about a hundred scenarios in his head, ranging from Belle running into his arms to the one where she found her inner warrior princess and went medieval on their asses.

Now that he was standing outside her darkened house, he really worried. He wasn't sure how the hell he would handle it if she told them to go to hell.

"Why are the lights out?" Kellan stepped up to a little carriage-style fixture affixed to the exterior that should have illuminated the area.

"The house hasn't been lived in for months," Tate explained. "She'll be lucky if the power is still on."

Standing here in front of the place, a chill swept through him, much colder than anything the fall breeze had swept in. Just a couple of yards away, the street was lit, looking bright and elegant, but here, a deep gloom clung.

He glanced around the back of the house, looking for any sign of life. Total darkness. There was a thin alley between Belle's house on one side and a neighbor's fence on the other. Just enough for a man to lay in wait. Belle wouldn't see anyone creeping through her yard. No one from the street would see a thing either.

If they couldn't persuade her to come back to Chicago with them in the morning, they would so be getting some lights to brighten up the alley and exterior tomorrow. And whether it lacked charm or not, he'd make sure the perimeter had a sturdy fence.

"I don't like it," Tate said. "It's too dangerous. This is just two blocks from that woman's murder yesterday, the one we heard about on the radio."

The death of Karen Ehlers had made a huge news splash across New Orleans. It had been all over the radio as they'd driven into town. The fifty-nine-year-old socialite had been discovered in her New Orleans mansion, strangled by unknown intruders.

She'd been one of the toasts of the city, known for her philanthropy and love of her home town. Turned out that she'd also been known for something else.

"Belle's not a hooker," Eric reminded him.

"She won't be turning tricks for strange men so that will reduce her odds of being strangled significantly," Tate added. "That's true."

The big guy hadn't factored him in. Eric was still really mad. And yeah, he hadn't done the best job of letting Belle know that he would treasure her virginity. Not as bad as Kell, but even so…she shouldn't have run off.

"But technically, Karen Ehlers wasn't a hooker. She was a madam." Tate was always so fucking precise. "Should we knock on the door or something, even if it's not the front? You two constantly tell me I can't just hang out around her house and look like a pervert stalker or the cops will arrest me."

Kellan was still fiddling with the light fixture. It came on suddenly. The old, dusty bulb bathed the door in a hazy,

yellow glow. "The bulb was out of the socket. That's odd."
At least they could somewhat see now.

An odd banging sounded from somewhere around the
house. Eric's instincts went on high alert. He dashed around
the side of the building and looked down the alley. The
illumination from the street didn't penetrate this far back. In
fact, it was eerily dark. If anything, the neighbor's interior
lights behind him blinded him just enough to make seeing
anything almost impossible.

Still, he could swear he saw a shape moving in that alley
in the distance.

He was just about to run after the asshole when he heard
a scream from inside the rundown house that made his whole
body freeze in terror.

Belle.

They had to get to her.

* * * *

Belle woke from her dream, certain that she was no
longer alone in the house. Her hands shook. Her heart
drummed in her chest. Pure fear threatened to choke her.

Move! Don't just lay here.

As quietly as she could, she kicked the covers away and
swung her feet, moving slowly so the wooden floors
wouldn't creak. Belle shivered with every step, but forced
herself to keep moving. When had the room gotten so cold?
She wrapped her arms around herself and she could
practically see her breath, as though the air around her was
freezing. She'd turned the ancient heater on a few hours ago.
Had it stopped working?

In the short time she'd been in this house, Belle had
quickly realized that she had plumbing, electrical, and
flooring problems. Now she could add the HVAC unit to that
long, expensive list. That was before she tackled updating the
décor.

Something loud banged downstairs, startling her. She shrieked. Her hands shook in a way that had nothing to do with the cold. Fear iced her veins. Someone was in the house.

Where the hell had she put her cell phone? Sir was suddenly right at her heels, yipping up at her. Did he think it was play time?

"Keep quiet," she hissed under her breath as she remembered she'd left her new cell phone on the charger downstairs since that seemed to be one of the few electrical sockets currently functioning. She'd decided to find the fuse box in the morning and see if she could trip the breakers and get some of the upstairs sockets operational. She'd been too tired to deal with it before going to bed.

The moment her head had hit the pillow, she'd fallen into a deep, thick slumber where she'd had horrible nightmares of dead women swinging from the rafters of her house. Different girls in different eras, but all hanged in the same room from the same beam. Creepy. She'd let Gates's warning get into her head. Even now, Belle tried to shake away the vestiges of the dreams. They had seemed so real to her.

The lawyer had said young women committed suicide in this house. Her dream had clearly shown a murder. Belle really hoped she hadn't gotten her grandmother's gift. She hoped even more fervently that she hadn't dreamed about her own violent end.

Was someone really in her house or was she just freaked out? Who would have broken in? Squatters? The place had been vacant so long maybe some of the homeless thought they could just move in. Despite what Mr. Gates had suggested, it couldn't really be ghosts.

She tiptoed through the bedroom and toward the stairs, trying to control her runaway breathing. Until she reached her phone, she didn't have a way to call 911. Right now, she didn't even have a weapon to fight off an intruder. What the hell was she going to do? What time was it? She wished she knew if there was any chance that there were still people on the street outside to hear her call for help.

Belle paused, trying to decide if she should risk going for her phone or just get out of the house. Then she realized that everything around her had gone quiet. She didn't hear footsteps, per se. She didn't see shadows or movement, but every creak and groan of the stairs brought fresh terror. Was someone here?

Maybe she really was just overreacting because the dreams had provoked her imagination. They'd started as soon as she closed her eyes. One vivid nightmare bled into the next in a terrible montage.

Helplessly, Belle had watched pretty young women being pulled through the house, screeching and pleading and fighting with every step. Each had been utterly helpless to stop a noose from winding around her neck before a dark figure hauled them high up the stairs. Finally, the assailant tightened the rope around the poor women's throats and shoved them over the banister, leaving them to dangle to their death.

As the last had been pushed, her neck broke. A jarring crack had jolted Belle awake.

Except that noise hadn't been a byproduct of her dream. Had it? She'd heard another sound awfully like it since she crept from her bed.

Even if the noise had been real, that didn't mean someone had broken in. Old homes shifted and groaned. She had to get used to that fact. Her newish apartment in Chicago hadn't been noisy until the middle school kid living with his single mom above her had taken up the sax.

At the top of the stairs—the very stairs she'd seen in her dream—was a small umbrella holder. She'd noticed her grandmother's canes stashed there earlier in the day and she inched one out of the little bucket triumphantly. At least now she had some kind of weapon.

Sir barked again.

"Shh." She tried to shush him, but if she died because her puppy couldn't stay quiet, she was going to kill Kinley. She just was.

She managed to sneak to the first floor, wincing with each step down. Just another few tiptoes, and she would have her phone in hand. If she was simply hearing things, who cared? She was terrified, and if the police laughed at her, so be it. She wasn't going to put off calling for help just because she wasn't absolutely positive she was about to be killed.

As her eyes slowly adjusted to the dim light filtering into the house from outside, she made out the small table in the kitchen where she'd stashed her phone. Ten steps to the table, then she could dash out the servant's door and call for help. It didn't matter that she was in her nightgown. This was New Orleans. Surely they'd seen freakier things than a woman in her PJs emblazoned with martini glasses and shoes all over it, decorated with the words *Girls Night In* across her boobs.

Once she was on the street, she wouldn't be alone, she prayed.

She was almost to the phone when the light over the back door flickered on, pouring light through the big kitchen window and blinding her for a moment.

Then she felt something—or someone—brush past her. Not around her ankles. Sir couldn't stir the air like that. No, this had been done by something terribly near her torso.

Belle screamed, the sound coming from deep in her gut. There was another loud crash, then something that sounded like metal wrenching, then a splintering sound. Sir barked madly, placing his little body in front of hers with as much of a menacing growl as four pounds of canine could manage.

Acting on pure instinct, Belle swung out, hefting the cane and trying desperately to whack whoever was coming after her.

"Belle, baby, stop," a familiar masculine voice commanded. Suddenly, warm, strong arms wrapped around her. "It's all right. It's just me."

Tate? When had he gotten here? How had he found her? Belle didn't care. She threw her arms around him, taking in his familiar scent, his comfort. His big body was warm and safe against hers.

"Let's go check the rest of the house to see if there's any sign of an intruder." Kellan brushed past her, leading Eric along. "Tate, don't take your eyes off her. If you see anything out of place, beat the shit out of it."

After a moment of fumbling against the wall, light flooded the L-shaped kitchen, and she could see again.

Tate's arms tightened around her. "Baby, what happened? You screamed, and we could hear you from outside."

"I think someone might have been in the house." Her words shook. Now that she knew she was safe, the adrenaline bled from her veins, leaving her weak with relief. "We should call the police."

Though she didn't know what they could tell her at this point. Whether there'd been some forced entry and where? Maybe she could hope for prints. Or maybe they would tell her there was no sign of anything other than her overactive imagination.

Kellan walked back in the room. "It was just the screen banging open and shut with the wind. Looks like it's bent and the latch is broken. The door itself was locked but the screen made a hell of a lot of noise. I'll jimmy it so it will stay secure for tonight."

"All the downstairs windows are locked," Eric said a minute later. "I checked. Are you sure someone was actually in the house?"

"I felt someone run past me." It had been a light touch, a stir of the air, then nothing.

Kellan looked around the room. "Did you do a thorough search of the premises when you got here?"

Why was he using his lawyer voice on her? She'd heard him use that quiet tone on many a skittish witness. "I checked a couple of rooms, but it was getting late and I was too tired to look everywhere. I focused on the office and master bedroom since I'm using them."

"What is this?" Eric picked up Sir, frowning. "Is this one of those puppies from the wedding?"

She grabbed her dog and held him close, crooning, "Don't you mind him."

"It's possible you've had squatters here, Belle," Kellan pronounced. "This place has been abandoned for months, right?"

"Yeah. I thought of that." She winced. Tate would remember that she'd inherited the house. They'd done their research—fast.

"We'll search every room before we go to bed, open every door and every closet. Tomorrow morning, we'll improve the security. We'll make a comprehensive list of everything that needs attention and break it out."

Kellan was in charge. It should have annoyed her that he thought he could just walk into her house and take over, but his authoritative voice calmed more than irritated her. Still, she couldn't let them stay here.

"Are you okay, Belle?" Tate asked, inching close again.

Was she? She'd been so terrified before they'd arrived. The door banged again and she jumped. Yes, that had been the sound. God, what was she doing? She pulled away from Tate. She'd had a bad dream and convinced herself she was hearing things that weren't there. The house was old and in need of repair. Exhaustion still weighed on her. She needed to turn on some white noise and go back to sleep.

After she figured out why they were standing in the middle of her kitchen at midnight. "What are you guys doing here? You were supposed to have flown back to Chicago already."

Eric shook his head as he walked back to the front door. "You were supposed to be on that flight, too, Belle."

"I canceled my reservation, but not yours."

They eyed her as she spoke. She wished again that she'd packed a robe. Though the nightshirt covered the essentials, she wasn't wearing a bra. She worried that her nipples would give away how glad she was to see them.

"We'll also have to replace the screen and the door," Eric said, walking back in.

"What?" She better not have heard that right. "That door looked like an original part of the house."

"Now it's kindling." Eric shrugged.

Tate frowned sheepishly. "Sorry. Once I heard you cry out, I didn't think about anything but getting to you. I'm really sorry about the door, but I was completely justified in breaking it down. Not only was that madam who lived two blocks away murdered just yesterday, but look at the overall murder rate in New Orleans. I probably should have done a quick assessment of the physics of busting that old slab of wood down. My shoulder really hurts. And then you clocked me with the granny cane."

"He hit that freaking door like a linebacker," Kellan agreed. "We should be glad there wasn't a glass screen in front or we'd be stitching him up. You know, a well-placed kick might have worked just as well, man. I'm also pretty good at picking a lock."

If she let them, they would devolve into an argument about how they should have broken into her house. "I quit, guys. Didn't Sequoia tell you?"

All three men zipped their gazes her way now, wearing scowls ranging from unhappy to forbidding.

"You quit to the intern. Does that seem like an adult way to handle this situation?" Kellan had dropped the lawyer tone and now spoke in pure, grade-A Dom voice.

She so had a way to address that concern. "The last time I saw you, you and Tate were fighting like a couple of school kids, so don't you dare accuse me of being unprofessional."

Eric shrugged out of his jacket. "That was sex, Belle. There's nothing professional about sex."

"Damn straight. And I want to know where the guy is," Kell said, his voice turning deeper, darker. "Why isn't your 'friend' here defending you."

"Who are you talking about?" She set Sir back down and he did a quick sniff of all three men.

"Kinley said you left with someone you called Sir," Tate said. "But you were just being polite, right? You're a very well-mannered woman. You wouldn't have just met some random man and run off with him. I mean, if you waited twenty-six years to have sex, you're probably not going to copulate with a stranger."

"Tate, you're not helping the situation," Kellan said.

Oh, her BFF was such an awesome bitch. Kinley had told them she'd run off with Sir without mentioning that Belle had slapped that name on her new dog. She had to hold in a little giggle.

Sir scampered around their ankles as Belle did her best to look innocent. "Of course I'm polite."

Tate winced as he moved his sore arm. "I simply pointed out that she's picky. Aren't you, Belle? That's not a bad thing."

"I'll get you some ice to put on that." She did feel bad about hurting Tate. She hadn't exactly held back. "If I have any."

She practically ran to the old fridge around the corner in the kitchen when the truth hit her. Her former bosses and almost lovers were here. All three of them. She wasn't sure what to do about it. On the one hand, she'd severed ties with them. None of the reasons why had changed.

Except...despite the house being locked up, Belle had still felt something brush past her. Surely the house wasn't really haunted.

She found a freezer bag in the dusty pantry and dumped some of the cubes from the trays to make a quick ice pack as she contemplated what to do. Let them stay...or make them go.

Tate stood in the doorway of the pantry, his face a weary mask. "Don't throw us out, baby."

Well, she'd never said they were stupid. They'd been smart enough to send in the one she couldn't turn away. Tate had always held a soft spot in her heart. He was awkward and a little weird and she adored that part of him. He was unlike anyone else.

"Here, put this on your shoulder."

He took the baggie out of her hand. "I won't sleep tonight unless I know you're safe. Please let us stay."

His dark, soulful eyes searched her face hopefully. Damn, the man was hot and there was something so earnest and sexy about the way he asked. It wasn't Tate's instinct to be polite. He was more likely to give a PowerPoint presentation about why he was right. He was thinking their interaction through, being careful with her. She found something about that so sweet.

Did she really want to stay here alone tonight? Sir bounced into the tight space, skidding to a stop at Tate's feet. If they left, she would be alone with an overly hyper puppy. "You can stay the night. I need someone to fix the door."

He nodded, looking so relieved. "I'll get it done in the morning. Kellan said he'd secure it for the night, and Eric is going to walk through the house once more. We'll make sure you're safe."

From everything but them. "Thanks."

"And we'll talk in the morning. Belle, you can't just run away from us. Leaving without a word wasn't fair."

She could still feel how vulnerable she'd been standing there naked while they debated the merits of her virginity. "Humiliating me wasn't fair."

Tate started to pace, a familiar habit but one that spoke of his frustration. "I didn't humiliate you. I was happy about your...news. A little surprised, but happy. I would have been gentler if I'd known. I've never slept with a virgin before, Belle. I should have studied how to do it properly. I'm sure I could find a book or two that explains how to make it as pleasant as possible. I don't want to hurt you. I'm…well, I have a large penis."

He was going to kill her. She so would rather deal with Eric's logic or Kellan's authority than Tate's brutal honesty.

She held up a hand. "Stop. I understand your reluctance, but you know damn well that wasn't Kellan's problem. Let's just get some sleep and we can deal with this tomorrow."

"All right." He leaned his good shoulder against the doorway, way too close to her for her peace of mind.

At their feet, her puppy hiked a leg.

"Sir, don't you pee on the floor."

Tate's eyes widened. "I wasn't even thinking about it."

Then comprehension seemed to set in. He snorted as she held her puppy. "Ah, hello, Sir. That is absolutely the meanest thing I've seen in a long time, Belle. You can't name the dog Sir."

He couldn't tell her what to name her puppy. She wasn't about to let him take away her little revenge. "I already did. And I need to start house training him. Can you walk outside with me while he does his thing?"

Tate grinned, and Belle's heart did an unwanted flip. "Sure, baby. And I'll let Kellan wonder a little longer about the mystery Dom Kinley said you left Dallas with. He deserves to stew for a while, but he's going to spank you for naming that little thing Sir. Is it really a dog? Have you checked to make sure it's not a rat with a bit of extra fur?"

He wasn't *that* ugly. "Be nice to my dog, Tate."

Tate opened the back door for her. "Yes, ma'am. That's a beautiful animal you've got."

At least one of them was listening.

She let Sir down, and he ran around the courtyard, looking for a good place to handle his business. She stood by Tate, feeling safer than she had in hours.

She was in so much trouble.

Chapter Nine

Belle woke to soft light filtering through the filmy curtains covering the windows. She glanced at her phone. One of the pluses of having her bosses show up was Eric's knowledge of fuse boxes. All the plugs worked again, so she'd been able to charge her phone while it sat on her nightstand.

Nine a.m. Wow, she rarely slept that late. She stretched and nudged Sir, who had managed to hop up on the bed with her. She'd tucked him into his little dog bed on the floor, but he'd chosen to cuddle up with her instead.

Despite having three gorgeous men in this house, she'd slept with the dog. Yep. Her life was surely looking up.

Stop it, Belle. You can't think about sleeping with them. Absolutely not. No way.

She had to be strong because she wasn't going to be a doormat, a novelty, or a friendship wrecker.

But would Kell drive five hundred miles to walk over a doormat he'd already wiped his feet on? Would Eric come all this way just to rubberneck at the silly virgin again? Would Tate actually tag along with them to declare his undying love once more if he thought their relationship was over? Belle doubted it, but even so she couldn't pretend that Saturday night in Dallas hadn't happened—or that it hadn't crushed her. In fact, that event had been a turning point. She needed to do more with her life than pine over them. Today, she would start.

As she climbed from bed, she glanced around the room she felt sure had been her grandmother's. The high ceilings with elaborate crown moldings and the fireplace gave the room such grandeur and elegance. All she had to do was rip down the yellow floral wallpaper that looked like spring had puked and the tacky green marble mantle and hearth. Otherwise, the lines of the room were classic and clean. The door to the balcony overlooking the courtyard invited her outside to bask in the bright autumn morning. Belle pictured sipping coffee there and never hearing the sounds of the city or seeing anyone go by. It would be her own private escape.

She needed a distraction, a creative outlet, something to launch her new career that would fund her life away from her former bosses, a project that would help her focus on something besides her broken heart. This place fit the bill. With enough money and a lot of elbow grease, she could make it something to be proud of again. As she made the house a home again, she could unravel the mystery of the past that had shaped her departed loved ones. Already, the snippets she'd read of her grandmother's journal hinted at the woman's life. The initial entries Belle had read had waxed positively poetic about how sweet her baby boy was and how much she loved being his mother. But soon, she'd begun repeatedly apologizing to him in her writings.

Her grandmother never once mentioned the child's father. The journal started the day of the baby's birth and lacked all mention of a man or her romantic life. Belle had to wonder how hard it had been to raise a child alone back then, when the stigma had been far greater. Her grandmother had clearly possessed backbone.

But how had a single mother afforded this grand house? According to the records Mr. Gates had sent her way, Marie Wright had paid cash for this house in 1960. No mortgage. Even then, this real estate would have been spectacularly expensive. Belle had never heard a whisper about her grandmother inheriting money. Had she been the mistress to a man who'd left her pregnant and given her the money for this house to ease his guilty conscience? Belle didn't know a lot about the woman, but somehow that scenario didn't seem right.

"Maybe Grandma really was psychic and she got stock tips from the dead," she murmured to Sir. "If not, she had to have read a whole lot of palms to buy this place. What do you say we explore it today and start adding to our to-do list?"

Sir wagged his tail and headed out of the room, more likely because he needed to scurry downstairs and heed nature's call than because he understood her.

As she stepped into her fluffy slippers, Belle kind of hoped the men had overslept or had rebooked an early flight back to Chicago. She wasn't looking forward to the coming confrontation, so the less time they stayed, the better. But she owed it to them to at least hear what they'd come all this way to say. Those three men had been better than good to her for over a year. One disastrous personal catastrophe shouldn't undo all her professional goodwill. The very least she could do was give them the courtesy of an exit interview and tips on finding a new assistant.

The idea of some other woman taking care of them made her heart clench and pang, but Belle did her best to ignore it. She'd made her choice to move on and find another happiness.

Sir scampered down the stairs on light feet. She wasn't quite so nimble, wincing at every creak she made with each step. On the second story landing, she peeked around, wondering where the guys had slept last night. According to the information she'd received when she inherited the house, it had four other bedrooms. No doubt, they'd all been dusty and not ready for guests. Guilt niggled her. Last night, as soon as she'd finished talking to Tate and Eric and they had restored the electricity, she'd run to her bedroom and locked herself in. Otherwise, Belle had feared she would be too tempted to see if there was any hope they could somehow reconcile. But no. She had to strip away her little-girl dreams and stop wishing for a happily ever after.

Running out on them probably made her a coward, but Belle had been so relieved to see them. She hadn't wanted to give them the wrong impression or lean on them. They made it so easy. Comfort her after a nightmare, secure a screen door, fix a breaker, check the windows... She'd had a long list of things to do and now? Poof. They were done. Last night, some part of her had craved nothing more than to let them shoulder her problems, but it would be unfair to rely on them now—to give Tate false hope, to wheedle Eric into giving her more elbow grease, to force Kell into the uncomfortable position of setting her aside again. Her heart probably couldn't take it either.

When Belle started down the second set of stairs, the smell of coffee wafted up from the kitchen. Damn. There went her hopes for a peaceful morning.

She really should have showered before leaving her room. But she still needed to clean the bathrooms and wash towels. No clue if the hot water heater was even working. With a sigh, Belle turned back, thinking a cold shower might do her some good, when the door to the kitchen swung open and Kellan stood, hands on hips, staring down at Sir.

"We need to have a talk, dog. I saw you sniffing around my dress shoes. Don't even think about it." He lifted his dark eyes from the canine and looked her over. Heat flared there briefly. Then he banked it. "Good morning, Belle."

No skipping out now. Eric might not press her to talk immediately. She could invent a reason to convince Tate that she needed to go upstairs. But Kellan would either tie her to a chair...or follow her upstairs. God knew what would happen then.

"Good morning," she murmured. "I was just going to

grab some coffee before I showered. I bought some things from the convenience store down the street, but I haven't made it to the grocery store yet. I'll go out in a few minutes to find us some breakfast."

That would take a chunk of time. Today was Monday, so she had to believe the guys intended to get back to work and Chicago soon. They wouldn't leave Sequoia alone at the office for long, surely. So if she could survive a couple of hours without pining for them too obviously, then she would be alone again. Rattling around all by herself in the empty house would be unnerving, so Belle promised herself that she'd call today to get a good security system. And find a nice bottle of wine because she was probably going to cry herself to sleep tonight.

Kellan shook his head. "Eric's already been to the grocery store. He cooked bacon and eggs. They're waiting for you. It's going to be a little simple for a few days, until we can get the oven working properly. You should get in there. Tate's already had a plate. He'll go back for seconds and thirds. Eric claims he eats like a hobbit. I don't know what that is, but apparently it's always hungry."

Kellan wasn't big on fantasy films. Tate really did eat somewhat like a hobbit. He was constantly snacking, but somehow that didn't affect his perfect body.

Belle walked into the kitchen and found utter chaos. The big table was covered by paperwork and computers. Cords slithered across the tables like snakes entwined with one another. Cups of coffee cooled in between all the other clutter. Someone had placed a TV on the counter. Currently, the little device spit out news and stock quotes while Tate and Eric both spoke into their cell phones.

"Don't you dare pull that clause on me. That is not the intent of the verbiage, nor is it the language. I will sue you so hard, your children will still be feeling it when they turn eighteen. Do you understand me?" Tate was a sweetheart with her, but he got pissed off when people used his words against him. Belle swore sometimes that he grew claws and fangs when he went into lawyer mode.

"No. No, I can't make that date. We need to settle this. I understand that we have science on our side, but they have a sick little girl with asthma holding her teddy bear. Have you looked at the visuals on this one? No one is going to listen to a bunch of boring medical journals. We're going to lose." Eric ran a hand across his head in an obvious sign of frustration. "We need a different strategy pronto."

Belle stared at her formally grubby kitchen. Every surface she could see appeared to have been wiped clean, then utilized as office space.

She turned on Kellan. "What the hell is going on here?"

He smiled sardonically. "Welcome to the New Orleans branch of Baxter, Cohen, and Kent. I think it's going well for a startup, don't you?"

She gaped at them. They could not be serious. In fact, she could think of a dozen reasons that was impossible— starting with the fact that they didn't have licenses to practice law in Louisiana. Not only that, they could not run a business out of her kitchen. What about their office and life back home?

Eric put a hand over his phone. "Belle, baby, did you get the latest numbers from the EPA on the Hanover case?"

She'd put them on his desk last week. Unfortunately, his desk was in Chicago. "This is my kitchen. There are no latest numbers on the Hanover case here."

Kellan reached over her toaster and pulled some paperwork off what appeared to be a damn fax machine. "Here you go. I had Sequoia fax them. What a surprise. He sent a note protesting the use of fax machines and said to pass that on to you, too. Apparently we shouldn't use hard copies because it's bad for the environment." He turned back to her with a sigh. "Give me one good reason I can't fire him."

Belle half heard Kell. What had these crazy men done?

Instead of using their heads and realizing they couldn't possibly run a practice from her house, they'd bought every piece of office equipment known to man and set it up in her kitchen. She was fairly certain she glimpsed a copy machine in the butler's pantry. "Given his connections, you know you can't. Don't forget, you have a very nice office in Chicago. Then Sequoia wouldn't have to fax you anything. Much comfier chairs there as well. This doesn't make a good office."

Eric covered his phone and murmured, "But you're here."

Belle didn't want to, but she melted a bit.

"See that you do, you piece of crap," Tate yelled into his phone, then paused. "Sure. Yeah, tell your mom hi for me." Another pause. "I doubt Wednesday will work. It looks like I'll be here for a while and the Internet sucks, but I'll see what I can do. Good luck on the raid." He frowned as he hung up the phone. "Sorry, that was Phil from Greene and Associates. He's such an ass, but he's in my guild. We're supposed to raid Jondor on Wednesday."

Most lawyers made deals on the golf course. Not the new geek. Instead, they made contacts in role-playing games online.

"There's something deeply wrong with you." Belle shook her head, trying not to smile.

Eric grinned, and before she could stop herself, her heart skipped a beat. "Hey, you should be glad you weren't around for his LARPing days. You think online games are weird, try a hundred geeks dressed in medieval wear, throwing little bags at each other and calling them spells."

Tate flushed. "I was trying to sleep with a girl. At least LARPing was more fun than those foreign films Belle made me see."

She narrowed her eyes. "I didn't make you do anything. You showed up at that festival and said you were a huge fan of Siberian cinema."

Tate groaned. "Babe, not even Siberians watch that shit. Seriously. It made me want to open a vein and bleed out." The sexiest smile heated his face, taking him from boyish to such a man. Then his voice dropped to an intimate growl. "But I was trying to sleep with a girl then, too."

Just like that her pussy clenched. Oh, they couldn't stay—or she'd do something she would regret. "You're going back to Chicago today, right?"

"Of course not." Eric frowned. "We need to put the HVAC unit on the list of items to have serviced. It seems to be malfunctioning. You look awfully cold." His glance lingered on her, and Belle had no idea what he was hinting at. "I've also felt icy spots in the house."

Belle wasn't worried about being chilly now, not when she was getting hot just being near them. "It's on *my* list. I'll take care of it."

She wasn't about to fess up that her room had gotten so cold the night before that she'd seen her breath. Surely, that had been a freak occurrence.

Fighting a smile, Kellan's stare caressed her chest before taking a slow path back to her face. "I believe Eric is referring to your nipples, Belle. They're very hard right now. If you're not cold, then you must have been having some juicy dreams."

She gasped and folded her arms over her chest. "The state of my nipples are none of your concern."

"I could warm them up for you," Tate offered. "Hands or mouth? Your choice."

She ignored him. "What am I supposed to do with all this stuff when you leave? You are flying back to your jobs and responsibilities soon, right?"

"Nope," Eric replied. "Like we said, you're here, so we're opening a practice in New Orleans. Unless you're ready to go home with us."

She held out a hand. "You were serious? No! You can't do that. This is my home now. Yours is in Chicago. And have your forgotten than you're not licensed to practice law in this state?"

"We're not trying cases here." Eric shrugged. "We're telecommuting until our office manager is ready to return to the office with us. When you won't come to the office, the office will come to you. We had a meeting last night after you went to bed and worked it all out. That's part of our new protocols."

Surely they didn't need her assistance around the firm that badly. "Guys, I resigned."

"We didn't accept your resignation," Tate replied cheerfully. He held up a stack of papers. "In fact, I had Sequoia fax me your employment contract. It's for two years, so you should probably pull up a chair and get busy."

"What?" She thought back, vaguely remembering something about guaranteed work. "That language was in there for my protection, not yours. You couldn't fire me for any reason other than gross incompetence for two years without penalties. I made you put that in because your last three office managers lasted a total of two weeks. You always found something you didn't like about them. If I recall, you fired one because he brought you the wrong soda."

Eric shook his head. "No, baby, we really fired that guy because of his outrageous body odor. Tate's got a very sensitive nose, and I'm pretty sure that guy thought he was allergic to deodorant."

"You smell like happiness," Tate supplied.

She almost laughed at his sappy grin, then she remembered they were trying to screw her over. "You can't use that contract against me."

"We totally can," Tate shot back.

He acted like a five-year-old sometimes—but he was a man with a spectacularly square jaw and amazing pectorals she could see all too well through his tight T-shirt. She turned to Kellan, who would surely be the reasonable one. "Explain to him that it won't hold up in court. That contract states you three can't fire me, not that I can't quit."

Kellan poured a cup of coffee and handed it to her. "As his lawyer in this matter, I really can't comment."

It took all her self-control not to scream. They were closing ranks to show her a united front.

"You can't hold me with that contract." She grabbed the document and shook it in her fist.

"We'll use whatever we have to in order to hold you," Eric replied solemnly. "Belle, where you go, we go. If you decide to stay in New Orleans, we'll just take the Louisiana bar."

"I'm excellent at taking tests," Tate said. "I'll look forward to it. I might even enter into criminal law down here since the cases are so interesting. I've been watching this madam murder case all morning."

Of all the conversations she'd imagined having with them now, this possibility had never crossed her mind. They had rejected her, so why had they come here and insisted on staying? God knew it shouldn't be that hard to hire another competent assistant. But Eric and Tate didn't act as if their interest was purely professional. Kell…she wasn't sure where he was coming from and she was too afraid to ask.

Belle set the coffee mug down and walked through the house, then let herself outside, determined to get some fresh air and figure out what the hell was going on.

The courtyard was blissfully quiet with the single exception of Sir yipping as he chased an insect and the gently trickling fountain. One of the men had let him out and turned on the peaceful water feature. Their thoughtfulness did strange things to her heart. They were so concentrated when they worked. They got involved in a case and rarely did anything penetrate their cone of concentration, but one of them had stopped to let her dog out and make her world a little more tranquil.

What was she doing out here? There were three

amazingly hot men inside her kitchen with varying degrees of interest in her, and she stood alone, mooning. Had they overreacted to that night in the suite? Had she? God, she wasn't sure what to think, what to do. All Belle knew for sure was that she could still feel their hands on her, their mouths seizing her own, claiming her down to her soul. After they'd arrived last night, she hadn't dreamed of dead girls hanging from the rafters, but of sharing a bed with them. Obviously, she'd felt safe with them in the house, so her mind had wandered—right back into their arms.

In her dreams, they'd surrounded her. Their arms had been the sweetest cocoon. Not only had they protected her, but they'd held her, pleasured her, loved her. She'd opened herself to all of them in turn, consuming the sustenance she needed from each: Tate's goodness. Eric's strength. Kellan's dominance. She'd surrendered, giving over her problems in favor of their affection.

The trouble was, in her dream, they had worked in tandem to complete her, body and soul. No one had thrown a damn punch.

"Hey." A dark voice skated over her skin, and Belle turned.

Kellan stood in the doorway. Instantly, she knew from the tight set of his lips that he had something on his mind. He wasn't going to just leave her in peace.

Belle steeled herself because it looked like the fight had just found her.

* * * *

Kellan looked at Annabelle and tried like hell to keep the longing off his face. In the early morning, her skin glowed a warm, golden brown that had always fascinated him. Her hesitant expression and wounded chocolate eyes made him wish so badly that he was a better man. Why couldn't he have met her before his marriage and the resulting disaster of his divorce? If he'd known her when he'd been a dumbass kid who thought the world was fair and wanted to make sure it stayed that way, he would have claimed Belle and never let her go. The cynic standing before her today wanted more than anything to believe in love and faithfulness, until death-do-us-part. But now, he couldn't just forget the lessons from his trip down the aisle with Lila. How would his life have changed if Belle had been the woman on his arm that day so long ago?

"Kellan." She put a hand on her chest as though catching her breath. "You scared me."

Oh, likely she wasn't scared enough of him. He intended to make her understand just how scared she should be, but first he had a case to plead. "Sorry. I just want to talk to you."

Those gorgeous lips of hers thinned to a stubborn line. "There's not much to say. You made yourself clear in Dallas. Message received. But now that I'm trying to leave, you're using that employment contract to force me to stay? It wasn't intended to force me to work for you."

She was certainly smart enough to know the contract was a Hail Mary play, but they were very good lawyers. Still, he understood the way the court system worked and how the game was played. "It could take a while to convince a judge of that, and the case would have to be heard in Chicago. Do you need the name of a good attorney?"

"I shouldn't need a lawyer."

Probably not, Kell conceded. But he couldn't let her ask Tate. The big genius would agree to represent her, then likely argue against himself in court.

"You're being an ass, and I don't understand why," she went on. "You're the one who wanted to be rid of me. So I left. Why does anything I do matter to you anymore?"

"Because they're desperate, Belle. Could you just hear me out? We might be able to avoid a crappy, embarrassing court case we're sure to lose."

"At least you admit I'm right." Arms crossed, she frowned and turned away from him, watching her dog-thing run around the tiny yard.

"It's a stall tactic, and you know it. You've watched us work enough to know that sometimes we wait out the opposition long enough to make them rethink their position." He sighed. "Listen, they can't walk away. They won't."

"They?"

This was the hard part. He had to be honest with her. "We. I should probably go, but I don't want to either, Belle. I need to talk to you before we make any decisions about the situation. But first, think about what Eric and Tate are offering you."

She turned to him, her eyes wary under the delicate arch of her brows. Even in a cartoonish nightshirt, she was so beautiful it hurt. "I've already had a dose of what they're offering me. I think I should keep waiting."

"You're not being fair, Belle. You are the singular most forgiving person I know, so why are you punishing them for my stance? You dropped a bomb on us that night."

"It wasn't a bomb, just the honest truth."

"Maybe, but the news hit me like a ton of bricks." He sighed because she was being naïve. "The honest truth is telling Eric that you liked the way he kissed or Tate that you swooned at the sight of him without a shirt, or even admitting that you enjoyed the spanking I gave you. Springing your virginity on us? That was a megaton bomb that blew up in my face. I admit that I didn't handle it well. Don't punish Eric and Tate for my behavior."

She sat on one of the white patio chairs in the shady courtyard and hugged herself in the morning breeze. She seemed almost frail in that moment, though it was an illusion. Belle was strong. Kell had no doubt she'd easily survive his stupidity.

As much as he hated to admit it, he was the fucking fragile one. He pulled out the chair beside her, legs scraping the flagstone gently, then sank down. He ached to hold her close, but he'd lost that right. Hell, he'd never had it in the first place, and it was time to let her know why. "You know I was married, right?"

Belle shook her head, her long black hair caressing her shoulders softly. "You don't have to explain yourself to me."

"Maybe I don't have to, but I should." Otherwise, nothing between them would work. She'd keep hoping for more from him because she always expected the best in others. And he'd just keep hurting her because he wasn't strong enough to walk away again on his own accord. "Belle, I'm trying to salvage any sort of relationship between us because I really do care about you. I don't even want to think about a world where I don't see you, but you need to understand why I can't do the hearts and flowers thing. Do you hate me so much that you won't even listen?"

Somehow he hadn't expected that of her. He should know better than anyone that a single moment could change a person for life. He should know that one betrayal could make an idealist bitter. He stood, sick to his stomach that he'd been the one to do it to her. Damn it to hell, he was going to have to find the strength to walk away from all of them because he was toxic if he could ruin someone as sweet as Belle with a few careless words. Destroying her would kill his best friends, too.

He just fucked everything up wherever he went.

"Never mind. I won't force you to hear this." He curled his fingers into a fist to stop himself from touching her. "I'm sorry."

Belle touched him, a hesitant caress of her fingertips on the back of his hand, so soft he almost didn't feel it. "Stop. You think I hate you, Kellan, and I don't."

When he looked down he saw that gorgeous face he knew so well, the one he saw every day while he worked and dreamed of every night when he slept. It tore at his heart. "I wouldn't blame you if you did."

She shook her head. "I know you were married. Since you're not anymore, I assume it didn't end well."

He eased back into the chair beside her, so close now their knees nearly touched. The intimacy of their closeness in the early morning light made it easier to confess his past.

"It was more than the end. Way more." He rubbed a hand across the back of his neck, trying to ease away the tension. "I met Lila in law school. We were the golden couple of our class."

The slightest smile tugged her lips up. "I can see that."

His head sometimes hurt just thinking about his ex-wife and her machinations. "My father is a judge."

"In DC, right?"

"Yes, he's a federal court judge, but before that he was a lawyer for years. Kent and Associates was a powerhouse firm. We made millions. When the president appointed dear old dad, I took over the firm. Well, Lila and I took it over. We hadn't been married long." He shook his head, thinking about all his stupid hopes and foolish dreams back then.

Belle tucked her hand in his. A stronger man would push her away, but damn, the world seemed like a better place when she touched him.

"Obviously, the divorce had a profound effect on you, Kell. You must have loved her very much." A well of sympathy filled her voice.

He winced. That had been part of the problem. Perhaps he could have forgiven himself if he'd been blinded by love. "I thought I did, but I'm pretty sure now that I chose Lila because she fit the bill, if you know what I mean."

"I don't."

That didn't surprise him. Belle wouldn't marry for any reason but pure, abiding love. "I was ready to start my life and getting married was the next step. I had a plan, you see."

"Not surprising. You always have a plan."

He was a list maker, a man who usually thought out his next twelve steps before taking one. He'd never been a fly-by-the-seat-of-his-pants thinker the way Eric could be. He'd never had impulsive moments like Tate. Nope, he thought through every pro and con, then made decisions based on his sometimes laborious risk assessment.

Loving Belle was too much of a danger. He'd decided that long ago.

"I wanted to go into politics. It probably sounds stupid, but I decided to seek office when I was a kid. I'm sure it had something to do with pleasing my parents. My mom was a wonderful woman. From the time I was little, she always said I should be president. We've had a few senators in our family, but Mom thought I deserved to be the first Kent to achieve the nation's highest office. She put it just like that, too. I was convinced I wanted to help people. So corny."

"Not at all. I think it's admirable."

Belle could be so naïve. "Did I really want to help people? Or was I just an ambitious fuck who had too much money and always wanted the best of everything? Being president looked like the best job, so I'd made up my mind to surround myself with the appropriate trappings and go for it. Lila was pretty and so smart it hurt. Hell, she was smarter than I was. Tate was top of our class, but she was right behind him. I trailed her academically, but she backed my dreams. So we became a pair. About the time I graduated, my mom died of cancer. Her last wish was that I pursue my dreams. She'd given birth to me and when she lay dying, I couldn't do anything but promise I would."

"Kellan, at the risk of sounding like Tate, it's almost statistically impossible to become president. Your mother wouldn't hold you to a deathbed vow, especially if chasing the goal was making you miserable."

He shook his head. "You didn't know my mother. She would be disappointed in me today. But at the time, I was determined to keep my promise. So I proposed to Lila, and we went to work for my dad's firm. After a year, we started planning my first campaign. State senator. We began fund-raising, and for a while we were really a team. I thought we were happy. I wanted to have kids, but she put me off at first. She agreed it would be great publicity for me to campaign with a pregnant wife, but she wasn't ready."

Belle's little gasp said it all.

"I wanted kids. Having them wasn't just about the campaign for me. Please understand that. I wasn't some party guy. I worked eighty hours a week and I was married. I wanted a family to come home to. For months after the wedding, Lila resisted even discussing trying to conceive. She didn't want to lose her figure in her twenties. She wanted to establish her career. She wanted time with me. That last one was a lie because she was always working. But she had every excuse to avoid becoming a mother. Then suddenly she was ready to throw away her birth control pills. I should have known something was going on, but I chalked it up to her simply coming around to my way of thinking." He snorted. "And I was a bit behind in the poll numbers."

Her brows came together in a puzzled frown. "What do you mean 'going on'? You two were practicing together at the same firm. Didn't you practically trip over one another all the time?"

He could see where she would have a few misconceptions about their careers. "You've only worked in a very small office. You don't know how easy it is to get lost in a big, corporate firm. We didn't work in the same division. We were both heading large portions of the busy practice and we were starting to campaign locally, each with different responsibilities. It's a lot of work. There are a ton of distractions, and one day I looked up and realized we didn't spend time together anymore. And I hadn't missed her as much as I should have. One Sunday, I sat her down and told her that she felt too much like a stranger to me and that we needed to make time to be together. She started crying and said she really wanted to have a baby."

"Some people think having a baby will save a marriage.

It rarely does, but…" Belle sounded as if she was making excuses for Lila's behavior because she knew something bad was coming. "Maybe she didn't know?"

"I wish she would have told me how she felt about us before I started the campaign, but I think she was hedging her bets. Turns out, she'd been having an affair for the past year. She'd gotten pregnant."

Belle's mouth gaped open. Shocked didn't begin to describe her expression. "And she wanted to pass the baby off as yours?"

Kellan gave a resigned shrug. Spilling all this to Belle actually felt odd because his gut wasn't churning the way it normally did when he thought of Lila. The guilt and self-loathing still felt toxic in his veins, but the mad rage was muted by Belle's soothing presence, by her hand in his.

"It would have likely been easy to do. I was just happy to have everything falling into place. I would have smiled and never questioned it. I like to think I would have been a good dad, but mine was pretty awful, so I have no idea."

"When did you discover the truth?"

"Three weeks before the election. That was when a staffer came to me and showed me the proof that my pregnant wife was having an affair." He rubbed at the back of his neck again. "With my father."

That day was still vivid in his memory. He could see the photos of his wife and father making love in the swimming pool where he'd played as a kid, where his mother had taught him how to swim. They'd had barbecues and family gatherings in that backyard, filling the expansive space with their big personalities. All of those memories had been burned away by a handful of photographs featuring his dear old dad happily plowing his beautiful bride.

"Oh my god, Kellan. That's terrible." Belle clapped her hand over her mouth and looked at him with an expression somewhere between horror and pity.

Once, he would have pushed her away, but now he

realized this was as close as he could allow himself to be with her emotionally. Sex... Now that was different. He could have sex with her all fucking day and night, but taking her comfort pushed at his very firm barriers. Allowing her soft empathy meant she could sneak behind his walls, and he couldn't allow anyone to do that again. He couldn't give her what she deserved, and letting her indulge in the fantasy that he was a whole man would just hurt them both.

Still, he gave himself one moment—just this one—to sink against her and feel her gentle caring.

"My pride was shredded, but worse than that, my campaign was over and not for the reason you'd think."

"Did someone leak the pictures?"

He huffed out a bitter laugh. "No, my father bought them. Then he sat me down and told me I was a disappointment, but he'd long known I would be. I hadn't been man enough for my dad and I'd proved it by not being able to take care of my wife."

Hell, son, I even had to get her pregnant for you. Maybe this kid will have some guts.

"Oh, Kellan, he was wrong." Belle put an arm around him and looked into his eyes as if willing him to believe her. "You have to know that."

Fuck if he didn't want to wrap himself up in her warmth. But all he could allow himself was to let her touch him—and steel himself so that her comfort didn't sway him. She really didn't know the whole truth, and Kellan decided to skip over the part where he'd nearly killed his father that night. After his dad had goaded him and told him how pathetic he was, he'd finally seen red and showed the old man that he could, in fact, fight.

"That Monday, Lila filed for divorce. The ink had barely dried on the decree when she married my dad. She runs Kent and Associates to this day. Dad is still a judge, and they have a son they'll ship off to boarding school about the time he turns four. He'll be given the best of everything with the singular exception of any kind of affection because Lila isn't my mom."

When he looked back on his childhood, his mother had been his only nurturer. He'd been shipped off to the same boarding schools his half-brother would one day attend because Kents always had prestigious educations, but at least he'd been able to come home for summers and make some awesome memories with his mom.

"I feel for the kid," Belle said, an ache in her voice. "And you, Kellan. You were the wronged party. Why did *you* have to leave everything behind? You could have exposed the truth and ruined them."

He shook his head. "You don't understand how politics work. My father had been playing this game a long, long time. He was appointed to the bench by the president. He has power and influence. Once Lila filed for divorce and Dad put an engagement ring on her finger, it made me look weak. The party forced me to drop out of the race in favor of someone who could win. Everyone loves a winner, you know." That humiliation still stung just under his skin. "I lost everything, including my ability to make a living. No one wanted to hire me, and if I had started my own firm, I would have been utterly without clients. I was done in DC."

"So you came to Chicago?"

"Yeah." He let out a long sigh. "I didn't know where else to go. Eric and Tate had been my friends in law school until Lila decided they weren't the type of friends 'we' needed. It wasn't like I dumped them. Lila just made it harder and harder to see them. When we graduated, we drifted apart. Eventually, I let their calls go to voice mail because I wasn't sure what to say. They moved to Chicago, and I settled into DC…and life went on."

Belle eased her arms from around his body, but remained close. "You know, I've always thought you three were an odd mix, but somehow you work."

"You have no idea. At first I thought they were freaks.

Then I wished I had someone like them in my life. They're weird halves of a whole, but sometimes I think I'm just hollow on the inside, so it would be better to be like them. They know who they are and what they want. They make no apologies for it."

Kell could hear the envy in his own voice.

"Eric called me after he heard what happened," Kell went on. "All those years I ignored them, but when I needed a friend, he reached out to me."

And changed his life forever. Kell might have helped their firm fiscally, but they had given him something he'd never had before: true, stable friendships.

"I can't repay their loyalty by ruining the one bond they desperately want. Belle, please don't blame them for my inability to be the man you need."

Tears shone in her eyes. "You don't think you'll ever trust another woman, do you?"

"I know my limitations. You've seen them. I'm damaged beyond any kind of repair. But I fully admit that I want you. That's probably not fair to you, but it's honest. I want to be your lover and your Dom, but you should understand my hard limits now. Do you see why a D/s relationship is all I can handle?"

"I understand why you believe that," she said carefully. "But I wasn't asking you for a ring."

"You deserve one. Hell, you deserve three. I just can't do it. If you want me to leave, I will. I can reinvent myself again. I'll go west, maybe California."

He hated the thought of moving, couldn't even imagine not seeing Belle every day. This was why he'd really put off Tate's plea to pursue her for so long. He'd been trying to delay this inevitable moment where he asked Belle to accept him strictly in her bed and she turned him down, forever changing both his relationship with her and his friends.

To his surprise, she didn't slap him across the face. "Why would you leave?"

"Because I think you'll forgive that horrible night in the suite eventually, but I don't expect you to forgive *me*. If leaving means you'll give them a chance, then I'll go. I owe them that."

She sighed and suddenly his arms were full of Belle, his whole world narrowing to the feel of her as she eased herself onto his lap and wrapped herself around him. Just like that, his cock sprang to full attention and he had to shift so he wouldn't grind himself against her. Instead, he wrapped her tight in his arms. Just a minute. He would let go in just one minute.

"I won't say I wasn't mad and hurt, but..." she sighed against him. "I don't want you to go."

Her whisper slid warm and tantalizing across his skin. She turned her face up to his, and god help him, Kell couldn't stop himself. She was right there, so close, her lips just over his. The world slipped away, and nothing mattered except the woman he held close.

He kissed her, his lips on hers, taking hers. The night in the suite had been incendiary, but this was softer, more intimate. So potent and wonderful...and dangerous.

She gasped as he claimed her mouth, but then she opened to him. She followed the rhythm and depth of his kiss with ease, as though they'd shared a thousand such kisses, danced the long slow grind of Dominance and submission together until they were in perfect harmony.

His whole body—not just his cock—reacted to her, tensing, shuddering, hardening. She made his heart pound, his brain haze over. Even breathing felt different when he had Belle in his arms. She made him feel more alive.

He was going to lose himself here if he wasn't careful.

Abruptly, Kell ended the kiss. He needed to maintain distance between them however he could.

As their eyes met, hers went wide with stunned hurt. "You can't even kiss me?"

He ached with the need to pull her close again, but the

pain hovered just under the surface and he never wanted her to feel the agony he'd endured. "Not like this. This isn't sex, Belle. This is more. These are feelings, and I can't do those. I want you so badly, but I can't have you in any way but sexually. I can't share more than passion and bodies. So it would be better if I left. You could be happy with them. They really love you, Belle."

With a long sigh, she let him go and shrank back to her seat, her eyes on the puppy again. He was now in a stare-off with an orange tabby cat dancing on the fence and taunting him. "I don't know if it will work, Kellan. I think you're more important to them than you think. From what I can tell, they were drifting before you came to Chicago. I worry they'll drift again if you leave. I've watched you guys for a year now. Your friendship is a delicate balance. You work as a team in every aspect of your lives. I really think it will be the same in a romantic relationship. I think it's why they've been so insistent about sharing."

He hadn't thought about it that way. Before they'd met Belle, the three of them hadn't tried anything beyond a one-night stand because Kellan had refused to try a long-term relationship. But before he'd come along, Tate and Eric had attempted to date women. Nothing had stuck.

What would it be like if Kell dropped out of the picture and his friends made Belle their woman? Tate was too soft around Belle. He just let her walk all over him. Eric didn't think about things like schedules. Belle would end up managing everything and that might become a burden. Kell recognized that he and Belle worked well together to juggle the details in their daily work lives. He enjoyed sharing that little bond with her. He'd never had a partner either professionally or romantically like Belle. Could he truly leave her and not be gutted?

Through the open door, he heard Tate and Eric start to argue about some case. It had to be getting heated because their voices could be heard over the ugly puppy's whining.

Apparently, furball had lost the staring contest with the cat and now seemed determined to prove he was louder, bigger, and badder. For her part, the cat just stared at some spot beyond the agitated dog. He could practically see the tabby rolling her eyes.

He was the referee, Kellan understood in that moment. He had been since he'd joined the firm. Who would arbitrate Eric and Tate's often lengthy "debates" if he was gone? They could lose hours of productive time because they'd bicker over tiny interpretations in the language of a contract. Hell, they could waste hours arguing over the latest episode of Game of Thrones.

"Could you at least think about staying for a while?" Belle asked, leaning against him again. "I'm not asking for anything except a little time so we can all figure this thing out. I'm not sure this can work, but I'm willing to think about it."

And that was all he could really ask. Time. He had a little more of it with her, and that filled him with a disturbing amount of relief. "Yes, I'll stay. For now."

He let his arm drift back around her shoulders and promised himself he would get up and deal with his partners.

In just a minute.

Chapter Ten

Three days later, Belle shook her head at Malcolm Gates, completely frustrated by his request. "Didn't you do an inventory of the house after my grandmother died? Shouldn't her insurance adjuster have one?"

The lawyer shook his head. He hovered just inside the foyer, but he looked deeply uncomfortable. It was obvious he would prefer to be anywhere else. "No, Miss Wright. The insurance company only had a very basic inventory. Your grandmother scheduled her jewelry and her collection of antiques, but nothing else. I'm afraid for the judge to finalize the will, we'll need a complete inventory of the house. I'm going to send some workers in to do it for you."

She saw a truck pull up, searching for a place to park. Her electrician. She definitely wanted to see him. The lights in the house flickered on and off at the oddest times. But other than the man who would ensure her lights worked properly, she didn't need anyone else tromping through her house.

Updating a place like this would be a painstaking and delicate process. She'd pulled all the furniture to the center of the living room and covered it with a plastic tarp so she could paint the walls the quietly elegant color it deserved. She'd selected a warm, pale gray. She intended to strip the sage-colored paint from the gorgeous original wood trim. Instead, she'd opted for a crisp, clean high-gloss white. She'd also bought a charcoal and white drapery fabric in a damask pattern, as well as a soft white sheer that would peek from beneath the curtains, enabling light to stream in but keeping prying eyes out. A simple plush black area rug would ground the space, and she'd ordered lamps with the same pop of color in their hand-blown glass bases. They'd been a little bit of a splurge, but everything she'd chosen would coordinate perfectly with the attitude of the room. Comfortable but elegant. New Orleans glamour.

Now she'd have to put off the project—and starting her new design business—if she had Gates's interns stomping around and getting in her way. God knew what they'd do to all this original hardwood flooring. It needed repair, re-sanding, re-staining, and a quality sealer. Until she could have all that done, she didn't want strangers walking on them, much less moving the furniture or knickknacks around. She already had three men and an eager puppy who wasn't housebroken running all over the place and causing chaos. Even more distracting, Tate had taken up working shirtless half the time just to tempt her.

"I'll get you the inventory." It might take her months, but she refused to have others pawing through her grandmother's things and slowing down her renovation.

Since moving in here, Belle had become very protective of the woman she'd never met. She'd made it through half her grandmother's journal, all the way to her dad's junior high years. Her grandmother had written about how much "her girls" loved him and gushed that he was the king of her castle. So apparently, Grandma had run a business of psychics out of this house. Hiring only females had been fairly smart. Women tended to be more empathetic and in tune with those around them, so they probably made better psychics. Obviously, she'd run a lucrative business, too.

Belle loved getting glimpses into her father's childhood. The boy her grandmother had written about had been a happy kid. She'd even found some pictures of her dad tucked into the volume. In one, he'd been in overalls, wearing a goofy grin as he hammed it up for the camera.

She often thought that her mother hadn't smiled much since the day her father died. So much of her life came back to that one tragic afternoon. Her mother had given her food and a roof over her head after his passing, but Mom had been a ghost flitting through life, allowing no one—not even her own daughter—to touch her.

Maybe if she brought her mom these pictures of her dad she'd smile.

Mr. Gates frowned her way. "I don't think you understand how much work this entails. How precise you must be. This is a big house, and the job is far too big for one person. It would be so much better if you let me handle this. I'll have it done quickly, but we must have an accounting of every possession, down to the last piece of paper."

That seemed a bit extreme, but she wasn't an expert in Louisiana inheritance laws.

Belle sighed, heartily irritated. "Fine. Send a couple of interns, but I'll be overseeing everything. Thank you, Mr. Gates. Now excuse me." She nodded toward the electrician, a big guy who made his way up the walk, toolbox in hand. "Hello, Mike." She opened the door wider, allowing Gates out so the electrician could enter. "I'm glad to see you."

Mike winked her way. He was a handsome blue-eyed devil in his early thirties with broad shoulders and a ready smile. He'd given her an estimate the day before, and Tate had been trying to convince her since then that Mike must be a lothario, a serial killer, or an escapee from a mental ward— whatever he thought would convince her to hire someone else. Eric had threatened to run a background check on the man. She sighed.

"Good to see you, Ms. Belle. I'm going to start in the bathroom today. You have a lot of old knob and tube wiring to bring up to code. You're damn lucky this place hasn't burned down yet. Don't be surprised if your homeowner's insurance won't renew you until it's fixed. It's happened to more than one resident in the Quarter."

She winced. Naturally, building codes had changed a great deal since the house had been built. Her grandmother had renovated the house since taking possession of it, but the wiring hadn't been terribly out of date then. Drywall and paint or wallpaper had covered what people now considered an electrical sin. Still, as low as Mike's estimate had been, it chafed. Satisfying the city and changing things she really couldn't see was rapidly depleting her design budget. Unfortunately, it was a safety issue, so she merely smiled. "Let me know if you need anything."

Mike shrugged. "Oh, I'm sure I'll see one of your…friends before I see you. They seem mighty interested in watching whatever I happen to be doing."

As he walked into the house with a grin, Belle groaned.

For three days, Eric, Tate, and Kell had been steadfast. They worked. They cooked. And they tried to seduce her. When she went out to buy supplies for the renovation, at least one of them came along. She'd tried sneaking out yesterday, but Eric had been smiling and standing by her car, swearing he needed a break.

Despite their argument about her employment contract, none of them had tried to rope her into resuming her old job. Belle had noticed a don't ask/don't tell policy. As long as she didn't ask when they were leaving, they didn't tell her to pick up a case file and get busy.

Instead, both he and Tate had caught her alone and done their utmost to tempt her to kiss them. They'd invaded her space with their big, male bodies and stared down at her with hungry eyes, reminding her of everything she'd almost had. When she'd weakened enough to melt against them, when she could feel her blood humming and her sex aching, then the bastards would walk away, reminding her that she knew where to find them and they'd welcome her anytime.

Something had to give, and she worried it would be her. She'd spent three restless nights knowing that they were just down a flight of stairs. She'd also spent three nights dreaming of dead girls swinging from a rope and the monster who dragged them to their deaths.

She shivered, despite the heat of the day. It was morbid, but she couldn't seem to stop the terrible dreams. She'd even gone so far as to check into the house's history on a local historical website. It hinted at the home's colorful past. Those tales were more rumor than anything, but the police reports on file corroborated Gates's story. All the deaths had been suicides, not murders.

"I'll be leaving now, Miss Wright. Thank you for allowing the interns to help with the inventory. We'll get this mess put behind us so you can move on. The most important thing is to find your grandmother's papers. She told me she had a life insurance policy, but I don't have the name of the insurance company or the policy number. I'll need to file on your behalf so you can receive the funds." Mr. Gates looked nervously around the house as though he thought someone might jump out and yell "boo." Belle found his demeanor unsettling.

A cool breeze brushed past her legs. Cooler than cool, really. In fact, it felt like an arctic blast. Mr. Gates obviously felt it as well because he stiffened and took a giant step back to the threshold of the front door.

"I think that's my cue to leave." The lawyer's eyes had gone wide. He swallowed nervously. "Expect the interns shortly."

Belle frowned. The guy was really freaked out about the house. She'd noticed that when she'd first come here. That cold draft probably wasn't anything more than the air conditioning being temperamental. The HVAC expert would be here in thirty minutes. Problem solved.

Unfortunately, now she'd have a group of wet-behind-the-ears wannabe lawyers parading through her house. So what was one more, especially if he managed to keep the temperature in the house stable? If necessary, she would shut off the rooms with exposed wood and pray she didn't have to spend more than the rest of the funds her grandmother had left.

"If you think your interns can find the insurance paperwork and it's worth some money, I'll dance a jig." Belle smiled, mentally making a priority list of all the things she could renovate.

Gates backed out of the house until he stood in the midmorning sun. Once he'd cleared the threshold, he visibly relaxed and regained his composure. "Thank you, Miss Wright. You know, all these repairs to the house will be quite expensive. My buyer is still willing to take this house off your hands and pay you in cash."

She shook her head. Even with the debt mounting, she refused to sell. Despite her bad dreams, Belle loved being here. The house had quickly grown on her, and she felt a connection to the place she never had before. Her father had grown up here, and being under this roof reminded her how much she'd missed him.

She looked up, and the sight caused every sad thought to dissipate.

Tate jogged up the sidewalk, his big body covered in nothing but sweatpants, sneakers, and a fine sheen of sweat. Every muscle on the man's body bulged. The definition of his shoulders and chest almost made her drop her jaw. Belle hoped she could remember to breathe. Damn, when he wore next to nothing, she needed one of those arctic air drifts blasting through the house.

A flirty grin transformed his face as he jogged his way up to the house. "Hey, baby. You should have worked out with me. I burned roughly seven hundred calories given distance, time, exertion, and my relative weight." He utterly ignored the lawyer nearly blocking the door and gave her a sexy little growl. "Although oral sex burns roughly a hundred calories per half hour, and you wouldn't have to do anything but let me love on you."

She gasped and slapped his perfectly muscled bicep. "Tate! Hush, you dirty man. Go take a shower. You're supposed to be the one with the delicate nose."

"I can't smell myself." He shouldered his way past Gates, who recoiled and grimaced. Then Tate leaned in and ran his nose along her neck, breathing against her and lighting up her skin. "But you smell so good." He turned to Gates, suddenly focused and protective. Tate morphed from horny man to shrewd lawyer in the blink of an eye. "What do you need with my client, Mr. Gates?"

The older man frowned. "If that's the way you treat a client, sir, then I'm afraid we have different ideas about professionalism. And my business here is done."

He pivoted on his heel and walked away.

"You didn't have to be rude," he called back. Tate tended to correct people he didn't like. He'd said he merely tried to make them more likeable, but Belle was pretty sure he did it to irritate them.

But that got her thinking... Maybe she should treat Tate a bit like Sir. When he was good, she'd toss a cookie his way. When he was rude, she could spray him with a water bottle. If nothing else, it would give her a giggle.

Tate eased inside and closed the door. "I don't like him. He sets off my douchebag radar."

Belle felt the same, but no sense in adding fuel to Tate's fire. Once they'd finished all the paperwork associated with her grandmother's estate, she'd never have to see Mr. Gates again.

"I need to get back to work."

"One second." He grabbed her elbow and pulled her so close the heat of his body wrapped around her.

God, even sweaty, he smelled amazing. So musky and manly... Her girl parts clenched in a silent pleading.

"What?" she breathed.

"Did you know that sex is one of the best workouts a man can get? I could burn a hundred and forty-four calories during actual intercourse and that doesn't include the hundred I would have shed from eating your pussy."

Heat flashed through her system again. The weak part of her longed to throw herself against Tate and forget prudence, but if she gave him an inch now, he'd more than take a mile. "You can't talk to me like that."

"Is he going on again about eating your pussy?" Eric asked as they meandered into the kitchen.

Crap, he wasn't wearing a shirt either. His thin jersey knit pants rode low on narrow hips. What had happened to her buttoned up, always-in-a-perfect-suit men? Now they walked around her house like super-hot cavemen, scratching their perfectly formed six packs.

"Neither one of you should be talking to me about any sort of sex. In fact, you shouldn't be here at all since this isn't your office. And why doesn't anyone wear clothing anymore? I thought you'd set up a legal practice, not a *Playgirl* cover shoot."

Belle hoped like hell that they couldn't tell how she'd flushed at the sight of all their muscles and bare skin. Her cheeks only grew hotter when they managed to wedge her in between them. Sandwiching her between them and the kitchen counter, they cut off her only avenue of escape— something they seemed intent on doing more and more these days. She constantly found herself surrounded by gorgeous men eager to verbally seduce her every chance they had. Even Kellan had developed an alarming problem with personal space. She'd asked him to stay, and he'd decided that meant right against her.

Eric grinned. "What's the problem? I'm enjoying this whole telecommuting thing. I could totally get used to ditching the jacket and tie. And baby, in case you hadn't noticed, it's way hotter down here than in Chicago. I'm too uncomfortable to wear clothes. When is the AC guy supposed to arrive? I hope he's more competent than that idiot Mike."

She sighed. "The electrician came highly recommended. I have a list of contractors. He was the first on the list."

"Seriously? Who gave you the list?" Tate sounded irritated.

"My grandmother's lawyer. You guys seem to have taken a dislike to Mike, but his quote is very reasonable and he seems to know what he's doing. So let him do it." The sooner she got the wiring fixed, the faster she could figure out how much money she had left for the pretty stuff. For now, focusing on prepping the living room walls for paint would force her to look at something besides the lovely male chests on display.

Another knock sounded on the door. Tate scowled. "I don't like all these people coming in and out. We don't know who they are. Baby, our place in Chicago doesn't need this much work. You could move right in. We'd make sure you were totally happy and comfortable."

She tried to squeeze between the two men to head for the door. But she brushed her breasts against Tate's chest. Then she felt *it*. He had a massive, gloriously thick erection that pressed against his sweatpants and prodded her belly. The feel of him, hard and wanting, caught her off guard and she stepped back—into Eric.

Eric laughed, glancing down at Tate's junk. "Dude, I have no idea how you run with that thing."

But she felt Eric's too, jutting against her ass. He wasn't at all small or flaccid either.

"I can't help it," Tate defended. "The average adult male gets approximately eleven erections daily during waking hours, but when I'm around Belle or think about her—or even remember something that reminds me of her—I get hard. I'm probably skewing the average." He shrugged. "I'm a guy who happens to be really crazy about a girl. Sue me."

"Nah, I'd have to sue myself, too," Eric admitted.

"No doubt." Tate slapped his buddy on the shoulder and headed toward the stairs. "I'm going to take care of this thing, then I need to conference on the Harrison case."

"Take care of what?" Belle just blinked. He couldn't mean what she thought he meant.

With a wink, Tate jogged up the stairs with more energy than a man who'd already spent an hour running should have. He would have that stamina in bed. The thought slammed her out of nowhere. This time, more than her cheeks flamed.

"He's going to go masturbate," Eric said matter-of-factly.

Someone knocked on the door again, this time more insistently.

"More information than I needed." She scurried for the kitchen door, trying to put space between them. They were driving her completely insane, and if she didn't spend the next hour imaging Tate bringing himself pleasure, it would be a miracle.

"We're in your face because you're being a stubborn little thing." Eric caught her before she escaped by placing a palm flat on the door, caging her in. "Come home with us, Belle, to a place we can all share. Give us another shot, baby. Let us show you this can work."

He was so close, his mouth lingering just above hers. She nearly lost herself in his glittering greenish eyes. All she'd have to do was lift her chin and inch up on her tiptoes to feel those firm, talented lips against her own. Already, her body prepared itself for him. She'd softened and had to force herself not to lean into him. Her nipples peaked. Her pussy moistened and throbbed.

Whoever stood outside banged impatiently against the door again, and the moment was broken.

Biting out a curse, Eric stepped back. "I'm going to set up that conference. This afternoon, we'll help you paint."

She shook her head. "You don't need to do that. I understand you have work."

"I said we'll help you after lunch. And I expect you to eat today. Lunch is at noon. See you then." Eric turned and planted himself at the breakfast table again.

Shaking her head, Belle pushed her way out of the room and hustled to the door, signing for an overnight package of new bedding she'd ordered.

As soon as she shut the door, she leaned against it and closed her eyes. What was she going to do? The guys weren't going to leave. They'd already made that point crystal clear. If she kept them here, their business would eventually suffer.

Or they might do exactly what they threatened and move the whole damn office here permanently. Tate had already bought a book on passing the bar in Louisiana.

She dug into the box, trying to busy herself...but in the back of her head, she couldn't help but wonder how much longer she could resist them.

"Belle!" Kellan strode down the stairs, her puppy in the crook of his arm. "Your rat-thing crapped in my dress shoes. Do you have any idea how expensive those damn loafers were?"

She did since she'd been the one to order them. "Sir, please stop that."

Belle refused to chastise the puppy too much. He still wasn't completely housebroken, and he'd likely forgotten to bark at her so that she knew he needed to go.

She reached for her dog, watching as Kellan's face went red. She winced inwardly because she'd managed to get through three whole days without the big bad Dom figuring out her little joke. But now the jig was about to be up. She winced.

"What is it you think I need to stop, Belle?" He clipped and carefully enunciated every word.

She scrambled to avoid answering him because she and Kellan had formed a decent truce and she was reluctant to upset him. "Uhm, you have to stop holding my dog that way. He needs to have his underbelly completely supported or he feels unsafe."

Sir proved her words a lie as he did everything he could to wriggle out of her grasp.

Kell ground his teeth together. "Annabelle, did you name that thing Sir?"

She tried to send him a bright smile. "I wanted to help his self-esteem. I'm sure he could be an alpha dog."

The puppy yipped, and Belle let him down. Immediately, he started chasing his tail. Somewhere beyond the kitchen, a door slammed shut. Sir scampered behind Kellan with a little whine.

He shook his head. "You're changing his name."

"Am not," she said quietly as he walked into the kitchen.

"You absolutely are. Now, Annabelle."

"My house. My dog." She marched toward the living room, Sir hard on her heels.

Kellan came after her. The ringing of his phone was the only thing that saved her from more of this confrontation. Belle left the room while she could…but she was pretty sure he would think of some punishment soon.

* * * *

Tate sighed and let his weary body slide into the chair across from Kellan. Painting sucked. It wasn't nearly as much fun as sex, but Belle probably didn't trust that there'd be no repeat of the debacle in Dallas. And she obviously wasn't ready.

The question was, would she ever be ready?

All Belle seemed interested in was reading that journal of her grandmother's and fixing up this old house, though they'd had a promising couple of minutes earlier in the day, so Tate had high hopes for the evening. But right after dinner, Belle had escaped into her grandmother's office and began browsing an old photo album she'd found.

Her father's mother had been a beauty who had

surrounded herself with other gorgeous women. Page after page showed pictures of Belle's grandma standing near women who looked like they belonged on the silver screen. He'd loved the smile on Belle's face as she pointed out her dad during various stages of his childhood and adolescence.

Again, Tate recalled the day she'd spoken to him about her father's death. She'd haltingly admitted that her mom had shut down after he'd died. Though she'd received basic care, Belle had been utterly alone. He related. Even in a house filled with family, no one who shared his flesh and blood had reached out to him as a child. He wondered if that festering hurt caused any of Belle's hesitation to dive into a relationship now.

Eric walked into their "office," yawning. "I got the briefs filed in time. I'm going to have to fly back next week. I don't want to, but I have to handle the court date myself."

After just three days away, the strain on their business was becoming evident. They could handle much of their case load via computer and phone, but Kellan and Eric still appeared in court routinely. Tate avoided it like the plague. Mostly because he'd come to realize that judges were pompous windbags who liked to hear themselves talk, and being forced to listen to other lawyers pontificate made him want to punch someone in the face. He preferred contracts and corporate clients to dealing with criminal cases. He usually ended up wanting to punch unscrupulous assholes, too. Tate understood the law. People were another matter altogether.

At the moment, that included Belle.

"Okay. Do you need me to schedule the flight?" He was probably the only one of them who remembered their passwords.

"Yeah. Fuck, we need a secretary." Eric sat in the chair beside him.

Kellan chuckled. "Yeah, I don't think any of us really understood until now how much Belle did for us."

"I would reward her properly if she would let me." In fact, Tate would reward her all night long.

Eric nodded. "Amen, brother. Did she eat anything tonight?"

He'd cooked a very nice roast that had filled the house all day with savory smells and made Tate's stomach growl.

"A little, but I found her asleep at her grandmother's desk with her plate half full," Kellan grumbled. "I'm going to move the office into another room. The four of us need to sit down together at meals. This whole grabbing-a-tray-when-we-have-a-minute bit isn't working, guys. We need to think things through."

Scowling, Tate almost objected. He was always thinking. "Sorry, I had a six p.m. conference call. I couldn't get out of it."

And he'd eaten lunch at his computer because he'd gotten an emergency e-mail begging for clarification on a contract some clients hadn't yet signed. Eric had been forced to leave to find a new router when the one they'd been using suddenly blew out. Tate blamed the flirty electrician.

"Clear your schedules tomorrow at eight, noon, and six. We'll force Belle to sit down with us," Kellan counseled.

"Yeah, like civilized people in a relationship." Eric looked like his patience was at an end.

"She won't admit we're in a relationship." Tate sure didn't feel like he was in one, either.

"I really thought she'd give in by now," Eric admitted, frustration contorting his expression and tightening his shoulders. His brows settled into a deep *V*. Tate might not be able to read most people, but he knew his best friend. "I hate how hard she's working."

"But she likes it. She seems happy." He'd noticed her smiling and humming while she painted. There was a peace to her he'd never seen before. "I think we have to really consider the fact that she's not going to leave this place. We fucked up."

Maybe he should have let Kellan go and wrapped Belle in his arms for good. He could have kissed her and told her what she meant to him and maybe they wouldn't feel as if they'd lost their chance with her. She could respond to his flirtations all day long, but if she didn't give in or let herself fall in love, it wouldn't matter.

And almost as soon as he finished the thought, Tate realized that he couldn't abandon his friend. He felt disloyal for even thinking it.

"I'm sorry, guys." Kellan stood up. "This is my fault."

"Stop. No more apologies," Tate insisted. "The question now is, what do you want out of this?"

Eric nodded. "Yeah, what do you want to do here? I think you should stay. Belle can handle you, but we've spent days just sitting around waiting for her to change her mind. It's not working."

"We need a plan." They'd thought she would come around quickly, but Tate saw now she'd been serious about her career change. Just like she was serious about the move.

"What if we can't get her to come home with us?" Eric asked.

"I don't know, but I know I'm not giving up." He loved her. He'd never felt for any woman what he did for Belle. He smiled more with her. He even liked himself better when he was around her. "If I have to move, I will. I love her. We need to put her first from now on."

Eric held a hand up. "I agree. Putting her first is the only way this works, I think. If I really thought she couldn't handle the type of relationship we want, I would allow her to choose one of us, but she needs us all. I think her reluctance now is about her wounded pride and her inexperience, not any fear she has about having more than one man."

"I don't know," Kellan hedged. "You two need to show her you can make her life better. That starts with being organized. You're right about putting her first and giving her what she needs. Any good Dom does. That means prioritizing her above business, too. Tomorrow we help her. All three of us. I've looked at your schedules and almost everything can wait."

Tate thought through his calendar tomorrow, then nodded. He'd helped with painting today, and he'd felt wonderfully close to her for those precious hours. They'd joked and bantered like old times, but a new awareness had hummed between them. While he'd worked beside her, he'd been almost perfectly content. If he could have kissed her when they'd finished and taken her to bed, he'd be the happiest bastard on the planet. Instead, when she'd tidied up for the night, Tate had sensed her pulling away. The distance between them gnawed at him.

But that wasn't the only thing troubling him.

"I want to look into that lawyer of her grandmother's. I heard some of their conversation today and I didn't like it. He told her he had to have an inventory of the house before the court will sign off on the will."

Sure, probate law differed slightly from state to state, but if Marie Wright had left everything to her granddaughter and Belle didn't have any contentious relatives to share the estate with, Tate couldn't think of any reason the state would need a complete inventory.

"What? That makes no sense." Eric frowned. "I guess that explains all the five-year-olds in ties crawling inside the house today."

"Yeah. Look into that lawyer," Kellan said. "These interns weren't just jotting down an inventory. They were poking and prodding and taking shit apart. And we should also look into our dear friend, Mike the electrician. He crawls up my back."

Tate kind of hated the fucker, too. He especially didn't like the way ol' Mikey smiled at Belle, as if the expression was a come-on. He was one charming asshole who needed to keep his eyes off other guys' girls. Except she wasn't really his. Crap, did she like the electrician? He probably didn't cite statistics or verbally offer his penis.

"I don't think he's very good at his job," Tate asserted. "He got lost all over the house. I had to tell him where to go three times today."

"I'd like to tell him where to go," Eric growled. "I know there are a lot of rooms in this house, but he seemed more interested in what was in Belle's personal space than any wiring behind the walls."

"I watched him, too. I agree," Kellan said, sitting back. "So are we all on the same page?"

Well, two of them were. Kellan just happened to write the page. He wasn't actually on it with them. Tate just had to keep hoping that Kell's feelings for Belle would eventually fix that. "Are you going to help us out?"

Kellan's jaw tightened. "I don't think that's a good idea."

"So you're going to let the bitch from hell keep defeating you." Tate was really sick of the excuses.

"You don't understand," Kellan shot back, obviously trying to be patient with him.

And he was sick of people's patient attitudes as they talked down to him, too. Yes, he was socially awkward, but he wasn't a moron. "I understand that if you let Belle go, your ex and your dad have won again."

Kellan forced his chair back, the loud scrape filling up the quiet room. "Again, you know nothing about the situation, so it would be best if you stayed out of it. You weren't raised the way I was. You weren't dragged through shit by your own family."

Tate couldn't stop his eyes from rolling. "Yeah, man, my childhood was a blast. So was Eric's."

"Your father didn't impregnate your wife," Kellan ground out.

"And your dad didn't lock you in a room for three days when you came home with a 92 on a test." Everyone had their troubles. Sometimes Kellan couldn't see past his, and

Tate realized he'd been treating his pal with kid gloves. Time to take them off.

"Your dad did that?" Kellan asked, horrified.

Tate could remember how humiliating it had been. "He left me with two bottles of water and a loaf of bread and he said that was how I would have to live if I didn't study harder. And your dad didn't tell you that you were a worthless wimp because you pulled out of football after your second concussion led to short-term memory loss."

Eric held up a hand. "That was my asshole dad. He was a man's man. Men played football. Brain damage was just a minor battle scar in his book. Look, none of us had it great in the dad department. My mom has only been a good parent since she left my dad."

"And you didn't have to contend with two brothers who called you a moron because you snuck in a little TV time at a neighbor's house. The brainless box rots intelligence, according to my mother. They forbid television, books that weren't academic, and most sports. Absolutely no girls. Hell, friends were even discouraged. I didn't really have one until I met Eric." The awkward day in high school when he'd been assigned to force some math into the jock's head had been the single biggest turning point in his life.

"Okay," Kell conceded. "So we all had some form of shithead for a father."

"But that's the past," Tate stressed. "I think our future is upstairs in bed by herself because we didn't handle her right. I don't want to be that kid stuck in a room again. I broke out of it a long time ago and I won't go back in. Whatever cell your bitch of an ex locked you in, you need to shove the door open. Otherwise, you're letting her trap you inside."

Eric's eyes went wide. "Wow, Tate. That is the most emotionally astute thing I've ever heard come out of your mouth, man."

"I *can* learn." He rolled his eyes.

He'd actually worked really hard to figure out why the

people he cared about did the things they did. He just wasn't always right. In this case, though, he was dead-on.

"I think Belle needs all of us, and that means you need to stop thinking with your PTSD-damaged heart and let your dick take over, Kell. Your dick is way smarter."

"And there it goes." Eric shook his head. "Obviously, his emotional intelligence comes in fits and starts."

Tate wasn't going to apologize for being blunt. He was right. If Kell would just follow his instincts and realize how much he valued Belle, they would all be happier. "Unless you really are turned off by the virgin thing."

Kellan growled his way. "Of course I'm not. But I don't think I can take care of her the way she deserves. I've explained that. She needs a husband and a family."

"She'll have one. Two actually," Eric replied.

At least one of his friends backed him up. Tate was pretty sure if Kellan managed to let go of his fear, he'd find himself in a happy place. But so far, he kept managing to overthink the situation and continually fuck it up.

"Fine. We'll take care of Belle," Tate offered. "You can show up just for sex."

But it wouldn't be just sex, he knew. Kellan would balk at the notion that making love with Belle would be therapy, though it would be. For Tate, it would be coming home. Still, Kellan needed to keep things casual because he wasn't over the hatchet his ex and his asshole of a dad had taken to his soul. Tate would give Kell one thing: at least he'd never had to see his dad naked and doing the nasty with his girl. Come to think of it, he was pretty sure even his mom had never seen his dad naked. Tate figured he and his brothers had been conceived in some petri dish because the idea of his parents boinking didn't compute.

His life would have been like that—sterile and void of emotion—if they'd had their way. He would have dedicated himself to solving intellectual problems without ever really understanding what life meant. It was incomplete without friendship and love. Sometimes that meant sitting around watching action movies on a Saturday night. Sometimes that meant taking stock of who and what was important to you. A million little details and moments made up a life. Eric had taught him that. In some ways, Kellan had, too. It was why he couldn't just let the guy simply drift away. Belle came first, yes, but his friends ran a very close second.

He wanted to have it all.

"I doubt Belle is going to be interested in that kind of relationship," Kellan hedged, though it was easy to see he was thinking about it and aching for it.

"Just come have breakfast with us." The first step to solving any problem was developing a hypothesis, and his was that Kellan wouldn't be able to resist if he stayed around a while longer. If he was sleeping next to Belle every night, he'd be unable to keep his distance for long.

Shit. Another problem hit him squarely between the eyes.

"Wait, guys. There are three of us. Where does number three sleep?" Tate shuddered a little. "I can't cuddle with Eric. It's just…no."

He'd had a vision of sleeping next to Belle, his arms wrapped around her. He could wake up to her sweet scent and the soft feel of her skin, then roll her over and slide inside her before they were really awake. That would be damn near impossible if his best friend was in between them.

Someone needed to write a book of ménage advice.

Eric laughed out loud. "I think we'll have to deal with that problem when we come to it, buddy."

Eric could laugh all he wanted, but this seemed like a real conundrum.

And then a high-pitched scream cut through the house. Tate's heart damn near stopped. He leapt to his feet. "Belle."

Eric and Kell jumped up, too. They were running for the stairs before the sound died, and Tate prayed he could make it to her in time.

Chapter Eleven

Belle lay a trembling hand over her mouth, then reached for her nightstand to turn on the lamp and crawled from bed. When a golden glow illuminated the room, she scanned it, panting wildly. But she saw no sign of the person she'd sworn had just whispered in her ear.

After an exhausting day painting—that reminded her she'd grown unused to physical labor—the comfortable bed had lured her. The quiet had enveloped her, lulling somewhere between awareness and sleep. Just before she'd dropped into the dark chasm of slumber, she thought she'd heard the menacing hiss of a warning.

Get out before he gets you, too.

Then an ear-splitting cry had jarred her awake.

Panting, Belle let her skittish stare bounce around the room. No one visible, but the idea of a stranger in her bedroom made her nauseous. Fear shook her. Had someone been here earlier? Her door was still shut, as was her window. How would anyone have gotten in? Where? It looked somewhere between unlikely and impossible. But she would absolutely swear that someone had stood over her in the dark and whispered the warning.

Maybe it had been a dream? It was possible that between Mr. Gates's warning that the house was haunted and total exhaustion, her imagination had kicked into overdrive.

Belle turned back to glance at the bed. Sir yawned, looking at her with a slightly enquiring gaze, mostly as if asking when she'd turn the damn light off again so they could sleep. But the dog wasn't barking. She let out a pent-up breath. If Sir wasn't yipping his little head off, then they were alone in the room. Heck, he sometimes barked even when no one was there. She needed to calm down and stop letting her weirdly vivid dreams get the best of her.

Belle decided to stop freaking out and let it go, but even as she began climbing back in bed, Belle found herself mentally replaying the dream. Had the scream she'd heard been a part of her nightmare…or something real? She couldn't remember.

Then as she turned to her nightstand, telling herself to kill the light and get some sleep, an unexpected sight snagged her attention. Written on the wall above her grandmother's antique vanity in a pigment that looked unnervingly red were the words *get out while you can.*

Belle opened her mouth to cry out again just as the door flew open. Tate ran in, his eyes wild. Clearly, the scream she'd heard had been real. Had it been hers?

Immediately, he strode to her, his big hands encasing her shoulders as he looked her over, worry written on his face. "What happened?"

Eric charged in right behind him, looking every bit as ready to defend her. "Is someone in the house?"

Kellan stopped in the doorway, gripping her grandmother's cane in one hand and his cell phone in the other. "Do I need to call 911?"

Heart pounding violently, she pointed to the opposite wall. As she read the warning once more, she sidled as close to Tate as she could, taking the comfort and protection his big body offered.

Kellan stormed over to the wall and studied the writing there. "What the fuck?"

"I was almost asleep. Someone whispered similar words

in my ear. At least I thought I heard that. I don't know. Maybe it was a dream, but..."

Tate wrapped his arms around her and brought her closer against him. Eric opened the doors to the adjoining closet and en suite bathroom. Both empty.

"Stay with her," Kellan told the other two. He didn't wait for them to answer. He immediately dialed his phone and paced to the landing. "I need the police, please. There's been an intruder in my girlfriend's home."

As she heard him walking down the stairs and answering questions in clipped replies, Eric approached, speaking in a tone meant to calm everyone. "Tate, why don't you take Belle downstairs and get her a cup of tea while we wait for the police?"

Tate nodded, taking her hand and linking their fingers. Eric tore his gaze from the warning on the wall before the two men shared a long, tense stare.

"What is it?" Belle asked, scooping Sir against her with her free hand. Something was going on, and they knew more than they were telling her.

Tate shook his head and urged her toward the door. "It's nothing, baby. We're going to let the cops take a look at this. Let's get you downstairs. I'm sure they'll have questions for you."

She dug her heels in. "Not until you tell me what's going on."

Eric's eyes closed briefly, but when he opened them he nodded, as though he'd reached a decision. "I'm pretty sure that's blood, Belle. The brownish cast to it makes me think it's dried though, so I don't think the person who did it is still here. But I want to check the rest of the house. We need to get you out of this room and let the cops do their job."

Blood? Belle hadn't let herself dwell much on that possibility, but in the back of her head, she'd suspected the same thing. Desperately, she'd hoped the thought was simply an illusion generated by her fear. Knowing the guys had drawn the same conclusion didn't comfort her. She shivered and let Tate hustle her down the stairs.

An hour and a cup of tea later, she was calmer as the police left with reassurances that the house was secure and they would start looking into everyone who had been there earlier that day.

"You really didn't see those words on the wall before you went to bed?" Kellan hovered above her, his tone pure interrogation.

Belle had already retraced the evening about a dozen times with the police, but she grasped her patience firmly in hand to answer. If one of the guys had woken up screaming, she'd likely be freaked out, too.

"No, but I was exhausted. I literally fell into bed with my clothes on, so I didn't have any reason to turn on the light." Of course if she had, she would have noticed the message someone had seen fit to leave her. But on the bright side, she'd already been fully dressed when the police had arrived. "I didn't see it. And I have no idea who would be trying to scare the bejeezus out of me. I don't have any enemies that I'm aware of, especially in this city. I just got here."

The police had done some quick forensic thing and determined the message had been written in pig blood. They said they'd investigate the vandalism and possible break-in, but much of the department was mired in the madam murder that had taken place a few blocks away and was now gaining national news attention.

"I think we should pack up and head home until we know who's trying to scare Belle and why." Eric paced the kitchen.

Tate nodded. "We can spend tonight in a hotel and catch a flight home tomorrow."

She was afraid, yes. Terrified that someone had come into her house, in her bedroom, intending to frighten her. But she wasn't leaving. Her future was here, and these men didn't seem to understand that she couldn't go back to the relationship they'd had before. If she followed them back to Chicago, she would be just their secretary again, taking care of their professional needs, but not really fulfilling any of her own.

"No. This is my home now, and I'm not going to let some jerk scare me out of it."

"Belle, someone broke in. It's not safe, especially until we know who and what we're dealing with." Kellan's voice sounded hard as nails.

"You know that's not totally true." She shook her head. "No one had to break in. Did you see the list of contractors and delivery people I gave the police? Probably twenty people were in and out of here today, including the creepy old guy next door who told me my grandma was a witch and I shouldn't follow in her footsteps."

Two of her neighbors had shown up in fact, one a very nice woman who wrote novels for a living and had brought her muffins. The other had thumped a bible in her face. Belle knew which neighbor she'd be inviting to dinner parties.

"There were the interns from the law office," she went on. "Don't forget the electrician, the plumber—"

Tate frowned. "Was that the guy with the beer belly and the mullet who told you to call him Captain Ron?"

"That's him."

"Was he in the military or something?" Eric looked confused.

"No, that's just what he likes to be called." Belle sighed. It followed that such an interesting city would have lots of colorful characters. She just wished they weren't all in her house at once.

Tate just shook his head. "And I thought I was weird..."

"Focus, guys," Kellan snapped.

"I remember everyone who came through—the UPS guy, the handyman who gave you an estimate, even the teenager who delivered our pizza."

"How about the three couriers who needed your

signatures on documents? There were tons of people here today," she pointed out. "Any one of them could have come into my room at any time. The house was wide open."

Tate tapped his fingers along the kitchen table. "The question is, why would someone do that? The weird neighbor and Captain Ron guy I can see since they kind of seem unhinged anyway."

"Which is what I told the police," she said to Kell.

"What's creepy neighbor guy's name? Did you catch it? I was on a call when he stopped by."

"He was an ass who maligned my grandmother. I blocked out his name." Belle smiled tightly.

"I'll find out tomorrow. I know the police say they'll look at everyone, but I'll put some extra effort into him," Eric promised.

"Or we could just walk next door and have a nice chat with him." Kellan had a placid look on his face that didn't fool Belle for one minute. If she let him, he would threaten the man next door with all manner of violence. After the guys had gone, she had to live next to the him. She couldn't let Kellan make a bad situation worse.

"No. We're going to let the police deal with him. Tomorrow morning, I'll let Mr. Gates know that I won't allow any interns back in the house. I'll watch every single delivery man. I've already called for a new security system. But for all we know, it was a prank," Belle theorized, though she suspected otherwise. "I can't let someone scare me away."

The memory of that ghostly voice floated through her brain again, but Belle shoved it aside. She was not "getting out." She also refused to let her active imagination run crazy. Of course she was scared. Whoever had done this could be a whack job of Manson proportions. She hoped this episode was simply the work of someone trying to rattle her. Her house wasn't haunted, and no ghost had written that warning on her wall.

"I still think we should go home," Tate said stubbornly.

Belle sighed. They'd been over this. "I'm going back to bed. I have a long day ahead of me tomorrow."

She stood and started up the stairs, weariness and disquiet both invading her system. Could she really sleep in that room alone tonight?

"No, you're not, Belle." That voice told her instantly that Kellan intended to put his foot down and defend his decision.

At the foot of the stairs, she turned. "I can't go to sleep? Really?"

He marched to her side, then ascended the stair above her, blocking her path, arms crossed over his wide chest. "Until we know for sure it's safe and that no one could possibly get to you, you can either sleep in one of the bedrooms on the second floor near ours or we can sleep on the floor in your room. Your choice."

Tate rushed to her side. "We're just worried about you, baby. If whoever wrote on your wall in animal blood comes back, what will they do?"

"Belle?" Eric approached, his expression both imploring and gentle. "I'm sure you're thinking we don't have the right to tell you what to do since you don't work for us anymore and we…well, we fucked up in Dallas. But as a favor? Please don't make us worry about you more than we already are. Thinking we may have lost our chance to be with you hurts, but imaging we could lose you forever…" He shook his head. "I couldn't take knowing that I hadn't protected you."

She let out a shuddering breath, trying not to be touched, but she was. Yes, they'd laid a fairly slick guilt trip on her, but their expressions also told her they really meant it. They cared. At least Tate and Eric had told her a dozen times that they wanted a chance to right their wrongs following Gigi and Butch's wedding. Kell had even bared his scars to her. She really did love these men.

So where did that leave them?

The guys were hoping to wait her out and wear her

down, she knew, so she'd come back to Chicago. That wasn't going to happen, but in the meantime, they crowded her half naked and whispered wicked suggestions. She would have done her best to keep resisting them. But she was a total sucker for their concern. She knew Kell well enough to know that this high-handed ploy was the only way he'd allow himself to express affection. The hard insistence on his face told her that he cared every bit as much as she'd suspected when he threatened to spank her for wanting to help Kinley a few months ago.

Belle teared up. What was she fighting exactly? She wanted them. They wanted her. She wasn't expecting them to stay forever and she wasn't intentionally holding onto her virginity. What if business called them back north? Her new life was here. Theirs was there. What if she never saw them again? The thought stabbed her in the heart. She hurt and bled, but forced herself to face reality. They would return home and find someone who was right for them, who could bring them all together. Belle knew they weren't really in love with her—lust maybe—but if Kell had actually given her his heart, she'd be able to heal him. She couldn't, but that woman was out there, just waiting for them.

But why couldn't she enjoy a few nights with them before they left and found the one who completed them? She was tired of being close to them and not touching them. Was it so bad to want to feel their protection when she was afraid? To ache for the chance to experience their passion while she still could?

Her stare caressed them. They were so smart, gorgeous, kind, funny… The woman who ended up with them would be lucky beyond compare, and knowing it wasn't her tormented Belle. She'd counted their friendships as some of the most important in her life and had hoped she could have Kinley's sort of happily ever after. But no. The best she could do now was embrace them and experience pleasure at their hands. Then she'd know what it felt like to be held and loved by them, what it meant to be their woman—even if it was only for a night or two. Once they'd gone, she'd have beautiful memories for the rest of her life.

"What do you say, Belle?" Eric prompted.

"All right. I'll stay in your room. But only if you stay with me."

* * * *

Eric stared at her. Had she just said what he thought she'd said? "You want me to stay with you?"

"Yes. Please." She bit her full lip, looking somehow incredibly sexy yet pensive at once.

Of course she was afraid. He shouldn't read anything sexual into her request.

"Sure. Let me grab some pillows and blankets. I'll sleep on the floor so you can rest easier."

He turned away to find what he needed. His back would probably hurt like a bitch tomorrow, but Belle was finally reaching out, finally softening toward them. Well, at least him. Surely it didn't matter to her which one of them protected her.

"Wait." She touched his arm—a whisper of her skin over his. Then she pulled away, looking downright nervous. "I want you beside me."

Eric stared. Had she meant that the way it sounded, like she wanted sex?

The room had gone completely silent. In fact, it seemed like the whole world had stopped. Tate stilled beside him, and Eric felt tension pinging through his best friend. What the hell would Tate do if Belle didn't want him?

Eric knew on some basic level that he was supposed to be happy that she might desire him above the others, but he'd stopped working that way a long time ago. Maybe he never had. When it came to Belle, he was possessive, yes. He'd caught that overly muscled electrician staring at her ass earlier in the day and it had taken everything he had not to kill the fucker. But Tate and Kellan were different. They were his partners.

He was crazy about Belle, but he didn't want to hurt his friends. He hadn't dated a woman without them in years. He wasn't even sure he could succeed at a solo relationship with a woman.

Tate deflated like a balloon slowly losing its air. He swallowed. "All right. I'm going to bed, then. Good night."

Shit. His buddy wouldn't recover from this rejection. One of the reasons Eric had fallen so hard for Belle was because she understood and embraced Tate's personal brand of crazy. In fact, she seemed to enjoy it. In the past, they'd dated more than one woman together who'd later declared Eric "boyfriend material" while shoving Tate aside. If Belle followed suit, his best friend would erect a fortress against the world and everyone in it.

"Tate, stop." Belle leaned closer, placing a hand on his arm. "When I said you, I meant all of you. It's just that Eric's is the biggest of the guest rooms. I would rather be near you three. I don't think I'll feel comfortable in my room until I clean it up."

Eric let out a sigh of relief. Tate's balloon was suddenly full again and he puffed up, ready to play protector—and lover, if she'd let him.

Kell wore a satisfied smile. "Good choice."

Belle was inching closer to giving in, but he was also thankful that she was going to let them watch over her.

Something about the house had made him edgy from the first moment. He hadn't said anything, but he'd often felt as though he wasn't alone in a room when logic told him otherwise. Sometimes, he'd even felt someone staring. Gates said the place was haunted. Eric wasn't a believer...but he wasn't a disbeliever, either. Belle's theory was that the zealot next door neighbor had caused tonight's ruckus to scare her into leaving. Eric didn't agree, though he didn't know who else to blame.

"Let's go upstairs," Tate directed. "We'll take care of you so you can get some sleep."

She seemed to falter, victim of some anxiety Eric didn't understand. They were going to watch over her and keep her safe. Wasn't that what she wanted?

"I don't want to sleep," she confessed, her voice breathy.

Eric felt as if a boulder had hit his chest—and liquid flame filled his cock. Holy shit, that really did sound like she wanted sex.

"Hot damn!" Tate grinned and lifted Belle off her feet. "You won't regret this. We're going to make you feel so good, baby."

"Stop for a minute," Eric insisted. "Put her down."

They all needed to slow down before they made the same mistake they had in Dallas by jumping in with both feet and not talking the situation through. They'd been so happy to have Belle naked and seemingly willing that they hadn't thought through the ramifications. Her statement just now could be taken in more than one context. No way could they leave any gray area or room for interpretation.

"Why should I do that?" Tate demanded, but he complied, though with obvious reluctance.

"Belle, what exactly are you asking for?"

She bowed her head slightly, as if she wasn't quite sure she could or should answer. "I want you all to be with me."

That wasn't a precise answer. They couldn't move forward until he knew the truth.

Kellan's eyes narrowed. Obviously, he wasn't happy with her reply either. "You don't have to sleep alone, Belle. We'll all get pallets made up. One of us will sleep in the bed with you, if you want. Or we can stay up and talk, take your mind off your fears until you're ready for a good night's sleep."

"That sounds horrible," Tate complained.

Eric saw Kellan's tactic immediately, and was glad the

two of them were on the same page with making Belle state her wants explicitly.

"But you'll survive, Tate," Eric promised, sending him a glare that demanded he get on board.

With a long, unhappy sigh, his big buddy put her down.

If Belle wanted to be held or kissed...or more, she would have to ask for it. Eric wouldn't take advantage of her vulnerability or give her any reason to wake up tomorrow and blame them for whatever happened.

Eric led an oddly quiet Belle toward his room on the second floor. Tate followed. Kell said he'd gather extra bedding and meet them back in the bedroom. Still she didn't speak up. Either she'd meant what she'd said literally and they were in for a hard night, or she was being a coward. He hoped they had some ibuprofen in the house for the inevitable backache he would have tomorrow. Nothing would relieve the ache in his cock. He doubted he would get a minute's sleep knowing Belle was so close and he couldn't have her.

When he led Belle into the bedroom, Tate prowled in as well, frowning with all the happiness of a thundercloud.

Eric put a hand on his best friend's chest, stopping him. "Don't look at me like I took your favorite toy away."

"You totally did. I didn't even get to play with it."

Sometimes he was far too literal. "What has Kellan been trying to teach us?"

Tate sighed. They'd been going to BDSM clubs with Kell for years, but had only recently gotten serious about topping when they realized Belle would likely be submissive in the bedroom. What they'd learned since was about far more than what flogger to use. Instead, Kellan had tried to teach them the value of communication.

"Damn it. Why can't we just fuck?" Tate put a hand up. "Don't say anything. I know the answer. If she wants sex, she needs to ask for it."

Kellan came in and dropped an armful of bedding on the

floor, then slapped Tate on the back. "Ah, he learns."

"He learns that he's likely going to remain horny and lonely. Sometimes, D/s sucks." Tate grumbled. "Vanilla guys just get to fall on the woman they want and enjoy her."

"You'll be fine," Eric assured, then turned to Kellan. "But you realize we'll have to listen to him complain about his penis all day tomorrow."

Kell snorted. "Probably so, but it wouldn't be the first time."

"It will be the loudest," Tate promised. "Belle, baby...just tell them what you mean and put me out of my misery."

"Don't push her if she's not ready," Kellan growled. "I'll sleep in front of the door. She'll feel better that way."

"No, she won't." Belle protested, looking frustrated. "I want you with us, Kellan, for however long we have. And I think it's embarrassing and slightly mean that you're going to make me admit what I want out loud. It would be easier if you would just toss me on the bed and attack me."

Eric's heart skipped a beat because there was no way to mistake those words. He stepped forward and crowded her, his cock coming to attention the minute he realized tonight might not end in sleep after all.

"Belle, I want you," Eric murmured. "I'm not going to lie about it or prevaricate. So I'm going to put all my cards on the table. I want everything you have to give me. I want to share you with Tate and Kellan. I want to top you. I want to be one of your Masters. If you can't admit what you want, then it would be best if we just watched over you tonight."

Kellan slid his fingers over the delicate slope of her jaw. "We really will wait for you to be comfortable and ready. We won't repeat our mistakes. We took things much too fast. We didn't talk."

"I think I talked too much," Belle said. "I wish I hadn't said anything at all."

Eric forced her to look into his eyes. She needed to

understand a few truths. "You should be very happy you did. We would have known the minute one of us got inside you, and there would have been hell to pay for keeping that secret from us. We could have hurt you Belle."

"I've heard it's going to hurt no matter what," she argued.

She was just begging for a spanking. Previously, she'd only taken Kellan's discipline, but Eric itched to take her over his knee, too.

"It's time to explain how this is going to work. Then you can decide whether you want to proceed."

He heard Tate groan, but then the big fucker was already out of his clothes. Stripping in record time around Belle seemed to be one of his new talents.

Belle turned, stopping to stare at Tate and his massive cock. Eric decided to make it a teaching moment.

"Do you see how eager he is? If we don't properly prepare you, that monster will tear you up."

Tate frowned and palmed his cock. "It's not a monster. That's totally rude. And it's going to be so sweet to you, Belle. Sorry. I thought we were getting to the good stuff. Should I get dressed again?"

Kellan sighed and sat on the small chaise across from the bed. "Don't bother. Belle, I'm here to help. You understand I can't commit the way they can. I would like to offer my services as a Dom to help them introduce you to the lifestyle. I think you'll find comfort and pleasure in it. Will you allow me to assist?"

She finally took her eyes off Tate's dick and faced him. "Yes. Kinley has made BDSM sound fabulous, and this is the way I suspect we'll all enjoy it most. So I want to experiment."

Eric didn't like the thought of being her guinea pig, but he understood. She'd been burned by them. She still clung to her pride and tried to hang onto her heart, but he would make her understand she didn't need to. He would strip away all the walls and barriers she put up because he didn't intend for anything to come between them again.

"Tell me about the experiences you've had," he demanded.

"Is that necessary?" Belle shook her head, obviously flustered.

"Yes," he volleyed back immediately.

Belle sighed. "I'm struggling to concentrate while he's naked."

"Get used to it. He's naked a lot." Eric took a seat next to Kellan, wishing Tate had never gotten so fucking comfortable with his body.

The big guy shrugged. "It helps me think."

"It's not helping *me* think," Belle replied.

"Come here and place yourself over my lap." He patted his thigh to underscore his command and remind her who was in charge. Normally, that would be Kell, but he'd obviously taken a backseat since he didn't intend to stay with Belle long term. Eric thought that was a crock of crap, but having the four of them all together and ready to take the next step was a big win. He wasn't going to push them anymore—yet.

Kellan smiled his approval.

"Are you going to spank me?" A breathless anticipation rang in her voice that calmed him considerably. She did want and need this.

"I'm going to ask you a few questions and you're going to answer me as soon as you do as I've asked."

With an endearing awkwardness, she draped herself over his thighs.

Because they were sitting so close, her head ended up in Kellan's lap. He immediately cradled her head, smoothing her hair from her face. "Very good, love."

She relaxed slightly, but he still felt a fine trembling in her body.

Eric ran a hand across her ass. So perfect. That ass was

round and juicy. He let himself touch her through the thin yoga pants she wore, cupping and molding her flesh as he spoke. "Tell me about your sexual experiences to this point."

She hesitated.

He gave her a few seconds more before he smacked her through her pants three times in quick succession. Belle stiffened for a moment, then released a shuddering sigh. Already, this was turning her on.

"Tell him what he wants to know," Kellan said, petting her hair. "Withholding information is not an option."

Tate knelt and kissed her forehead. "Belle, we really do need to know."

"Once I have, are you going to tell me all of your sexual experiences?"

Eric repressed a smile. Her bratty mouth was going to get her in so much trouble. He delivered three more smacks, these a bit harder. When he'd finished, he pulled at the waist of her pants, lowering them over her backside and exposing it to the cool air. He loved the way she gasped and shuddered when he touched her hot skin.

"I'll answer any questions you like later, but tonight is about you. We need to know what you're seeking, Belle. What you respond to. I'm not asking you these questions to embarrass you. I know it's not polite, but it's necessary. So start spilling and don't you dare give me sarcasm. Tell me why you waited."

She hid behind her smart mouth. He'd figured that out a long time ago. She was bright and quirky and she usually made him laugh, but this wasn't the time or the place for her sharp wit.

A long moment passed, and he worried she would ask to be released. Finally, she sighed. "I didn't mean to. It just happened."

Belle relaxed again, likely because Tate and Kellan were both stroking her. Kellan rubbed her scalp and massaged her neck over and over. Tate kissed her shoulder as he put his hand under her shirt and eased the muscles of her back. The touching seemed to ease her.

"No high school boyfriends?" Eric couldn't deny his curiosity about how a woman as beautiful as Belle managed to stay a virgin for so long.

"I dated a little, but my father died when I was young. My mom needed help around the house, so I often did laundry and started dinner. I also worked a part-time job at the library and I went to school. I was on the debate team, and in high school, I got involved in academic decathlon. It took up most of my time."

His heart softened further as he imagined a teenaged Belle, so sweet and studious. "You were a mathlete?"

Tate grinned. "Me, too."

"That doesn't surprise me." Belle chuckled. "But I was more of a history and literature expert. I dated a guy on the team, but we mostly studied together."

He gave her three more smacks, just for fun. "Keep talking. Tell me about college."

"It was more of the same. I dated but I didn't find the right man. I don't know. Maybe I had an unrealistic vision of what a relationship should be. I wanted to be in love, but I'm too practical to fall easily. I've always wanted something that lasts."

Eric wanted that too, and he knew he'd found it with her. He just had to make sure she saw it that way. "So there's no particular reason you chose not to have sex."

Her head came up a little. "There's no dark past that made me avoid sex, guys. I just wanted it to be special and I didn't find it."

Kellan eased her back down and petted her. "Good. We were worried there was, so we all backed off. I'm pleased to learn it was just you being your picky self."

"How are you feeling, Belle?" It was something Kellan had taught him: always ask where the sub was emotionally.

"I feel achy and a little scared. I want to feel the way I

did the other night. Can't I have it? I'm not asking for more."

"Belle, I want to give you more," Tate said. "A whole lot more, baby."

"There's more to this than an orgasm." Eric soothed his hand over her flesh. "But you'll certainly have that, too. How do you feel now, knowing that?"

"Better," she admitted. "Talking about my past wasn't as hard as I thought. I just don't have that much experience, so it's embarrassing. I mean, I've kissed before. I've had some heavy make-out sessions."

"Did you let a man touch your breasts?" He wanted to know everything she'd experienced so they could do it better, make her forget any touch but theirs.

"I don't know that I'd call them men. I had a couple of boyfriends squeeze my breasts in the past, but it usually hurt."

They'd likely moved far too fast. A woman had to be aroused to really enjoy rough play. Once they got Belle hot enough, she would accept clamps on her nipples. Without proper preparation, she'd likely just slap them. "How about your pussy? Ever had a man finger you before the other night?"

"No. I never let it get that far. I didn't really want any of those boys touching me there. I thought it would be messy and nasty."

Kellan chuckled. "It is messy and nasty. It's also fucking hot. That's why I licked my fingers afterward. You tasted so good. I suppose that means you've never given anyone a blow job, huh?"

"No," she replied. "I've never wanted to before."

"Before what?" Eric hung on her answer to that question.

She hesitated only a moment before she answered. "Before I met you three, I hadn't thought about sex for a long time. I didn't miss it. I didn't care that I wasn't having it. I certainly didn't think about spanking or letting anyone tie me up. But now I like getting spanked. Does that make me weird?"

"It makes you perfect." Eric gave her another three in rapid succession, loving the way she wiggled and squirmed. "It makes you perfect, Belle. And you're going to love it when we tie you up."

He was satisfied that she wasn't trading sex for comfort. He could smell her arousal, but he wanted to feel it, too. Her legs were trapped, the pants holding her thighs together, but the way she was lying across his lap placed her sweet pussy on perfect display. He ran his hand down the swell of her ass until he reached the soft, slick heat of her pussy.

Belle gasped, but Tate and Kellan were there to settle her down with soft words and strokes. Tate lowered himself closer to the floor so he could kiss her. His lips brushed hers as Eric started to work her pussy, spreading the arousal he found there.

"Did she really like her spanking?" Kellan asked, his eyes on her ass.

Eric pulled his hand out and showed his partner her wetness on his fingers. "She can't fake that. She's ready, so I think we should give her a few firsts tonight."

He didn't just want her to lay back and take pleasure. That wouldn't tie her to them. She needed to be involved.

"Get up, baby," Eric ordered. "I want to watch you give your first blow job."

Chapter Twelve

Kellan watched as Belle eased off Eric's lap and into Tate's waiting arms. The big guy covered her back with his body, almost eclipsing her as he wrapped an arm around her waist and bent to feather kisses along her neck. He fanned a hand under the hem of her shirt, skimming his palm up her abdomen, then peeled the garment off her body, apparently determined to get her as naked as he was.

Eric claimed Tate had once been self-conscious about his body, but by the time Kellan had moved to Chicago, all trace of that insecurity had left the building. The upside was that it made Tate perfectly comfortable in BDSM clubs. Belle, on the other hand, curled her hands over her chest, already looking a little unsure.

"Don't try to hide. Tate is going to undress you," Eric said, his voice reassuring but firm. "Let us see what's ours."

Belle exhaled and lowered her arms to her sides again, visibly relaxing as Eric took control of the scene. Pride and desire both stabbed at Kell. Not only had Eric come a long way from the anxious kid he'd first met in college, but Belle surrendered herself a little at a time, her submissive streak so natural and beautiful. No, they hadn't asked a lot of her yet. Her emotional triggers would trip her up at some point. Kell had no doubt of that.

She claimed she'd only remained a virgin because she'd

never had time to pursue romance and hadn't found anything special enough. Maybe that was somewhat true, but he was a betting man. He'd put money on the fact that Belle had been scarred by her father's death. Tate had once told him that her mother had checked out after her husband's demise. Belle had been a mere child. It must have been bewildering and painful to go from being loved unconditionally to damn near being orphaned. No doubt she'd learned to hide in her shell to protect her heart. Kell vowed to make sure Eric and Tate gently pushed her boundaries and opened her up.

If he were a better man with a different past, Kellan would relish the opportunity to participate. But it wouldn't be fair to Belle to top her and build her trust in him when he had no intention of staying. So he'd simply support his friends in their efforts and envy their happiness while cherishing what little time he had with her.

He watched with greedy eyes as Tate unhooked the clasp of her bra between her shoulder blades. It sagged against her body, the straps clinging to her, as he plucked at the string of her yoga pants and shoved them down the lush curve of her hips. Once they reached her ankles, Belle stepped out of them. Eric stood and drew her bra from her body, tossing it aside and leaving her gloriously naked. Kell wondered if he would ever forget the sight.

Raven black hair curved around her shoulders. Her skin was the most beautiful color he'd ever seen. The contrast of its mocha tone against Tate's tanned flesh was striking. But her plump breasts with their pert chocolate nipples looked downright sexy. The little nubs strained for attention, begging to be taken into his mouth and sucked until she screamed with the pleasure he ached to give her. Her flat belly led to a dark pussy, engorged and lightly covered by a trimmed fringe of hair that fascinated him.

With a low groan, Tate wrapped her in his embrace, plastering himself across her back and kissing her bare, delicate shoulder as he palmed his way up her abdomen. Fire shot through Kellan's blood as he watched Tate cup her breasts in his big hands. The luscious mounds just fit in his grip.

Eric stepped against her, crowding her, and staring down with demand in his eyes. "You're going to kiss me, Belle."

She looked breathless, overwhelmed. So ready and beautiful. So perfect for them. "Yes."

"You're going to give me control of your mouth while Tate touches you wherever and however he wishes."

A shudder went through her body. She closed her eyes. "Yes."

At her shaky whisper, satisfaction lit Eric's eyes. He plunged his fingers into her hair and tugged her head back. When he'd positioned her to his satisfaction, Belle strained up to meet his kiss, lips parted in silent but unmistakable invitation.

Eric seized her mouth with his own, taking her lips and stealing her kiss, stripping her of restraint.

Eric took ownership of Belle's mouth as Tate skated his hand back down her torso and right between her legs. As he strummed her clit in a slow, rhythmic circle, she tensed and gasped into Eric's kiss, standing on her tiptoes. Kell didn't know if she meant to get closer to Eric or prevent Tate from learning just how wet she was, but it didn't matter. She had to learn that she didn't have control of either man.

"Flat on your feet," Kell growled in her ear. "If Tate wants his fingers in your cunt, aren't you supposed to let him?"

She whimpered...but slowly lowered down on her heels again.

"Such a pretty pussy," Tate murmured in her ear. "So wet, baby."

Eric ate at her mouth, then drew back to nip at her bottom lip before he bestowed a lingering brush of his lips over hers and pulled back.

"I've wanted that for days. Sometimes I would watch

you talk and just stare at your mouth, fantasizing about it," Eric admitted.

She blinked, once and then again, obviously flustered. He laughed, then turned her to face Tate, who took hold of her shoulders and dragged her close.

"I've totally masturbated thinking about your mouth, Belle. It's perfectly symmetrical. Your full bottom lip will cradle my cock and increase the sensation. At least by ten percent."

"Tate..." Eric warned.

The big guy shrugged. "Just being honest."

"Sometimes too much. Wouldn't you rather kiss her?"

A wicked grin crossed Tate's square face. "Absolutely."

Belle smiled up at him. Her shining dark eyes silently said that his eagerness both amused and endeared her. As Tate swooped down and captured her mouth in a ravenous kiss, she moaned and met him, opening to his need.

Kell could almost see them begin to heal the wrongs of that night in Dallas and start to bond. He gritted his teeth. Fuck, he wanted to be with them. In the past, he'd always believed that he used Eric and Tate as cover so he wouldn't have to be responsible for any woman. Now he realized he liked being a part of this weird family. He didn't want cover; he wanted partners. He wanted this woman.

He couldn't have them, of course. He couldn't trust anymore. Truthfully, he didn't even know how to try. But that didn't stop him from wishing he could bond with them.

For a moment, he considered walking out. These three didn't need him. Leaving later, after he'd tasted Belle, would only hurt more.

As Tate ended the kiss with a little growl, Eric placed a hand on her bare hip possessively and swiveled her in his direction. "What do you say, Kell? You want to teach her how to suck a cock?"

His breath nearly left his body. He'd likely had a hundred subs get to their knees before him, but the thought of

Belle being there threatened to unman him.

Shit, he had to get out of here now. If he were a strong man, he would tell Tate and Eric to care for her always, never to let anything come between them. Then he'd exit stage left so he could keep his soul intact.

His feet wouldn't move. They were planted here, along with his fucking cock, which didn't care that he would be devastated later. It only knew that she was here and she was naked and that he wanted her more than his next breath.

Just a couple of nights. That was all he could have.

"Belle, do you want this?" The words fell out of his mouth.

"Do you?" She bit her lip nervously.

She doubted her appeal? After the way he'd treated her in Dallas, no wonder. Remorse lashed him. He'd shoved his baggage on her. For the hundredth time, he wished he'd handled that night better. Since he'd been an ass then, all he could do was try to reassure her now.

Kell brought her close and cupped her face in his hands. "I've never wanted anyone more. But I'm leaving this up to you."

"Then yes. I'm nervous, though. What if I'm not any good at it?"

"We'll teach you." Tate smiled her way. "I'm a really patient tutor. Ask Eric. I got him through Algebra II. But this will be way more fun. I'm going to like grading your homework."

Tate's humor broke the tension in the room for a moment, and Kell rolled his eyes, then grinned affectionately. "Crazy nerd."

With a shrug of his big shoulders, Tate smiled. "You know me…"

Kell did, and his friend would treat Belle the way she deserved. For now, he was just glad they were all allowing him this opportunity, this moment.

"All right, then. Come with me, Belle. The only thing I

require is your promise to tell me if you're uncomfortable at any time." He gave her an expectant look.

"I promise," she murmured.

"Good. I want this to be pleasant for you."

He settled back on the chaise while Eric and Tate brought her forward. She was a beautiful, luscious gift, and he couldn't be more thankful they were giving her to him—at least for now.

"On your knees, Annabelle," Kell instructed. "Unzip my pants and take my cock in hand. Unlike our overeager friend there, I want you to undress me."

Belle fell to her knees, her hands shaking just a little. Something inside him softened. Kell had grown so accustomed to subs who performed this task simply because they liked turning over their power or wanted their itch scratched in return. This meant something to her.

He took her hands in his own. "Are you scared?"

The thought that she might be afraid of him crushed Kell. He couldn't accept her love, but he wanted her trust. It was imperative she knew that he would shelter and protect her.

"I'm nervous. I've wanted to be with you all for months. I never imagined you'd want me back."

"Why not?" He frowned.

She shrugged and couldn't quite meet his gaze. "We come from different worlds. I was your secretary."

"Office manager," he corrected with a little smile.

Her lips, swollen from kissing, curled up. Kell wanted to feel them on his own. Before he could bend to her, she said something that shocked him to the core.

"You're three white guys and I'm—"

"Beautiful to the men who think the world of you?" he countered sharply. "That better be what you meant to say."

"C'mon, Kell. I don't have a problem with it. I know that attraction is attraction and most people these days feel the same way, but not everyone. Some of your clients might have a problem with it."

"You haven't seen the way some of our clients look at you then," he said with a shake of his head because half the time he wanted to chuck them right out of the office. "All they tend to see is that we have a luscious assistant. You're our lovely Belle. Period."

"If anyone has problems with it, they're small-minded assholes and we don't want them as clients," Eric growled. "We want you just as you are. I wouldn't care if you were purple."

"I would!" Tate looked at them like they'd gone mad. "If Belle was purple, that could indicate some life-threatening respiratory issue."

They all laughed.

"Figure of speech, buddy." Eric clapped him on the back.

"Oh. Then, what they said. I think you're beautiful and I wouldn't want you any other way."

Her eyes slid away from them. "Are you sure?"

Kell tugged, pulling her into his lap and settling her head on his shoulder. "Why don't you know how gorgeous you are to me?" He tilted her head up. "You're the most beautiful thing I've ever seen. God, Belle, you make me wish I was a better man. If you get anything out of this, know that you are everything I could ever want. I'm so sorry I made you feel bad that night in Dallas. It was about me, love, not you."

Belle teared up. "That's very kind."

No, it was the truth. But words wouldn't show her how he felt. He brought his mouth down on hers, reveling in the soft feel of her body against his. He licked at that sexy bottom lip and growled, letting her know he wanted inside. Her mouth flowered open, giving him access. Kell moved in and dominated the kiss, sinking deep and drowning in her flavor, his tongue dancing against the silk of hers.

She softened against him the minute he took control. Belle was so naturally giving, so perfect. She breathed into him, her nipples hardening against his chest. His cock, already rigid, turned to stone.

Over and over, he kissed her, caressing her back, saying without words how precious she was. She melted into him a little more. This was what she needed, to know how beautiful she was, how much he wanted her. Now that she was in his arms again, he realized that her sexual experience—or lack thereof—didn't matter. She could have fucked a thousand men—or none at all—and she would still be Belle. That innocent light would still be a beacon to assholes like him because she was a good, lovely soul. No amount of sex would ever change that.

He brushed her lips again, then looked deep into her eyes. The connection between them tugged at something in his chest. "Belle, can you forgive me for the hurt I caused you?"

She blinked at him and sent him a small, forgiving smile. "It's all right, Kellan. I understand. Will you stay with us as long as you can?"

God, he'd basically admitted he was going to use her body without giving her his heart, and she still wanted to touch him, comfort him, share herself with him. He was so fucking selfish, but he couldn't walk away yet. Later, he would find the strength to do it, but not tonight. Right now, he needed to show her just how amazing she was.

"I want to feel your mouth on me, Belle. I want you to take those sexy lips and wrap them around my cock. Lick me all over. Taste every inch of me. There's no wrong way for you to do it. I'll love everything you do to me. Are you ready?"

"I am."

"Good," he murmured. "There's one thing I need you to do."

"What's that?"

"Let go of your inhibitions. They don't have a place here. With us, you can explore safely because you have three men who want you so badly. Together, we'll help you find what works for you and what doesn't. So put your mouth on me. We'll go from there."

When Belle nodded, he saw a contentment in her eyes he'd never seen. She wanted to please and serve, and now he was giving her an outlet for her submissive nature.

As she slipped off his lap and to the floor, naturally bowing her head, Kell sighed. Shit. She really was just perfect.

Out of the corner of his eyes, he caught sight of Tate and Eric, preparing the bed and ensuring they didn't have to stop later for condoms. Eric had ditched his clothes as well. Kell would have smiled at his friends' eagerness if he wasn't so desperate to feel Belle's hand on his fly and her mouth around his cock.

Her hands weren't shaking as she eased down the zipper of his slacks and folded over the sides. Though he wanted to growl and demand she move faster, he forced himself to remain still. His cock strained against his boxers, but he couldn't stop her exploration. There was a look of wonder on her face as she drew his cock into her hand and stroked up, causing him to shudder. As she stroked down, he really had to concentrate on not coming in her hand like some teenager. It would be downright embarrassing. He'd wanted her for too long to end it so soon.

Her fingers played over the sensitive skin of his cock, little brushes that only made his struggle for control even more difficult.

"Do you like what I'm doing?" Belle whispered.

"I love it." His voice was a guttural groan. "But you don't have to treat me like I'm breakable. Grip me. Squeeze me in your hand."

Tate sank to his knees behind Belle. "I just want to touch you, but don't stop what you're doing, baby. When you're done with Kellan, I'm going to put my mouth on your pussy and eat you until you come just for me."

Belle shivered, but her eyes were dilated. No doubt about it. Dirty talk did something for her. They might have to be careful with her body, but she wasn't going to run away because they showed her how hot and dirty sex could be.

She gasped suddenly, and with his eyes rolling into the back of his head, Kellan could only guess what Tate was doing to her, probably rubbing her clitoris, getting her even wetter than the spanking.

"Belle, he'll stop if you don't take care of Kellan, and we'll start all of this over again." Eric's voice was a firm warning as he dropped a hand on Belle's head and nudged her closer to his waiting cock. "You'll be spanked again, with less thought to pleasure and more about punishment. There will be no release for you until you take care of Master Kellan. Understood?"

Kell loved the thought of being her Master, but Eric was handling her well. It took everything inside Kell not to take over, but he was determined to honor Eric and Tate's claim on her since they intended to stay.

Belle took his dick in a light grip, as though she was afraid of scaring or hurting him.

"Eric?" His partner would know what to do.

Eric tugged on Belle's hair until she craned her head back to stare at him. "Do we need to start all over? Maybe skip the orgasm Tate was planning to give you to make you understand Kellan wants it harder?"

"No." She looked distressed that Eric wasn't pleased with her.

"Reply with a 'yes, Sir.'"

"Yes, Sir," Belle said, downright breathy.

The sound just reinforced Kell's cock with more blood-laden steel.

"Good. Stroke him harder. He won't break."

She licked her lips, obviously trying to focus. "Yes, Sir."

Her small hands tightened. Sensation immediately shivered up his staff. He hissed, then let out a breath, wrestling for control again. "That's it. So fucking good. Now lick the head of my cock."

Blinking up at him, Belle watched with slightly anxious dark eyes as she leaned in and swiped her tongue across the sensitive head of his dick. Heat burst through his system. Before he'd even recovered, she enveloped the wide head of his cock into her little mouth. Watching her struggle to open wide enough to take him all in at once turned him the fuck on.

Finally, she managed, and he groaned at the feel of her soft tongue cradling his cock as the heat of her mouth bathed him with sizzling need. It took everything he had not to grab a fistful of her hair and thrust up and deeper, past her lips. She was new at this and a little nervous. Kell knew he had to restrain himself and talk her through this, build her confidence so her first experience bolstered and pleased her.

"Suck me deeper inside your mouth." He wasn't going to last forever. Hell, as on edge as he felt now, Kell feared he wouldn't even last long, especially not when he watched more of his cock disappear between her lips and she sucked him deeper.

"Ah, god, Belle. Yes. Now stroke the inches that won't fit in your mouth and suck in all you can." She did exactly as instructed, and he sagged back on the chaise with a groan, losing himself to the sea of pleasure drowning him. "That's a good girl. Fuck... Now use you free hand to cup my balls."

He was pleased his voice remained steady and that he didn't sound like a maniacal pervert ready to growl and fuck her throat. Later, he would. He didn't want to use Belle now, but he ached to share this experience with her.

Over and over, she dragged her mouth up, then slid back down his sensitive length. The wetness, the heat, that goddamn suction that had him losing his mind... All her anxiety seemed to have evaporated, and she began to suck his cock in earnest, finding her rhythm.

Belle groaned as she glided her teeth across the tip of his

cock ever so gently. The tiny bit of pain blended with the soft brush of her thumb over his testicles. Oh hell, he'd never felt anyone attend to his pleasure in this particular mind-blowing way. In the middle, she wrapped her palm even more tightly around the base of his cock. The friction from that touch matched the drag and pull she administered to his sensitive head. God, she seemed to understand what he wanted perfectly. Her tongue rolled over his flesh, drawing him closer and closer to the edge. Kellan wondered how the fuck he'd ever do without this—without her—again.

Blood thundered through his system. She sucked harder, whimpered around him, laved him with her tongue again—and he was fucking gone.

"Belle, I'm going to come. Suck me down. Take everything I give you."

She didn't lose a beat, just bobbed her head as she drew even harder on him. His whole body seized up as pleasure coursed through his veins, heavy, drugging, dizzying. Amazing. What he and Belle had shared was far more than a blow job or a mere orgasm. This was...pure connection that jolted him straight down to his soul. He'd never felt it before. Likely, he never would again.

As she slowly drew away, Belle smiled up at him. "I liked it."

He smoothed her hair back. "Oh, damn. Love... I more than liked it."

And he more than liked her. Lila had put a dent in his heart, yes. But once he walked away, he worried now that Belle might put a hole in the damn thing that would never heal.

* * * *

Belle couldn't breathe and she didn't care. She licked her lips, still able to taste Kellan there. She hoped she'd pleased him, that the act they'd just shared meant far more to him than an orgasm. It certainly had to her.

The moment she'd taken his cock in her hand, she'd felt the intimacy of the moment, not just that she touched the most manly part of him, but that he trusted her to give him satisfaction. She'd trusted him to guide her gently. They'd both lowered their guard to share this experience. Because of it, they'd connected on a deeper level than they ever had before. Tonight, she'd seen a side of Kellan she was sure few did. That precious fact had given her confidence…and a bit of dangerous hope. Kellan Kent truly wanted her. And he cared. He'd sworn he wasn't staying and didn't intend to share forever with her, but…

Belle stifled her encroaching anticipation. She shouldn't expect forever from him. Better to simply bask in the time they had together. No way would she put a halt to this night just because she wasn't sure if Kellan would be here tomorrow. She was done with waiting for the future to happen to her. From now on, she'd grab life with both hands and live it.

She gasped as Tate's fingers returned to her clitoris. It wasn't as if she'd never touched herself, but his big fingers felt utterly different—and totally mesmerizing. Beside him, Eric rubbed his broad palm over her burning backside. Everything they'd done to her this evening had heightened her senses. Her skin tingled, feeling completely alive. A pleasant ache thrummed in her system.

"You did so well, baby." Eric kissed her forehead. "You definitely deserve a treat."

Before she could respond, he lifted her in his strong arms, cradling her against his warmth. She missed Tate's fingers on her most sensitive parts, sure. But Eric replaced that, his embrace making her feel feminine, petite, and treasured. Safe.

He carried her across the room as if she weighed nothing. Somehow she'd imagined sex would be all passion and intensity, but she loved the unexpected adoration and surprising sense of togetherness. They'd even laughed some. The guys hadn't thrown her on the bed for rapid-fire thrusts and grunts. They'd chosen to take their time, and what she'd experienced so far had proven so much better than anything her imagination had conjured up. All the awkward talk in the beginning had brought them to this place. Now, Belle was greedy to experience more.

Eric lowered her to the bed, and the soft satin sheet cradled her back. He loomed over her, so gorgeous with hazel-green eyes and short sandy hair that made him look utterly sharp and masculine.

"Do you know what it did to me to watch you suck Kellan's cock?" He stroked his own stiff flesh, his stare never leaving her.

Belle couldn't take her eyes off him. From his bulging shoulders to his firm pecs, down to his stunning corrugated abs, he had an athlete's body. She kept following the visual trail down. Her gaze glued itself to his cock. His very maleness was a thing of beauty, long and thick with a big plum-shaped head. Maybe she should be intimidated by the thought that something so large would eventually thrust inside her. Instead, she was just excited.

Being naked was easier when they were, too. Tate approached the end of the bed, every muscle in his body rippled, easy, and fluid as he moved. That huge erection of his matched the rest of his sizeable body. She should probably be daunted, but Belle had a feeling she was going to enjoy it before too long.

"Spread your legs for me." He dropped a knee to the bed and prowled across the mattress in her direction.

Why wouldn't he just grab her ankles and spread them himself? Because her men didn't play that way. They wanted her conscious of her choices and involved in everything. She had to offer herself before they'd take her. They might call it submission, but they were giving her the power to say yes or no, to decide for herself.

Conscious of their gazes fixed on her, Belle tried to ignore the riot of nerves in her stomach as she bent her knees and eased her feet apart. As cool air kissed the damp folds of her pussy, she wondered exactly what they were seeing and thinking. Anxiously, she watched Tate's face for any reaction. She'd seen a few of the women they'd dated, and she didn't look anything like them. Her insecurities threatened to undo her, but then Tate gave a rough groan of pleasure. Belle couldn't mistake his approval. She let out a shaky breath of relief.

They followed you here because they want you. Remember that. Stay in the moment.

"I can't wait to taste you, baby." Tate sank to his stomach, arms curling under her thighs, palms looping around to the top and clamping down. His face hovered right over her pussy. She felt his hot breath on her flesh.

Shock and desire flared at once. Belle gasped. This position was so intimate, the space he sought to invade incredibly personal.

"You've gone tense. Relax," Eric urged, smoothing her hair from her face. "You're definitely going to like this. And if you don't, he's doing something wrong."

"Please…" Tate scoffed. "She'll love it. I've studied this way more than I cracked books for the bar."

Which had to mean that he was an oral sexpert.

Tate nipped her thigh playfully, and Belle couldn't help but giggle. Just by being himself, he had broken the tension and made her shiver all at once.

"That's better," Eric praised. "Let him have his taste, then I'll take mine."

No doubt, Eric was the bossy one tonight. That surprised her. She'd expected Kellan to take charge, as usual. But he'd nodded at Eric earlier, as though giving his friend permission to take over. That made Belle's heart hurt. Kell had probably only ceded control because he intended to keep his distance. What would it take to make him change his mind? How dangerous was that thought?

She glanced over to find him shedding his clothes. Instead of dropping them with abandon, Kellan slid each piece off, then carefully folded it. Despite the sublime moment they'd shared, she could see he held himself remote once more.

"Attention on me, Belle," Tate demanded.

The moment she cut her gaze back to him, his face disappeared between her thighs. She held her breath, wondering how quickly Tate would dismantle her restraint. Then as his tongue lapped at her pussy, she wasn't thinking about anything but the fire that flared through her body.

The sensation of his mouth working her little bundle of nerves sent a shiver zipping up her spine. She tensed, spilling out his name in a moan. But Tate paid her plea no mind. He simply showered attention on her pussy with soft, repeated lashes of his tongue. His hungry groans reverberated under her skin. He overwhelmed her. Belle shook. She had no defenses to handle an onslaught so targeted and devastating.

Tate hadn't been exaggerating; he was really good at this.

"That's it, baby. I'm thrilled to see you enjoying his mouth worshipping your cunt. Get used to it. It will happen a lot." Eric bent and lowered his head to her breasts.

"She tastes like honey." Tate growled the words against her flesh, then parted her with his tongue again, tasting every swell and crevice. "She's so fucking sweet."

Belle closed her eyes and drowned in pleasure. She would have been far more self-conscious if she hadn't put her mouth on Kellan just minutes before. But she'd loved the closeness, the direct correlation between the swirl of her tongue and his reaction, having the power to bring him pleasure. She'd known instantly that he'd enjoyed her touch. And she'd been shockingly thrilled by his taste.

Tate was doing the same to her. His gusto made her feel beautiful and treasured. God, now she knew why Kinley smiled all the time, why she winked at her husbands. They shared something more than pleasure. Yes, she'd known they were in love, but now she understood the intimacy. They gave and took bodies and hearts. They'd created a bond stronger than steel, and soon they would add to their family. Though thrilled for her bestie, Belle had been the teeniest bit envious. Eric, Tate, and Kell were giving her a little nibble of that same joy now.

A mouth fitted over her left breast, enclosing the bud and giving it a long pull. A zing of sensation zipped all the way to her clit and made her moan. Tate increased the sensation by flicking her flesh with his tongue. The tandem manipulation didn't just double her pleasure, but multiplied it. Her blood surged as Eric scraped her nipple with the edge of his teeth. The feeling was completely unexpected and just on the right side of pain.

Belle cried out, writhed. Desire climbed and clawed, almost too overwhelming. Yet she wouldn't change a thing.

Tate didn't let her divert her attention from him for too long. He redoubled his efforts, licking her, tucking his tongue between her swollen folds, sliding the tip inside her, deeper than she'd imagined possible. Fire shot through her veins. She grabbed at the sheets, mouth gaping with a silent whimper.

She was on the precipice, burning and half out of her mind, willing to do anything so Tate would bestow that dazzling pleasure on her, but he knew exactly how to keep her on the edge, withholding the climax she craved just out of reach.

Bracing on her heels, Belle tried to lift her hips, circle them, anything to increase the pressure on her clit. Just a little more was all she needed… But Tate held her effortlessly with strong arms, caging her down.

"Stay where you are, Belle. Let Tate have his fill. If you're good, he'll make you come. If not…" Eric let the warning hang. Then he helped his buddy by gently anchoring her left arm to the bed.

Kellan circled to the other side of the bed, pinning her right arm down and bending toward her breast. As soon as he enclosed it, the suction, coupled with the rest of the stimulation, had her crying out.

They had her deliciously trapped. No way to escape or move or manipulate the sensations they heaped on her. Belle could do nothing but accept pleasure—in whatever time and way they chose to give it.

If she'd been in actual panic or pain and she told them to stop, they would, but she didn't want them to let her go. She trusted them. These men would never hurt her physically. Her heart was another story, but even then, she knew they'd never mean to harm her. Kell had even explained his terrible past—a feat he obviously hadn't found easy—so she wouldn't be too devastated when he left. Wishful thinking, but Belle knew one thing for certain.

She'd waited for the right men.

Something blunt began to breach her aching sex. A cry escaped her throat as she jerked her gaze down to see that Tate had lifted his head. Now his fingers probed her, gently stretching her opening, preparing her for what came next. Though Belle was nervous, she already felt empty, greedy to be filled.

"Hurry," she begged.

"Patience," Eric insisted. "You're not ready. Tate will get you there."

Then the conversation stopped as he slid his digits deeper and suckled her clit once more. Eric and Kell each plucked on a nipple with their fingers, then with their mouths. The men moved in perfect harmony. The feel of them all drawing on her most sensitive spots at once had her holding her breath, euphoria dancing just under her skin.

Tate sucked her harder, fingers sinking deeper. Tingles swelled, spread. Her body tensed. Heat everywhere. God, she wondered if she'd ever recover from this avalanche of a climax when it finally rolled over her. The need gathered and grew as it accelerated, almost overshadowing her ability to breathe.

"Belle," Eric murmured in her ear. "Come."

Almost instantly, the ache behind her clit turned sharp and burst through her system, making her arch and scream. The hot shock of something far beyond incredible consumed her. She'd never even fantasized that the heavens could sing like this—or that anything could unravel her body so completely.

Panting, she lay spent as the sensations subsided. Belle didn't even know what to call that. Orgasm seemed weak, like calling a massive quake a tremor.

Before she recovered, the guys went into motion. She tried to catch her breath as Tate lifted himself off the bed, then dragged her into his arms. Thankfully, he held her up, giving her strength since her whole body had gone limp with sweet lethargy.

He tilted her chin to meet his kiss and devoured her mouth. Belle smelled and tasted herself on his lips. Just like when she'd put her mouth on Kell and laved him to climax, everything felt intimate. A part of her marveled that this man could—and would—give her the sort of pleasure that shook the earth and rocked her soul.

Tate broke the kiss with a grin and a wink, looking really pleased with himself. Before she could think of a reply, he turned her to face the other two. Eric's expression was every bit as hard and hungry as Kell's. Belle's stomach dipped and rolled with the knowledge they all intended to become her lovers tonight.

Practically bouncing on the bed, Tate settled himself against the headboard, then pulled her between his long, muscled legs, resting her head on his thigh. She was on her back, looking up at him. He brushed a palm over her cheek, and she sighed, clinging to the warmth in his stare.

"Eric will do this right," Tate promised. "I'm so thrilled

you're about to become ours."

She was, too.

Through half-lidded eyes, she watched Eric at the foot of the bed as he worked a condom over his angry, vein-laden cock.

Kellan leaned closer, brushing his lips over hers. "Thank you for letting me be a part of this, love."

Even though he hadn't promised her anything beyond right now, Belle softened. This night wouldn't be complete without him.

She threaded her fingers through his. "Thank you for being here. I know it's not easy for you."

Tate brushed his knuckles across her cheek. "I can't wait. It seems like I've waited a lifetime for this. Ready?"

She didn't reply. She couldn't as Eric climbed onto the bed between her sprawled legs. Her heart pounded too hard.

"Baby?" He glided a hand up her thigh, to her hip, caressing it as though he couldn't stop himself from touching her. "Second thoughts?"

"None."

The sense of connection to all three of them bound Belle. She wanted them, felt them. After this, some small piece of them would always belong to her. And no matter what happened later, a piece of her would always belong to them.

Eric smiled as he eased deeper into the *V* between her legs and covered her body, nudging her opening with his cock. She whimpered. This was it.

She'd wanted this moment since she'd laid eyes on them. They surrounded her, their big bodies warming and protecting her. With them, she felt not just beautiful, but like the only woman in the world.

"I'll be as gentle as I can, but if it hurts more than you can bear, Belle, you have to tell me. You'll do that, right?"

She assured him with her smile. His voice might sound a tad stern, but concern shadowed his hazel eyes.

"Women have been losing their virginity and living to

tell the tale for millennia. I'll be fine." When he opened his mouth to rebut, she cupped his shoulders. "But I will tell you. I promise."

"Excellent." Eric didn't waste a second before he sandwiched a hand between them and aligned their bodies, then began working himself inside her. "Oh, baby, you're so tight."

"Gently," Tate warned his friend.

Eric nodded, focusing on her completely as he lifted up on his arms and watched his cock begin to disappear into her body. The head stretched her, burning a bit as she opened to accommodate him. He inched inside her with a hiss, tensing and bracing himself above her with bared teeth.

"You already feel amazing." He sounded strained.

Belle found it endearing. Some guys would only care about getting off. But his every thought now seemed focused on her comfort and pleasure.

He was barely in, and she already felt awfully full. As he pushed deeper, panic threatened. She whimpered and gripped Kell's hand in hers. But she refused to say the words that would stop Eric from breaching her completely.

Kellan squeezed back, letting her know he was there. "It's okay. We're going to take the time to let you get used to sex. It's only going to be uncomfortable a few moments the first few times. Just remember, your body was made for this."

Her head knew that, but it wasn't prevailing now. Her body insisted Eric was too big, too much. Her heart thundered, seizing up further in an attempt to keep him out.

"Shh," Tate whispered, caressing her breasts, gently playing with her nipples. "Belle, baby, it's going to feel so good soon. You're so fucking beautiful. I can't wait to be the man inside you, loving you. You mean everything to me."

He meant an awful lot to her, too. His devotion warmed her. His touch relaxed her. Belle forced herself to draw in a deep breath and let go of her tension.

"Watch what he's doing, love." Kellan looked down her body. "Seeing you and Eric come together, witnessing your first time... It's amazing. Look."

She glanced down, fastening her stare to the spot where Eric's cock slowly disappeared inside her body. She forced herself not to think of the invasion, but of getting closer to them, of being theirs tonight.

Spreading her legs wider, Belle welcomed him. He sank in just a bit more. Suddenly calling it sex seemed silly. This moment was so much more. Not only was she inviting him inside her body, but her soul. She was giving him something she couldn't give again. She was telling him without a word how much she cared. That was more than worth a moment's discomfort.

His face was a mask of concentration as he nudged at her opening again, but the barrier inside her stopped him. And knowing it would cause her pain, he looked reluctant to break through. He needed reassurances, too.

She let her free hand drift up, touching his face. "I'm all right, Eric. I want this. I want you—all of you. Take me."

Belle lifted her pelvis, unwilling to wait a moment longer to have him inside her. Eric groaned out her name and gripped her hips, piercing her hymen and surging into her.

A flare of pain lit inside her, a tearing sensation as he thrust all the way to the hilt. She yelped as he took complete possession, filling her to capacity and beyond. She struggled against him.

"Eric!"

"I know, baby," he soothed. "I'm sorry it hurt. Take a deep breath. That's it. Now exhale."

She did exactly as he demanded while he remained totally still. Slowly, her body adjusted, stretched to accommodate his cock, softened, reshaped around him. Her mind calmed.

"You better now?" he asked after a long moment of nothing but harsh breaths filling the air.

"I think. Yeah." She hoped.

"Thank god. You can't know how fucking good it feels to be inside you."

As he held still, forging himself deep inside her, his cock pulsed, a rhythm her heart matched. But sex involved far more than him staying stationary with his flesh buried in hers. Now that the pain had subsided, she wanted to know just how fabulous him being inside her could feel. She wiggled her hips to entice him.

"Shit. Baby, if you don't stop moving, I'm going to come. I don't want to do that yet. Let me make this good for you."

The feel of him submerged inside her was already reigniting her desire. Knowing they were joined charged that desire into need.

"I'm ready. Eric, don't make me wait."

He seemed to take forever, his head bowed as he worked to take air into his lungs and grab hold of his self-control. Tate continued his gentle adoration of her breasts, all the while telling her how beautiful she was, how much they wanted her.

Finally Eric raised his head. Anticipation thrummed through her. "I'm going to make love to you, Belle, soft and sweet."

Her sex cramped. Her heart caught. "Please."

Oh so slowly, he withdrew almost to the edge of her cunt, dragging his cock over the sensitive flesh inside her. He took in a shuddering breath, then eased back in, dragging over nerves now tingling and spreading pleasure throughout her. Eric repeated the motion again, giving her more of his weight, arching his pelvis against hers and twisting slightly. The motion pressed on her clit as he forced his dick higher inside her.

Following her instincts, Belle worked with him, matching him thrust for thrust. The movements stimulated spots that fingers, lips, and tongues could not. Eric had barely introduced her to the gentle feel of his thrusts, and already she was soaring so much higher. Instead of someone heaping ecstasy on her, he was sharing it with her.

Belle curled her fingers into his shoulders and began spreading kisses along his jaw. Between deep, measured thrusts, he took her mouth, the kiss rough, punctuated by a long groan when he completely seated himself again.

"More." She closed her eyes as a rush of euphoria heated her blood, wanting everything he had to give her.

Eric picked up the pace. She was still so achingly full, but she enjoyed the sensation now. The contact, the friction, the closeness. This was even more pleasurable and profound than she'd hoped.

Over and over, he thrust into her, and she slammed back up to meet him. They crashed together in unison. He grunted as she gasped. Then he took another hungry swipe at her mouth as he shoved deep.

Tate's fingers were still wedged between them, twisting her nipples. He found a tempo to match Eric's thrust. He plucked at her, the pleasurable little pain jolting straight to her pussy.

"I've never seen anything sexier," Kellan growled in her ear. "I can't wait to get deep inside you and fuck you, love."

"You won't believe how good this is, Kell. Nothing has ever felt this amazing," Eric moaned.

"I'm dying to be inside you, Belle." Tate's voice almost sounded like a plea as he twisted her nipples, adding more pressure and a bit of pain. The edge was right there. She held her breath, then keened out with need. The next touch would send her over.

Kell nipped at her shoulder, breathing on her skin.

Eric slammed inside her and ground down, finding a place deep, shocking her with an exhilarating sensation that swirled and gathered, tight, tighter. Then it released in a torrent like a giant storm. Belle gave a long, guttural groan, her head thrashing as the rapture drenched and drowned her, pulling her under in a consuming wave.

Eric stiffened, his face contorting as he thrust one last time into her. His entire body seized up. He shuddered, cried out, then poured his body—and soul—into her.

An electric moment later, he released a heaving breath, then fell on her chest. His heart still thundered against hers. Their bodies remained connected. Belle suspected that, from this moment on, their hearts always would be.

Peace filled her now. Every cell in her body exhaled as though she'd been waiting for this feeling—for them—all of her life. Such dangerous thinking, but no sense in lying to herself.

Finally, Eric lifted his head, his lips tugging into a satisfied grin. "That completely blew me away, baby. Being your first was so special. I'll never forget it."

He gave her a lingering kiss, so tender that tears stung Belle's eyes. As he ended it, he rolled away. A chill hit her damp skin, but she didn't stay cold for long. Tate slipped out from behind her, then rolled a condom on in record time and covered her body with his own. Wow, he was big and heavy, and his cock prodding at her would stretch her even more. But Belle didn't panic this time. She knew they'd all work together to make this fabulous.

A wickedly sweet smile lit up Tate's face. "My turn. I've wanted to offer my penis to you for a long time."

Belle grinned. "I accept."

"Thank god."

He covered her lips with his own, his tongue finding its way inside at the same time his cock began to. Gasping at the sweet burn as he stretched her opening to accommodate his girth, he tunneled in deep, deeper, so deep she could almost swear he was about to hit her tonsils. Surely, he couldn't fit another inch in. He did. And more. When he tilted his hips to grind into her and she felt their bodies totally merged, she whimpered in delight and wrapped her arms around him. It was going to be an amazing night.

Chapter Thirteen

Tate stretched as he walked into the kitchen, every muscle in his body suffused with a happy ache. He wouldn't need to work out today. He'd gotten the workout of a lifetime fucking Belle the night before.

Fucking. Maybe he hadn't really known the meaning of the word until her. Strictly saying he'd had sexual intercourse with Belle wasn't accurate. He hadn't merely inserted slot *A* into tab *B*, but connected with her on a level he'd never experienced with another woman. Fucking Belle meant more than ever before. Because he'd opened up and poured himself into her. He'd made love to her.

His only regret was that he'd had to wear a condom. Once they got her home, they would all schedule checkups. Once they proved their clean bill of health, they'd put Belle on the birth control of her choice and toss out the condoms. He'd never taken a woman bare, but he didn't want anything to come between him and Belle again.

Of course, she might not want birth control at all.

A vision of Belle, round and soft with a baby in her arms, floated across his brain. He'd never considered children much in the past, but now that the concept was crossing his mind, he loved the idea of creating life with her.

"I suppose I should be glad you put on pants." Eric's voice brought him out of his thoughts.

Tate ignored his friend's acerbic glance with a yawn as he ambled to the coffee maker. "Too many strangers in this house to be naked. I don't want to freak out some poor delivery guy, but I still think clothes are unnatural. Humans walked around naked for far longer than they've covered themselves up."

Eric shook his head, clearly in disagreement. "After it calms down around here, we'll have to accustom Belle to you walking around with your junk hanging out."

He shrugged. They would be back in Chicago before too long. "I think we should accustom Belle to walking around naked. When she's alone with us, she doesn't need clothes, man."

He wasn't the dominant of the group. He liked to top a woman, but not the way Eric—and especially Kellan— needed it. But he loved certain aspects of the lifestyle.

Eric's hair was still wet from his shower, but he was dressed for the day in slacks and a dress shirt. "I don't hate that idea. We need to start thinking about a collar for that beautiful girl. I thought I'd go shopping and pick up a few things. I considered asking Sequoia to grab some stuff from our stash back home, but god only knows the lectures he'd give about the plastic found in anal plugs killing the environment."

But anal plugs would get Belle's sweet ass ready for play. With just that thought, his cock wasn't tired anymore. It strained against his sweats. Unlike Eric, he wasn't about to get all dressed up to spend the day in front of his computer, but he'd toss on something acceptable for that errand. "I'll go with you. We definitely need to get her ready, but don't you think we should consider a ring before a collar?"

Eric raised a tawny brow. "You think so?"

He poured himself a cup of coffee, hoping the answer he got matched his own. "Yeah. I want to marry her. Don't you?"

How had they not talked about this? He'd just assumed

they wanted the same thing. They'd talked endlessly about getting her in bed, moving her into their home, having a future with her. What the hell was he going to do if that future didn't include marriage for Eric?

"Of course I do," Eric shot back. "And I think we should do it fairly quickly because she deserves to know the men she gave herself to want to marry her. She waited a very long time. She should never question that we love her."

Love. Wow. Tate had never believed he would find it. He'd basically been programmed that love was detrimental to one's ambitions. But he had no doubt now that he'd totally fallen in love.

"This is what my mom and dad warned me about," Tate admitted. "I can't think straight around her. I think love is turning me into a Disney character. Damn it. I always thought I'd be someone interesting out of a *Star Trek* episode, but I kind of want to break into song a little. Just a little."

Eric stared at him. "I've heard you sing. Please don't."

Belting out a chorus of "Can You Feel the Love Tonight" might be fun, but it would probably scare Belle away. "I'll hold it in."

"Yeah." Eric nodded. "Shove it down, dude. *Way* down."

The door opened, and Belle dashed in. His damn heart skipped a beat because he knew they were meant to be. He'd spent many an awkward morning with a woman who didn't mind him in bed, but completely ignored him out of it, preferring Eric's company after sex. Belle wouldn't be that way. She didn't mind his quirks. He could be himself around her, and it felt totally freeing.

She blinked up at them before her gaze skittered away. Obviously, she felt a little bashful.

"Morning, guys." She stole another glance at him. He loved the way she sighed. It made all that time at the gym worthwhile. "You...um, look good this morning. I mean you look well rested. You slept okay? I didn't kick or snore or anything?"

With a laugh, Tate scooped her up in his arms, enjoying her squeal as he hauled her against his chest. "Last night, I slept better than ever. You are the perfect body pillow."

She relaxed in his arms. "I was so warm in between you and Eric."

Eric grinned, looking happier than Tate could remember. He took Belle's hand in his and kissed her fingers. Even her hands were small and adorable.

"We were very happy to keep you warm, baby," Eric murmured. "Now, we have to talk about those interns from the law office because they are not returning to this house today."

Belle frowned. "I've been thinking about that... I know they're an inconvenience and I didn't want them here last night, but I really don't have time to do the inventory."

Tate was with Eric on this one. "Then I'll help you. I can take the weekend and get it done."

"It'll be fine. I doubt any of them wrote in pig's blood on my bedroom wall. Why would they have a beef to pick with me? I don't know them."

"You don't know anyone in this town, but that doesn't matter. Someone is out to disturb you—at least. At worst..." He shrugged. "I'm not taking chances. In fact, we're going to vet everyone who walks in this house, including that douchebag electrician who stares at your ass."

She huffed. "He does not."

"Oh, he does." Eric opened the fridge and pulled out the eggs. "And when you're not looking, he's staring at your boobs, too. Next time he does it, I'm going to kick his ass. God, I hope he has a record. Maybe he's on the lam. Then we could kill him and claim self-defense."

Belle looked horrified.

"He's teasing, baby. At least kind of." Tate settled himself on one of the kitchen table chairs and looked at the mess of computer equipment, legal files, and writing implements all over the table. He couldn't see a single inch of the antique cherry surface anymore. Frowning, he made a mental note to clear off the dining room table and relocate the office elsewhere so they could all sit down and eat together. Kellan was right. They needed to behave like a family.

It would just be so much easier if they were back home, in their recently constructed suburban paradise, instead of this never-ending home improvement project.

"You can't kill Mike. I need him." Belle rested her head on his shoulder. "I have to get the electricity working properly. Have you noticed that power works selectively in certain rooms? And some spots are just weirdly cold."

"That last problem is HVAC. The vents are probably screwed up, baby." Eric put a cup of coffee in front of her. "It's one more hassle and expense to add to the list that you don't need."

"You know," Tate began, "we could hire someone to revamp the whole place, find someone capable of handling everything."

Belle's head snapped up, and he felt her whole body stiffen. "Are you saying *I'm* not capable?"

A voice in his head told him he was walking into dangerous territory. That same voice always told him he wasn't going to get the girl or say the right thing. But he had Belle now, and she wasn't like every other bitch who'd snubbed him after sex. She didn't expect him to say the right thing all the time. That stupid voice was the product of self-doubt, and it had to go.

"Of course you're capable. I know you want to stay here, but we need to get back to Chicago, baby."

Hadn't they settled this last night? Yeah, she'd said a few days ago that she wanted to stay in New Orleans, but surely she wouldn't have gone to bed with them if she didn't intend to share a future. Chicago was home, and he was anxious to get back. Although he kind of loved that it wasn't cold here yet. He also dug the nifty, weird vibe and charming architecture of New Orleans. When he jogged, he always found something new to see. The city was a chameleon, changing on a daily basis. Tate found it a little weird and wonderful. He'd even found himself running down Royal Street beside a group of dudes in red dresses the other day. He didn't know what the hell was up with that, but they'd looked as if they'd been having fun. Pretty soon he wouldn't have anything in Chicago except frigid temperatures and another average season for the Bears, but everything they'd worked for was there.

She slid off his lap, looking incredulous. Tate wished he hadn't brought the subject up.

Belle took a long sip of her coffee, her stiff body suggesting she grappled for patience as she turned back to them. "I know you need to get back. I'm glad you stayed here with me for a while. I really enjoyed your visit and appreciated your help with the house."

Tate frowned, his whole body going on alert because he'd heard that flat cadence coming from a woman's mouth before. Just before she broke up with him. Just before she explained all the reasons it wouldn't work between them. "What is that supposed to mean?"

Eric stood, putting a hand on his shoulder. "Hey, buddy. We can hang out here for as long as necessary."

"As long as necessary for what?" Belle's lips firmed.

"Nothing, baby. Just as long as you want us here." Eric seemed determined to keep everyone calm.

Tate couldn't let it go. Dread churned an ache in his gut, and it wasn't going to go away until he knew the truth. He'd thought everything had been settled the night before, but maybe history was just repeating itself. "I want you to explain yourself, Belle. I deserve the truth. I've never lied to you. Not once. I've always been straight with you. What are your plans?"

"I've said for days that I'm going to work on this house and set up a design business." She squared her shoulders. "Don't look so shocked. I told Eric in Dallas this is what I wanted. I quit, Tate. Just because you didn't accept it doesn't make it less true. I don't want to be a secretary for the rest of my life."

He tried to force down the panic invading his system. *Keep cool. Don't blow it.* She deserved the career she wanted. Her desire and his didn't have to be mutually exclusive.

"I understand. You've got a dream," Tate acknowledged. "We'll help you find a space in Chicago. Baby, you have to understand that everything we've built is there. We can't drop our livelihoods to move here."

"I didn't ask you to." She pressed her lips together in a grim line. "But I'm not going back to Chicago."

"We don't have to decide any of this right now," Eric interjected.

Tate ignored him. "Seriously? What about last night?"

Making love to Belle had meant everything to him. His whole life had built up to the one moment he'd joined his body to hers and found what he truly wanted in life. All the hours sweating in the gym and enduring the users who'd wanted him just for sex had shaped him. Until last night, he thought he'd put up with it because that was the cost of getting some. Now he knew he'd unconsciously done those things to become the man for her. He'd found his calling. Practicing law was great, but he wanted to make Annabelle Wright happy. He wanted to be her husband and build an extraordinary life with her and his best friends.

How could she not want that, too?

She shrugged, her gaze sliding away from his. "I enjoyed it, Tate. But you can't expect that I would give up all my hopes and dreams because I liked what you did in bed. Can't you see that I have a chance to create my dream here?"

"And if I offered to move? If I gave up the practice?" He

hated how pathetic he sounded, like that five-year-old he'd once been, praying that his mom would hug him, just once. Like the kid yearning for his dad to play catch with him.

Belle sighed, hesitated. "I don't think it would work."

Of course it wouldn't work. She would need to socialize with clients. She would want a wide circle of friends, and he struggled in those situations. He was a liability. He was a nerd without a filter. No amount of muscle he packed on was going to change what he was. He couldn't magically transform into Eric.

He was good for sex. That had been a shocker. He'd been a sexual savant, easily learning how to please a woman because he was willing to do just about anything. He loved to eat pussy, loved the little sounds a woman made, the way she squirmed on his tongue. He had a big cock and he'd learned how to use it. When he was in bed with a woman, there was no doubt he excelled.

They just didn't want him out of bed.

Apparently, he'd been naïve to think Belle would be different.

Tate pushed his chair back and stood, his gut heavy and knotted and dragging somewhere near his feet. How the hell had he gone from believing he was getting married to breaking up in less than ten minutes?

She stepped forward, the sympathy on her face almost too much to take. "Tate, I don't mean to hurt you. I just don't think it would work in the long term."

He suddenly realized he would do it. He would give up his practice and start over again here. He would sell his house and follow her if that's what she needed. He could beg, but it wouldn't change the outcome.

Belle just didn't want him.

"Hey, it probably wouldn't." He wasn't going to make a bigger fool of himself.

She reached out to touch him, but sighed again when he moved away. "Tate, if I asked you to move here, you would eventually resent me. I know it worked for Kinley, but I doubt Eric wants to give up his practice for a woman he spent one night with. I don't see how it works, especially since Kellan isn't interested at all."

Ah, so it was Kellan she truly wanted. He'd known it must be one of his two friends. They were smooth. They wouldn't embarrass her by doing anything painfully awkward. Now that he really thought about it, she would never have gone for their type of relationship. Almost no woman actually wanted to deal with more than one man. They were demanding, obnoxious at times. He might be the most demanding of all, following her around like a sad puppy or the horny mutt trying to hump her leg. Most women preferred men like Kellan.

He held a hand up. "Whatever. It's cool. I'm going to take a shower. I'll look into flights out of here this afternoon."

She looked startled. "I thought you were going to stay for a few days."

"That was when I thought you gave you a shit, Belle. Now, I think I'll let you get on with your life."

Eric tried to step between them. "Tate—"

"So we can't be friends if you don't get your way?" Belle cut in.

"My way? You want to make me sound like a kid who throws a temper tantrum because I had a toy taken from me? I wanted to marry you, build a life with you. I wanted to take care of you and make you the center of our world. But I guess you just wanted a man to pop your cherry and we were handy."

Belle gaped at him. "That's not true! I never said that."

"You don't have to. I know the drill, baby. So I'll make it easy on you. I won't tell you I love you again. Clearly, you don't want to hear it." Trying to hold himself together, he whirled away to leave.

She grabbed his arm. "Tate, stop. Will you sit down so

we can talk? I care about you. I'm not trying to hurt you, just be realistic about this. I can't let you give everything up for me when it can't work. You would hate me."

He could never hate her, but he damn straight could hate himself. At the end of the day, this mess was his fault. He was the real reason it wouldn't work.

"I'd rather not rehash this shit." He yanked away from her grip. "I need to take a shower and get back to work. I'll be out of your hair as soon as I can."

He walked out without another word, letting the door shut behind him.

"Tate!" he heard Eric's oh-so-reasonable voice but kept walking. He needed to be away from her, away from all of them. In his suitcase, he found a tank top, then he thrust his shoes on, his whole body numb. In moments, he headed for the door.

Kellan walked in, a white bag in his hands. "Hey. I got us beignets. I thought we could sit down and figure out what we're going to do about the house situation. I have some thoughts on vetting the people who've been in here in the last twenty-four hours. The cops are going to be useless. They have a high-profile murder to solve. They aren't going to waste many man hours on what amounts to vandalism."

Of course, Kellan would take charge. He usually did. Often, Tate found a deep and grateful comfort in it. Not today. Instead, it was just another way he didn't measure up.

"Do whatever you want." He shouldered his way past Kellan and slammed out the door. Then Tate did what he always did when the world pressed in on him.

He ran.

* * * *

"Do you have any idea what you just did to him?" After the door slammed behind Tate, Eric snapped around and drilled his stare into Belle. He had a point to make to her.

238

Yeah, he'd have to go after his best friend very soon. Tate wouldn't talk about this argument now. He'd need hours, maybe days, to process it. He might say he planned to take a shower, but he would find his sneakers and run through the streets until he couldn't see straight. Only when he'd pounded out every ounce of his frustration would he come back.

Of course, he also might just run to the airport and leave for good.

Belle shook her head, looking perplexed. "What? I shouldn't be honest? I wasn't trying to hurt him. Damn it, Eric. Did you really expect me to wake up this morning and give up this house? Is one night supposed to make me believe this can work long term?"

"You could have mentioned how you felt last night." Eric forced himself to take a deep breath because he was brutally angry, too.

Of course, he and Tate had already written the fairy-tale ending in their heads without telling her, either. Still, hadn't she felt the magic between them when they'd made love to her? Hadn't it made her rethink staying in New Orleans at least a little?

Kellan pushed the door open and walked in, looking deeply concerned. "What the hell happened to Tate? He took off running. The last time he was that upset, he'd just watched the last *Star Wars* film."

"No jokes. It's not helping right now." Eric ran a frustrated hand through his hair. He knew Kellan wasn't intentionally being insensitive, but now sure as hell wasn't the time for a ribbing.

Kellan stared, then cut his gaze to their aloof lover. His face lost all amusement. "What happened?" His eyes narrowed. "What did you do, Annabelle?"

She loosed an exasperated huff. "Why do you think *I* did something?"

"Because there's only one person in the world with the

power to crush Tate like that, and I'm looking at her." Kellan set his bag down and prowled toward Belle. "Tell me how you hurt him this morning. I have a suspicion, but I hope you prove me wrong."

Belle opened her mouth. "I-I—"

Eric saved them all the time and her the effort. "She explained that she didn't want anything but sex from us."

Belle would probably choose different words, but he cut to the chase.

The distance she'd forced between them had completely shocked him. While he hadn't thought Belle would immediately begin packing to head back home, he sure as hell hadn't thought she would pronounce that a relationship between them couldn't work.

It had worked pretty fucking well last night.

"Oh my god, I didn't say that—at all," she shot back, tears shining in her eyes. "Tate started talking about me going back to Chicago or him moving in here. I just… He blindsided me. I tried to explain why that wouldn't work, and Tate took off."

"You told him that you weren't interested in a relationship." Tears or not, he refused to let her sugarcoat what had happened.

"No, I told him I didn't necessarily see a future for us."

Kellan shook his head, a tight fury all over his face. "Well, that's perfect. Hey, at least she told him to fuck off before the wedding."

Hurt ripped across Belle's face. "That's not fair!"

With a shrug, Kell turned to him. "Look, man, I should go. I'll do nothing but make this worse. Sorry."

Crap. At the moment, Eric wanted to throw down with both of them. He'd been prepared for Kellan to shy away or bow out. He'd always known that bringing his friend into the relationship after his bitter divorce would be difficult. He'd never imagined Belle would wake up after the best night of his life and declare that they could leave whenever because it didn't matter to her.

Kellan paused, gripping her shoulders and staring into her eyes. "Think about what you're doing, Annabelle. There's a reason you're driving away men who love you. Think hard and fix it. Don't end up like me."

"What does that mean? You said yourself you didn't think it could work," Belle replied.

"I still don't, but then it's occurred to me very recently that I might not be the most optimistic person about love." He withdrew. "Besides, we're not talking about me. Really think this through before you break anything off. Make sure there's not even the smallest part of you doing this for revenge."

"Revenge?" Confusion widened her eyes.

Eric had been thinking along the same lines. "Back in Dallas, you were very upset with us. You thought we were rejecting you. Maybe you think it's a good idea to reject us right back. It won't work, Belle. You'll regret it."

"I am *not* doing this for revenge."

"Then you're pulling away because you're afraid," he shot back. Those were the only two reasons for her to be so standoffish.

"She is and she won't admit it." Shaking his head, Kellan headed for the door that led to the dining room.

"Afraid of what?" she challenged.

"C'mon, Belle. You're too smart to play stupid." Kell pushed the door open. "I'm going to start background checks on everyone who was here yesterday."

Belle opened her mouth to say something, but Kell left.

And Eric shut her down. "Don't. Do not be stubborn enough to stop us from watching out for you. Think very carefully before you say whatever is about to come out of your mouth. The last twelve hours aside, we've been friends for a long time, and I will be deeply offended if you choose your pride over your safety. Before you told Tate he could leave on the next plane for all you cared, did you think about the fact that someone broke into this house and tried to scare the hell out of you?"

Tears spilled from her dark eyes, down her cheeks. "Damn it, Eric. You make me sound cruel and awful. I did not say that."

"Not in those exact words, but I assure you that's what he heard. And you're probably about to tell me to get out, too."

"No, I appreciate you looking into the suspects. If there's any help I can give you, let me know." Her big, hurt eyes were like a punch to the gut. He wished he could take back the whole morning. Or that they'd just stayed in bed. "I can't keep you here, Eric. And I can't lie to Tate and tell him I'm willing to do something I'm not. If that means he has to go, I'll understand."

Pain wracked his system. "You're not even willing to see what we could have?"

"What do you think we could have? I can't go back to Chicago. I really believe I need to be here. But I can't let you guys give up your careers to move because I can't promise a relationship will work out. Tate wanted commitment from me this morning. We've never even gone on an actual, romantic date. I have no idea where you stand, and Kell is out on the whole relationship thing, so why should I be thinking about cohabitation already? I don't know that I'm ready. It would be unfair to ask you guys to give up everything back in Chicago when we might not have a future."

Eric sighed. That's how she saw the situation? So maybe they hadn't exactly communicated their wants and expectations to her. But she also hadn't tried to meet them at least a little closer to halfway. Either she was getting her revenge or she was terrified. His money was on the latter.

"We can't leave until we know you're safe. That's not open for negotiation," Eric stated unequivocally.

Tate wouldn't be able to leave her vulnerable and alone

either. Sure, he could threaten to walk away, but he would stay here tonight and every night until he was sure Belle was safe.

It wouldn't matter that she refused to love them back.

More tears spilled onto her cheeks, and it took everything Eric had not to brush them away. "What do we do, Eric? I don't want you to leave, but I can't tell you that I'm ready for anything more than a casual relationship. Maybe you think this is stupid, but I don't think it's going to work without Kellan. You three are a team. I've watched you for a year. You're happiest together. You'd resent me if I came between you."

She looked so miserable, Eric couldn't stop himself from cupping her cheeks and wiping her tears away. "But you hurt Tate. You have to understand that this isn't the first time a woman has pushed him out of the relationship."

"What do you mean?" she frowned.

"We've dated women who didn't want to see Tate outside the bedroom. Once we explained that we wanted a more established relationship, they quickly let us know that Tate could pop in for sex, but they didn't want to see him socially."

Belle gasped. "That's terrible."

The utter horror in her voice made Eric breathe a little easier. "It's true, and now he thinks that's what you're doing. He's convinced you prefer Kellan to him, but that you're willing to fuck him because he's good in bed." At Belle's shocked frown, Eric shrugged. "It's exactly what our last girlfriend told him."

"I didn't mean anything like that. I had no idea anyone had treated him so awfully. I just need time to figure out where this is going, Eric."

"And for that you want us all to go back to our corners and pretend like last night didn't happen?" He wasn't sure he could do it.

"You keep assuming the worst. It's nothing like that.

Whatever time you have, I want to spend it with you, Tate, and Kellan. Honestly, I wasn't trying to shove anyone out the door. I just can't give you the assurances you want right this second. I get the feeling you guys have been thinking this out for months. I haven't, and everything in my life has changed suddenly. Maybe I would feel different if I hadn't inherited this house, but I did and I already love it here. I've been ready for a change. I can't go back to being just your secretary. Can't you see that?"

"We've been slowly preparing you to be with us for almost a year. We waited until you wouldn't think we were lecherous bosses like your last one and until you really got to know Tate. We waited for Kell to trust you. But we always had a plan. We might not have been traditionally dating, but we've spent every spare second we had with you."

"While you 'dated' other women." She made air quotes with her fingers.

"What other women? Name one."

"I know about that skinny paralegal at Johnson and Forbes."

So she wanted to debate? This was so up his alley…

"That ended about two weeks before you came to work for us. Next?"

She crossed her arms over her chest. "Are you going to tell me you don't go to that club? Or that there are no women there."

Apparently, Belle was under some very mistaken impressions. He'd be more than happy to correct them. "No, we went because Kellan has been sponsoring our training. But that isn't what's bothering you, is it, Belle? You think we were out having a grand old time while you took care of the office. I'd like to know why you think any woman is more important to us than you. We haven't brought one female to the office who wasn't there in a professional capacity. We answer your calls at all hours of the day or night and drop anything we're doing to take care of your needs. One of us takes you to lunch nearly every day and dinner at least once a week. We've spent a year taking care of you. What makes you think we were sleeping with other women?"

Her brows rose as her jaw dropped. "Are you trying to tell me you haven't had sex in a year?"

"I'm telling you I haven't had sex with anyone but you since the moment I laid eyes on you. Neither has Tate. After his divorce, Kellan fucked everything in sight. But shortly after you came to work for us, he tapered off. He hasn't slept with anyone else in easily six months. For a guy who used to get a different piece of ass every night, that says a lot. We all knew who we wanted and we were willing to be patient until the time was right."

"The time was never going to be right." Tate shoved the door open and stood, his eyes flat.

"I thought you went for a run." Eric stared at his best friend.

Tate looked dangerous, his eyes predatory, every muscle in his body still as though ready to strike. Suddenly, Eric was worried that Belle was Tate's prey.

She looked hesitant, but raised her chin and approached him. "Tate, we should talk."

When she reached for him, he jerked away. "Nothing to say. We're not going anywhere until we're sure you're safe. In the meantime, you want to explore sex? You can do it with us. I was gentle with you last night, but if this is just a fuck, then we're going to do this my way—hot and dirty."

Tate didn't wait for her reply, just swept her in his arms, against his chest, and headed for the stairs.

"Hey," Eric called, following after them.

Kellan met him in the hall, and Eric wondered if he'd been listening on the other side of the door since he supposedly left. "Don't. He might be right, and Belle isn't exactly protesting. Let's join them and see where this goes."

"I don't know. He's emotional." When Tate exploded, it could get spectacular.

"In normal circumstances, I'd prevent him from sceneing, but maybe this is what Belle needs. She's shut down. Make her feel, force her to open up, but you have to break through those walls or you have zero chance." Kellan stared after Tate and Belle. "I can stay down here, if you'd rather. But you definitely need to get upstairs."

He slapped Kellan on the back. Maybe they could break down some of his walls, too. "Come on. Help me see if we can save this."

They walked up the stairs, Eric's heart pounding.

Chapter Fourteen

Arms hooked around Tate's neck, Belle looked into his face, her heart softening even as she told herself this was an absolutely terrible idea. He climbed up the stairs two at a time, her weight seemingly not a burden to him at all.

"Tate," she called softly. "We really should talk. I didn't mean to hurt you."

He didn't break stride, didn't acknowledge that she'd spoken. He just stared straight ahead, his strong face closed off. "Tell me whether or not you want this. That's the only conversation we need to have."

Belle bit her lip. She'd done a number on him. She hadn't realized it at the time, but now she understood that he'd misinterpreted everything she'd said through his own filter. Unwittingly, she'd pushed his buttons. "I don't even know what this is anymore, Tate."

"Sex. That's it."

No, it wasn't. He might be angry, but he couldn't stop caring for her in the blink of an eye any more than she could stop caring for him. He was simply hurt, and she'd have to help him understand that she wasn't pushing him aside for Eric or Kell.

That realization helped her find an inner well of calm, even as he kicked open the bedroom door. The knob bounced off the wall, but he either didn't notice or didn't care, just strode into the room and headed for the bed. Given his predatory mien, she should probably be trying to escape or at least balking, but Tate would never hurt her, even if she had wounded him deeply.

She palmed his nape and tried to catch his remote dark stare. He looked past her, and that made Belle ache. He was a little too good at shutting her out. Then again, growing up he had probably learned from the best.

What had his childhood been like, raised in a cold household by unfeeling parents who had valued only his intellect while repressing his big heart? Eric had been his first—and for years, his only—friend. They balanced one another.

How would she feel if she'd constantly been told that she was the inadequate half of a whole? Belle kind of understood how crappy that must be. Kinley had always been far more outgoing, the fun, bubbly blonde people gravitated to. If she and Kinley had shared the sort of life Eric and Tate did, she would have been the one on the outside looking in. She'd tasted how bitter that was over the years. Those memories made her ache for Tate even more.

"Those women were wrong to reject you in favor of Eric. You're so wonderful, Tate. For so many things besides sex."

He settled her onto the bed where they'd made love the night before. He could call it sex, but they both knew better. They'd made love. She wished she knew how to open herself, embrace the experience, and trust that it could last.

As Tate followed her to the mattress and pinned her under him, she lay in his arms, offering her acceptance. Even when he was mad at her, he treated her with such care. She blinked up into his dark eyes, hoping he could see her welcome.

"It doesn't matter, Belle. Are you saying yes or no? If you say yes, then you should prepare to submit. If you say no, understand that I won't ask you again. I'll leave you to Kellan and Eric. No matter how you answer, I'll make sure you're safe. But I will keep my distance."

Belle hated ultimatums, but she understood. If she said no, Tate would put a wall between them. Not to punish her, but to protect himself. He'd done a remarkable job of making her feel safe with him, but she hadn't tried to do the same for him. Remorse stung her.

What did she want, to risk her heart for something that probably wouldn't last or to open herself up and surrender to the men she loved for whatever time they shared?

Eric entered the room. Kellan hovered in the doorway. All eyes fastened on her. Expectation hung in the air.

These men really would put their lives on hold until she was safe. After that, they would return to their homes and their careers. They'd leave her. If by some miracle they didn't, their little quartet wouldn't work if Kellan wasn't even willing to try.

Of course, could she really expect complete security in the relationship? No one had that. She especially couldn't expect it if she wasn't ready to commit herself. And she didn't need a commitment to have sex.

Belle's thoughts raced. Did she want to go back to simply sharing a roof with them? Most likely, they only had a few days left together. Hell, even if they'd promised her a lifetime, that didn't always work out. Her father had vowed to love her mother forever and he'd died. When her mom had given birth, she'd committed to being a parent, but after her dad's death, she hadn't lived up to that obligation. Her mother's detachment had hurt and confused Belle. She'd shut everyone out after that. With the exception of Kinley, she still did.

But now, these three men tempted her. Not just sexually. She could really be herself with them—a rarity for her. They set her at ease. Why shouldn't she experience what they shared to the fullest while they were here? Find pleasure and joy? Her skin heated at just the thought of feeling them deep inside her again. Her heart warmed at the thought of being close to them. Even if it didn't last, she'd have these days to hold close to her heart.

"Yes." There was nothing else to say.

"Do you understand what you're saying yes to, love?" Kellan stepped into the room. His whole body hardened, his previous calm gone. Before her stood a Dom.

Her Dom.

"Yes. I'm agreeing to submit to you in the bedroom." Elsewhere, she would insist on being an equal partner for as long as it lasted or she'd be unable to live with herself.

Eric let out a sexy growl. "In the bedroom, the living room, the bathroom—whatever room we want. We're not going to always carry you to the comfort of a bed, Belle. We'll have you in every room of this house. We'll take you wherever we want you. I'll flip up your skirt or pull down your pants, and you'll take my cock. Do you understand?"

She would be theirs to play with at their whim— whenever they wanted. The thought more than excited her.

"I understand," she murmured.

"Good. I want you now, Belle." Tate pulled his shirt over his head with an impatient yank. "Strip and present yourself to us."

She sat up and unbuttoned her blouse with shaking hands. "How?"

She'd read descriptions of it in erotic romances, but being this close to the guys made her feel too jumbled and hot to remember the details.

Kellan dipped into her personal space. "First of all, look at your Dom when you ask him a question. No more hiding. We've let you slide by on that for too long."

She bit her bottom lip and stared at his chest, finding it difficult to meet his stare. "I'm not hiding."

Gently, he cupped her chin and forced it up. His stare bored into her. "You are right now. Look at me, not away, when you should connect. There will be no more dodging us. When we speak, unless you're told otherwise, look directly at us. Do you understand?"

She hadn't realized she'd been avoiding eye contact. But somehow, when they flipped her submissive switch, that backbone she'd relied on since her mother had withdrawn in grief after her father's passing just seemed to go on hiatus.

Belle sucked in a deep breath and forced herself to nod, their gazes still connected. "Yes."

"Yes, *Sir*," Eric corrected. "When we're playing, you're to call each one of us Sir or we'll punish you."

"Yes, Sir." She could remember that. It would be harder to constantly make eye contact. The visual connection could be so squirm-worthy, so intimate.

Kellan released her chin. "Now ask Tate your question."

They were going to make this difficult for her. She could tell because Tate didn't come to her rescue the way he normally would by volunteering the information. Instead of telling her how to present herself, he simply stood over her, arms crossed, watching and waiting. Standing on shaking legs, she tangled her gaze with his and studied him.

Little lines feathered around his eyes, along with a few others that had formed around his normally big smile. Now, his expression looked somber, lacking his usual spark. Already, she missed the Tate she'd come to know and love. Funny, gentle, considerate and earnest. God, she wanted that man back. She didn't know this one at all. The fact that she'd helped create him killed her.

Belle edged closer to say something—anything. She watched him closely, heard his breath hitch slightly the instant she drew near.

"How do I present myself, Sir?"

His jaw firmed, forming a straight, stubborn line. She had the sudden desire to run her hand across it, to brush her fingertips there. To reassure him. She stopped herself. He was too angry and hurt to want her softness now. She would have to be patient and find other ways to prove that, even if she couldn't commit to forever, he still mattered.

"Take your clothes off. Get on your knees and spread them wide. Place your hands on your thighs, palms up. Remember this position. You'll greet your Doms like this to show us you're ready to submit." Every word came in the same staccato grind he used when explaining a point of law or lecturing a client.

She never looked away, focusing solely on his instruction and his dark stare. Their deeper visual bond made her aware that, without uttering a sound, he said so much. Words could lie, but his eyes didn't. Tate might try to put forth a cold façade, but the sweetheart she knew was still in there. Belle's heart melted.

Now that he'd been hurt by women, including her, sex seemed like the only way he could connect with her and retain his pride. Surrendering to him might not fix everything wrong between them, but she could give him her body, her warmth, her comfort, and hope that would help him find a better place.

Belle shrugged out of her shirt and turned to toss her clothes on the bed. Instead, Kellan held out his hand. Without a word, she draped her blouse across his palm and looked his way for confirmation.

"Yes, love." He snagged her stare and fused them together. "This is what we want and what you need. Give me everything else you're wearing."

She didn't try to look away.

Pride gleamed in his eyes. The knowledge that she pleased him calmed her. Eric's expression was a mirror of Kell's. Even Tate looked grudgingly satisfied with her progress.

Making eye contact helped Belle to understand them so much more clearly. How had she not known it would? Because she'd avoided a lot of connection and closeness for most of her life. She'd let that tragic autumn when she'd been eleven change her. But all her questions about her lovers' feelings seemed to have answers when she really looked into their eyes. The adoration she saw there took her breath away.

Belle realized now that they didn't just watch her because they thought she was pretty, but because they cared for her and wanted to make her happy. They might not know it, but those desires went both ways.

Kinley had explained the power exchange. She submitted. They supported, protected, and cherished. They gave her what she needed. Right now, she wanted that so badly.

"Start with the bra, Belle." Eric stepped closer, caressing her with just a look.

He was the glue holding them all together. She hadn't realized that until just now, but she could see that Tate and Kellan were the real opposites, while Eric provided the middle ground. He bent, compromising his own wishes to suit the needs of the group. He would always put his family first. Belle admired him so much.

She worked the clasp of her bra, allowing her breasts to spring free. As the cool air brushed her skin, she breathed deeply, feeling the weight of her breasts against her body and the nipples peak under their stares. They made it so hard not to want something with them beyond the here and now. They made it hard not to love them.

She shoved her pants off her hips, along with her underwear, before handing everything to Kellan. Two days before, she couldn't have imagined being so comfortable naked, but now she liked how natural she felt. The appreciation on their faces and the satisfaction her submission seemed to give them filled her with a confidence she'd never had. In this moment, she wasn't worried that her imperfections made her unattractive. Instead, she just breathed into her body, concentrated on the beating of her heart, the tightening of her nipples, the clench of her aroused pussy.

She felt perfectly at peace as she found the center of the room and sank to her knees. It felt awkward at first, but she spread her knees and placed her hands on top, palms up. She glanced up at them for approval.

"Eyes down," Tate said, his voice hard. "Kellan said to look at us when we're talking, but when you're presenting yourself, you look down until your Dom chooses to acknowledge and accept you."

The minute she lowered her gaze, a blanket of vulnerability fell over her. Tate's sneakers came into view as he stood over her. Belle knew his stare roamed all over her, but she had no idea what he was thinking. That connection she'd had with him earlier seemed to have vanished and she wanted it back.

"Spread your knees wider so I can see your pussy." Without seeing the softness on his face, he seemed harsh.

Still, she dredged up her courage and spread herself open further because, deep down, she suspected that pleasing him would please her, too.

"Straighten your spine," Tate continued. "Let your head fall forward."

She did as he asked, her whole being now centered on his voice. He sounded rougher, less collected.

Then again, so was she.

With every breath and every command, they opened her up—not just to them, but to the deepest parts of herself she'd kept closed for so long.

She felt poised on the edge of something amazing—life-altering—as she submitted her body to their pleasure.

"That's it." Tate's big hand covered her head. "You look beautiful like this."

Even when he was angry with her, he still made her feel special. She wanted to take back everything she'd said to him, but she couldn't do that unless she was absolutely certain she could keep whatever promises she made. Instead, Belle swore she'd take whatever time they shared and give as much of herself as she could. "Thank you, Sir."

"It's a simple truth." His sneakers exited her line of

sight. "If we're going to continue this sexual relationship, we need to prepare you. In the past, we've always taken a lover together. That means using more than just your mouth and your pussy. Do you understand what I'm saying?"

Tate clipped every word with a distinctly academic tone, as though he were discussing some intellectual problem, not explaining that he wanted to have anal intercourse with her.

Maybe it was time to show him she was learning. She didn't normally curse, but the night before had been dirty and glorious, and there was nothing wrong with the truth. She wasn't the same reserved girl whose virginity they'd taken. These men had changed her for the better. "You want to fuck my ass, Sir."

The whole room went still, as though not a single one of them could believe she'd uttered those words. At their shock, Belle had to stop herself from giggling.

"That's correct." Tate's voice was a little higher than before. It was nice to know she could get to him with a few well-chosen words.

"Belle, what Tate is trying to explain is that we'll first prepare you by inserting a plug in your ass that will stretch you to take a cock there." Eric circled around her until his feet came into view. He wasn't wearing shoes. How could his bare feet seem so masculine, so sexy? No clue, but they were.

She felt his hand sink into her hair, then he gently tugged until she was looking up at him. "When Kellan went out for beignets, he bought you a set of training plugs. This city has a surprisingly large amount of sex shops. And voodoo shops. Sometimes I couldn't tell the difference."

Belle would have to hope that no one had placed a curse on her anal plug. "I understand, Sir. I want to be able to take all of you. I'm ready."

He tipped her chin up and stared into her eyes as though he could see her down to her soul. "You're ready for sex with all of us, but not commitment?"

"I can't promise more now, Eric. You've had a year to

255

think about this. I've had a few days. I need time to figure us out."

"I should probably step back until you do, but I won't. Instead, I'm going to show you absolutely everything we can give you. I'm going to show you what it means to belong to us. You won't be able to send us away."

Belle was already afraid of that. She didn't want to find herself swept back to Chicago and giving up her design dreams. She couldn't run their lives again and not have one of her own. Even if they did help her find an office close to theirs so she could go into business for herself, as Tate suggested, it wouldn't be what she needed. Fate, her grandmother—something—had called her to this place. She had to make them see that. Besides, even if she was ready to jump into the relationship...well, Kell still wasn't. These three men wouldn't be right without one another. She didn't want to be the reason they were no longer a unit.

"I can't do this." Kellan shook his head.

Couldn't what, even sleep with her anymore? Now that he'd had her, did he not want her again?

Panic encroached. She studied Kell's face, wishing he would look at her. She couldn't read him beyond agitation. His jaw firmed. He paced, shaking his head. Her stomach knotted, and she barely held in a sob.

She'd thought she would have more time with him, that she could build up memories with him before he left her. How had everything gone so wrong so quickly?

"If you want to bail, there's the door." Tate's face had gone harder, his eyes downright stony as he glared Kellan's way.

Kell rolled his eyes. "Stop being a drama queen. I wasn't talking about leaving. We're going to shove a plug up her ass. Don't you think I'm staying around for that? I was talking about this whole 'Sir' thing. She ruined it for me." He pointed at her. "Now when the word comes out of her mouth, it's like she's addressing that little rat-thing that hikes its leg and pees on my shoes."

A great well of laughter burst from Belle. She tried to press it down, but couldn't. Her reaction might annoy him, but she couldn't stop it, especially not when he looked so righteous.

Even Tate cracked a smile. "How about Master? Except we haven't earned it."

"I can call you Master," she interjected quickly.

It felt right, like a formal admission of their sexual relationship. They would be her Masters...for now.

"I like the way that sounds. Hands and knees, baby. Let's get the rough part over." Eric moved to the dresser where someone had lain a plastic bag. He retreated to the bathroom, and Belle heard the water begin to run.

Rough part? They were really going to impale her backside with a foreign object. She wasn't entirely sure how she should feel about that, but she'd seen Kinley blush and stutter when the subject of anal anything came up. Belle didn't have any hang-ups about it being "weird." It was simply new, but she wanted to know what it meant to be in between them, to have them love her all over. If she had to allow them to plug her before that could happen, she'd manage.

Belle leaned forward, placing her palms on the carpet. It was plush against her skin, between her fingers.

"She needs a safe word." Kellan sank into the chair opposite her, obviously preparing for a show.

"Belle, select one," Tate commanded. "Make it something you wouldn't typically say during sex."

"Aquamarine." It was the color of Kell's eyes as he stared into hers now.

Tate nodded, his face still grim. He'd shrugged out of his shirt, but his sweats were still on. The night before he'd been so eager, he'd tossed off his clothes with abandon. This morning, she felt distance between them—and she hated it. Her eager lover had been replaced with a wary man, and she wished she'd had more time with the fun-loving Tate before they'd confronted the issue of forever. Last night, he'd been all over her, caressing her body as if he couldn't stand not to touch her. Today, they'd barely shared any contact since reaching the bedroom.

"Fine. Everything stops if you say that word," Tate explained.

The water shut off, and Eric returned with a piece of pink plastic in one hand and a tube of lube in the other. "Exactly. At that point, we talk about what made you uncomfortable and how to rectify that. In exploring your submission, we should find your boundaries and push them. We'll discover what works for you sexually. So if you don't like something or find it uncomfortable, we hash it out until you're ready. For now, I'm going to work the plug inside you. You're going to keep it there until we take it out. You'll wear it a few hours each day until we decide you're ready to handle a cock."

She wouldn't say that she wasn't a little nervous, but she didn't shy away. "Yes, Master."

Eric held out his hand. "Suck Tate's cock, Belle. He's had too much stimulation for one day. He'll be cranky for his one o'clock phone conference with these new clients about their multimillion dollar case if he doesn't release this tension."

Belle slanted a glance in Tate's direction. His eyes lit up briefly before he seemed to remember he was crabby. Instead, he pulled up a chair and plopped in front of her, then settled in to work his sweatpants down.

Eric edged behind her, his warm hand on the small of her back. "Spread your legs a little wider, baby."

She did as he asked, moving her knees further apart. At the same time, Tate pushed his boxers down and released his cock. He was so beautiful—big, strong, stalwart. She couldn't help but lick her lips. She hadn't really gotten to explore his body yet. The previous night, he'd taken her with his mouth and driven her to insanity before spending half of the night inside her. Belle looked forward to paying him back.

He stroked himself, staring down at her. "Suck me until I come."

A drop of fluid already pearled on the head of his cock. More than ready to taste him, she began leaning closer when she felt Eric pull her cheeks apart.

Surprise and more than a little embarrassment made her clench down instinctively to keep him out.

A loud smack cracked through the room, then pain flared across her ass.

"Don't fight me," Eric growled. "Arch your back and push down."

"Seriously?" She wasn't sure what she'd expected. "I thought you would just push it in."

Kellan chuckled. "Push it in? Love, it's not just going to fall into your backside. Eric will have to coax that pretty little hole into opening for him. He'll spread you wide and use his fingers to distribute the lube. He'll rim and stretch you. You'll shudder and gasp a little, but eventually you will let him in."

Maybe it shouldn't, but the demand in his speech made her squirm. "But does he have to look at it?"

Her question might annoy them, but Kinley had always stressed communication in BDSM.

"Fuck, yeah, I'm going to look at it," Eric said, his hand heavy on the curve of her hip. "Every single part of you is gorgeous, Belle. Watching you take our plug will be sexy as hell. Do you know how long I've dreamed about getting my cock up there?"

When he talked that way, her heart rate zoomed. Her skin felt too tight.

Tate tangled his fingers in her hair. "You pay attention to me, Belle. Let Eric do what he needs or we'll give you a nice long spanking and you'll still take the plug."

Put that way, she leaned forward and raised her ass in the air, trying to relax. Vulnerability washed through her, but as she took his cock in one hand, she smelled the musk of his arousal blending with the clean smell of the soap he'd used during his morning shower. She found Tate's scent a comfort.

Belle licked him, using the flat of her tongue to rub along the *V* on the back of his cock. She settled there briefly, rubbing that little indention, learning its depth and feel. She laved the thick head, then sucked, enjoying the way he fidgeted, then tried to force himself to still.

Behind her, Eric parted her cheeks. Belle resisted her instinct to flinch away.

Something cool coated her opening. Lubricant. It wouldn't be long now before Eric breached her with that plug. She fought a shiver. She needed to pay attention to Tate, take her mind off Eric's inevitable penetration.

Belle bathed the head of his cock, lovingly saturating it, before bobbing her head to take more of him in her mouth. Rolling her tongue around him as she sucked, she forced herself to remain still even when she felt Eric's fingers circle the rim of her back passage.

She immersed herself in Tate's scent, texture, and flavor as Eric's fingers explored where no one had touched. Repeatedly, he worked his fingers around that spot, feeling her flesh part as he began to push his fingers inside.

As he deepened the penetration, it became an odd pressure—not unpleasant. In fact, it soon had her gasping at the shockwave of sensation. That caused her to swallow more of Tate's cock into her mouth.

"Fuck, baby." He pulled on her hair, drawing her closer, forcing his cock deeper. "Suck me hard, until I can't hold back another second. Oh, yeah. That's what I want."

And he tasted so good. She lapped at him some more, then drew him all the way to her throat, forcing herself to breathe through her nose. The slight tang of his salty essence coated his cock and teased her tongue. She stroked him with her tongue in passion, trying to give him all the devotion she couldn't promise with words.

As she sank into the experience, something hard pressed against her ass, then began to pierce her. Oh god, he was breaching her with the head of the plug. Belle held her breath.

"Open up." Eric pressed his hand into the small of her back, forcing her to arch for him. "Breathe out and let me in. You'll not only be full, but satisfied. Don't be afraid. Let it happen."

She concentrated on the task at hand, sticking her butt even higher in the air and sliding her tongue around Tate's thickening dick. He groaned low as he pulled at her hair.

Then the plug began to breach her, sending a new and dazzling pressure deep inside her. She whimpered as the sensation snaked to her quivering belly, warmed, then settled into her clit. Slowly, Eric fucked her with the plug, little thrusts, each time deeper, that made her moan against the cock in her mouth.

"Fuck, that feels good," Tate said.

"It's so pretty." Eric pressed in again.

Out of the corner of her eye, she saw Kellan stand and disappear behind her. "Damn, that's a pretty sight."

"She's taking the plug beautifully." Eric made another pass with the plastic device, penetrating her more deeply. As it slid out again, she clenched down to keep it inside. When he pushed in once more, she relaxed and let the protrusion slide home.

"It's in. Damn that's hot," Eric groaned. "You keep that plug in place or there will be punishment."

Belle barely had time to bob her head before Tate tugged on her hair again. "Deeper. Take me to your throat."

Eric twisted the base of the gadget impaling her. She felt it even deeper. It ignited nerve endings she'd never known existed and revved her arousal in a way she'd never imagined. The plastic wedge held her open, not allowing her to hide from Eric and Tate. Nor did it give her any respite from the constant barrage of tingles and the delicious feeling of fullness. The penetration was so primal, she could only imagine how taken she would feel once real flesh filled her.

Frantically, she worked Tate's cock over and over, taking him a bit deeper and harder each time. She wanted to please him so badly, especially after their terrible argument earlier. Being on her knees, having her ass filled, gave her a completely new sense of her body and of the sensual power she had right now. It also made her deeply aware of how thoroughly they controlled her orgasms. She'd happily do just about anything for one soon.

With fingers thrust in her hair, Tate guided her, his hips moving in short thrusts. She finally worked her lips all the way to the base of his cock. He filled her mouth completely, and Belle held her breath as he prodded her throat. Her body conformed to the plug, hugging it, craving more. What would it be like when one of them replaced the plug *and* one filled her pussy? Already, she felt so tightly packed. Would she be able to truly take two of them at once? Belle doubted she would be able to breathe or think or move—and she didn't care. She couldn't wait to feel them deep inside, connecting her to them in a whole new way.

She dragged her mouth back up the length of Tate's cock until only the head remained cradled by her lips. With a little sigh, she swiped her tongue across the head.

"Oh, wow. Damn." Tate let out a harsh breath. "Belle... Baby, you're killing me. I can't hold—"

One more pass was all it took. The minute she sucked him back in and swallowed around his cock, his entire length stiffened and pulsed. Hot splatters filled her mouth. He tasted rich and salty as she drank him down while he groaned low, long, and loud.

The minute Tate sagged back into the chair in a spent heap, Eric held a hand out to her and helped her to her feet.

He led her to the bed.

"You're too sore to fuck this morning."

She wanted to feel them inside her so badly. The urge to meld with them once more surged like a craving. "But—"

"No, we won't let our impatience cause you more pain, Belle. Soon, when you're less tender, we'll fill that pretty pussy again. Now, we're going to try something else. Lie back. Don't lose the plug. I don't want to have to start your training all over again. I'm serious about fucking your ass— and soon." Eric eased her down on the bed, looking her body over. Kellan was suddenly beside him, both men appraising her with their hungry stares.

"You're such a beautiful sight." Kellan reached down and gripped a nipple between his thumb and forefinger. He twisted slightly, the sensation zinging straight to her pussy.

"Please. I'm not really all that sore." She was, but surely it wouldn't be uncomfortable for long. She wanted them, needed them. After all the emotion of the morning, she needed to be close to them, feel that they were still with her.

Eric tweaked her other nipple. "I said no. Tomorrow will be soon enough, but there are plenty of other ways for you to please your Masters. Tate, can you get me the clamps? I think it's time for a little nipple torture. These jewels are so sensitive. I think we'll have her squirming and begging in no time."

Her eyes widened. She already felt as if she was begging. Then Kellan eased beside her, his mouth hovering over her nipple. She gasped as he ran his tongue over the little nubbin, making it stand at attention.

"These are tweezer clamps." Eric took the small metallic thing Tate handed him. A chain connected the two silver objects to one another. "Kell bought them for you, along with that plug in your ass. You still feel it?"

"Yes," she breathed.

"We have a huge kit back home, all brand new and waiting just for you, Belle. We began buying the items months ago. Every time I shopped for you and added more goodies to the pile, I just got harder and harder imagining all we could do to you."

"Why would you have bought things like that for me back then? We weren't… It wasn't like *that*. I just worked for you." She fought to concentrate while Kellan nipped at her breasts, every pass of his mouth and teeth shooting arousal through her system.

"Because we're optimists," Eric explained. "Whenever I went to the club and trained, I did it because I believed I would be your Master. Even before I met you, I knew there was a you out there. I knew I would find the one submissive who truly belonged to me. I never imagined she wouldn't see the truth. So listen up, Belle. I intend to make you realize that you belong to us. You're ours, and no amount of success in business will make you as happy as we can. Although you might curse my name in a minute before you admit I'm right."

He handed the first clamp to Kellan, who slid it onto her nipple and let go.

Pain flared through her, biting at her and making her gasp. "Damn it."

Eric held up a hand when Tate moved toward her. "No. We didn't tell her she couldn't curse, and I kind of like knowing I can make her say all those dirty words. Does the clamp hurt, baby?"

It did and it didn't. The erotic pain sent a sweet ache twinging through her pussy. Like everything they did, that little vise on her nipple forced her awareness. Her very skin felt alive and awake. Her blood hummed.

"A little, but I can handle it." And the more moments that slid past, the more she actually liked it.

The minute the words slipped from her mouth, Eric dropped to his knees and suckled her free nipple. His teeth lightly bit at her, gently preparing the other bud to take the pain of the second clamp. He clipped it on. With rapt eyes, he watched the chain stretch from one nipple to the other, the cool silver snaking across her chest. The clamps bit. One individually tested her pain tolerance. Two at once somehow magnified the sensation. But the pain morphed, dropping from the intense bite at her nipples to a lip-biting pressure that joined up with the fullness in her ass to send a shocking jolt straight to her clit.

Kellan reached down and gently tugged on the chain. "Are you ready for more? This little work of art isn't finished by a long shot."

Tate passed him another clamp, this one a single pair of tweezers on a longer chain. Kellan carefully attached the silver length to the middle of the chain running between her breasts and laid it in a cool, thin line down her torso. She shivered, feeling them everywhere, touching her, arousing her, filling her.

She watched as Kellan tugged on the chain over her belly just enough to make the pleasure-pain surge to life again as he rested the final clamp just above her pussy.

"Where does that go?" She had a suspicion. It made her both worry and ache. He couldn't clamp her there, could he?

"You have another sweet jewel for us to adorn, Belle." Kellan moved between her legs. "While I work on this, I think you should take care of Eric."

She turned her head to find that Eric had shed his clothes. He stood beside the bed, beautifully naked. She stared at the slab of ridged and notched muscle covering his powerful torso. It was easy to see he was a former athlete who hadn't let himself lose any of his form or prowess.

"Touch me, Belle." He grasped her hand, bringing it to his abdomen and pushing it low.

She allowed her fingers to run down his magnificent six pack. So much muscle, steel covered in the softness of warm flesh. She loved how he felt, could spend days just touching him, but Kellan was right. He needed more.

His cock strained, almost reaching his navel. She let her

hand slide down, brushing against him. His cock jumped as though electrified by her touch.

"Suck me, Belle. I need to feel your mouth on me."

Kellan had moved between her legs, but she didn't feel anything except his heat near her pussy. The waiting for more made her eager, jumpy. She glanced down, noticing that he'd placed the clamp just above her clitoris, but he made no move to slip it on. Instead, he just stared at her pussy, settling on his stomach and rubbing his nose along her labia.

"Fuck, I love the way you smell, Belle. But you taste even better." He ran his tongue the full length of her pussy, sending a flare of desire through her.

She cried out his name.

Someone tugged on the chain between her breasts. Tate. He'd moved on to the bed, sliding into the spot Kellan had vacated. Pain flared, snapping her attention back up. "Kellan is readying your clit to be clamped. He'll stop if you don't behave. Would you rather have a spanking? Do you think you could hold that plug inside for that? I think it would be very difficult. And you won't get an orgasm until your Masters are pleased with your progress. Do you understand?"

She understood that there was no way she would be able to keep that damn plug in if she was suddenly tossed over one of their knees and had her backside smacked. "Yes, Master."

Though she really wanted to watch what Kellan was doing, she looked away. The three of them were keeping her on edge, forcing her to focus on Eric so she wouldn't know what Kell or Tate intended next. They were forcing her to trust them, to give herself over.

Eric held his cock in hand, sidling closer so she could easily lick and suck him. Slowly, he stroked his length, and she couldn't help but watch in fascination at the way his fingers traveled over the ridge and his thumb traced his veins. She wanted him in her mouth.

Drawing in a deep breath, Belle relaxed, giving herself over to all of them and the sensations wracking her body. She closed her eyes and leaned in.

"That's right, baby," Eric groaned. "All you have to do is obey and feel." Eric put his cock to her lips. "Relax and let me fuck your mouth. I want your lips around me so badly."

Kellan chose that moment to lick her, his tongue painting her flesh with pleasure. He sucked her clit, niggling and prodding it, drawing her closer and closer to climax. Belle tried to keep her attention on Eric, sucking and swirling her tongue all over him, and to ignore the dazzling pleasure Kell heaped on her.

Suddenly, something hard and metallic cut into her needy little bud. The clamp. She shuddered as it bit into her tenderest flesh. The pain burned and sizzled and then sank into her skin until she buzzed with need. She arched and writhed, trying to breathe through the pain.

"Hold still so I can look at you." Kellan waited impatiently while Belle whimpered and tried to still her body. "So pretty." He touched the aching point with just the tip of his tongue. "I agree that your pussy is too sore to take a cock, but I think you can ride my tongue nicely, love."

He closed his mouth over her and speared her just as Eric began feeding her his length again. She curled her tongue to conform around the underside of his cock. When he began to withdraw, she pulled on him furiously, sucking until her cheeks hollowed, trying to keep him inside. Tate alternately plucked at the chain between her breasts and caressed the bare flesh surrounding it.

This was what she wanted. All three of them, touching her, connecting with her. She let all of her worries go. For this moment, she was theirs and they were hers. Tomorrow didn't exist.

Eric fucked her mouth, thrusting in and out, gently forcing her to take him to the root. Kellan kept up his tender assault on her pussy, owning her with his mouth while Tate showed his continued fascination with her breasts. She held her breath, on the edge, never sure if she would get pure pleasure or the burning erotic pain that only seemed to take her higher.

Eric groaned above her, his thrusts losing their smooth rhythm as his cock pulsed in her mouth. "I'm going to come, baby. Your mouth is too sweet. Take me. Take all of me."

She sucked hard as he began to coat her tongue. Lovingly, she laved the head and worried the little ridge just underneath that made him shudder. He held her hair in his grip and groaned, spilling even more. Knowing she could affect him so deeply sent a thrill through her.

Just as she swallowed down the last of his release, Kellan rewarded her with a long kiss of her clit and she went soaring over the edge. Her body twisted, bucked. The ecstasy mixed with that sensual torture ate through her, grinding her resistance and chewing up her composure. Pure pleasure screamed through her system. She couldn't think, couldn't breathe. She existed only in that moment.

Finally as the wracking pulses began to trail off, she lay back, panting, her body surfeit with sensation.

"Don't scream, baby," Tate said.

Just as Belle wondered what he meant, he released the first clamp.

The blood flowed back to her nipple, and she slammed back against the bed with a yelp. As he sucked her nipple into his mouth, her cry turned to a scream. Then tapered off to a gentle lick, his tongue easing her pain.

Eric dropped to his knees and worked the other nipple, laving her with affection. Sensations churned, meshed, growing exponentially. Then Kellan released the final clamp.

Her whole body clenched. His mouth covered her clit, drawing it in with a soft suckling. After a sharp spike of tingles and another high racing through her blood, Belle sank into the comforter, all of her men surrounding her, wishing this could last forever.

Chapter Fifteen

Belle sighed deeply as she dried the last dish and put it away. Dinner had been another awkward affair, full of stilted conversation where everyone avoided talking about the future. Instead, they'd discussed the tile she'd chosen for the downstairs bathroom and the removal of the hideous vomit yellow floral wallpaper in the master bath, but she knew they'd been half listening, more frustrated that she wasn't budging about returning to Chicago.

How long could they remain in this limbo? They no longer mentioned their work to her, even though she'd told them she was interested. In fact, Belle was beginning to think they weren't talking much at all. They definitely weren't communicating.

The sound of her grandmother's old television filtered in from the living room. Ah, the news. At this time of the evening, the broadcast was local, the usual fare that attempted to be hard-hitting while forcing in odd banter now and then.

After she'd painted the living room, the men had moved their office there. The space was far larger and contained more work surfaces, so they could spread out. Unfortunately, it also meant she couldn't walk in and see them five times a day. She didn't have a logical excuse, as she had in the kitchen. None of them were gullible enough to believe that she'd come into the living room for a drink of water or a nibble to tide her over until dinner. The formal space was in a corner of the house, so she couldn't just happen by. When Belle did gather up the courage to enter their new "office," she didn't know what to say. So she'd stopped going. Other than meals, she barely saw them during the day. But she missed those men so much.

It had been over a week since she'd discovered them on her doorstep. She'd grown accustomed to finding them all over the house—maybe talking on the phone in front of the refrigerator or huddled in her favorite chair in the parlor with a laptop and coffee. But since she told them she didn't see the relationship lasting, something had shifted. They'd relegated themselves to a room far out of her way and rarely left there unless they retreated to their own bedrooms. If she worked up the courage to ask for their help with a task, they graciously agreed to do it, but they no longer sought her out for a morning flirtation or an afternoon chat. They didn't try to make her laugh or steal an afternoon kiss. They didn't crowd her or watch her with hungry stares. Some days she wondered if they really even looked at her anymore.

After the work day, the men had fallen into patterns. They all had their assigned chores and performed them with the politeness of good roommates. They gave her every distant courtesy. She couldn't fault them in any way—except the emotional chasm they seemed to be digging between her and them.

From the moment she woke until the time she went to bed, Belle's frustration made her want to scream. And her heart felt so close to breaking.

At least until deep in the night. Then they ceased being distant roommates and came to her as lovers. Every night, they seduced her, touched her, groaned about how good she felt until she couldn't think straight. They took her with their fingers, mouths, and cocks repeatedly. They impaled her ass with progressively larger plugs and they spanked her. They tied her up and forced her to take them in any and every way they wanted her. They consumed her completely as they made love to her.

Had sex, she corrected herself mentally. They had sex with her. They never mentioned love anymore. They cuffed her and teased her until they made her shout out their names. They grew their collection of toys a little each day and used them on her relentlessly. They taught her the intricacies of a D/s relationship, playing the role of her Masters every single night. And though Eric and Tate still slept in her room, they no longer cuddled her the way they used to. They merely stayed close so she would feel safe. Tate had even dragged an overstuffed chair into the room and began sleeping there.

Kellan always left the moment the orgasms ended. He would make her cry out until her throat felt scratchy and raw. Then he would depart for his own room, and she wouldn't see him again until he nodded her way as they passed in the hall the next morning like relative strangers.

When they shared their bodies and such pleasure, Belle thought only of how they made her feel. When they were in bed together, she didn't think about the future. She lived in the moment. But the moment was starting to confine her. Oppress her. Depress her.

With a weary sigh, she stepped away from the kitchen sink and sat at the eat-in table. Restlessness settled over her. She couldn't seem to quiet the voices in her head. It had been days since she'd told Tate, Eric, and Kellan that she couldn't return to Chicago with them. Belle still knew she couldn't resume her old life, but she now dreaded the moment they would walk away. Because they would. Soon they'd realize she wasn't the woman for them. Despite Tate's idiosyncrasies and Kellan's reluctance to get involved, they were a packaged deal. They would never be happy any other way. When they realized she couldn't fulfill them, they would leave her for good.

Life wasn't fair. She'd learned that at a young age. She'd

watched fate snatch away her mother's happy ending. After her father's death, Mom hadn't believed she had anything to live for. When her men had packed up and gone home, Belle feared she'd feel the same.

Sir scratched at the back door and she got up to let him out, closing the door quickly to keep out the humidity of the night.

At least the air conditioner seemed to be working now. It was a small miracle. Sir barked, and Belle saw the outline of that damn cat prowling around in the dark. The thing seemed to delight in making her dog insane.

The kitchen door swung open, and Eric strode through. He grabbed a beer from the fridge. "Thanks for doing the dishes."

His tone was so polite, it hurt. "Thank you for cooking dinner. Are you still working?"

He nodded. "Yeah, my hearing got postponed until Monday, but I've got to be there. I bought my plane tickets this morning. I'll only be gone for two days. Will you be okay here?"

She nodded, but the thought of not seeing him even for a few days made her anxious and achy. "Sure. Things should settle down now that the A/C is fixed and the wiring finally seems to be up to code."

"I won't be sad to see that pervert go." Eric had never warmed to Mike. "What's your next project?"

She hated the distance between them. He didn't move closer to her, didn't reach out to take her in his arms. The abyss seemed to widen every day. "The parlor. I'm going to sand the wainscoting and strip the paint from the crown molding so I can stain them and restore both to a more period-appropriate color."

He nodded again, but it was a negligent gesture. "I'm sure it will be lovely."

And then he was gone once more, heading back to the living room and leaving a terrible void in his wake.

Something had to give. Right now, she just hoped Eric actually came back from Chicago. What if he got there and remembered how much he loved it, how much less complicated everything was in his office? How much he enjoyed the comforts of his home? What if he called in a few days and told her to have a good life? Kell and Tate would leave shortly thereafter.

At the terrible thought, a sob rose up inside her.

Once, she'd thought they'd all be better off if the guys left. Now, Belle wasn't entirely sure she'd live through their parting. She'd gotten so used to being with them, to having them in her everyday life. She couldn't imagine how quiet the house would be without them. But her feelings stemmed from more than a worry about being lonely. Belle would miss them like she'd miss the beating heart they'd tear from her chest when they left.

She took a deep breath and picked up her tea mug. Weariness threatened to invade her bones. Despite the fact that she wasn't alone at night, what little sleep she got wasn't restful. Her dreams were still haunted by swinging ropes and screaming women as they were dragged to their deaths. She still heard those whispers in the night that warned her to leave. Often, she'd sit straight up in bed. Then the voices would stop, only to start again when she settled back against her pillow.

The sound from the television drifted from the living room.

Police are still investigating the murder of local madam, Karen Ehlers, age fifty-nine. Ehlers allegedly ran the most upscale brothel in New Orleans. She was found strangled in her home just over a week ago amid rumors that she was preparing to write a tell-all autobiography that would have outed several of New Orleans's most powerful men as her clients. The police haven't made any arrests. In a press conference earlier today, they requested that anyone with information about Elhers's infamous client list or the murder contact them.

Belle shuddered as she walked into the parlor and saw another dead woman center screen. The last thing she needed before bed was to listen to tales of death and mayhem. She already had them running through her head every night.

Belle stretched as she walked into the parlor and turned on the overhead lights. They illuminated the room with warm, golden light as she headed for her favorite chair in the house. It was a big comfortable wingback in the corner. The fabric was an eye-assaulting brocade, but she couldn't bring herself to change it. Big bookshelves full of eclectic tomes flanked the chair, and the prettiest Tiffany lamp decorated the adjoining side table.

At some point, her grandmother had begun using this space less as a room to greet guests and more as a cozy place to relax. She could envision her grandmother sitting in the comfy chair while reading. Belle had taken to curling up there in the evenings and reading her grandmother's journal before she retired.

The woman she'd met only at her father's funeral fascinated her. The diary hinted at some big and slightly scandalous parties back in her day. Belle had wondered more than once what her grandmother would say about her unusual relationship with Kell, Eric, and Tate. Oddly enough, she had the sense that Grandma would have understood.

The overhead lights flickered, blinked twice, and died, sending the room into gloom again. Belle sighed. Maybe they weren't done with Mike after all. She reached over and pulled the chain on the Tiffany lamp. Luckily, it came on, giving her a small circle of light. Belle settled against the back of the cozy chair, deciding the little pool of illumination was actually quite nice.

She opened the journal, flipping to the place where she'd left off last night, and settled in eagerly.

My darling boy, I hear you had a baby girl. Annabelle. Oh, my son. I'm so proud you named her after my dearest

Belle. She loved you so. I sent a gift, but I don't expect you to receive it well. If you send it back to me, I'll give it to the orphanage. They can always use the money. I wish I could see her, see the smallest piece of myself in her beautiful, tiny face. You won't allow it, but know that I love that child like I love you, son. Tell her to have the best life she can. Tell her to find love and when she does, you tell her to never let it go. You tell her to fight in a way I didn't. I let your father go too easily. You tell her she'll never regret that she fought. She will only mourn if she doesn't.

Would it please you to know I sold the business? Likely not. I'm too old to control those girls anymore. I'm far past my prime. I'll just read my cards in the Square from now on. I'll tell tourists the futures they want to hear, then maybe—just maybe—they'll create their own self-fulfilling prophecies and make their dreams come true. Sometimes all a person needs is a little faith. I have the greatest faith that someday you will forgive me. Someday I will prove myself and my adoration to you. I love you, my boy. Take care of your baby girl.

Tears sprang to Belle's eyes. She sniffled, the words in front of her watery but seared into her heart. She flipped the page to read on, to find out why her father had never forgiven his own mother. But that was the last page of the entry. The rest of the pages remained void—like their mother-son rapport.

Why had her father been so angry with Grandma? Belle couldn't understand why he'd kept her from a loving grandmother. It was so obvious the woman had adored her only son. In earlier entries, she'd written tearfully about sending him away for boarding school. She'd missed her son desperately, but wanted what was best for him. How had her father not seen or believed in that love?

Belle read the entry again, looking for clues. The words seemed to swell off the page and into her consciousness. Fight. Fight for the love she wanted and deserved. Risk her heart. Take a chance.

It scared her. She'd already seen what life looked like when one didn't. Her grandmother had ended up alone. Her mother, too. Her father...she recalled his occasionally withdrawn moods. Had her family all walked away from love and lived to regret it? Could she break the cycle?

On the other hand, she'd tried so hard as a child to make her mom love her again following her father's passing and she'd failed. After that, she'd stopped trying at all, refusing to let herself be hurt again.

Was she playing out the same patterns as her ancestors? Sure, she'd listened to Kellan's terrible past, even empathized with him, but had she fought for him? Really? For all of them to stay and love her?

No. She'd pushed them away to protect her heart, but it was already breaking. And if she didn't change something now, she feared she'd soon mourn the fact that she had not done absolutely everything she could to keep them.

The light in the room flickered on again. Belle glanced up at the big fixture dangling from the ceiling. It flared and died, a popping sound splitting the air.

She stood. Damn it. Mike had sworn everything was up to current code. He'd smiled and taken her check, and now Belle kind of wanted to punch him in the face. Guess she'd be calling him again in the morning.

With a sigh, she leaned back against the chair, wishing her other problems would be half so easy to fix.

Suddenly, every hair on her body stood up. The air seemed to turn electric. Goose bumps covered her body.

A shadow snagged her attention, and Belle zipped her gaze to the far wall in time to watch a dark mass move across the area. She gulped in a silent breath, her eyes widening as the figure moved toward the window. The whole room seemed to turn cold.

There was no way to deny what her eyes were seeing. That shadow moving across her wall didn't move like a person. It seemed to float off the ground. It didn't have defined legs.

It wasn't of this world.

A cold menace snaked across her skin. All the air in the room was suddenly sucked away. Her lungs ached. Time slowed to a stop as she watched the black mass pause, turn. Was it coming her way?

She felt a cold touch on her shoulder, almost like an icy finger passing through her flesh. She heard a scream. Then the whole world went black.

* * * *

Kellan's heart threatened to stop when he heard the blood-curdling scream fill the whole space as though the house itself was screaming.

He dropped the file he'd been studying and ran because Belle was in trouble.

"Belle!" Tate yelled for her as he jumped to his feet.

"The parlor." Eric picked up his cell phone as they all sprinted toward that section of the house. "She always reads in there at this time of night."

Kellan got to her first. She looked so frail and delicate, her body slumped over in the big chair. He got to his knees, feeling for a pulse. Praying for a pulse. God, what had happened?

"Kellan?" Her lashes fluttered, her eyes opening slowly.

"I'm here, love."

With a cry, she threw herself against him, wrapping her arms around his body as if he was a life preserver in the middle of a raging sea.

"I'm calling 911," Eric barked.

"Do you see something? Someone? I'll do a search." Tate stood tense as he stared down at her.

"Don't," she said quickly, sniffling slightly as she shook her head. "Don't call anyone. They'll just think I'm crazy."

"Love, we need to get this on record. Who was in here?" It had been so quiet the last few days, Kell had almost believed that whoever had tried to scare her previously had moved on. He'd hoped that whoever wanted her out had realized that scare tactics wouldn't work. No. They'd just been waiting, plotting, and escalating. He was going to kill whoever had rattled her with his bare hands.

Belle pulled back, trying to stand on shaky feet. "No one. I mean no one alive."

Had she been drinking? "What?"

She scanned the room fearfully, as though trying to find something no longer there. "It was here. A big shadow... I-it was shaped like a man mostly, but I felt its evil. God, Kellan. The room got so cold. I felt him touch me and it nearly made me sick."

His heart was still thundering in his chest, but he frowned. Was she implying that she'd seen a ghost? He wondered what exactly her grandmother had been writing about in that journal of hers because it was making Belle's imagination run wild.

"I'm sure you just fell asleep and had another bad dream."

Her eyes narrowed into a stubborn glare. "I did *not* fall asleep." She frowned, swallowing. "I didn't want to believe it myself, but I think this house is haunted and by more than one entity."

Yeah, what the hell did he do with that? "Okay, maybe we should have you talk to someone. You're under a lot of stress."

Tate cleared his throat and suddenly looked sheepish. "I might need to talk to someone, too."

Belle turned, gasping as she reached for Tate's hand. "You've seen something?"

Kellan frowned at Tate. What the hell was he up to? "Are you serious?"

Tate flushed slightly, his big shoulders shrugging in a

self-conscious gesture. "Maybe. Look, there are some weird things going on in this place."

Eric pocketed his cell again. "It's a historic house, man. You've never lived in a really old place like this. There's always settling, and the electricity is obviously still faulty. There's a logical explanation."

"Okay, explain why the dog barks at shit that's not there," Tate shot back.

It took everything Kellan had not to roll his eyes. "Uhm, because he's a dog and not a very smart one."

Seemingly of its own accord, Kell's head jerked slightly to the right. Damn it. He was going to have to get that checked out. He seemed to have developed a tic in his neck that caused him to jerk occasionally.

Belle stood by Tate, obviously picking her side of the fence. "Sir is not stupid."

Oh, she was going to change that dog's name if it was the last thing he did. "Love, he's out chasing a cat across the courtyard. He's not exactly a Rhodes Scholar."

Eric crossed his arms over his chest. "It is a little creepy how he acts sometimes. I caught him growling at a closet the other day. Like really growling. He was ready to attack."

"A lot of people believe animals see things we can't," Belle argued. "That animals have extra or heightened senses."

"And some people think Santa Claus is real. It doesn't change the fact that he's not." His head jerked again. Damn it. Maybe there was something neurologically wrong with him.

"Are you okay?" Belle's eyes softened with concern.

"It's a just a tic, love. Sometimes I get them when I'm stressed." Though usually it was in his left eyelid. He'd never had his neck jerk like someone had slapped him upside the head.

Tate held up a hand. "Look, all I know is there are creepy parts of this house."

Kell glared. Tate was supposed to be the logical one. "What does science tell you, man? I really thought you would be on my side. You were raised by scientists."

"Yeah, uhm, what science tells us above all else is that we don't know everything. The Greeks explained thunderstorms as Zeus getting pissed off and throwing lightning bolts around. How do we know that the ghost thing isn't a way of explaining something we don't understand yet? A truly good scientist leaves room for possibilities."

"Do you really think that Belle saw a ghost?" Eric asked, shaking his head. "Because that seems farfetched."

"To you, sure. But an iPod would look like magic to someone who lived a hundred years ago. I'm just saying there are more things in heaven and earth than are obviously a part of the grand philosophy of Kellan. Forty-eight percent of all Americans believe in ghosts. And this particular one seems to like to pat my ass," Tate said with a sigh. "It's happened more than once."

"What?" Belle's eyes widened.

"Dude, come on." Kell frowned. Was Tate trying to get in good with Belle or had he just lost his mind?

Even in the dim light of the room, he could see Tate's face flush a bright shade of red. "I started feeling it a couple of days ago. A cold spot drifts around me. I don't feel...alone anymore. Then something pats me on the butt. I don't know how else to say it. I also think I saw the shower curtain moving on its own today. Baby, did you sneak in and write *nice ass* on the bathroom mirror this morning?"

"No," Belle assured. But she looked alarmed.

Eric held up his hands. "Dude, I try to not look at your ass even though you walk around with it hanging free most of the time."

They all turned to stare at Kell, and he rolled his eyes. "Do you honestly believe I would come up with a practical joke like that? I have no sense of humor."

It was a sad fact of life. He'd lost his sense of humor

when he'd lost everything else. Though the idea of some perverted ghost having a fixation on Tate's butt was kind of funny.

Eric mumbled something completely incoherent.

"What did you say?" Belle asked.

Eric seemed to find his feet very interesting. "I'm saying something keeps patting my butt, too. It's weird. And sometimes I think I hear a voice saying I'm a good one. I don't know what that means."

Belle's eyes lit up and she raced across the room to pick up her grandmother's journal. "That's what my grandma used to say about the men she liked." She flipped through the pages. "Look here. She says her friend, Harrison, was a good one. One of the good ones. My grandma is here."

"And she wants to pat their butts?" he asked incredulously. "Belle, really?" Maybe he should call in a shrink.

"I know it sounds crazy, but there is something happening in this house and I'm going to figure it out. I need a computer." She looked up at Tate. "Would you help me do a little research?"

The faintest hint of a smile lit his lips, the first bit of happiness he'd seen out of Tate for days. "Yeah, let's do it."

They walked out, hand in hand. Belle might have scared the shit out of him, but at least she and Tate seemed to have put aside their problems. That alone might make the whole near heart attack worthwhile. Although if she got truly close to Tate and Eric again, where would that leave him?

"You okay?" Eric asked.

"I'm fine. I'm a little worried about her. I think the pressure must be getting to her. It's the only way to explain this sudden belief in ghosts."

Eric's brows rose. "I don't think it's sudden. Have you ever seen all the shows she tapes? Mostly it's shows where people buy houses and then like wreck them and shit, but she also likes shows where people hunt for ghosts. But that's not what I'm talking about. What are you doing, man?"

"I'm trying to figure out how to help Belle." What was Eric's problem?

"Belle's fine. You're the one with the problem."

"What do you mean?"

"I mean that Belle's surrender is inevitable. She won't hold out on us forever."

He hadn't really thought about it. The truth was he'd been happy the last couple of days. Well, he'd been happy at night when they took her and he could be close to her. There had been a deep sense of loss every time the sex ended and he left her bedroom, but he couldn't do much about that. Sleeping next to her seemed even more intimate than fucking her, so staying the night cuddled up beside her would be implying a promise he couldn't make.

And now he realized just how little time he had left with her…maybe with all of them. "Do you think her belief that the house is haunted will send her back to Chicago with us?"

If she came back, Kellan had no doubt she would move right into Eric and Tate's house. What would he do then? Show up for sex? He couldn't see that working for long. And the night she finally shut the door in his face would fucking hurt.

"Hell, no. I don't think anything will induce Belle to leave this house. I've been thinking… Next week, I'll be applying for my license to practice law in Louisiana. I'll take the state bar exam as soon as possible."

Kellan felt the bottom drop out of his stomach. "Are you serious? What about Tate? Have you told him?"

"No. I just decided today."

"Tate won't leave Chicago," Kell pointed out.

"He fears change and always has. Do you know the anxiety he went through when I bought a different brand of toilet paper? But there's only one thing he fears more and that's losing Belle. She's going to soften and let us into her lives. Once she does, he's going to give in. It's inevitable.

She's the one. At least, she's the one for us."

"Oh my god," Belle stuck her head back through the door looking more animated than she had in days. There was an excited light to her eyes. "I saw a shadow person tonight. Tate just found all this information. It's so cool. Apparently when really bad things happen in a space, sometimes energy lingers and forms this creepy paranormal entity that appears as a black mass. It can sometimes feed off of negative energy in the house or the bad moods of people in it. Isn't that amazing? I also ordered a ghost hunting kit off the Internet. It gets here tomorrow. In the meantime, I have a dictation tape recorder. I'm going to see if I can capture some EVPs."

"What?" Kell wondered if she'd suddenly decided to speak a foreign language.

"Electronic voice phenomenon. Even if the human ear can't detect them, recorders have been capturing compelling sounds and voices for decades." Tate poked his head in, looking just as excited as Belle.

"Ghost voices?"

"Yeah." Belle nodded. "It would explain so much around here. I mean, when Gates first brought up the idea that the house might be haunted, I didn't want to believe it, but…it really makes sense."

Eric laughed indulgently. "Then I guess we're going into the ghost hunting business, baby."

She bit her bottom lip, looking almost apologetic. "Is it wrong that I'm a little excited?"

Eric shrugged. "I'm getting used to having my ass patted." His face went blank. "Yeah, there it went again."

"I think that particular ghost is harmless, babe. Come on. You have to see what we found out." She gave them a brilliant smile and ran back toward the living room.

No doubt about it. She was the one. He just wasn't good enough for her.

When should he pack up and leave? Tonight? Tomorrow? Maybe she'd grant him one last night.

Eric put a sympathetic hand on his shoulder. "Come on. Let's go and try to figure this out. Ghost or no ghost, I think an actual person left the message on Belle's bedroom wall right after we arrived. I would feel better if we found out who wants her gone from here. Maybe we should research the house and see if we can find out if any of our suspects have hidden attachments to the place."

"Eric, there's an app!" Belle yelled.

Kell stared, astounded. Eric's smile could only be described as joyful. "Man, ghost or not, I'm just happy to see her smile."

He walked away, joining Tate and Belle.

For a deathly quiet moment, Kellan stared at the place where his friends and his love had been before they'd left him behind.

His time was running out.

His neck jerked again, this time stronger than the last. It felt like someone had just roughly smacked him upside the head. "Goddamn it."

He really needed to get that looked at.

* * * *

Tate stretched as he closed the laptop and glanced at the clock. It was after two in the morning, but he'd found an enormous amount of information on the house he now lived in—and possibly shared with a bunch of creepy shit and one slightly sexually forward ghost grandma. Was he really thinking about ghosts? And was he really thinking about bringing some psychic in to do a house cleansing? All the sites he'd read had suggested he should, though some of the same sites also told him what to do in case of a Bigfoot attack.

Where was he going to find the psychic equivalent of a Swiffer?

"Hey, why don't you come to bed?" Belle stood in the

doorway. She and Eric and Kellan had gone upstairs an hour before, but he'd stayed behind, his brain running too fast to sleep.

She looked gorgeous standing there with her hair mussed and a sleepy expression on her face. Clearly, she'd been tossed a time or two, and his dick got hard, despite his weariness. It was never tired around Belle.

"I'll be up in a minute. I just want to make some notes for when I head over to the city records building tomorrow." He'd discovered some very interesting facts about the house, including several rumors that the girls who committed suicide had actually been killed by their father. The incident had happened back in the fifties, before Belle's grandmother had bought the place. In fact, after the father of the dead young women had passed on himself, two other people had bought the house. Both had sold it again within a year. Belle's grandmother had paid far below market value for the house. That explained how she'd managed to afford it. But Tate felt sure he was missing more, something that explained who wanted Belle gone from here now. He needed to delve into city records to see if he could find any clues.

He also needed a little space. He'd gotten close to her again tonight and not in a physical way. Over the last several days, he'd managed to put distance between them. She wanted him in bed. He wanted her, too. He could handle that. He could fuck her every night and do his job in the morning, putting her out of his head until it was time to fuck her again.

When she was safe, he would walk away and sink himself into building the firm. He would keep all of his relationships purely physical. Eric could date, and if the lady felt adventurous, Tate could join them for sex. At least that had been the plan he'd been brewing for days. Hearing her scream tonight, holding her and researching crazy shit with her—yeah, that had screwed with his perfectly good strategy.

She moved in behind him, cupping his shoulders in her gentle hands. "I'm having a hard time sleeping without you.

I've gotten used to having someone on both sides of me."

"Well, maybe you can get a body pillow." He hated the fact that he sounded like a sulking kid, but he hurt inside in a way he hadn't for a very long time. Maybe when she saw how childish he could be she would kick him to the curb and put him out of his misery. Staying here with her was like living in purgatory.

She wrapped her arms around his neck, laying a kiss on his cheek. "A body pillow wouldn't be as warm as you. Nor would it be as sweet or funny or perfect. Come upstairs with me. I hate the thought of you down here alone."

He sighed, unable to stop himself from letting his head roll back until their cheeks brushed. He closed his eyes, damning himself. He was addicted to her. He could keep telling himself he'd walk away, but every time she offered him even the smallest taste of her, he took it greedily with both hands.

"I'm not alone," he said. "I have Sir. He sleep barks by the way. And I think he's sleep running. His paws keep twitching."

Belle laughed and let him go, moving around the desk to see Sir asleep on the couch. "Thanks for letting him stay in here."

He'd gotten used to the mutt. Another thing he would miss when he was back in Chicago. He was getting used to New Orleans, used to living with her…used to having this little slice of heaven. "No problem."

Belle scooped up her puppy, who looked at her with sleepy eyes before giving her a lick. "Did I ever tell you about what happened the day my dad died?"

He sat up straight, his whole being focused on her. She so rarely talked about her past that he knew she was about to tell him something important. "No. I know there was a car accident."

She nodded, stroking Sir as though finding comfort in the action. "Yes. I was just a kid. It was raining that night, but I wanted to go to my friend's slumber party. I didn't usually get invited to stuff like that. Kinley did, and she talked this girl into asking me, too. I think her name was Brianna, but I can't remember. How sad is that? I can't remember her name. I should remember everything about the night my dad died."

"You don't have to, baby. All you have to do is remember he loved you. What happened?" He had an inkling, but she needed to say it.

Her eyes took on a far-off look as though she wasn't really there with him, but lost in the past. "My mom thought the storm was too bad to drive in. She told me I couldn't go. She wouldn't drive me. My dad came home from work early and I cried and threw a temper tantrum and I got my way."

"Baby, it was not your fault. You were a child."

She sniffled a little. "He lost control on his way home. He died at roughly eight pm according to the police reports. I was playing with lip gloss and listening to music when he died and do you know how I found out? She came and got me the next morning. She didn't even tell me that night."

His heart ached for her. "Maybe she was trying to give you one last night."

"I wish. She claims she had a lot of things to do concerning the accident and dad's body. She said she thought it would be best to tell me after I got a good night's sleep." Belle shook her head. "That wasn't it. She shut me out, Tate. She pulled her grief around her and she wouldn't let me in. She blamed me."

He couldn't keep his distance when she looked so miserable. He stood and crossed the empty space between them. "Baby, it wasn't your fault."

She sniffled, tears welling in her eyes. "One day I was a kid with two parents who loved me. The next day my mother resented me, and I was alone." Her voice shook. "Tate, I'm so scared it could happen again."

He hugged her and sighed, an odd relief filling him.

They were finally at the heart of the matter. "You think if Kellan leaves, we'll resent you."

She closed her eyes, letting her forehead rest against his. "You guys are so close. You all need one another."

Belle was also afraid she would lose the little family they'd formed. She was afraid she would be all alone again with no one to blame but herself. Tate wanted to rail at his own idiocy. He'd been so hurt by her rejection—seemingly like every other one he'd been dealt—that he hadn't thought to look for the real reasons behind Belle's refusal to let them close.

"Do you know what I'm going to feel if Kellan leaves us? I'm going to feel sorry for him, Belle. I'm going to pity him because here's the truth: we could have an amazing family and a beautiful life."

"But—"

"No, let me say this. Eric and I have been talking. If you'd let us, we would be together for as long fate allows. If anything happened to one of us, we'd cling to whoever is left because that's what family is supposed to do. Mine didn't. My parents' version of love and support was to punish me when I didn't perform perfectly. Eric was only valued athletically. We could be different. We wouldn't have to do anything the way they did. In fact, we wouldn't. If you agree, we'll figure this out. The one thing I do know is that I won't hate you if Kellan leaves. You didn't push him out the door. He's a grown man choosing to let his past hurt him. That's not your fault."

Tears splashed on her cheeks, and Tate knew he was making the right decision. Now he just needed to make Belle understand that he wasn't walking away. Too many people had disappeared from her life. He refused to be another.

He tilted her chin up, forcing her to look in his eyes. "If you let me into your life, Annabelle, I will never leave you. I love you. I won't regret anything except losing you."

Her eyes closed briefly. "I hope you mean that."

It wasn't exactly what he wanted to hear. She hadn't told him she loved him back. She hadn't agreed to marry him, but she also hadn't run away. She stood here with him. As long as she was in his arms, he had a shot and he intended to take it.

Sir lay between them, but he didn't seem to mind being squished. The puppy simply chose the most important moment of his life to start licking his ankles. "Belle, look at me."

Her eyes opened and widened before she laughed. "Sir, stop."

Instead, Sir pranced with a happy bark, then tried to mount his leg. Tate sighed. "I'm pretty sure he licks his own butt, and I may die of some horrible puppy venereal disease. Would any man who didn't love you to the core of his being allow himself to be molested like this?"

"Definitely not. Will you come to bed with me?"

He would go anywhere to be with her. He would even study for another damn bar exam. "Yes."

He took her hand and led her up the stairs.

Chapter Sixteen

Kellan frowned as he looked down at the massive stack of information Tate had compiled in a short period of time. "I don't see how this changes anything."

Afternoon light filtered through the stained glass, making the floors Belle had splurged on to have sanded and stained again absolutely gleam. Another knock sounded at the door, and he heard Eric begrudgingly welcome back the electrician inside the house again.

"Where's Belle?" Mike asked with a grin.

Kell wanted to punch him until he lay flat on the floor. "Busy."

Mike shrugged. "Tell her I said hi."

"Maybe we should try someone new," Tate muttered as Mike made his way toward the stairs. "I don't care how old and complex the wiring is in this house, he should have fixed it by now. And you should really read all of that info before you start telling me I'm wrong."

Between the endless contractors and Tate's newfound belief in the paranormal, Kellan's day was rapidly going to hell. "I don't see how a bunch of rumors help us figure out what's going on in this house. I don't need to know the history. I need to know who's trying to scare Belle out of it right now."

Eric shouldered his way back into the kitchen. "That's

an electrician, a plumber, a carpenter, and some woman with a god-awful amount of something she calls swatches. Belle's trying to pick between five colors that all look the exact same to me, but apparently they have different names so the decision is massive. Who are our most likely suspects here?"

So many people walking in and out of the house. Every single one of them was a suspect in his mind. "Don't forget the landscaper she brought in. And someone's coming in today to look at all the old photos. Belle wants to restore some she found in the attic. I put them over by the copy machine."

The photos didn't matter now. "Process of elimination. Who was here that first day? Mike, Gates, Captain Ron—"

"Who?" Tate looked confused.

"Mullet guy," Kell supplied. "Big belly, lots of crack."

"Oh, the plumber." Tate sighed. "Who else was here that first day? The interns."

"They haven't been back," Eric pointed out.

"And nothing else has happened." Kell crossed his arms over his chest. "Any one of them could have done it and none of them appear to have a motive. This isn't getting us anywhere."

"Wow," Tate exclaimed, looking at a framed photo in his hands before he passed it over.

Kell took the big black-and-white picture of Belle's grandmother and a bunch of women. They were all standing in front of the house, smiling and looking like they were ready for an evening at the disco. It had been taken in the seventies from all appearances. Wow was right. Belle's grandma had clearly had some gorgeous girlfriends. Every single woman in the photo was stunning.

"See? Maybe we can't find a motive because none of those people left Belle the warning on the wall." Tate looked more animated than he had in days, surprising Kell.

"You're back to the ghost theory?"

"Hear me out. So a few owners before Marie Wright

291

bought this place, a man named Fredrick Peterman lived here with his two daughters. Peterman was rich, and the rumor around town was he was involved in the local voodoo scene."

Kellan shook his head. When was he going to wake up? Obviously, he was having a really weird dream. Logical, rational Tate believing in ghosts and now this? "Voodoo? Seriously?"

Eric shrugged. "Hey, it's not a game down here. These are hard-core believers."

And his friends weren't going to shut up until he heard them out. "All right so Peterman was into voodoo before he died?"

Tate shook his head, an amused light in his eyes. "At one point, yes. The word is, he ran afoul of the local voodoo priestess. According to local legends, the Peterman family had been in New Orleans for years and made their money in shipping, but the times changed and so did their fortunes. One Madame Charitte went to the local police and claimed that Peterman had come to her and asked her to summon the devil to make a deal with him to restore their fortunes. She refused to be involved in dark magic. The cops claimed she was a kook and ignored her. Of course, Peterman was a long-standing donor to their charities, if you know what I mean."

Kellan didn't like where this was heading. "So Peterman had the police in his back pocket. Got it. But do you really think the man would try to call the devil? That sounds insane."

"According to Madame Charitte, Peterman had brought her a detailed spell to work that involved a very nasty sacrifice," Tate explained.

"He had daughters, two of them," Eric reminded. "Both supposedly hung themselves."

Kell gaped. "Like the girls in Belle's nightmares." She'd finally confessed this morning that she'd been having terrible dreams since she'd first moved in about two girls being hanged to death. But... "You can't think for a minute that the man sacrificed his own daughters to the dark side and got away with calling it suicide."

"This was back in the fifties. Peterman was considered an upstanding citizen. In the wealthy community, there was an outpouring of sympathy when both of his daughters committed suicide." Tate pointed to the headlines. "So tragic, right? All evidence of ritual sacrifice was covered up. Although, if he managed to make a deal with the devil, ol' Lucifer didn't keep up his end of the bargain. The business went belly-up within a year, and Peterman shot himself in the library. Police reports suggest his body was discovered roughly where Belle said she saw the shadow person."

"Come on, Tate. Don't get distracted by this. It's a great campfire story, but totally illogical. There's something else going on here." He turned to his other friend. "Give me something real, Eric. Has Sequoia run all the searches we asked for?"

Eric chuckled. "Yes, but he says it's bad karma to invade someone's privacy. So here's the rundown. The plumber is clean. Captain Ron had a couple of parking tickets and was cited for public intoxication years ago, but that's all. The landscaper got sued for stepping on someone's prized hydrangea. But Mike, our friendly neighborhood asswipe, has a little more on his record."

Something akin to joy lit Kellan up inside. He really hated that asshole. "Please tell me he killed someone or something juicy we can use against him to keep him far from Belle."

"Sorry. He was convicted of bribing a city official to turn the other way on code violations for a wealthy client. He did six months, but it looks like he had a lot of trouble in jail. While there, he had multiple trips to the infirmary because the dude got his ass handed to him. Other than that he's sadly clean. No violent offenses. I don't think we can bury him or that Belle will kick his ass out. He's doing all the follow-up work under the original contract so it's not costing any extra money."

Tate glanced through the folder. "It looks like Grandma's lawyer has some unsavory connections."

Kellan snorted. He didn't know a lawyer who didn't. "Well, we can ban him from the house. I think he's got a meeting with Belle this afternoon, but it's just to pick up the final inventory list since we all pitched in to finish that. I found the insurance paperwork so he should be satisfied. He won't need to come here again. From now on, we'll take meetings at his office."

And that was about all he could do. Frustration welled. Who the hell had left the note on her wall that day? True, the warnings seemed to have stopped, but Kellan didn't like unanswered questions. They tended to come back to bite him in the ass.

He didn't care how quiet this person had gotten. The situation could be dangerous and whoever the hell masterminded it was human, not some shadow person or ghost.

"So have we looked into Helena?" Eric asked.

"Who is that?" Kell snapped.

"The psychic." Tate acted as if he should know. "Mike, the perverted electrician, recommended her to Belle. I'd call another psychic if I knew one, but I don't. This one seemed all right."

Oh, fuck. Could his day get more surreal? "We have a psychic now?"

Tate waved them both off. "Yeah, she's a psychic medium, dude. She does house cleansings. I talked to her this morning and, lucky for us, she's free this evening."

"Yeah, lucky, man. I'm shocked she doesn't have a full schedule of house cleansings. Uhm, you do know that grifters tend to make room on their schedule for naïve idiots, right? It's kind of how they make their living."

Tate rolled his eyes. "I don't know if any of this is real or not. I only know what my instincts tell me and I've decided to start listening to them. This will very likely make Belle feel better about living here. Helena asked us to clear the house of as many people as possible or it interferes with her reading."

"Whatever. So you're really not even going to try to get Belle back to Chicago?" Kellan asked with dread in his gut.

"Nah, I like it here. I've gotten used to beignets," Tate explained, reaching across the desk for a file. "I know I said I wanted to go home, but home is where Belle is."

He knew it made him a sick bastard, but he went a little nauseous at how settled Tate seemed. He was a fucker because he should be happy for his friends, but all he could think about was his own despair. If Tate and Eric really settled down with Belle, where would that leave him? Would he ever be truly content to be their "roommate"? Would he be the creepy dude who lived in their house and showed up for sex, only to slink off to a lonely bed afterward? No, she'd shut him out quickly. At the end of the day, Belle was a woman who had sex because she felt something for her partners. Getting off wouldn't be good enough for her for long.

He forced himself to smile. He was not going to ruin their happiness. "That's great. Have you thought about the firm? You can't run it from here forever."

The lamp on the desk tilted as Tate knocked it over. It began a long fall to the floor before Eric threw himself across the room and managed to catch it. There was a collective sigh of relief. Belle took those damn antiques seriously.

"That was close." Eric managed to sit up and glared at Tate. "Dude. Bull. China shop. Watch what you're doing."

Tate flushed sheepishly. "Sorry. It's crowded in here. We need to find office space."

Eric set the lamp on the floor and got to his feet. "Yeah, we do. As to your question, Kellan, we have a proposition for you."

His stomach took another nose dive. He'd been afraid

they would do this. "You want me to buy you out?"

Eric reached down and brought the lamp back up to its original position. "Yeah, but not all at once. Obviously we're not going to pressure you for capital. I'm going to make a list of lawyers I think you would work well with. You'll still need partners. Unless you change your mind and decide to stay here with us. Come on, man. Southern gentlemen lawyers? We can get our mint juleps on."

He ran a hand through his hair. He couldn't do this now. He thought he would have so much more time.

"Hey, what the hell is that?" Eric stared down at the lamp.

"Uh, it's a lamp. You turn it on and it provides the room with illumination and aides the human eye in seeing things," Tate said with a big "duh" in his voice.

Eric threw him his happy middle finger. "Fucker. I'm talking about this thing inside the shade."

He walked across the room, leaping at the chance to do anything but answer the question Eric had posed. "There's something in the lamp?"

Eric pointed to the inside of the shade. He unscrewed it, lifted it off the lamp, and handed it to Kellan.

Peering inside the lampshade, he saw a small round device. Holy shit. He knew what that was. A bug. He'd seen his father's private investigators use them many times before when attempting to get dirt on rival politicians. He put a hand to his lips and bade Tate to look inside, too.

Tate stared for a moment, then stood. He pointed toward the back of the house. Kellan followed him, making his way to the kitchen and out to the back porch. After the door was closed, Tate and Eric both turned to him.

"That's a fucking bug, isn't it?" Eric asked.

"I think so. It looks like the type my father used to listen in on his adversaries. Or his mistresses. He didn't mind cheating on my mother, but he demanded he was the only customer when he was paying." Someone was listening to them.

Tate held a hand up. "I think Kellan's right. That technology has got to be ten or fifteen years old, and it looked like it had been there for a while. I would bet it's been there at least a couple of years."

"Who would be listening in on Belle's grandmother?" Kellan asked. A couple of ideas hit him at once. "We need to learn more about her life. Who did she associate with? What business did she sell off? Did she have any enemies? She couldn't have been just a psychic. Haunted house or not, there's no way a street psychic could afford this place. She had something else going on. Whatever it was, someone was interested enough to bug her place. Check with your fed contacts. I want to know if there was any reason for the feds to be investigating her."

Tate huffed a little. "That would explain the crappy technology. I'll sweep the house and find out if there are any other bugs. I suspect so. What do we tell Belle?"

She was worried enough as it was. He didn't want to put more stress on her shoulders. "How do we tell her we think her grandma might have been involved in something criminal?"

"Maybe it wasn't criminal," Eric said.

Eric was being naïve. "Something went on in this house, and you know damn well it's not about ghosts. Spirits from the beyond didn't plant that device. A person did, obviously a while back. But someone wanted to keep tabs on Marie Wright. If that bug belongs to the feds, then she was involved in something nasty. If it doesn't, then it's very likely she was still involved in something nasty. Completely innocent people don't normally have bugs in their houses. I don't want to tell Belle anything until we at least know what Grandma was involved in."

"Belle doesn't have much family." Tate looked back toward the door. "She's been reading her grandmother's journal. I think she's really starting to admire the woman. I would hate to crush that. Kellan's right. I'll see what I can find out before we say anything."

"What are you going to tell her when you walk through the house looking for bugs?" Eric asked.

"That I bought a ghost hunting kit and I'm looking for evidence," Tate shot back. "Which is kind of true. I'm looking for spooks."

The door creaked as it opened. They turned to see Sir running by as Belle let him out of the house. She smiled a little. "If you need fresh air, you could always open a window."

That restless feeling was back. The minute she walked into a room, he felt antsy, anxious. There was so much he wanted from her and so much he didn't deserve. "It got crowded in there."

She joined them. "Well, the good news is, the whole house is empty now. Mike got an emergency call. The draper left. Everyone else went to lunch. We should be quiet for a few hours."

Eric sighed with obvious relief. "Thank god. I have a conference call in five minutes. I thought I would have to yell over the sound of that saw whining." He strode back into the house.

Tate leaned over and gave Belle a kiss. "I have errands to run, baby. I'll be back in a few hours. I'll be here in time for the cleansing."

She nodded. "Okay, but she said I needed to clear out the house. The fewer people here, the better."

Tate left, and he was alone with Belle. How could it be more awkward to talk to a woman than to make love to her? He hated the fact that he felt anything but comfortable with her. She was one of the few people in the world he could really relax around, and now all he could think about was the fact that he was going to be the outsider, the interloper. Tate and Eric would be here with Belle—live with her, love her. They would be her family, her men. He would be back in

Chicago with new partners. He'd be alone again without friends. Without a woman. He'd have nothing.

"Hey." Belle approached him, putting her hands on his waist and tilting her face to his. The sun hit the glowing brown hue of her skin, making it come alive. So fucking gorgeous. "We have the whole house to ourselves. What should we do? Have any ideas?"

He knew what he wanted to do. He wanted to lay her out and take her over and over again, as many times as he could until she shut him out in favor of the men who gave her love and forever. His cock twitched, but his heart took a nosedive. "Belle, I don't know if that's a good idea."

He'd never made love to her without Eric and Tate around. He wasn't sure he should. They knew what they wanted. They wouldn't hesitate to tell her they loved her, worshipped her, and wanted to spend the rest of their lives with her. He was a sad sack who could never give her what she deserved.

Belle went up on her tiptoes, brushing her lips against his. A light touch, almost a whisper, but it made his cock go instantly hard as a rock. "I think it's a brilliant idea. It's the best I've had all day. Tate and Eric won't mind. They've got things to do."

He wanted nothing more than to toss her against the wall and force his way deep inside her body. When he was inside her, everything made sense.

She took his hand, and before he had time to protest, she was pulling him into the house. They walked through the kitchen, toward the hall.

"Eric!"

What the hell was she doing? She pushed through the kitchen door and led him out into the main hallway.

Eric stepped out of the living room, his cell phone in hand. "Yeah, baby?"

She wasn't going to ask him, was she? "Do you have a problem with me taking Kellan upstairs and blowing his mind for an hour or so? It's been a stressful morning. I could use a little relief."

What the hell was wrong with her? He shook his head. "Man, I…"

Eric grinned and winked at Belle. "Go for it, baby. If I can knock this call out in less than an hour, I'll join you." He nodded Kellan's way. "Take care of our girl, man."

Belle blew him a kiss as she started up the stairs. Kellan found himself following, dumbfounded. Were they all out of their minds?

She was making their problems sound easier than they really were. She was taking something complex and making it so simple, as though all they had to do was love each other to make this work. As if the other guys wouldn't mind because she was their girl and all that mattered was working together to make her happy.

The trouble was, she wasn't his girl. He hadn't earned her. She belonged to Eric and Tate.

Belle grabbed the bottom of her shirt as she entered the room and pulled it up and over her head, tossing it to the side. Every inch of skin she revealed made his cock jerk.

His mouth started to water as she unhooked her bra and her breasts bounced free. She gracefully stepped out of her pants. What the hell was he supposed to do? Turn her down? Maybe she wasn't his, didn't belong to him, but she wanted to be with him. He hadn't lied to her, hadn't told her one untrue thing. Why shouldn't he take her?

He came up with a hundred reasons why he shouldn't leave the bedroom now, but only one of them really counted. He had so little time left. He couldn't waste a minute. He wanted her more than he wanted just about anything.

"Undress me." He didn't know how long he would last. They didn't have the time to do all the things he really wanted, like tie her up and spend hours torturing her with pleasure. Clamping those magnificent breasts would be the first on his list. He would use diamond clamps because they would set off the deep, rich color of her skin. A platinum chain would run between her breasts and down to the clamp he would affix on the jewel of her clit. It would bite into her, a pleasurable pain that would lead to the sort of orgasm that made her cry out and twist and plead for mercy. When it came to her, he didn't have any. He'd love to keep her on the edge all afternoon. She would scream his name out over and over again.

But the freaking contractors would eventually show up after their lunch break, and Belle would be angry if she got caught naked and tied up and bejeweled like the BDSM princess she was. He had an hour with her—max. Greedily he wanted to spend every second of it inside her.

Belle sauntered to him, lifting her shaking hands to the buttons of his shirt. Every second she worked to bare him, she blinked up at him, her unwavering stare allowing him to see the honest desire in her eyes. Gone was the shy girl who hid her emotions. He could see them playing out, could feel the caress of her hands over every inch of skin she uncovered. This wasn't a selfish girl trying to take her pleasure, but a woman offering all of herself to him. Kellan was suddenly humbled by her.

He caught her hand, some unnamable emotion welling inside him. "What are you doing, Annabelle?"

A glance around confirmed that this wasn't a mere haphazard encounter. She'd already turned the bed down. He could see a box of condoms lying on the nightstand. She'd planned this.

Her rich chocolate gaze never faltered. He'd taught her well—and she'd learned quickly. "I'm seducing you."

"You don't have to. You know I want you."

A little grin curved her lips up. "It's harder than you think. You're still fighting me."

"Did you send everyone away?" How far did her plotting go?

"Yes."

He sighed but let her hand go. She immediately went back to working to free him of his shirt. She pushed it off his shoulders, then dropped to her knees, touching the button of his slacks. It was the first time she'd broken eye contact, and he found himself breathing again. When she watched him with her big dark eyes, he got lost in her.

"Why the big production number, love? I admit, it worries me that Eric and Tate might think I'm being presumptuous, but other than that, I'll take a nooner."

He purposefully used casual words. Nooner. Quickie. Roll in the hay. Hookup. He could toss those words out all day long, but deep inside he knew where this was heading. He was making love to the only woman he would ever care about. Might as well admit it… She was the only woman he'd ever love.

Belle lowered his zipper. It hissed in the silence, broken only by their ragged breaths. He sighed as she pulled his boxers past his hips and toward the floor. She knew exactly how to make a man feel good. He would give her that. Over the course of a week, she'd tossed aside her inhibitions and become the lover of his dreams. Giving. Open. Honest. Passionate.

How was he going to leave her and not fucking fall apart?

"Eric gave you permission."

He felt his jaw clench as his cock sprang free. "I'm sure Tate would like to have a say. He's a possessive bastard."

She tilted her head up, giving him a brilliant smile. "He is, but he's okay with this. Who do you think plugged me earlier today? He took me into the bathroom and spent a lot of time working this plug inside my ass. He talked about you and Eric the whole time, about how he hoped we'd eventually all be together. But he also knew what I wanted today. He thought you would find it hot."

Hot? He found it scorching. His cock strained up, twitching as though trying to get to her on its own. "You're wearing an anal plug?"

She licked his cock like a treat she wanted to savor—slowly, lovingly, making him bite back a moan. "Tate thought it might spice up the encounter for you. It's the large plug. I've run through the whole training set. Tate says this is the last one before we get to the real stuff. According to him, it will make my pussy very tight. Interested?"

Fuck, yes. Well before she'd said any of that. All Annabelle Wright ever had to do was look at him and he burned.

She took the head of his cock into her mouth, and he closed his eyes. He had the terrible suspicion that she meant to seduce him into some sort of forever. It wouldn't work, but he couldn't say no to her. His dick was already threatening to burst. His heart...not far behind.

"Come up here." If he let her, she would suck him until he came deep in her mouth, and he really wanted to fuck her with that plug. They'd been progressing her through the training set, each plug a little larger to ready her for the anal sex he ached to give her. He wished he'd been there when she'd taken the large plug. He would have deeply enjoyed the way her eyes had to have widened and her breath must have caught as Tate had slid that plug home.

She rose to her feet, and he kicked away his shoes, slacks, and boxers. Normally he would have folded them, but he didn't give a shit today. They weren't playing. They were stealing time. He had an hour or so to have her all to himself. Eric would try to rush through his call. Tate could come home at any time. The minute they could be up here, they would. It made him a selfish bastard but he wanted all the time alone with her he could grab.

He kissed her, letting himself really revel in her for the first time. He'd been viewing the encounters with the four of them as very pleasurable teaching sessions. He'd distanced himself by playing the second-fiddle Dom, letting Eric take the lead, but here and now he was just Kellan and she was just Belle. Just a man and a woman with only these moments together.

The minute the others showed up, he would have to take on his hands-off role because they deserved her and he didn't. He would have to honor their claim on her.

His tongue delved deep, rubbing and playing against hers. He felt the nubs of her nipples against his skin. He reached down, cupping her breasts. They were soft, but firm. They nestled so perfectly in his hands as though she'd been made just for him. He kissed his way from her mouth to her neck, burying his face in her shoulder, inhaling the sweetness of her scent.

He'd never wanted any woman as much as he wanted Belle. What if he'd met her before Lila? He could rewrite his history. Why couldn't he have found her before he'd attached himself to that ball and chain, then jumped into the drowning pool? Before he'd been ruined. Before he'd been utterly broken.

How different would his life be now?

"I need you," she whispered. "Please, Kellan. Please take me."

He watched as she moved away from him, settling herself on the bed with a siren's smile. She held a hand out to him.

She could ruin him in ways he'd never even imagined. If Lila had taken his family and his pride, Belle could kill his soul. If she chose to, she could rip him apart, and he would never be able to put himself back together. He would lay down and die if Belle betrayed him.

That summed up why he had to leave.

But not yet. Not fucking yet. He wasn't walking out until he absolutely had to. He could have one more taste of heaven before he resigned himself to a lifetime of hell.

He cursed, hating that he was even thinking about anything except the ecstasy she offered him here and now. Only that mattered. Right now, he had no past and no future.

Just the beautiful present.

Kell pulled a condom off the strip, opened it and worked it over his straining cock. Desire pounded through his system, and he wondered what it would be like to take off the fucking piece of latex and take his chances. How good would it feel to come deep inside her knowing there was nothing in between them. If he got her pregnant, there wouldn't be any question of him leaving. He would have to stay. He would be obligated to remain in her life. They would be connected by a child who would need them both.

But he couldn't do that to her. She deserved to know that any man in her life was there because he couldn't live without her, not because he'd knocked her up.

"Please, Kellan. Give us just a few minutes. We don't have to think about anything but right now. Just...be with me."

She offered him everything he wanted. He couldn't stay away. He fell on her without an ounce of his usual finesse. It was raw and real, and he couldn't seem to make himself stop. When he took a lover, he thought about technique and forced himself to be patient, but he couldn't with Belle. He kissed her again, needing to be as close to her as possible.

He covered her body with his, holding none of his own weight. God, she was small against him. Small and beautiful and so welcoming, but she could handle him. She wasn't fragile or delicate. Everything about Belle was strong. She didn't hold back. Instead, she opened her arms and her body, allowing him inside. Not just for pleasure. He'd had that so many times before. Women asked him to please them. They wanted to be taken care of sexually. But Belle offered to take care of him. She offered to join with him, to merge with him for no other reason than she cared.

He touched her womanly folds, wondering if she was really ready. He was moving so fast. The last thing he wanted to do was harm her in any way. His fingers found the petals of her flesh. They moved easily inside, sliding all around.

Her pussy was soft and wet. Ready for his cock.

He spread her wide, unable to wait. He usually had such patience, but now it was blown. He needed her.

She reached around him until her hands found his ass. Her nails sank in, giving him a little jolt of pain that quickly flared into pleasure. She wanted him, too. Belle was with him completely, touch for touch. That made him even more crazy.

He aligned his cock with her sweet opening and started to sink in.

So tight. As he pushed in, Kell closed his eyes in bliss. The plug dragged against his cock, adding another layer of sensation. It would feel the same way when they shared her, when his best friends were right here with him, pleasuring their woman.

Belle pushed up, forcing him in further. He knew he should take more control, but this was different. This was wild and candid, and he didn't want to change it. He wanted Belle fighting for her pleasure, for the sharp satisfaction they could find in one another's arms.

He loved the fact that every time seemed different with her. They didn't have to play the same way. They could explore, give in to their instincts and let their emotions guide them. There was no book he had to follow on the proper way to make love to Belle. They wrote it themselves with every joining, each time a new expression of his feelings for her.

"You feel so good." Belle looked up at him, desire softening her face.

He thrust deep, his heart thudding in his chest. Even as he penetrated her with slow, hard thrusts—one after the other—she looked up at him with such innocence and trust that she took his breath away. For the first time, he realized that he could take her every day of her life and she would still be innocent and beautiful to him. Belle's purity was soul deep. She loved with her whole heart, offering every bit of her gorgeous self, inside and out, to him.

"Stay with me." Belle held him tighter.

Though she asked him to be in the moment with her, the underlying question ripped through him. Stay with her—beyond now, beyond next week or month. Stay with her forever. He wanted to. Fuck, he wanted to be worthy of her, to be the man she needed him to be.

Kellan held her stare as he dove deep and watched as her eyes flared. She tightened around him, whispering his name like a plea.

Between the tight clench of her cunt and the drag of the plug, he couldn't last long. It was too good. Too right. The only things missing were his partners. He'd thought having her all to himself would be perfect, but he missed his brothers, his best friends. He and Belle were only a part of the puzzle. They weren't complete without Eric and Tate.

And then it didn't matter. Nothing did except for her as his balls drew up and his spine tingled. He thrust deep one last time, emptying himself with a shout. She followed him over with a whimper. Then he let himself sink against her, vowing to hold her as long as he could.

* * * *

Belle sighed and sank her fingers into Kellan's hair, reveling in the softness. It felt like dark silk. She breathed him in, his clean masculine scent mingling with the musk of their sex.

Her heartbeat pounded in her chest, the remnants of pleasure still running through her veins. She loved this time. She loved the sex, but she also craved the soft time afterward, when she was surrounded by her men.

Of course she only had one of her men this time, and if he had his way, she would only have him for a brief time.

Belle had decided that Kellan's way sucked.

Between reading the last entry in her grandmother's journal and looking back at her parents' miserable choices, she'd realized that nothing was certain—except that not fighting for love would lead to heartache. She'd been looking for proof that these three men would always want to be with her, that they would never leave. She'd demanded that the universe guarantee her happiness before she was willing to try grabbing it herself.

It was an arrogant thing to ask. No one got guarantees.

When she'd taken Tate's hand the night before, she'd finally realized something. Life was an adventure. It was mysterious and could be dangerous. And it was utterly meaningless without them by her side.

All of them.

Her grandmother had left her with far more than a haunted house. Instead, she'd left a legacy of words and pictures and the poignant sadness of her regret. Marie Wright had wanted to reach out to her son, but she'd been afraid for years. Then it had been far too late. Clearly, she'd thought she had more time, but the universe had other plans.

Life didn't care that she was afraid. Life moved on and it would leave her behind if she didn't make the choice to fight for her happiness.

Kellan didn't know it yet, but she wasn't letting him go without one hell of a fight.

With a long sigh, he rolled off her, taking his warmth with him. He sat up and dealt with the condom, tying it off and wrapping it in a tissue before throwing it into the small trash can by the nightstand. There was something wary about the way his back curved, as though he was trying to protect himself from something. From her.

"Are you going to walk away again?" Belle murmured. She could ask more delicately, she supposed. But he'd asked for her honesty. It was time he repaid the favor.

He turned back, his eyes hooded. "Why did you do this, Belle? Why send everyone away to be with just me?"

"I wanted to. I want to spend time alone with each of you. It doesn't have to be a crazy orgy every time we make love. Sometimes it can just be the two of us. Tate and Eric both get that. You're the only one who doesn't."

He sighed, but he lay back on the bed, working them both under the covers. "It's a bad idea. Eric might be fine for now, but Tate won't like it over time. It'll make him crazy. Unless you're planning on keeping this thing casual."

Kellan would probably love that, but she'd finally figured out that there was nothing casual about any of this. There was nothing casual about love, especially not the depth that she felt. They wanted her to treat sex with reverence. Well, for her, sex came with love, and her men were going to learn that.

"Tate is going to be fine once he realizes he's going to get what he wants. Mostly, I think he'll come to love New Orleans. We all have our flaws. One of his is a fear of changing his habits. He's a moody, broody man-child half the time, but I love him anyway. Eric can play the martyr to perfection. He won't tell anyone what he needs. I love him anyway, too. And you…"

"Don't say it."

She turned on her side, staring down at him. This was exactly the way to have this conversation, naked and with nothing between them. She needed to touch him, hold him. "Why not? You taught me to be honest. You taught me to take this seriously. I'm serious about this, Kellan. About us."

"I thought you were just playing around. I was under the assumption that you didn't believe a relationship with the three of us could work long term. I rather thought we were on the same page here."

"I'm still not sure it will, but how can I know if I don't try?"

Looking back, she saw that life hadn't taught her to try. She'd spent her childhood attempting to please a mother who had shut her out. She'd done everything she could to try to get Mom's attention after her father had died—for a while. Then she'd quit, resigning herself to loneliness and hurt. Was she willing to spend the rest of her life shutting out anyone who might want her because deep inside she was still that kid whose mother couldn't love her? She had to leave her childhood behind. Comfort the girl by embracing the woman she'd become.

And not everyone had abandoned her. Kinley had still stood by her. Her grandmother had remembered her. Her father had left her a life lesson, if she chose to see it. Would he be proud of the woman she'd become or would he be disappointed that she'd closed herself off?

If she never opened up, maybe she wouldn't feel pain, but she also wouldn't feel joy. Belle was rapidly realizing that joy was worth the risk.

So was love. Kellan had to see that.

"There are a lot of reasons I believed it couldn't work, but I was wrong. I thought I wasn't the woman who could heal you." She willed him to understand.

Kellan turned to her with a frown. "Love, it's not that."

"No, it's not. I realize that now, too. It's not that I can't heal the pain from your divorce. It's that you don't want to heal. You think you're safer in your nice little cocoon."

He frowned and sat up suddenly. "Cocoon? You make it sound like something pleasant, Annabelle. I assure you, it's not."

A hard edge sharpened his tone, letting her know that she was pushing his boundaries. He'd pushed all of hers, but she'd known he would probably react poorly. Still, she pressed on because this was too important to let go. "I don't think it's pleasant at all. I think it's lonely, but you've gotten to a comfortable place. I know because I did the same thing."

He huffed, sounding deeply frustrated. "Annabelle, you weren't wrong to think it couldn't work. You were just being realistic. Most marriages fail, and they only have two people involved. Putting four people in a relationship, much less any sort of marriage, makes it exponentially more complex."

She understood that he was attempting to protect himself, but she had to make Kell see that wouldn't lead to happiness. "So that means we shouldn't try? It's gotten easy for you to not try. I know that's the way it was for me. After my father died and my mother got lost in her own grief, I decided that I couldn't win, so I withdrew. That way I couldn't get hurt anymore. I thought it was better to be numb. It's not, Kellan."

He stood up and grabbed his boxers, shoving his legs into them. "I've never been anything but honest with you, Belle. I told you where this is going. I explained what I could give you."

The old Belle would have covered up and hidden, accepting that the fight was done. The new Belle could definitely kick the old Belle's ass.

She rose on her knees, giving him what she hoped was a spectacular view of her body. She was satisfied when he lost a bit of his normal grace and stumbled while reaching for his slacks. "You never lied to me, Kellan. But I think you're lying to yourself. I am the woman for you and you know it deep down. If you walk away from me, from this family we could have, you're going to regret it for the rest of your life. Do you want to know where this is going for me? What I intend to do?"

He jerked on his slacks, his face flushed, his every movement a testament to his anger. "Please, tell me, Belle. You seem to know absolutely everything. Enlighten me."

She ignored the sarcasm. He wasn't going to go down easy. She'd always known that, but she also didn't miss the way his stare found her breasts. And she definitely couldn't ignore the fact that he was already getting hard again. He had to carefully tuck his cock away.

"Here's how it will go, Kellan. I'm going to marry Eric and Tate, and we're going to live right here. You'll be more than welcome in my bed for as long as my husbands allow it. They'll never bar you for the same reason I won't."

A bitter laugh choked from his throat as he picked up his shirt. "And what reason is that? Because you like the D/s play, and I'm the only one whose been fully trained? You think they'll need me to train them for any length of time? Eric's already a good Dom. Tate can learn from him."

He didn't understand a thing and that made her soften utterly toward him. "No, they'll never bar you from our bed because they love you, too."

That made him stop. He stared at her, obviously at a loss for words.

Good thing she had plenty for them both. "I love you, Kellan Kent. I want to marry you and your best friends. But if you choose to hold on to what that terrible woman did to you, if you choose her over us, then I think you'll come and see us for a while. I think you'll go back to Chicago, but you'll visit. We'll come see you, too, and it could work the way you want it to...until we have babies. And we're going to have them, Kell. I want kids. I want to raise a crazy family, but I know that the minute I have that first child, you'll be gone. So I'll have to choose between you and having babies with the men I love."

"I'm not asking you to choose." The words rasped from his throat.

"Good, because you would lose, my love. I'm going to choose the future, even if it means putting you in the past. It will hurt like hell and I will love you until the day I die. I will always miss you and I will always wish that you wanted our family as much as we want you to be a part of it."

There was a suspicious sheen to his eyes as he stared at her. "That's not fair, Belle."

"Life's not fair, Kellan. And I'm not going to play fair with you. I'm going to fight dirty because this is the fight of my life. I love you. I'm going to tell you every day, all day long. I'm never going to let you forget it. And if you let that bitch win, if you walk away because you can't get over what she did to you...well, you should know that I'll still be here loving you. No woman in the world will ever love you the way I do. And you won't love anyone else the way you love me."

His head shook, seemingly interested in the floor suddenly. "I never said I was in love with you, Belle."

"Not aloud. But like I said, I think you're good at lying to yourself. Come back to bed."

Those words seem to jolt him, and he practically ran to the door. "I have to think, Belle. I didn't want to make this decision yet, but you pushed me. I just... I don't..." He plowed a hand through his hair. "I'm going out. I don't know when I'll be back."

"Kellan," she started, lunging closer. She wasn't sure she could stand to watch him walk away. She needed more time with him.

"No. You've said what you needed to say. Now I need time to figure out what the hell I'm going to do because you've put me in a goddamn corner. I don't need to hear another word right now." He walked out.

And Belle was alone. She stared at the door. Logically, she'd known he might get angry and leave, but somehow she hadn't really expected it to happen. Maybe she'd watched too many romantic movies or believed in too many fairy tales.

The reality was, she may have just driven him away for good.

Tears brimmed in her eyes as she climbed from bed. She hadn't meant to corner him, just let him know that her plans had changed and that she hoped he could be a part of them. Somehow she'd been unable go to Eric and Tate until she talked to Kellan. Her decisions affected him, too. And now, she'd probably ruined everything.

She forced herself to plod across the floor, dread and anxiety lashing her. She was weary, but resolute. She was going to move toward the future and make the best of it she could.

She opened the closet door to grab her robe—and she stopped short at the sight inside.

A small doll swayed from a tiny noose attached to the

rod. The doll had pitch black hair and dark buttons for eyes. Someone had sewn it a little outfit that looked suspiciously like something she'd worn a few days ago.

A chill swept through her as she realized she was looking at a voodoo doll of herself hanging, just like the Peterman girls had.

Her trouble wasn't over yet.

Chapter Seventeen

Eric hung up the phone and was just reaching for his notes when Kellan stormed by. Frowning, Eric paused and stared for a moment, noting the flushed grimace on Kell's face.

Damn it. That couldn't be good. He'd expected Kellan to take his time with Belle. Hell, he'd half expected to have to pull them off one another when the contractors returned. They'd designated this time for the two of them to be alone and to hopefully work through their issues. So why was Kell walking out?

Sir trotted in and jumped up on the couch. He was getting used to the mutt. The puppy had two levels of activity: full throttle or dead-ass asleep. Actually, Sir kind of reminded Eric of Tate. Since coming to New Orleans, his brainiac friend was either moody as shit or ridiculously happy.

Eric definitely preferred ridiculously happy.

"Hey, what crawled up Kellan's butt and died?" Tate asked as he walked in carrying two bags from a local electronics store. "I tried to talk to him, and he said he was going to get a drink. It's barely one o'clock. I thought he was spending the afternoon with Belle."

Something had gone very wrong to make Kellan rush out like that. "Maybe we should go check on her."

"No need. I'm fine." Belle stood in the doorway, lips turned down, shoulders slumped. She looked disheveled, delicate, and gutted. She'd thrown a robe on, but there was no way to mistake the sorrow in her eyes.

Eric's heart sank. He seriously thought about charging after Kellan and beating some sense into him. Letting Kellan spend alone time with Belle should have softened him up and helped change his very stubborn mind. Instead, it looked as if Kell had managed to break Belle's heart. Eric bit back a curse. Would Belle toss up her hands and say she was done with them all?

Mentally, he prepared the argument of a lifetime. He had to make her understand that whether or not Kellan stayed, he and Tate could form an unbreakable bond—if she let them. He intended to stay with her and make her happy. No fucking way was he going back to Chicago alone.

"Talk to me, baby."

"What do you have in the bags?" Belle asked, changing the subject.

Eric looked at Tate, who appeared just as tense as he felt.

With a sigh, Tate set the bags down and spoke carefully, as though trying not to upset her. "Just some new computer stuff. You know how I like to play around with all the new toys."

She gave him a sad smile. "I do. I thought you should know I found one of my own."

Belle dangled something from her hand. A doll formed of plain fabric with a bit of yarn for hair and two dark buttons sewn where the eyes should be. The doll was damn creepy. Whoever had made the thing obviously didn't believe in the pretty princess toys.

"Is that what I think it is?" Tate bit out.

Belle laid it on the desk, then joined Sir on the couch, scratching his belly when he rolled over. "If you think it's a voodoo doll, then you're correct."

"Your grandmother has voodoo dolls?" Eric frowned.

He thought she'd been a psychic.

"No." Belle shook her head. "Someone left this hanging in my closet for me. It's even wearing a replica of the same clothes I had on the other day. But I didn't see this when I got dressed this morning. Believe me, I would have noticed."

Eric stared, anxiety compressing his chest. His previous fear morphed into lava-filled. Someone was playing with them again, trying to frighten his woman away. "Hanging, you say? Like, by the neck?"

"Yep. From a noose." Belle looked every bit as pensive as she sounded. "I guess we should call the police again?"

Eric didn't see why. They hadn't done anything the first time, and based on the news, they were still mired in the madam murder case. "Let's take another look at Captain Ron and Mike because they've both been working in your bedroom and bathroom."

"And I took the draper up there so she could get a look," Belle added.

Eric shook his head. "She wasn't here when someone wrote the message on your wall. We need to figure out all the people who had access to the house on both instances."

"Or I could just install some hidden cameras and catch the fucker in the act." Tate pulled a teddy bear out of one of the bags.

"Am I supposed to cuddle with that?" Belle asked.

Tate started to fiddle with the bear, his fingers moving a switch. He opened his laptop and typed something into it. Less than a minute later, he turned the computer around and Eric saw himself on screen.

"A nanny cam?" Eric asked.

Belle peered over his shoulder. As she leaned in, she balanced her hand on his shoulders, and he was relieved she'd come to him for support. "This will be way more helpful than the voodoo doll. Where are we going to put it?"

Eric knew exactly where he wanted it. He turned when he felt Belle meander away. "This asshole seems to really like the master bedroom. I think we set up in there and watch who goes in and out. This way you can still have the house remodeled without us having to formally check everyone's backgrounds or kick them out altogether. We can monitor everyone's activity in your bedroom via our laptops. We'll know exactly when this sick creep goes in and what he does."

"God, I hope it's Mike so I can kick his ass," Tate muttered under his breath.

"You be careful. Both of you." She sent them stern glances. "I'll go along with this idea, but only if you promise not to do anything dangerous."

Something inside him eased, some kernel of doubt. She wasn't pushing them away or telling them to leave. The worst seemed to be over. Kellan had been an ass, but Belle wasn't letting another man affect her relationship with either him or Tate. He wound his arms around her, embracing her, adoring the warmth and feel of her. He loved how comfortable she'd become with his body and the fact that she no longer hesitated to show affection.

"Promise me," she demanded softly. "I couldn't handle it if anything happened to either one of you. Don't do anything reckless."

That was an easy promise to make. Eric had no doubt Tate believed it would be intensely logical to beat the shit out of the man who was trying to scare their girl. He felt the same. Nothing foolish about doing what made sense. "I promise."

Belle cocked her head and looked at Tate expectantly.

"I promise," he grumbled.

Eric elbowed his buddy. "Tell me what happened with Kellan."

Tate watched them with narrowed eyes. "Do we need to punch him, too?"

She softened against him, resting her head on his chest, seeking support and affection. "No. I told Kellan the truth about his future as I see it and explained how this was going to work from now on. I believe he's weighing his options, but you should know he's probably going to leave." She lifted her head, her expression filled with regret. "Maybe I shouldn't have pushed him."

Risking her heart only to have it stomped on was exactly what she'd been afraid of all this time. Eric hated to see Belle facing one of her worst nightmares, especially when one of their own had tossed it in her face.

He stroked her hair, trying to soothe her. "I'll talk to him."

"Don't. I knew I was taking a risk and that there was every possibility he would walk away, but I couldn't keep going the way we were. I need to move forward. We all need resolution. The decision has to be his, but he needed to know that I'm going to do everything I can to make sure my husbands are happy, and that means I'll only sleep with him when you two say it's all right."

Eric's heart nearly stopped. Had she said what he thought he'd heard?

"Belle?" As he moved to stand beside Eric, Tate fastened his incredulous stare on her. "You just said husbands."

She pulled back just enough to meet their gazes. "I love you. I was afraid for a long time, but I've learned that I can't live like that. What we share isn't just sex. We make love, and I want to honor that. I want to spend the rest of my life with you. I told Kellan I want him, too, but I'm going to move forward with you even if he refuses me."

No wonder he'd run out of the house like he was on fire. Belle had upended Kellan's whole world. Eric had no illusions about Kellan's feelings. The current arrangement suited him. Kell didn't have to make a commitment or even think about the future. He just had to watch over her and fuck her every night. Belle had changed the game.

Kellan's loss...but Eric celebrated his victory. This woman belonged to him and to Tate. It was about time she recognized that. He'd only known her for a year, but he felt as if he'd waited his entire life for her.

"You told Kellan you were going to marry us." He spoke the words slowly, savoring each and every one.

"Yes. If you'll still have me." The tremor in her voice told Eric that she was nervous.

He hauled her close again, pure joy in his heart. "Oh, I'm going to have you, baby. I'm going to have you over and over and over again, for the rest of our lives."

He felt her sigh in his arms and wondered how she could possibly have thought they would reject her. She was their whole world. He kissed her firmly, then allowed Tate to sweep her up in a bear hug. The big guy wore a huge grin as he whirled her around and finally planted his mouth on hers.

Their girl. Finally. Forever.

"We're getting married," Tate said, holding her close.

"You better marry me," she teased. "Because you've ruined me for all other men."

There would be no other men for Annabelle Wright. If Kellan was a stubborn idiot, then Belle would have to be satisfied with him and Tate. He vowed they'd make it worth her while.

Belle turned to them with a coquette's grin when Tate set her down. "We still have a little time, you know."

Heat darkened her eyes, and his cock was immediately engaged. "How long?"

She swayed to the door and lingered at the bottom of the stairs, giving them a sultry smile. "Long enough."

He chased her up the stairs, laughing with Tate all the way.

* * * *

Tate stared down at his fiancée. His almost-wife. God, Annabelle Wright was going to be his wife. How far he'd come. He'd grown up in a house utterly devoid of anything but intellect and duty, and somehow he'd found the one woman who could make up for everything he'd been denied before. He almost couldn't believe it, but the proof was lying there in his arms. Belle's eyes had closed after he and Eric had both taken her. She'd curled up next to him, and he watched her breathing turn slow and even. She slept, pressed against him trustingly. Afternoon light streamed in, caressing her mocha skin, making every inch of her gleam. She was so fucking beautiful. Even though he'd just made love to her, his cock was already straining to have her again. He would never take for granted that she was his. Every day, he intended to make sure Belle felt valued and loved.

He cuddled her close, loving the feel of her nipples against his chest. He wanted nothing more than to slide inside her again. Leaving the damn bed was the last thing he wanted to do, but work called. If they were going to renovate this big old house and make it a family home again, that was going to take money—lots of it.

On Belle's other side, Eric stirred and met Tate's questioning stare. "You going to set up the camera? We've only got about twenty minutes before the contractors return. I don't want to miss a chance to catch whoever is behind this shit."

The contractors would be here soon, and they only had three hours before their appointment with the medium. He had a plan to figure out who was trying to scare the hell out of Belle and he was eager to get started.

Then, they could focus on finishing the house, passing the Louisiana bar, and taking a long honeymoon, maybe a staycation in their new master bedroom and bath—just him, Belle, and Eric. He'd make the time to explore his new city—and his new wife. They'd spend lazy mornings in bed, learning every inch of Belle's gorgeous body. In the afternoons, they could hold hands and walk around, taking in all the famous New Orleans charm. Now that he was here with her and settled, it seemed right to make a fresh start at the beginning of their new life.

First, they had to take care of business.

"Yes. I hope we can catch the fucker today."

"Me, too," Belle murmured. "Let's end this because I want to feel safe in here again. I like this room best."

They'd all taken to sleeping in one of the guest quarters because Belle had bad dreams in the master bedroom. Hopefully the house "cleansing" would help cure her of that so she could feel comfortable enough to move back in here. It was the biggest of the rooms, the only one with a bed they all fit comfortably on. Though they were going to have to expand the closet.

Shit. He didn't like the thought of more work, but Belle really liked clothes and she would take up most of the space. His princess deserved a grand dressing room.

He kissed her lightly and rolled out of bed, not bothering with his own clothes. He didn't need them in this room. Once the contractors were gone, he intended to spend a good portion of his time naked—and keep Belle bare as well.

He'd brought up the nanny cam when they'd chased Belle up the stairs. The little teddy bear looked utterly harmless. A tiny camera dotted the bow tie around its neck that would catch the culprit on film. He placed it on the bookshelf next to a picture of Marie Wright and another woman. He glanced at it briefly, but then turned to study the layout of the room so he could position the bear for maximum visual coverage. He needed to capture an image of the sucker's face.

"Do you have to point that thing at the bed?" Belle asked, resting her head on Eric's chest.

He couldn't help but grin. "It's the best place. Anyone who walks in the room will have to walk by the camera. But beyond the practical, I think we should record our lovemaking. Baby, we could make so much money off a sex tape. You're so hot. I could call it Nerd Gets His Girl and it would be a best seller. Think of the download potential. We wouldn't have to work at all. We could just sit back and let the cash roll in."

"No!" She threw a pillow his way. Tate ducked and the pillow sailed by him, knocking over the nanny cam and the photo beside it. "I'm not making a sex tape."

He would have to work on her inhibitions because something about watching Belle on film got his motor running. But then, everything she did made him hot. She was it for him.

He reached down and picked up the pillow, tossing it back to his girl. He straightened the nanny cam and made sure it was switched on before picking up the frame. He was damn glad it hadn't cracked. Belle loved these old pictures of her grandmother. She hadn't spent time with the woman so Tate rather thought these pictures were Belle's way of making a connection. He glanced down at the picture in his hands.

Marie Wright was smiling at the camera, her arm around a younger woman. They were both in cocktail dresses and made up like they planned to hit the town. The blonde next to her seemed to be in her mid-twenties. Something about her looked very familiar.

Shocked, Tate stared at the photo, searching his memory. It was right there, on the tip of his tongue. A name. He knew that woman's name. Why would he know anyone Belle's grandmother had known?

"What is it? Did I break it?" Belle asked.

"No, it's just the woman with your grandmother looks familiar." Where had he seen her before? He couldn't put his finger on it, but he knew unequivocally that he'd met the woman.

Eric climbed out of bed, reaching for his pants. "I looked at another picture with her in the shot earlier, the one I set by the copy machine. It was taken in the late seventies, I'd guess. You weren't even born then. How would you know some psychic woman from New Orleans?"

There was something about the face. He'd seen those eyes somewhere. They were an odd color, almost turquoise. She was pretty, but there was something hard about her that he couldn't define. She would be in her late fifties today.

The name finally hit him. He'd been watching her picture on the television for weeks. He'd seen her as an older woman, the victim of a vicious murder and a whole lot of gossip.

"Holy shit. This is the madam. This is Karen Ehlers." So much fell into place. All the pictures Belle had found of her grandmother and the groups of beautiful women. He finally understood how her grandmother had really afforded this place. Marie had been a madam, then when she'd decided to retire, she'd sold the business to Ehlers. He opened his mouth, but Eric, who'd obviously just made the connection too, shook his head, his eyes wide with warning.

He and Eric had been best friends so long they sometimes didn't have to talk to communicate. That look on Eric's face was a stop sign. Do not pass go. Do not tell the secret.

Belle had never guessed her grandmother's past.

Eric had a point. Maybe telling Belle that her grandmother had been a prostitute wasn't the right move at this juncture. Their fiancée was just settling in and getting comfortable with her past. She was under a lot of stress and anxiety about the house, and now they were getting married. More stress. She didn't need to know anything except that her grandmother had loved her. He closed his mouth, and Eric gave him a supportive pat on the shoulder.

"That's very interesting. I suppose they were neighbors. I bet she had a lot of stories to tell," Eric said. "Why don't you put on some pants, buddy?"

He didn't want to. Eric was just going to have to get used to that because they had a girl now. It was perfectly normal for him to be naked around a girl. Sort of. He did sometimes struggle with social niceties.

324

Belle took the frame from his hands. Her mouth dropped open as she stared at the picture. "Oh, my god. That *is* her. That's the woman they're talking about on the news."

Tate shrugged it off. "Looks like your grandmother had some interesting friends."

And a whole bunch of employees who had specialized in giving dudes head. As family histories went, having a grandmother with a background in prostitution made her unique. He didn't really see a problem with it, but it might not be something they shared with their kids.

He thought back to the picture in the living room of Marie and all those gorgeous women. Who were prostitutes. When he really thought about it, those women spread joy. They performed a service. They were almost like ambassadors for goodwill.

Belle's eyes went wide. "Oh my god. They weren't just neighbors or friends. This explains everything. My father wasn't mad at my grandmother. He was embarrassed."

"What do you mean, Belle?" Eric asked benignly.

Tate thought that was a good ploy. Make sure Belle had reached the same conclusion they had before they opened their big mouths.

She ignored them both, shaking her head as she looked at the picture. "Grandma said she sold the business to one of the girls. Obviously, that girl was Karen Ehlers. Oh, my gosh. My grandmother was a madam. She just never stated that in her letters to my dad. She always talked about irritating clients or the ones who were kind to her. My dad grew up in a brothel. Wait. Do you think she just, like, ran the place? Or...?"

Belle looked a little shocked. Tate didn't want her upset.

"Absolutely," he and Eric said at the same time.

Belle rolled her eyes. "Oh, please. I wasn't born yesterday. You don't apply to be the manager of a brothel. You work your way up from the bottom, so to speak. She was a call girl. Clearly, a high-class call girl. Wow. I'm really shocked. Grandma was a bad, bad girl."

Belle bowed her head and her shoulders shook. Tate lunged at her, certain she was crying. Damn it, he shouldn't have said anything, just kept his big mouth shut. Belle hadn't needed this truth about her grandmother. They couldn't change it, and the knowledge didn't negate the fact that Marie Wright had adored her family.

She snapped her head up. Tate saw her laughing, her gorgeous body moving with the force of her amusement. God, she looked beautiful. "My grandma was a lady of the night. Holy crap."

Tate relaxed slightly. "Honey, it's obvious she loved you."

Belle met his gaze, her eyes soft. "I know she did. I've read her journals. She and my dad were estranged for years, but she loved him too. So very much. I think Grandma did the best she could. From what I can tell, she was an orphan herself. She got pregnant young, and my grandfather didn't want a family. So he left her alone and pregnant and she wanted to make the best life she could for her kid. And she did. He never went hungry or homeless. In fact, he went to the best schools. I loved my dad, but he was wrong to shut her out. I guess he wanted to distance himself from his upbringing and live a reputable life."

He pulled her close. "He wanted to do what was best for you, baby."

She nodded. "I know. But I've figured out that what society demands and what my heart needs aren't at all in synch. I finally figured out what I want to be when I grow up."

"And what is that?" Eric asked, getting close.

"Happy. I think that might be all that matters. I'm going to marry you both because I love you and you make me happy. I hope our kids don't react the way my dad did to my grandmother's choices, but I really think if he'd lived, he would have forgiven her at some point." She gave him a

326

brilliant smile. "So that explains a whole lot. I need to take a shower before the contractors come back and kick me out of the bathroom. Can someone figure out where Kellan is? I hate the thought of him being out there all alone, especially if he's drinking."

Eric nodded. "I'll find him. Tate can stay here and do the cleansing thing with you. I'll have a nice long talk with our partner."

Belle smiled and disappeared into the bathroom.

He held out his hand, shaking Eric's. "I'm going to set the camera up properly with a motion detector and attach the feed to our phones. We'll get a text when movement kicks it on. I'll set it to start running after Belle's ready."

"Perfect. I'll find Kell."

"Do what you need to in order to get his ass home and some sense into his brain."

If he couldn't, Tate knew Belle would always miss Kellan. Hell, he would miss the bastard. There would be a piece of them missing if Kellan wasn't with them. They would go on without him, but Tate thought they should at least try to talk some sense into him.

"Will do." Eric sighed and shook his head. "But please put on some pants."

Tate shrugged, promising nothing.

Chapter Eighteen

Eric stared at the bar where he'd tracked Kellan's cell phone. He was pretty sure the cell would be attached to Kellan since he never went anywhere without it. That made him easy to find.

The bar was a seedy little place a few blocks off the Quarter. Blinking neon lights illuminated the soft evening. It wouldn't have taken Kellan long to walk here, but he would bet every single step of the way had been hell on his friend. It had taken him away from the place—and the woman—he truly wanted. Eric had to believe that or his plan would be for nothing.

He texted Tate, letting him know he'd made it to the bar. Tate's deep need to always know where the people he loved were was slightly stalkerish, but it had proven to be helpful on more than one occasion, so Eric vowed to stop ragging on him about it. Tate was serious about his family and their well-being, and he trusted that Eric could bring Kellan home.

God, Eric hoped he was right. Otherwise, he was fairly certain the next time they saw Kellan would be when he bought them out of the firm. Then he would be gone.

If that happened, he was pretty sure Kellan would spend the rest of his life alone. He would take a sub here and there. He might find some partners he could have a beer with from time to time, but Kellan would retreat into his hard shell and never emerge again. Eric didn't want that for his friend.

Eric pushed through the double doors and looked around the place. It wasn't much better on the inside. It certainly wasn't the sort of place Kellan normally frequented. An air of weariness lingered, from the dim lighting and shuttered windows to the dark, stained carpet. It took his eyes a moment to adjust to the darkness, but he finally found the man he sought.

Sighing, Eric studied his friend of more than ten years. Kellan sat at the bar, hunched over the beer in front of him as if the weight of the world pressed down on him. Kellan looked like hell for once—a tough feat for a good-looking SOB. Normally, he appeared perfectly pressed, but his suit coat was missing, as was his ever-present tie. His shirt was wrinkled, too. But it was the look in his eyes that really stopped Eric.

Kellan Kent looked absolutely fucking lost. He hadn't looked this bad since right after his divorce. Eric winced.

Somehow, he had to make Kell see that Belle wouldn't hurt him the way Lila had. Something he said had to reach the stubborn ass. It had to be brilliant, too. Emotionally intelligent. *Shit.*

"You fucked up," was what actually came out of his mouth.

So much for emotionally intelligent. He slid onto the stool beside him, figuring he'd better try again. Sometimes he hated being the reasonable one. He wasn't always good at it. He used to be the jock. Football players weren't known for their dazzling communication skills.

"I know. You don't have to tell me that." Kellan grimaced and resumed staring glumly into his beer. "How did you find me?"

"Tate used an app to locate your phone."

"He has to have my password for that."

Eric just stared. "We're talking about Tate here."

"Fucker should have been a spy." Kellan took a swig of

his brew. "Remind me to get a new phone. Then none of you will be able to find me."

Kell didn't seem too drunk. He'd probably been nursing that same beer all afternoon. Eric would be happier if he'd been out getting shitfaced. It would mean his friend would be willing to give up some of his control. But that would never happen.

"No, you won't. You would hate changing phones. At the end of the day, I think you hate change as much as Tate does."

Kellan turned weary eyes on him. "What the hell is that supposed to mean?"

"It means you're set in your ways, my friend, and it's going to cost you everything. I don't think you're really ready to sever all ties to me or Tate. You're especially not ready to give Belle up. If you were, you'd be looking at New Orleans in your rearview mirror, not brooding in this shithole. You need to think about the future instead of being mired in the past."

Kellan tipped back his beer again and drained some, then took a long, settling breath. "She gave me an ultimatum. I don't take well to those."

That was news to him. "Did she? Tate and I heard a different version. According to Belle, she explained to you that we're getting married and you would be welcome to stay with us for as long as you like. That doesn't sound like an ultimatum. That sounds like an open invitation. She gave you everything you wanted."

"As long as you say it's okay. You *and* Tate." There was no way to miss the bitterness in his voice. It gave Eric hope.

Kellan was jealous, and that was a good thing. He could work with jealous. "Then what are you upset about, man? I've never cut you out. Tate won't do it, either."

He huffed a little. "Yeah, am I going to have to ask permission? Am I supposed to beg my way in every night?"

Eric sighed. Kell was going to heap on the drama. "I

haven't asked you to beg before. I wasn't planning on starting. What's really making you act like an asshole? Belle told you that you would be welcome. You can come and go as you please. That's what you wanted. Isn't it? No strings."

He didn't answer for a long minute. The bar got quiet momentarily as the jukebox shifted from jazz to the blues. The beat thudded through the place, setting the scene for Kellan's misery.

With a sigh, he shook his head. "I don't know what I want anymore."

Now, they were getting to the real problem. For a control freak like Kell, not understanding his world was bad enough. Not understanding what was going on in his head would be catastrophic. "You don't have to know this instant. You just have to come home and give it some time. That's what Belle is offering you."

Kellan shook his head. "There's no time. There's no way you're not going to marry her right away. You'll have her in front of a justice of the peace before she can change her mind."

"She's not going to change her mind." He knew his Belle. Now that she'd committed, she'd stay that way until the day she died. She would love them all with every breath and every beat of her heart. Now that she had agreed to marry him, he felt a deep conviction that everything would be all right. "We're still going to marry her as soon as possible. I think we've waited long enough. Even when we do, that won't change our offer."

Kell didn't appear to believe him. "If you say. And what about the firm? You're just going to throw out everything we worked for in Chicago?"

It hadn't been easy, but Eric had made his peace with that. He could find work here. "It's not as if Louisiana has met its quota for lawyers." And even if he convinced Kell to stay with them, he didn't see a reason they couldn't keep the branch in Chicago going, too. "I know she's asking us to uproot our lives and careers, and it's not easy. I think if we pushed her now, she'd return to Chicago with us. At the end of the day, she won't choose this place over her husbands. That's exactly why I'm going to move here. I'm going to support her and help make her dream come true, but if you'd rather go back to Chicago, do it. You can come and go from her bed as you please. You can run that office and visit us whenever you like. I'm not going to stop you. As long as Belle wants you around, I'll say yes."

A nasty frown crossed his face. "And what happens when you start popping out kids? She mentioned that would be an issue."

Eric leaned forward, getting a little angry himself. There was only so much he was willing to take. "I'm sorry. Did you mean to ask what happens when we decide to start a family?"

Kellan flushed guiltily. "Sorry. I really didn't mean any disrespect. I…I just haven't thought about a family in a long time. The idea of you and Tate starting one with Belle is disconcerting."

"You can't expect us to wait, man. We're not getting any younger." He was ten years older than his parents were when they had him. It was time for him to start building his future, and that began with Belle and some kids he could raise, mold, and love.

Kellan ran a weary hand over his face. "Well, I'm not ready—for any of this. I don't know if I'll ever be ready."

Eric had an easy answer for that. "No one ever is. No one. Do you think I'm ready for kids? It scares the holy hell out of me. What are we going to tell them? How are we going to explain the fact that they have a mom and more than one dad? We're going to have to try to fit in at PTA meetings and neighborhood block parties. The idea that we could make our kids' lives hard makes me sick, but that won't stop me from trying. Because I love that woman and I'm going to love our kids. After that, being ready has nothing to do with it. I'm just going to lead with my heart. But I think everyone who's ever had a kid worries about being a good enough parent."

"It's more complicated than that," Kellan shot back.

"Only if you make it that way. I think it's pretty damn simple."

"You don't understand what happened to me."

Frustration welled inside Eric. "I know exactly what happened to you. You were humiliated. You were betrayed. But most of all, you were embarrassed. And guess what? It doesn't matter. That's what you've never gotten. It doesn't change who you are to me, to Tate, or to Belle. You think you looked like a fool. You're wrong. We think Lila and your father are terrible human beings who didn't give a shit about you. None of that was your fault. Even if it had been, we wouldn't give a shit. We just love you. You're letting a woman who didn't give two shits about you—not even for one second—win over three people who have always loved you and always will. For a Dom, you sure are giving her all the power."

Kellan flushed, his mouth firming to a hard line. "I'm not giving her power. That's such a fucking simplistic thing to say. This is about more than just Lila."

"You're right. This isn't really about Lila at all. This is about *you*. You can walk away from what Lila did. You can even walk away from your father. You think it's Belle you don't trust."

Kellan slapped a hand against the bar, the sound jarring. "I trust Belle. I don't trust me."

Finally, he was being honest. "You blame yourself for everything, but it wasn't your fault."

"I should have seen it coming. I should have seen through her."

"You have to forgive yourself. God, Kellan, do you really think this self-flagellation hasn't affected the rest of us? You seem to think you're the one on the outside, but you're wrong. You are and have always been a part of this family, and we need you. You think your choice won't hurt anyone except you. You're wrong. And Tate and I will miss you. Belle will regret losing you until the day she dies. Here's what you really don't understand: our kids are going to miss you too because you would be a spectacular father."

Kellan closed his eyes, but not before Eric saw a sheen of tears there. He swallowed it down. "I don't have any idea how to be a father. Mine was such a crappy example."

It was easy to see he wanted it though. Eric relaxed. This wasn't a case of Kellan being stubborn. He was scared, but that wouldn't last forever. The situation called for a little patience and kindness. But then, he'd learned the hard way that patience and kindness were two requirements to make a functional, happy family.

"My dad was an asshole, too. He wanted to live through me. He expected me to do all the things he wasn't able to and he didn't care if I got hurt in the process. My last concussion put me in the hospital. My dad was there when I woke up, calling me a pussy and telling me to get my sorry ass back out on the field. I refused. He won't talk to me anymore. He didn't want a son, just a star athlete. He was a horrible role model. He taught me nothing about being a good parent. But he showed me exactly what *not* to do. I can figure out the rest because I'm going to love that kid like I love his mother."

Kellan set the beer down. "I don't know what to do. I…I care about Belle. I really do. You and Tate are the brothers I never had. I don't want to lose you all, but I don't trust it either. I couldn't make a lasting relationship with one person. How do I do that with three of you? If it falls apart, it will happen in spectacular fashion because of me."

Eric couldn't help but roll his eyes. "This will work because we all want it to. We're stronger than you think. Yeah, we're all broken, but we need each other. We prop each other up. Where one of us fails, the others take over. Belle needs all three of us. This family needs all of us, but you have to be willing to try, put some faith in yourself and us. More than anything, you have to forgive yourself or you will never move forward."

"I don't know that I can. How did I miss the signs? Hell, I knew the marriage wasn't normal. I knew I didn't even love her. I didn't even want to. Maybe that's the worst part; I wanted an easy marriage. We had the same goals. I wanted her to be a good political wife. I wanted her to be a good mom, but I expected any kids we had would be raised by nannies and likely go to boarding schools. I wanted us to have good sex. In exchange, I was willing to support her career goals. I thought we'd make a good team."

Eric couldn't imagine such a cold exchange of loyalties. He'd always known he wanted a real marriage, even if it was messy and hard. Before he'd really understood what love was, he'd wanted caring and kindness in his life. "I know you *think* you wanted that, but I firmly believe you would have found it empty and left anyway in the end."

"What if that kind of marriage is all I'm capable of? This is the first time in my life I've ever had a relationship with someone who wants something real from me. Not money or power. Not connections or my family name. Belle doesn't want a teammate. Belle doesn't care that I can take care of her financially. I sure as hell don't think Belle is going to want the same kind of childhood I had for our kids."

Eric ached for his friend, but he had to be utterly honest. "None of us wants that, man. What Belle requires from you is simple. She wants love and honesty. She wants to love you back and won't accept anything less than your all. But here's the thing: she'll give you everything she has in return. Always. She won't ever leave us. She won't cheat or stab us in the back. She would never whore herself for money or fame or anything the rest of the world can give her. Belle will love you for you. She'll do it whether or not you're brave enough to try. Just because you walk away, doesn't mean Belle will love you less."

"The sharing thing could make us all outcasts," Kellan

countered.

Eric was done with that argument. "I don't give a shit what others think. We'll make a great family. There will always be people who don't understand. I won't live my life by their standards. I want to live my life so fully that I have no regrets at the end. If you leave now, do you honestly think you'll never regret it."

"And if I fail? What if I'm only really built for the type of one-sided relationship my parents had?" Lines of worry creased Kellan's face as he spoke, the heavy weight of his fears apparent.

"How many close friendships does your father have?" He had to get Kellan to see he wasn't his dad. It was the only way they had a shot at moving past this problem. Kellan wasn't his father any more than any of them were the sum of their parents.

Kellan suddenly found his glass infinitely fascinating. "None. My father believed in allies and he would be loyal until he no longer needed them. Then he would walk away and never look back."

Rather like Kellan had done after law school. He'd found the woman he thought would be a perfect mate and he'd left Eric and Tate in the dust. He hadn't even invited them to his wedding. They had been the best of friends in college until Kellan had found a new life.

He would have been alone from that point on if Eric hadn't reached out to him after the divorce because Tate had found the article about it online. Tate hadn't called because he'd assumed that if Kellan needed him, Kellan would say something. Eric had known better, so he'd been the one to reach out. The two of them had worked together to help Kellan in his time of need.

Friendship was a delicate balance. Today proved it all over again.

"Is that what you're planning on doing? Walking away and never looking back?" Eric knew the answer, but Kellan needed to figure it out for himself. Then what?

After a long pause, Kellan turned his way. "I might not be able to live the kind of life Belle needs, but I can't just walk away. Whatever you need, all you have to do is call me. I'll stop whatever I'm doing. If I'm somewhere else, I'll come to you. I will never let you down. I'm done with that."

Because they were family. "Come home with me. If we're all committed, we'll work it out. Just give it some time."

Kellan finally nodded. "All right."

* * * *

Belle answered the door, eager to get the evening's meeting over with. The contractors had come and gone, and nothing had been settled. No one had tripped the cameras, so they still didn't have any evidence. Belle found the not knowing so frustrating, especially when all she wanted to do was bask in the glow of her new future, glimmering just over the horizon.

Of course, that future would be dimmer if she couldn't have all of her men.

Eric had left a while back. Perhaps he would find Kellan and bring him home. Then they could talk everything out. Or maybe she would just make love to the man until he couldn't walk. She could completely exhaust him so he couldn't run. That would be one way to keep him close.

"Annabelle Wright?" The woman was younger than she'd seemed on the phone. Somehow, Belle had thought she would be more like her mother's age. The face that stared back was perhaps a year or two older than her own. She was dressed in a business suit and carried a briefcase. Her blonde hair was in a careful bun.

All in all, not what she'd thought a medium would look like.

"Yes. Won't you please come in?" The faster she got

this started, the quicker she could set the scene for Kellan. Seduction might be the best way to go. She'd been honest with him about what she wanted. He knew the score. She could see if an enormous amount of really filthy sex would help him see that she could be his kind of woman. Now that she knew exactly what she wanted, she found herself eager to start making a home with her men.

The medium stepped through, her nose wrinkling delicately. "I'm Helena Rhodes. So you've been having issues with the house. I'm really not surprised. It's a bit infamous. Rumor is, there've been several suicides here, and some people who owned the house afterward complained of disturbances and unexplained activity."

Belle was fairly certain some of her issues were entirely human, but she couldn't ignore the feelings she got in the house. There was no way the shadow that had passed through her the night before had been human. There was definitely a presence or two in the house. Hopefully between the nanny cam Tate had set up to catch whoever was trying to scare her away and Helena, she could finally get some help on the ghost front. "Yes, we've had several incidents. There are cold spots all over the house and I can hear whispering at night when I sleep in the master bedroom. It always stops the minute I get out of bed. Did Tate explain what happened last night?"

Helena looked around the foyer, one brow elegantly arched. "I was told you were visited by an entity. It doesn't surprise me. I can feel it from here. There's a lot of darkness in this house. Do you know the full history of the house?"

Belle nodded as the medium walked into the hallway. "I've done some research. I know two young women supposedly killed themselves here. Two sisters."

Helena turned back, her eyes slightly narrowed. "Supposedly? You think you know something different?"

"I think they were murdered by their father." She'd seen it over and over again in her dreams. She'd even read some reporter's theories on the incidents. Her grandmother had also written about the house being haunted in her journals. She had never had the place cleansed because she'd attempted to communicate with the entities. Her grandmother had believed that all the women in her family had a touch of psychic power and owed it to the world to help the dead to move on.

Of course, her grandmother had also said that the ghosts of this house were terrifically stubborn.

Belle really hoped the medium knew what she was doing.

Sir scampered into the room, giving a little yip at her feet.

Helena stared down, then lifted her nose in the air. "No one mentioned an animal."

Belle frowned. Apparently, Helena wasn't a dog person. "He's actually been really helpful since we moved in. I'm pretty sure he knows when the entities are around. I think there are a couple of ghosts here. One is really nasty and likes to hang around the library. Sir won't go in there. He just stands outside the door growling sometimes. Sir here seems to like the one who drifts around. That one he follows around most of the day. It concerned me at first, but he's happy enough. There's a place upstairs he doesn't like, right in front of the master bedroom. He'll bark at it from time to time. I think it might be the spot where the girls were murdered. They were found hanging from the third floor staircase."

"Well, he's a dog. I think I should be the one to decide how many entities and what they're like. I'm the one with experience." With a sigh, she set her case down and pulled out her cell phone. She flicked her hand across the screen, either texting someone or writing an e-mail. "I have an associate coming with the rest of my equipment. I wanted to get a feel for the place before I set up. Is everyone gone? I was told you live with several men."

Belle was starting to think she should handle this herself

since the medium seemed awfully judgmental for someone who talked to the dead. "It's just me, Tate, and Sir tonight. The others are out for the evening."

Tate chose that moment to step out of the kitchen. He smiled and looped an arm around her shoulders. "Hey, are you the one who's going to de-ghost us? Because we could use it. I just got that blast of cold air thing. It's freaky. It's unseasonably hot. I shouldn't be scrambling for a sweater. Also, I'm pretty sure one of the ghosts keeps patting my ass. That weirds me out a little, but I do understand it. I really work on these glutes."

The medium stared at them, looking just shy of annoyed. "You should have told me there were extra people here. I explained that I need the house cleared. This is going to work best if there are no disruptions."

Tate seemed utterly unfazed by the woman's obvious irritation. He simply smiled. "This is as cleared as we get. Trust me, this is quiet for us. It's usually a madhouse. I'm surprised we don't scare off the ghosts. I turned all the ringers off on our phones so we shouldn't have a ton of noise."

Helena was texting again, her fingers moving in an almost angry fashion.

The hair on the back of Belle's neck started to stand up. Something was off about the medium. She seemed stiff, and there was something about the way her eyes darted around that made Belle wary. Helena kept looking from her phone to the door as though she couldn't wait for her assistant to show up.

Perhaps the house was overwhelming her?

"Can I get you a drink? Anything while we wait?" She had to give the woman the benefit of the doubt. Sometimes the house seemed oppressive to her, and she wasn't even psychic.

Helena's jaw tightened. "No. Perhaps Tate here could take the dog for a walk. It really would be better if we were alone. I sense this spirit doesn't appreciate the presence of males. Yes. Please take the dog out the back and give us an hour or so."

Tate's hold tightened and he looked down at Belle. "Is she serious? I mean I know they cleared the place out in *Ghostbusters* but that was because they were worried about crossing the streams. I don't think we're worried about that here. I'd rather stay with you."

Sometimes it was hard to keep up with Tate's pop culture references, but he was on par now.

"I'd like you to stay as well. Sometimes, the house scares me," she lied.

Something told her not to separate from Tate. Besides, Helena seemed to have it wrong. The ghost hadn't been bothering the men. Every instinct she had told her the malevolent spirit had a problem with women.

"Then I'm not going anywhere. The ghost will just have to deal," Tate pronounced. He turned to Helena with a shrug. "And so will you. I understand if you can't work under those circumstances. We can find someone else."

Helena held up a hand. "No. I'll work around it."

There was a brisk knock on the door, and Tate walked toward it, his hand outstretched.

"That's my assistant," the medium explained quickly. "Let him in. Just tell him to set up, starting in the bedroom."

"But the library is the worst room," Belle began. Something chilly ran through her, causing her to shiver. Something was wrong. So wrong. Her heart started to race— and it was all centered around that door. Instinct flared inside her. "Tate, don't open that door!"

But he'd already had the knob turned. Belle watched in horror as a man's silhouette loomed in the doorway.

"Oh, crap. Not you again. What do you want?" Tate groused.

Her grandmother's lawyer stepped up, leveling a gun at Tate's chest. "I want to get this piece of shit job done."

There was a tiny ping.

Tate turned to her, his eyes wide. He pointed toward the back of the house. "Belle, run."

There was an odd capsule-like dart sticking from his chest. Tate took a single step in her direction before his face went slack, his eyes rolling to the back of his head. Tate went down hard, his big body sliding to the floor.

What the hell was going on? Belle screamed as the man pointed the gun her way.

Chapter Nineteen

A hand clapped over her mouth, stopping Belle in mid-scream. Something hard pressed between her shoulder blades.

"Shut up or he'll hit your boyfriend again," the so-called medium hissed into her ear. "And I'll have to put a bullet in your spine, too. I don't want to do that, so you'd better stay calm."

The world seemed to have stopped as she turned to stare at Tate's unmoving form. Was he dead? How could he be gone? He'd held her not an hour ago. He'd promised her a life together, that he'd never leave her. How could it be over? Would she end up like her mother, mourning and bitterly shutting out the other survivors?

Tears made the world blurry as Belle stared at Tate, willing him to live. Then Gates stepped over his prone body and into the light.

Her grandmother's lawyer was dressed in all black, looking totally unkempt. All traces of the polished professional he'd been before were gone. He'd always put off a weird vibe, but now, with his fierce frown, he was downright nasty.

What was he doing here with a gun?

"Move him out of the way," Gates sneered with a glance at Tate. "We'll need to stage this properly, damn it. He's a complication we didn't need." His cold eyes raked the woman behind Belle. "You said she would be alone."

Sir scampered over to Tate, sniffing and whimpering as he tried to rouse his master. The puppy whined and looked to Belle, as though she could fix the problem. She wished with everything in her heart that she could because Tate still wasn't moving. Fear spiked through her veins. She needed to get to him, but the supposed psychic gripped her too tightly. Belle's brain whirled. What the hell was going on here?

Helena huffed. "She was supposed to be. I told the man who called to make the appointment with me that the house had to be cleared. It's how I usually work. It's way easier to con a single person than a whole group. There's almost always a skeptical friend the mark will bring along, if you let her."

So Helena wasn't a real psychic? Why had Mike recommended her? And why was she here with Gates? Had her grandmother's lawyer been behind the attempts to scare her off all along?

"You?" she asked him in horror.

"Me," he said simply.

"W-why?"

Gates stopped in the middle of the hallway and checked his gun. "Your grandmother had information I need. I've had this place bugged for years, hoping I'd figure out where she kept it hidden. Eventually, I figured out that she passed it on with the business she sold. But Karen brought it to her in the end. She considered the bitch her mentor or some shit. In fact, she came here at least once a week, but they talked mostly about the old days and their families, even the fucking weather. I think they knew someone was listening in."

Belle bit her lip to hold in a gasp. Grandma's own attorney had been spying on her?

"Are you going to do your job?" Gates asked Helena in a sour tone. "If not, I could have you tossed in jail. My client can make that happen, you know. He's a very important judge. He has favors he can call in everywhere. If you turn on me, you won't see the light of day for a long time, you con artist."

Belle really didn't know what they were talking about, but it all sounded ominous. Two against one, and they had weapons. The odds weren't looking good.

"Like I said, I'll do the job," Helena shot back, and Belle didn't think she meant cleansing the house of spirits. "I have zero interest in going to jail. I don't look good in orange. Where's your friend? I told you how we should set this up. I studied up on the suicides and the haunting. We can set this up to play straight into the legends about this place."

Meaning that someone would have to die by hanging, like those two Peterman girls? Belle's blood ran cold.

Gates nodded. "Everything we need is on its way. I told him to park far from the house so no one remembers his truck being here this evening. We'll set everything up right. But first I need to get that list. You know what could happen if that fucking thing gets out. It would ruin my client and many of his very powerful friends."

"I'm sure," the medium murmured. "Tell me something, Gates, are you on that list, too?"

What list did they keep referring to? Was that the all-fired important information Gates had been spying on her grandmother to obtain?

Sir suddenly barked, and Belle felt a chill pass through her.

The woman behind her shivered. "Fuck, I hate this place. If I didn't know better, I would say it's actually haunted."

Gates barked. "You bought the act, too? Christ, I'd have thought you were too jaded to believe in things that go bump in the night. This place is no more haunted than my ass."

So his refusal to step foot in the house earlier had all been an act? Belle felt foolish for having fallen for it.

Helena looked skeptical. "Just walking in here makes me sick. We need to get this done as quickly as possible. What are you going to do with that guy? Is he dead?"

The door opened again, and all of Belle's questions about who had left her the frightening messages since her arrival were answered. Mike, the electrician, stepped in, carrying a heavy bag. No wonder he'd recommended Helena. They were all in this together.

Mike blanched and clenched his fists when he saw Tate lying in the hallway. "You said no one would get hurt."

"Oh, boohoo. So I lied." Gates rolled his eyes. "He's alive. I just hit him with a tranquilizer. I brought it along in case Miss Wright proved difficult, but now we've got to figure out how to include him in the scenario. I think I have a way to make this work. Hand me the gun."

Mike set down the bag and Gates exchanged his tranquilizer pistol for what looked like a real semiautomatic.

Belle glanced Tate's way and her heart soared. Finally, she saw what she'd been looking for: Tate's chest rising and falling slightly. He was alive—at least for the moment. Hope flared inside her. There was still a chance to save him. She'd have to get out of this mess first.

Gates moved into her space. "Yes, Miss Wright. Your lover is still among the living, but if I hit him again, I assure you his status will change. This one fires bullets. If I hit him in the chest now, he won't get up again. You don't want that, do you?"

Belle shook her head. Tate's death would devastate her.

"Excellent." A reptilian smile passed over the lawyer's face. "Then you're going to cooperate with me. If you tell me where the list is, I'll make sure this goes easy and quick. We'll finish our business and be out of your hair."

The only thing quick and easy would be her murder. There was no way he could leave her alive after all she'd heard. He'd just committed assault and threatened murder. Now he meant to burglarize her home. He'd admitted to planting listening devices around the house and spying on her grandmother for years for his client, a powerful and obviously corrupt judge. There was no chance he'd let her live. But he needed her cooperation before he offed her.

She just needed to buy some time to hatch a plan or give Eric a chance to get home. "Of course I'll help you. Just please don't hurt him again."

She had no idea what drug they'd given him. He could have a bad reaction to it. As still as Tate was now, if they even gave him another dose, he might overdose. It could kill him. He looked so vulnerable, and Belle knew that only she stood between Tate and death.

"Stop yakking and hurry up." Helena loosened her hold. "I want this over with. The other two men are out, but I don't know for how long. We need to be gone before they return. Why are there so many men living here anyway?"

Gates sneered Belle's way. "Because she's a whore, just like her dear old grandma. You do know your grandmother ran a house of prostitution, don't you? But when she retired, she sold it to her protégé."

"Karen Ehlers?" The infamous madam. Several things fell into place, and Belle got an inkling of what they were looking for, but it was probably in her best interest to play dumb.

"Yes, Karen Ehlers." Gates nodded toward Mike. "Get set up while I talk to our friend here. You know what to do."

Mike looked a little green in the dim light of the hallway. His hands shook as he held his bag and walked toward her. "I just want to go home, man."

Gates wouldn't back down. "If you don't do what I tell you to, you'll go to jail. Did you forget that I have your parole officer in the palm of my hand? One word to him, and you go back to prison. I know how life was for you there. You spent a lot of time being passed around, didn't you? Maybe you liked it. Is that what you want? Do you want to be someone's bitch again?"

Mike came to stand in front of her, his face hardening as he obviously made his decision. "I'm sorry, Annabelle. I don't want to do this, but I'm on parole. He works for people who can send me back to jail. I can't go back. Give him what he wants. Please."

Mike walked away, his footsteps heavy on the stairs.

Gates got in her face. "I want the list, bitch."

Belle's brain went straight back to her first night in the house. She'd found a weird list written by two different hands in the desk, along with her grandmother's journal, in some sort of hiding place. She'd taken the journal, but put the list back because it had seemed like nonsense at the time. It was very likely some sort of code written by Grandma and Karen Ehlers. Their client list? She wasn't sure, but that seemed likely, given how badly Gates wanted it.

Her grandmother and Karen Ehlers would need some way to keep track of their transactions. Maybe they'd even dealt in information as well as pleasure. According to the news, Ehlers had decided to write a tell-all book. To ensure her retirement? Had someone learned of her plans and silenced her for good?

"What list?" She couldn't let on that she knew where to find it. *Play dumb. Buy yourself time.*

Gates slapped her face. A hard crack rent the air before the pain bloomed in her cheek. Belle bit back a groan because her skin was on fire—and not in a nice way. The difference between violence and what her men shared with her was massive. They were careful to bring her up to the edge of pain. Gates just wanted to torture her.

"Give me what I want or it gets worse from here." Gates smacked her again, and she couldn't stop her startled gasp. "Your grandmother started a list of clients, then sold it to Karen Ehlers with the business. I have every reason to believe it's in this house. I want it now."

She cupped her hot cheek. "Why would it be here?"

"Because Ehlers told me she gave it to Marie before she died. Your grandmother was her momma whore. When Karen got worried about her safety, she hid it here, a sort of insurance policy. You might have heard that Karen had decided to write an exposé. She thought that list would ensure that no one came after her, a sort of mutually assured destruction. She promised not to use real names, but everyone would have figured out her clients' identities."

Belle shrank back. "I don't know anything about it. I only met my grandmother once, when I was a child. We didn't keep in touch. I was surprised she wrote me into her will at all."

Gates frowned. "But you've been living here. You must have seen something. I found a draft of that Ehlers bitch's actual manuscript. She'd written the part that identified her clients and their sexual preferences in code, based on that list. I destroyed the manuscript and all the electronic copies of it I could find. I need to do the same with that fucking list. The elite of New Orleans are on it, and being exposed would ruin them."

Belle wasn't so sure about that. New Orleans wasn't exactly known for being uptight and prudish, but Gates clearly wasn't willing to take any chances.

And that was when she remembered the camera.

If she could trip the motion detector, at least she could capture her attackers on video and they would be identified. They wouldn't get away with murder. And leading them upstairs would take them further away from Tate. She had no idea how long it would take him to metabolize the drug, but she didn't like that gun being so close to his helpless form.

"I haven't found anything like a list." The minute she gave it up, they were both dead. She couldn't imagine how Eric and Kellan would cope if they had to walk into this house and find her body, along with Tate's. They would be devastated. She had to fight for every second.

"Well, that is very bad for you," Gates snarled, raising another hand to her.

She raised her hands to ward him off. "But I haven't searched her bedroom."

Gates's eyes narrowed. "You've been sleeping there."

She shook her head. "No. Not since the first couple of nights. I moved into one of the smaller rooms because I couldn't sleep in the master. I heard voices."

Gates chuckled, a nasty sound. "Yes, I had Mike set an audio device in the ceiling above the bed. It was tripped after the light was off and the room went still. The device would whisper when you were asleep and turn off the minute you moved. It was supposed to make you want to move."

Clever, but she would try to use it to her advantage. "It scared me. I didn't like to go into that room, but I know my grandmother kept a lot of very personal things in there."

She'd found pictures and a box of little keepsakes. The closest was big, and Belle hadn't even started to clean it out yet. There were storage boxes under the bed, as well. With any luck, she could keep them upstairs and searching for a very long time.

Gates nodded toward Helena. "You look through the office and the library. I'll take her upstairs. Don't make a mess. Our scenario is not a burglary. The last thing I need is for the cops to go over this place with a fine-tooth comb."

Helena let her go, obviously secure in the fact that Belle had another gun pointed straight at her chest. "I thought you had your interns looking through there last week."

So that's why he'd insisted on "taking inventory" of everything in the house. They might have looked through drawers and rifled through closets, but they had obviously missed her grandmother's hidey-hole.

"I couldn't actually tell them what I wanted them to find. I told them to bring me anything that looked like personal notes because Marie Wright might have jotted additional instructions about the division of her estate. Of course, the idiots didn't find anything. Start looking for hidden compartments," he instructed Helena. "Wright was a whore for a long time. She ran a brothel herself. She knows how to keep a secret."

"What about him?" Helena frowned as she looked toward Tate's body.

Gates waved off the worry. "He'll be out for hours. Don't worry about him."

As her grandmother's lawyer marched her up the stairs, Belle prayed Tate had the chance to wake up again.

* * * *

Kellan shuffled along the sidewalk, wondering if he was doing the right thing. It might be best if he just walked away. Belle needed a man who had a whole heart to give her, and he wasn't sure he'd even been born with one.

Fucking coward. Eric's right. You like things easy. You like not having to open yourself up. You're so fucking scared, you're going to let the best thing that ever happened to you slip through your fingers.

He might not have been born with a whole heart, but his inner voice seemed to be totally intact and brutally honest.

Eric stopped at the small gate that separated the courtyard from the street. The moon had come out, washing the brick in a silvery glow. He never noticed the moon in Chicago. Somehow it seemed bigger in New Orleans. The air felt heavier, almost mysterious, but there was a sweetness to it. And the heat seemed to seep into his bones, drugging him until all he wanted was to toss off his clothes and be naked with Belle. If he stripped down, past his clothes, past his skin, if he offered her every piece of himself, would it be enough? Could Belle heal that essential piece of him that had been damaged for so long? He'd long thought that a part of him was missing, but now he wondered if maybe what he'd always been missing was Belle herself. What if that crap about soul mates was true and he wouldn't ever feel whole without her?

The thought of her holding a baby conceived from their love did weird things to him. His gut tightened and turned, then did a little dip that didn't feel at all like anxiety. It felt more like anticipation. Hope.

He would be a terrible dad. Wouldn't he? But was he really willing to leave a child alone with Tate, who would have that kid geekified and speaking nerd before he even had a chance. Tate would dress his kid in snarky T-shirts and sweatpants that may or may not be clean.

And Eric? Eric would try to teach the kid to get along with everyone. Eric's willingness to compromise was a necessity to making this relationship work, but who would help the kid learn to stand up for himself, to protect his mom and siblings? Who would teach him how to throw a decent punch?

Eric would teach him to toss a football, while Tate would instruct him on the finer points of wielding a lightsaber.

Maybe he wasn't so unnecessary after all.

"You're thinking about something serious, man. Want to talk about it before we go inside?" Eric asked.

Yep. Eric would teach the kid how to express his feelings. That was nice and all, but there were times to man up and just do something.

Except he wasn't sure he was ready.

"Nope." He hated the way Eric's eyes tightened in disappointment. "Just give me a little time, okay? I need a day or two. I don't process shit like this the way you do."

"Shit like emotions?" The dry tone of Eric's voice made him smile tightly.

"Yeah. Shit like emotions. Just give me a day or two."

Eric sighed. "Fine. Take some brooding time. Just know that I'm willing to talk to you whenever you want. I know it probably sounds dumb, but you really will feel better if you talk it out. If it makes you more comfortable, I'll find us a gym and we can spar while we talk."

Punching and talking. That might actually work for him. "Okay." It would do him good to get out a little aggression.

"Only if I can work Tate over, too."

Eric chuckled. "Oh, I think Tate would love to beat the fuck out of you for a while."

It was what men did, what brothers did. It was what he'd never done. In the past, a fight meant an ending. It had never been simply a way to work through conflict. Any fight had been nasty, low down, and permanent.

His family could be different. *He* could be different, better.

"I think I might love her," he admitted quietly.

Eric's smile nearly lit up the night as he slapped him on the shoulder. "Of course you do. She's incredibly lovable, man. She's the best thing that's ever happened to any of us. She's the one. And the best part is that she wants all of us, too. We can have everything we've ever dreamed of. All we have to do is reach out and take it."

A buzzing sound emanated from Eric's phone. Frowning, he pulled it out of his belt clip and studied it.

"What is it? Belle calling?" Kellan asked, more than a bit hopeful.

He liked the idea that she wanted to know where he was or wanted to know what he was thinking, feeling. He wasn't used to having anyone give a shit when he came home. He would have to change if he stayed. He would have to check in and let his family know where he was all the time. It wasn't enough that Tate would likely hack into a satellite and direct it at all of them twenty-four seven. Kell needed to show them that he cared by checking in.

"No. It's not Belle. It's a nanny cam alarm Tate set up. We placed it in the master bedroom, and it's alerting me that something just triggered." Eric flicked a finger across his phone. "Weird. I thought we agreed not to go in there. All the contractors should be gone by now."

"You set up a camera? In the master bedroom? Did Tate find more bugs in other rooms?"

A massive wave of guilt crashed against him. He'd

walked out when Belle was still in some sort of danger. They couldn't be sure of when those bugs had been placed there. Tate suspected they'd been planted in the house a while back, but who knew for certain? Someone was trying to scare Belle, and no matter what she'd seen in the library, he couldn't accept that a ghost had left a message on her bedroom wall from beyond.

His departure at such a critical time proved how selfish he could be.

Kell had a sudden and deep need to see her. He might have no real right to do it, but he wanted to hold her in his arms. To apologize.

He glanced up at the house as they walked through the gate and into the courtyard. The glow of a light illuminated the living room, and a lithe figure moved across the shade, a shadow that was an illusion. His Belle wasn't that twiggy. She was solid and sexy as fuck. But then again, shadows could be distorted.

"I think Belle's in the living room. Do you think Tate's upstairs?" Kellan asked.

"Maybe." A concerned frown crossed Eric's face. "They were supposed to be with the medium, who was cleansing the house. Why would they split up? Belle was a little scared about the whole thing. That's why I left Tate with her. I didn't want her to be alone with anyone we don't know."

Kellan walked faster toward the house. Something wasn't right. He didn't like it. The sooner he saw Belle, the better he would feel. He was going to talk to her, try to get her to go back to Chicago. Not forever, just until they caught whoever sought to scare her. Wouldn't Belle have a few things to clear up at her old apartment or something? He would bring her back to New Orleans, to her new home, when they were all certain it was safe. They could call in the guys from Anthony Anders. Surely, Dominic, Law, and Riley could figure out what was going on.

He strode toward the door, Eric right behind him. As he

clasped the knob, something stopped him. The air around him became icy cold, his breath visible, despite the fact that the humid autumn evening was well above freezing.

Something moved through him that made him shiver. He felt his spine ping with fear. He could only focus on one thing: Belle. He wasn't sure why being cold made him so very aware of her. Then he heard a whisper in his head.

Save Annabelle.

"Belle's in trouble," he murmured just above a whisper.

The more he thought about it, that hadn't been Belle in the window. The medium might be in the house, but why wasn't his love with her? He suddenly felt certain that whoever he'd seen in the living room was dangerous. That woman threatened Belle.

"Open the door quietly." Eric's voice was low, tense. "Stay next to the wall. The floor creaks in the middle. God, I hope you're wrong, but I feel like she's in danger, too. I can't explain it."

Because some things defied logic. This was one of them. So was love. Reason told him to deny it, but his instincts were too pure, too strong. He might end up looking like a fool for bursting in on the house cleansing, but he'd look like an idiot a hundred times over to keep Belle safe because nothing was more important than Belle.

That truth hit him like a sledgehammer.

Kell turned the doorknob, his heart threatening to pound out of his chest. Unlocked. He prayed the creak of the old metal and wood wasn't as loud as it sounded in his head.

His warning instincts went off again when he remembered that Belle always locked the door behind her. She'd lived for far too many years in big cities to ever get into the habit of leaving any door to the outside unlocked.

He pushed the door open, anxiety churning. He had to be quiet, had to get into the house without anyone knowing it. Surprise was his only weapon.

The first thing he saw made his blood go cold.

A big body on the floor, crumpled and still.

Tate.

Kell barely managed to restrain himself from running over to his friend. Dread torqued up his gut. Not knowing if Tate was alive ate at him like he'd swallowed battery acid.

"Fuck." Eric cursed quietly behind him before he stepped back outside.

There was no question he had to call the cops, an ambulance—anyone who could help them. He couldn't wait. They all knew the drill. Call for help, then intercede until reinforcements arrived. Kellan would do just that, fight until his dying breath.

He tiptoed over to Tate and dropped to one knee, his whole body tense. God, what was he going to do if his friend was dead? The thought was surreal, unimaginable.

He put a hand on Tate's body. He was still warm. Kellan couldn't see any blood visible, but there was something sticking out of his chest. A dart of some sort.

Tate's chest moved slightly in a shallow attempt to breathe.

He was alive, but he'd been hit with some sort of tranquilizer. Who the hell was here? What the fuck did they want? Where was Belle?

"Is he alive?" Eric whispered, his voice shaking. He was pale as he stared down at his best friend.

Kellan nodded. "Yes. Cops?"

"On their way," Eric breathed.

"Go around the back of the house and see if you can figure out where Belle is." Kellan reached into the antique umbrella stand by the door. He pulled out a sturdy-looking umbrella and wished he knew exactly what to do in this situation. His friend Dominic Anthony would. He'd bet Dominic never got caught without a weapon. He would never have to defend his woman with a freaking umbrella.

"Will do. If you can, search the third floor. Something tripped that camera," Eric suggested, then slipped out the door again.

The master bedroom. Of course. The alarm had gone off on Eric's phone. He had explained the whole nanny cam plan to catch whoever was stealing into the room and leaving Belle frightening messages during their walk home.

Someone had taken Belle upstairs.

A million horrifying thoughts ran through his head. Why? What were they doing to her? Was she silently crying out for him? Was she hurting, and he wasn't there to save her? Had she watched Tate go down and known she would be next?

He hugged the dark wall, keeping his step light, but the person in the next room had no such qualms. He heard a squeaking from the living room as the woman he'd seen from the shadows exited the formal space, turning her back to him to call up the stairs.

"If it's down here, it's hidden, Gates. Damn it. We're running out of time," she hollered up the stairs. "We have to get out of here."

Malcolm Gates, the lawyer. What the hell?

"Keep looking, damn it." The lawyer's voice floated back down. "If we don't get our hands on that fucking client list, my career is over. If I could kill that whore again I would."

The woman mere feet away from him gave a frustrated huff. "Why the hell did you kill Ehlers *before* you had her notes?"

Fuck. Gates had killed the madam because she'd planned to go public. And they thought Belle had the woman's client list? Kell wasn't sure why they'd believe that, but no way he could leave Belle alone.

Or had the lawyer already killed her?

"Well, when I had my hands wrapped around her throat, she swore she'd brought it here," Gates growled. "Shut up and keep looking."

"The bitch granddaughter hasn't even found it," the

woman argued. "So maybe it's not here. We need to kill her and her boyfriend, then get the hell out of here. You can set this place on fire in a few days after the cops declare the whole incident to be a murder-suicide. Call it faulty wiring or something. We can make that happen. Then if the list is here, it won't ever be found."

There was a long sigh. "My client won't accept that. The judge wants the list in his hands."

"Then we make one up, and we're all off the hook. You don't think very creatively for a lawyer. All I know is if we get caught in here, we're all going to prison. We need to cut our losses. She doesn't know where it is."

"One more chance," Gates said. "I'll give it one more shot—literally. Maybe if I put a gun to your boyfriend's head, it will spark some memory, Miss Wright? Turn that idiot over, Helena. I want her to see his face when I blow it off. We'll be down in a bit."

Kellan's blood froze. He heard Gates moving upstairs. Belle must be with him and searching for the client list in her grandmother's old bedroom. At least she was conscious.

Kellan stuck to the darkest part of the gloomy foyer. The cover of shadow would buy him some time.

Helena's shoes clacked along the hardwoods, and Kellan made himself go very still. Silent. He had to be so quiet, not alert them that they were no longer alone. He had to save Belle and Tate. They were his family.

God, what would have happened if he hadn't come to New Orleans with them? If he'd listened to his fear and gone back to Chicago? Eric would have been here. Would he have been on the ground with Tate, leaving Belle alone to fend for herself. They would all likely die.

He'd spent all his time wondering how a relationship between the four of them could work, but now he saw plainly that it would work however they worked it. The universe didn't give everyone the same life. Love wasn't some cookie cutter that he had to mold himself into. He'd spent his whole time on earth plotting and planning his life, ruthlessly controlling it to reach some grand destination, all the while not understanding that the ending he'd chosen wouldn't make him happy. Belle was the destination he'd been unconsciously seeking. Her love and the family he'd share with his buddies were the end-all, be-all of his existence.

He couldn't control them, but hopefully, he could damn well save them.

"God, how did I get into this shit?" The woman turned the corner.

Kellan struck, cracking the umbrella over her head. It made a dull thud. Nothing that would register upstairs. Her eyes widened and her mouth fluttered open, but she didn't emit a single sound. He caught her before she hit the floor, then he eased her down.

She would live. More than likely, she'd have a massive headache, but the medic in the NOLA jail could deal with that. He pushed her body against the wall. In the shadows where he was hidden, it would be hard to see.

Kellan heard a yip, and he whirled around only to realize Sir was trapped in the kitchen and barking behind the door.

"Damn it!" Gates screamed from the top of the stairs. It was obvious to Kellan that he was losing patience. It would cause him to get sloppy, make mistakes. Unfortunately, it also likely made him more violent. "Shut that fucking dog up, Mike!"

Mike was here? Mike had been the man on the ground, the one doing all the grunt work? It fit. No wonder neither he, Tate, nor Eric had liked the asshole. Sure enough, Mike came rushing down the stairs, jogging toward the kitchen.

Sir growled.

Kellan crouched into a dark corner behind a grandfather clock just as the kitchen door began to open.

He was going to owe that damn dog a treat. Sir kept barking, making himself a target as a big shadow moved through the open door. Kellan got the glimpse of something metallic in the moonlight.

Mike wasn't packing an umbrella. It looked like the asshole was way better armed than him.

"Shut the fuck up, dog." The big guy took aim.

Oh, that was so not happening. Belle would murder him if he allowed that fucker to kill her ridiculously ugly, seriously brave little mutt. Like it or not, Sir was the family dog and he wasn't going down tonight either.

With as much force as he could muster, Kellan brought the umbrella down on Mike's head. It met with a crack just like the last time.

Unfortunately, Mike was harder a target to fell.

With a growl, he whirled, his eyes narrowing as he raised the gun.

Sir rushed forward and suddenly snarled at the guy's ankle. He shouted out as Sir's teeth sank into his flesh. The gun fell from his hand, thudding to the floor.

Kellan attacked, punching the man with a quiet grunt. He tried to get to the gun, but Mike threw him back with a fist to his face. Pure pain flared, making his head spin. He heard Sir yipping, but as he opened his eyes, all he could see was that big fist coming toward his face again.

"Mother fucker," Mike cursed before making contact again. "I'm going to kill you."

Then he heard the shocking sound of a gun discharging. It cracked through the small space. The punch that might have knocked him out never came.

Mike's whole face went blank as he listed to one side and fell.

"Are you okay?" Eric asked quietly, reaching out to help Kell up.

"You idiot!" Gates yelled down. "Someone's going to call the cops if you don't keep the goddamn volume down. I told you to shut the dog up, not shoot him."

Fuck. If "Mike" didn't answer, Belle would be in trouble. He lowered his voice and tried to sound like an idiot douchebag. "Sorry. Dog's no trouble now."

Eric had picked Sir up, who was enthusiastically licking his face, but at least he was quiet.

There was a long sigh. "Get your ass up here. I have one more place I want to look before we finish up. Tell Helena to get everything ready."

The door shut upstairs.

He looked at Eric. "Give me the gun. You've done your part. I'm going to go get our girl. You make sure no one else comes after me."

Eric nodded, and Kellan started up the stairs.

To save his woman. To make sure his family was safe again.

Chapter Twenty

Tears filled Belle's eyes. They'd talked about killing her little dog. Her sweet little Sir was just a puppy. She'd heard the gunshot...then she hadn't heard Sir bark again. She tried not to sob.

Gates had yelled to Mike about finishing up, so he'd shot her dog. He would kill Tate next, regardless of whether or not she found the list. They were determined to take everything from her, even her life. Belle felt helpless, and it was a small consolation to know that Tate wouldn't suffer. Knowing that nothing but death awaited for her and Tate infuriated her. Damn it, she refused to go down without a fight.

Unfortunately, Gates had never taken the gun off her. Even when he'd been yelling at his cohorts, he'd watched her carefully. "Move the mattress. I want to see what's under the bed."

"You're going to kill me anyway." Maybe it was time to take a stand.

"No, I'm not. If you give me the list, I'll walk away," he said in what Belle bet he considered a soothing tone. She noted that he didn't point that gun elsewhere, though a tremor shook his arm. He wasn't a young man. He likely wasn't used to holding heavy objects for long periods of time.

"I'm not stupid. I know you won't leave me alive." She listened for the sounds of movement downstairs. It was faint, but she could almost hear them moving, the wood floors creaking as Gates's two accomplices searched the downstairs. Well, Helena was searching, but Mike seemed to be preparing for her inevitable murder. How did they plan to finish her off? Another hanging murder designed to look like a suicide?

Belle couldn't wait to find out. She had to make a move. She wasn't sure she could live knowing Tate was dead. How much time had passed? Where were Eric and Kellan?

Gates shrugged a little, giving up his previous act. "Fine. Of course, I'm going to kill you. If you give me the list, I'll make it quick. If you give me trouble, I'll draw it out. You won't like that. I can make you feel pain like you've never felt before. I'll give you over to Mike. He seemed to really like you. Although you might enjoy that since you like sleeping with a lot of men."

She ignored his insults. They didn't matter. She had to think. Her brain raced. She'd screwed up his plan by having Tate in the house. He'd wanted to catch her alone. He'd intended to only have to deal with one body.

And with the history of this house, it would be easy. The story itself would be so spectacular—history repeating itself and all—that the truth might be easily concealed and forever buried.

"You're planning to hang me." She'd wondered why Mike had laid out a white sheet on the floor in front of the banister.

Now that she thought about it, she could see the whole scenario play out in her head. They would make a noose out of the sheet. Pristine white. Like a cloud. They would pervert it and slip it over around her neck before tossing her over the banister and completing the act.

Belle felt an odd chill go through her, though there was nothing truly sinister about the feeling. Strength. She felt a weird bolt of it run through her, giving her energy, straightening her spine.

Belle suddenly realized she wasn't alone. The house might be haunted, but not all ghosts were evil. Some simply wanted to right the wrongs done to them—like the Peterman girls who'd been hanged by their own father. They could right those terrible wrongs by saving someone else, by not allowing what happened to them to happen again.

A nasty smile lit Gates's face. "Everyone knows this place is haunted, Miss Wright. Your story will make headlines for a day or two, then it will fade into New Orleans lore. Then you'll be just another young girl who committed suicide in this house. Just another ghost."

But the ghosts weren't on his side. He couldn't know that, couldn't know they had been coming to her each night in her dreams, trying to tell her that they had fought and she should, too. She got that now. They hadn't come to scare her. The thing in the library, yes. That entity wanted to hurt her, but not the girls from her dreams. They'd come to warn her, to make sure she didn't suffer their fate.

A deep peace settled over her as though she was finally in synch with the house she'd come to call home.

She didn't have to die. Neither did Tate. She could fight and she could win.

She looked briefly around the room. It was in complete disarray. He'd forced her to ransack every inch of the place looking for his "list" and now she had to walk gingerly around the piles of her grandmother's clothes and keepsakes that had absolutely nothing to do with the list.

She decided to obey him for now, to buy a little more time while she sought a weapon. There had to be something heavy and blunt among all this stuff.

What if Eric walked in first? Would he walk in and immediately be killed because he had no idea what was going on?

She had to prevent that, too.

Belle pushed at the mattress, pretending it was far heavier than it looked. She made a big show of straining to move the thing while she pointed out certain truths to the lawyer. "It's not going to work. Why would I hang myself?"

She'd just gotten engaged. She had everything to live for. And she had friends. What Gates didn't realize was that if anything happened to her, Kinley would never stop trying to find the truth and she would sic her very-good-at-their-jobs husbands on the case. Kinley wouldn't believe that she would kill herself. Not for a second.

Gates huffed, his stare utterly derisive. "You live with three men. Your lifestyle alone will make people shake their heads. Obviously, they didn't want to stay with a whore, so you did yourself in. I was intent on simply killing you, but if I have to, I'll take out your boyfriend. But I'd rather let him live because he'll make a perfect fall guy. I have some interns ready to testify about all the fights the men have over you. Mike is going to tell the cops that he overheard you crying because you couldn't choose between them. Your boyfriend down there could have murdered you in a fit of rage. Do you want him to live or not?"

She didn't believe a word he said. He would kill them both and come up with a story he hoped would hold water. With corrupt officials in his corner, he had reason to be smug, but it wouldn't work because he didn't understand the nature of the relationship she shared with her men. He didn't understand that no one who knew her or Tate would believe a word Gates said.

Belle pushed at the mattress again. "It's so heavy."

Gates sighed. "Try harder. We're running out of time."

Yes, he was definitely getting tired. She pushed again, pretending great frustration. She finally groaned and stood back up, her hand on her lower back. "I can't. It's too heavy. You need to help me."

She needed him closer. She needed to close the distance between them.

She needed to get that gun. It was the only way she could protect herself and Tate.

Gates stared at her as though trying to decide whether or not he believed her. He was a lawyer, and like her men, he would be damn good at sizing up a witness.

Belle let her emotions show. Vulnerable. Kellan had once told her that the best witness was a vulnerable witness. Juries liked witnesses who seemed a bit fragile. They wanted to empathize with the person on the stand. Belle allowed tears to fill her eyes, let her shoulders slump as though she was utterly defeated.

"Move away." He rolled his eyes as he pointed the gun toward the corner of the room. "I swear, if you want anything fucking done...I should have burned this place down a long time ago."

She stepped back to the corner, between the far wall and the open bathroom door. He'd already made her search the master bathroom. She thought about the high window, but even if she could get it open, there was a three-story fall she was pretty sure she wouldn't survive. Still, there were things she could use as weapons in that bathroom. It was just a few steps away.

Belle felt that cold chill slide across her skin again. It seemed to press against her as though it tried to tell her something.

Out of the corner of her eye, she caught sight of one of her grandmother's canes, propped against the wall, just a few steps away. Grandma had left them all over the place, and Belle hadn't gathered them up on these upper floors. Could she reach it?

"Don't you fucking try anything, bitch. You stand there." Gates moved to the bed, gun still in hand. "Mike, get your ass up here. I need help."

She heard the stairs creak. Mike was heading up. She had only a moment or two before she would have a noose shoved around her neck and she'd be thrown over the banister, either before or after she was forced to watch Gates kill Tate.

Her heart started to pound in her chest. Adrenaline flooded her system as she took a step toward that cane. It was right there. One more foot and she would be able to grab it.

Gates looked up suddenly. "I told you not to move."

Belle stopped, thinking on her feet. "Sorry. I fidget when I'm nervous."

His eyes narrowed. "Maybe the time has come to call it a day. Helena was right. This is useless. Maybe Ehlers was lying and she never gave your grandmother the fucking list. Stupid cunt." He stepped forward and pointed the gun her way again. "Maybe I don't need such an elaborate setup. I can kill you and the one downstairs and make it look as if one of your other lovers couldn't take the jealousy. Your freaky living arrangements will play in my favor."

The footsteps drew closer. Her time was over.

She had to get out of that gun's line of fire. She threw herself toward the bathroom door as the crash of gunfire filled her world.

* * * *

Kellan cautiously made his way up the stairs, willing himself to be methodical and not simply run in shooting. He had to take it slow, careful. He had no idea where Belle was in that room.

In the distance, he heard the wail of a siren. His time was running out. The second Gates realized the cops were closing in, he'd want to tie up his loose ends, then cut and run. That likely meant shooting Belle on his way out.

From the second story landing, Kell looked down at Eric, who stood at the bottom of the stairs, an umbrella in his hand. His friend nodded, silently telling him that he didn't sense anyone else in the house.

They only had Gates to contend with, but the fucker had

a gun and he wouldn't hesitate to use it. Kellan was fairly certain the only reason he hadn't killed Tate yet was that he'd chosen the big guy as a scapegoat. He was likely going to make it look like a murder-suicide. Belle and Tate would need to die in the proper order for that. As a lawyer, Gates would know what the forensics guys would be looking for.

As he moved up the next set of stairs, Kellan envisioned how he would plan it. He would keep Belle alive, searching for whatever he was looking for. Then he would make sure her prints were on the gun, residue found on her hands when they killed Tate. He'd force her to write a suicide note and hang her himself, just like the house legends.

Or they could do the opposite, and have Tate "kill" Belle in a fit of jealousy.

Either scenario was logical, but that plan wasn't going to work.

He was on the stairs to the third floor when Gates started talking again. "Maybe I don't need such an elaborate setup. I can kill you and the one downstairs and make it look as if one of your other lovers couldn't take the jealousy. Your freaky living arrangements will play in my favor."

Kellan picked up the pace because he didn't like the sound of that. He took the rest of the stairs at a jog. Then it happened.

A crack split the air. Gunfire. It was so loud. It made Kellan's blood run cold.

He took the final steps at a dead run because surprise didn't matter anymore. He had to get to her, had to find her, save her.

He heard someone on the stairs behind him. Eric, who apparently refused to wait either. Kellan couldn't expect him to stand around when someone was firing a gun at Belle. At least he would have some form of backup. If Gates shot him, perhaps Eric could finish the job and save their girl.

It felt damn good to know he wouldn't be alone. No matter what happened to him, someone would take care of their family.

He shouldered into the room with the full force of his body and darted right past Gates, who never saw his face.

"Mike?"

Thank god he and the electrician were roughly the same size and had the same coloring. Kellan had just one shot.

He turned, raised his gun, and fired in one move.

He wasn't a cop. He wasn't a damn sharpshooter. He'd barely handled a gun before and instead of hitting the asshole's chest, he only managed to get Gates's left arm—not even the one holding the gun.

Gates gasped but lifted that weapon and fired.

Kellan felt something shove him. Someone. Just as the bullet would have hit his chest, someone he couldn't see threw him, and he fell to the side and hit the ground on one knee, pain exploding along his leg.

"Kellan!" a feminine voice screamed.

Belle. He whirled to the sound of her voice. She looked terrified and worried, but she was alive. And that made her so beautiful to him.

Kellan lifted the gun again and fired, aiming at Gates. He could see Eric moving through the door, trying to sneak up behind the bastard. Just a few seconds more.

As he fired, he felt something hit his shoulder. There was a burst of pure fire across his skin before an odd numbness settled into his bones and the gun clattered from his hand.

"Stupid fuck." Gates was bleeding but still on his feet. "I'm going to kill you all."

He stood over Kellan, pointing the gun straight at his heart. Kellan swallowed, couldn't breathe. It felt like there was a hundred pound weight sitting on his chest.

"I already called the cops." He forced the words out. He couldn't move his damn hand, but he could buy Eric a second or two. All that mattered was Belle.

The sirens were growing closer, the wail distinct now.

Gates's eyes narrowed. "Fuck. You stupid son of a bitch! Now I just have to kill you faster. Mike!"

"He's dead. And Helena is passed out. You're alone," Kellan warned.

Gates leveled the gun. Then suddenly, his head snapped forward, his eyes glazing over.

Eric stood behind him, the umbrella in his hand. He might have been a football player before, but the man could bat like a fucking pro.

His partner. His friend.

Gates fell to the side, and Eric kicked both of the guns out of the way and raced toward him.

Suddenly, Belle was there too, tears in her gorgeous eyes. "Oh, god, Gates shot his lung. What do we do?"

Kell could hear the panic in her voice, but the world seemed to be retreating. Darkness started at the edge of his peripheral vision and began clouding his sight.

And that was when he saw them. Three women. They stood behind Eric. One was older, but still incredibly beautiful. She wore a pretty white dress and a delicate straw hat on her head. Belle would look like this woman one day, when age had matured her, giving her a countenance of beautiful wisdom. Two younger women stood beside her. They were also dressed in white, though they seemed to be wearing clothing from an earlier decade. They looked like sisters.

What were they doing standing in this room?

The older woman smiled at him, giving Kellan a look of such beatific peace that it filled him, warming him when he'd been getting so cold before. She looked down at him.

Thank you.

She held out both of her hands and the girls took them, threading their fingers together.

We're done here, son, but you're not. You hold on. My baby girl needs all her men. And you tell her a cleansing will work now. The demon who lives here has been defeated. He

370

can't hurt these girls anymore. They're free, and so am I. Bring new life to this place, son. It's a good house again.

What the fuck? That couldn't be Belle's grandmother. He didn't believe in ghosts.

She frowned. *Such language. And you might not believe in ghosts, but this one believes in you. Hold on, Kellan Kent. If you want a future, fight for your life now.*

Just before he passed out, he could have sworn he saw a light.

Yeah, he wasn't going to walk into it. He had things to do here like marry the woman of his dreams and live happily ever after with her and his best friends.

Kellan let the darkness take him.

Chapter Twenty-One

Kellan frowned at Eric. The sounds of the party around him filled the space and made it hard to hold a conversation with someone two feet away. When Belle threw a party, she got serious. Now that the common rooms of the house had been painted and furnished, their floors refinished to a gleam, she'd insisted on planning a party for all their friends to show off the house.

But only after he'd assured her he was going to make a full recovery from his bullet wound. At the beginning of his recovery, Belle had proven to be a hard taskmaster when it came to his rehab.

"Are you absolutely sure it wasn't you?" Kellan asked, searching for Belle across the crowded room.

When he found her, his heart seized up. She looked luminous in a snowy white cocktail gown, the color contrasting with the gorgeous mocha of her skin. It skimmed over her every curve and showed off her truly juicy ass.

"I swear to you I didn't push you out of the way," Eric promised. "I had barely gotten up the stairs when that first shot rang out. I was behind Gates. How would I have pushed you? Your memory of that night is probably fuzzy. Are you sure you're feeling all right? Maybe you've done too much too fast."

Besides the fact that he was becoming more and more

certain that he'd been saved by a trio of sweet-faced ghosts, he was feeling positively chipper. Well, his body was in good condition. His head was still fairly messed up, but he was going to deal with that problem tonight.

"I'm fine. I saw my personal physician when I was in Chicago." He'd only gotten back to New Orleans a few hours before. He'd been surprised to realize just how much he'd missed the place. A week back in the city he'd called home for the last several years had proven to be illuminating. He'd thought he'd easily settle back in, but he'd longed for the sultry heat of New Orleans, for the smell of strong coffee and beignets in the morning. He'd missed so much about the city. He'd especially missed hearing Belle laugh.

Eric's smile became tight, a sure sign he was annoyed. "How was Chicago?"

His friend likely thought he'd spent his time there working to reestablish himself. Kellan had given that notion some thought. Even after his near-death experience, the need to build walls, to make himself safe had been so strong. He'd awakened in the hospital with Belle asleep at his side, while Tate and Eric paced the floor. They had been steadfast through his recovery, and yet some part of him had still felt the urge to distance himself. He'd been so savaged by Lila and his father that he'd been reluctant to jump into his forever with two feet.

"It was nice. The office was actually in pretty good shape. Sequoia has strewn plants all around the place though," Kellan said, taking a drink of the rum punch Belle had made. "Says the environment is more organic that way."

Eric shook his head.

New Orleans jazz played through the living room, but the sweetest sound was Belle's giggle as she joked with her best friend. Kinley Anthony-Anders said something else, and Belle threw her head back and laughed with unselfconscious joy.

There was a deep part of him that would likely always

want to hide and protect himself, to build those walls no one could climb. He wasn't listening to that bastard anymore. How could he? Forced to choose between that voice and Belle... No contest. He was home now and he was going to stay here. But it was fun to fuck with Eric's head.

"We need to decide what to do with Sequoia actually. His internship is supposed to last another six months, after all." There was a little question in Eric's voice.

Well, if he wanted to know what Kell intended to do with his future, he would have to be more straightforward. "He's cool. I mean, he's still fucking weird, but I think I can handle him for another couple of months. I left him with enough to do until I can get back up there."

Which would be next week. It was past time to start hiring associates who would run the Chicago branch. Sometimes Eric and Tate just didn't think big enough. They didn't have to lose their clients. They simply had to grow.

The way he had to grow.

Eric frowned. "Well, I hope you're here long enough to see all the indictments come down now that we've turned the client list over. You know Gates is already behind bars, as is Helena. The judge Gates had been protecting got arrested last night. He was a very frequent customer, from Marie Wright's days, all the way until just before Karen Ehlers's murder. They've barely scratched this guy's surface, and already it looks as if the feds will file corruption charges against him. Some other names are being tossed around as clients of Ehlers—senators, athletes, university officials, even a rock star or two."

"I'd definitely enjoy seeing what happens with the case," Kell said with a grin.

Tate approached, wearing a big, sloppy grin. Damn. When Kell had first started hanging out with Eric, he'd tolerated Tate because they'd seemed like a package deal. The big dork had grown on him quickly. Now Kell couldn't imagine living without him.

"Hey, how was Chicago?" The shit-eating grin on Tate's face let Kellan know the big guy was far more aware of what he'd been doing up north than Eric.

The fucker still had him tagged. At one point, Kell would have regarded it as a horrible invasion of his privacy, but now it just felt like someone gave a damn about him. "I don't know. You tell me."

Eric sighed. "You didn't."

Tate shrugged. "He's been in the hospital. He shouldn't have been traveling. I had to keep tabs on him. Besides, I didn't need to tag his phone to hear what he was doing. I just had to talk to Jeremy from Petty and Associates."

Yeah, he was never going to be able to slide much past Tate. "I thought he would be good to head up litigation. He got passed over for partner and he's hungry."

Eric's eyes widened. "You're taking on new partners?"

Tate grinned. "Nope. *We're* taking on new partners because we won't be in Chicago enough to keep the firm running, but I don't want to give up the income. Do you?"

A huge grin broke across Eric's face. "Now that you mention it, Belle has very expensive tastes. Do you know how much this master bedroom renovation will cost? We need the money just to feed her need to make things pretty."

Eric had accepted him back. Kell was finally coming home. A weight lifted off him and he felt lighter than ever.

From the other side of the room, Belle looked up and her eyes sparkled as she caught sight of him. He could see her relieved sigh. She'd thought he wouldn't return. He couldn't blame her for fearing he would walk away for good. He'd started to a hundred times. But the thought of never holding her again had stopped him. He intended to prove to her that he was a changed man. He'd changed for her. Because of her.

After a quick hug, Belle left Kinley and approached him with a wariness in her eyes that saddened him. She slid into his embrace, but didn't give him her usual full-body cuddle.

Obviously, she had no idea he'd come back to stay.

"Hey, Kellan. I'm so glad you could make it back for the engagement party." Her smile was gorgeous but didn't quite reach her eyes. "How was Chicago?"

His whole body went on alert the minute she got near him. Blood thrummed through his system, racing to get to his cock because it had been far too long since he'd been inside her. "Chicago was fine, but DC was a little more interesting."

Everyone stopped, all three of them staring at him. It was good to know he could still surprise them.

Eric reared back in shock. "What on earth did you do in DC?"

"Shit. Did you kill someone?" Tate looked wide-eyed. "Because you really should have called us, man. We would have helped bury the body."

It was good to know he could count on Tate if he ever needed to murder someone.

Kell laughed. "I didn't kill anyone." Though he had laid a couple of his demons to rest. "I went to see my father."

Belle had tears in her eyes as she looked up at him. "You wanted to mend the rift between you?"

He hadn't changed that much. "Hell, no. I looked the asshole in the eye and told him what I thought of him. And then I told him I wanted to be part of the family again—and not because I'm desperate to get in good with dear ol' dad."

Belle reached for him. "You want to know your brother."

His brother. Harrison Kent was a toddling ball of energy being raised by nannies and housekeepers. He would be sent to boarding school in a few years, poor guy. His brother was innocent, and he needed to know that he always had a place with someone who would care no matter what. Kellan intended to give his brother what he'd never had—someone who understood him, someone who loved him for who he was, not what he could accomplish or who he could crush on his rise to the top.

"I do. I don't know how much contact Dad and Lila will

let me have, but I'll take whatever I can get."

He'd finally figured something out. He didn't have to be perfect for the people he loved. He just had to be there. With them. Through everything.

"I'm so glad," Belle said. She kissed him on the cheek. "Kellan, I'm truly happy for you."

"How long is this party going to take?" He was anxious to get to the good part.

"It's winding down now," Belle explained. "Kinley's getting tired. The pregnancy is rough on her, but she's so happy I don't think she cares."

Tate leaned over and kissed her. "I'll have the caterers start wrapping up."

Eric shook his hand. "Good to have you back. I'll start gently moving people toward the exits. We have a lot to talk about."

They did.

And Belle had to answer a question before she spent the night serving her Masters.

All three of them.

* * * *

Belle tried to calm her shaky nerves as she let Sir back inside. The house was quiet, the guests and caterers gone. The place was back into shape for the next day. She was going to start meeting with clients tomorrow and her first ones would likely prove to be fairly easy, since Eric and Tate wanted her to decorate their brand new offices here in New Orleans.

She would miss having them with her all day, but she wouldn't miss the masses of paperwork and computers underfoot and on her grandmother's antique surfaces. They were all starting fresh.

How long would Kellan stay with them?

She patted her puppy's head and settled him into his

little dog bed they kept in the kitchen. She would have let
him sleep in her room, but Eric had nearly killed the little
thing by rolling on top of him because Sir wouldn't stay off
the bed. Despite the fact that their new bed was built big
enough for four, Sir always tried to sleep right against
someone.

Was Kellan going to take her up on her offer? Was he
going to visit her for sex, then go back to his life in Chicago?
It had seemed all right when she'd made the offer weeks ago,
but now she wasn't sure she could surrender herself to him
all night, then watch him leave the next morning.

After discovering that none of the men were in the living
room or the library, Belle started up the stairs. She'd watched
them talking together through the end of the party. They'd
had their heads together, and their conspiratorial air had
given her pause. What were they up to? They'd given every
appearance of plotting and planning together. Had they been
deciding how to tell her she'd have two husbands, not three?

Belle stopped just short of the third floor. When she
closed her eyes, she could still see Kellan lying on her
bedroom floor, wounded. Bleeding. That night, she'd been so
scared he would die. She'd pressed her hands to his body, as
if trying to push her life force into him. She'd refused to let
him go then. She wasn't sure she could do it now.

No matter what he told her tonight, she couldn't give up
on him. He had a second chance. So did she. Belle intended
to fight harder than ever.

Resolve settled over her like a warm blanket. Kell was
evolving. He'd gone to DC and confronted his father. He'd
reached out to start a relationship with his brother. Those two
things had been inconceivable a few weeks before. But now,
Kellan was accepting his past in a way he never had. She had
to believe he'd come around in time. She would wear him
down, give him so much love he wouldn't be able to say no
to her in the end.

She opened the door, ready to don something sexy and

fight for her reluctant man as she seduced the other two.

But Kellan stood in the middle of the room, looking absolutely perfect in his suit and tie. Eric and Tate flanked him. Someone had transformed the place.

Belle looked around in complete wonder. "How did you do this?"

Everywhere she looked, the room seemed soft and romantic. At least a hundred candles lit the room with gauzy splendor. And dozens of bouquets of her favorite flowers, calla lilies, lay all around the room.

"Haven't you figured it out yet?" Kellan asked, his voice tight with some unnamed emotion. "This place is magical."

Tears filled her eyes. "I thought it was haunted."

"Not anymore," Eric said with a gentle smile. "Not since we found a real medium to cleanse the place."

Tate frowned. "I knew I should have researched Helena… Geez."

Belle laughed. These men were the magical ones, all so different and yet somehow they made each other complete. She couldn't live without any of them. She hoped like hell she wouldn't have to.

Her heart nearly stopped when Kellan dropped to one knee.

"Belle, I know you've already answered this question for the other two, but will you marry me? Will you be my wife, my sweet submissive, and my partner in life?"

Shock broke through her. Her heart caught. She'd never imagined that she'd hear those words tonight. Tears sprang up and fell to her cheeks.

She bit her lip. "Well, the other two didn't actually ask me."

A gorgeous smile lit Tate's face as he dropped to one knee, too. "Belle, will you marry me? Will you be my wife, my best friend, the person who grounds me and shows me that life is best lived through the heart?"

He really had a way with words when he wanted to.

Eric stepped forward with a velvet jewelry box in hand, though it looked too big for a ring. He lifted the lid and diamonds sparkled in the candlelight. "Belle, will you say yes? We're a package deal."

She gasped at the gorgeous diamond choker and three interlocking rings. A wedding ring and a collar. Proof that she belonged to them and they belonged to her.

"Yes, yes, and yes. A million times yes." She gave them a tearful smile, joy bursting through her. Then she turned to Kellan, looking into his eyes. "You came back for me."

He closed the distance between them and gripped her shoulders. "You are my home, Belle. I'll always come back for you. I will always choose you."

Belle didn't think she could be any happier. She opened to him as he swooped down and his lips took hers in a kiss that promised he would choose their future over his past.

As she sank into him, he kissed her again, this time sliding his tongue against hers and deepening the contact. He skimmed his hands down her body, lowering the zipper on her dress. The electric current of arousal flooded her system. Cool air hit her skin, but nothing could cut the sizzle from the heat of his fingers on her bare flesh. Her body was suffused with it. Kellan traced the line of her newly bared spine, bringing the dress with it.

She felt someone move in behind her, another body against hers.

"You looked so beautiful tonight, baby," Tate said. "That dress was gorgeous on you, though everything you wear is amazing. But I like you best with nothing but this dazzling skin. Sometimes I just stare at you and wonder how you got to be so luscious."

He unclasped her bra and let it drop to the floor. Immediately, he cupped her breasts and thumbed her nipples. They stiffened with pure pleasure, and she couldn't help but sigh.

As she let her head drift back, Kellan began kissing her

neck. His lips caressed her skin, leaving a trail of tingly arousal. Tate turned her head gently, pulling her lips to his. As he covered her mouth, he groaned. His tongue surged inside as he toyed with her nipples, plucking at them with his fingertips, keeping the sensations just shy of pain. Her whole body came to life.

She stood before them in nothing but a tiny thong and her Prada heels, her breathing shallow with excitement and her heart full of love.

Eric moved in at her side. He slid his hand between her and Tate, cupping her rear. "I love this ass. Time to lose these, sweetheart. You won't need them, not for a long time."

She shimmied out of her undies, stepping out of the heels at the same time. She lost several inches of height, but that just made her feel more delicate and surrounded by her men. In every direction she turned, a gorgeous chest or broad shoulders filled her vision. She loved the differences between all her men. Tate was so big all over, while Eric had a lean athleticism. Every sinew in Kellan's well-muscled body screamed dominance. Any one of these men could take her apart if they chose. Instead, they completed her life and offered her the freedom to discover the woman and submissive who lived under her skin. They accepted her with all her flaws, which made it so much easier to accept herself. When she was naked with them, she didn't think about her faults anymore, just about the pleasure they found in her body. It was a gift she could give to them, one they treasured.

"I love you." She breathed the words like they were the oxygen she needed to live.

Because she needed these men.

"We love you, too, Belle." Kellan had the collar in his hand. "You know we love you completely naked, but we want you to wear this collar and the ring we had made for you. We want you to always know that you belong to us."

She shivered as he placed the collar around her throat. She reached up to touch it and caught a glimpse of herself in the mirror above the dresser. She felt beautiful and the woman reflected back at her looked that way. How far she'd come from that young woman who couldn't find her place in the world. That girl hadn't thought she was pretty, couldn't imagine she really deserved this crazy relationship with these three wonderful men. The woman who looked back at her now practically glowed—with love, with confidence, with joy.

She'd found her place in the world, and it was between them.

Tate slipped his section of the ring on her finger, then Kellan eased his into place.

Eric stood in front of her, the last piece of the ring in his hand. He smiled down at her, love shining from his eyes. "You're everything to me, baby. Thank you for bringing us together."

He slid the final shining circle onto her finger. Somehow, the three pieces fit together perfectly. The individual pieces were pretty, but together they created something new and utterly unique. Each were stronger together than they were apart—rather like her men.

"This is beautiful. I'm nearly speechless. When did you have this made?"

Tate flushed. "I might have thought about this…oh, a month or two after you came to work for us. I might have talked to the others about it off and on for the past few weeks. Eric might have found a jeweler here to make it. Kell might have picked up the beautiful collar in Chicago. You know, just maybe."

Belle laughed and rose on her tiptoes to kiss them gently, one after the other. "You three are my whole world."

And they always would be. No matter what happened.

"Then you should prepare to serve your Masters, love." Kellan's voice had shifted from smooth lover to hungry Dom in an instant, and Belle's whole body tightened.

This was what she'd missed when Kellan was away. Eric

spanked and played with her. Tate dabbled. But only Kellan could truly top her from a soul-deep place.

She dropped to her knees because she couldn't think of any other way she would rather celebrate her engagement than serving the men she loved. It was an easy thing to do since they served her so well in return. They took care of her, saw to her needs and her pleasure, kept her safe.

She bowed her head submissively and spread her knees wide. It no longer felt odd to be in this position. Before, she'd felt vulnerable with her body on display. Now she found her feminine power here. She found the beauty. Being on her knees for them allowed her to focus on her body, the way it felt, moved, loved. She could focus on the pleasure and comfort she took and gave. When she was in this position, she was safe.

"Do you have any idea how beautiful you are to me?" Kellan asked.

She could see his perfectly polished dress shoes. They were joined by Eric's loafers and Tate's sneakers. She let her hair fall forward and cover her smile. Tate would wear sneakers with a tux. She would have to make sure to pick out his footwear for their wedding. He wasn't going to be allowed to wear high-tops on their big day.

"I know how beautiful you make me feel." When she was with her men, she really felt like the sexiest woman in the world.

They stepped back, and she could hear them undressing. She wanted to look up so badly, to see their magnificent bodies as they stripped down, but she'd pledged them her obedience here in their bedroom. They had sacrificed so much to be with her, to share her, to teach her that they could last. She didn't need her eyes to see them. Instead, she waited patiently, allowing memories to fill her mind. Every inch of their bodies was emblazoned in her brain, on her heart.

"Look up, love," Kellan commanded. "It's time to get your men hard and ready to fuck."

She glanced up. They didn't need any help being ready for sex. Three very erect cocks stared back at her, straining her way. She wasn't about to argue though. She was their submissive and she couldn't wait to bend to their will.

Kellan stood in the middle, his strong legs apart as he stroked his cock from base to head. "Suck me, Belle. I want to be so hard I can't see straight when I finally take your ass."

Anticipation thrummed through her system. She would finally have them all. They'd been together in bed before, taking turns, but that wasn't how they wanted it. That wasn't how she wanted it either. Since she'd met them, she'd dreamed of the night she would finally make love to all of them at once—one each in her mouth, her pussy, and her ass. She would be filled with them. They would fit together like the ring on her finger, nestled and interlocked. Complete.

She leaned forward and licked at the head of Kellan's cock, reveling in his salty taste. Her tongue spun around the plum-shaped head, licking as if she tasted a sweet lollipop she couldn't suck deep enough. That wasn't far from the truth. She loved the way he tasted.

Belle took him in her mouth and drew on him, lightly at first, then in a stronger rhythm as she began to work her way down his stalk. Over and over, she sucked him in long passes, letting her tongue play against his smooth skin.

Kellan's hands found her hair, pulling gently so she would take more. She wanted to take all of him, to suck him until he couldn't take another second of her torture and filled her mouth.

"Time for a change, love. I'm not the only one who needs you tonight."

And then he was gone, and Eric took his place. He stood tall and proud in front of her, his cock in hand. "Suck me, too, baby."

Belle licked the underside of Eric's dick with the flat of her tongue, rubbing and laving her affection. Eagerly, she took half his cock on her first try. He rewarded her with a deep groan, tangling his hands in her hair and pulling gently. The little pain lit up her scalp, making her shiver, even as she sucked his cock deep again. They found a sultry rhythm. He pulled and she sucked, every motion of his expressive hands cradling her face or pulling on her scalp, sending signals to her pussy, to soften, to get wet, to make itself ready for what was to come.

He filled her mouth, his cock swelling inside.

"You feel so good. No one but you has ever made me feel this amazing." Eric pumped his hips, begging her to take more. "Don't stop. Don't ever stop."

She had no intention of that, but when she glanced up, she noticed Tate had moved to stand beside Eric. He watched as his best friend's cock sank in and out of her mouth. His hand was on his own dick, stroking himself as he drank her in with his stare. He was so hot, and all that masculine desperation was for her. She sent him a come-hither smile, reveling in playing their vixen.

"You know I love it when you get saucy, baby." Tate groaned as his thumb worked across the head of his cock, gathering the little bead of moisture and using it to ease his strokes. "But don't forget about me. I need your attention, too."

"Now I remember the crappy part about sharing my wife." Eric moaned as if in pain, but he spoke with a smile on his face. "Come closer and we can share at the same time. I think Belle can handle us both. She's a hell of a woman."

As excitement ripped through her, she felt someone moving in behind her. A big hand touched her back.

"Keep sucking Eric and Tate while I get you prepped, love. Don't falter or we'll stop the whole process and you'll get a good, long spanking," Kellan said, sliding his hand toward her backside. "You don't want to have to start over again, do you?"

"No, Master. No, I don't."

While she kind of loved the idea of a good, long spanking, it would have to wait. She needed them too much. She longed to finally be with them all together. Fate willing, she would have plenty of time to misbehave and earn her "funishment," but tonight was all about the togetherness they'd all waited so long for.

Eric and Tate moved close, their hips nearly brushing. The position allowed her to touch them both. Belle studied them, still unable to believe these beautiful men were all hers.

She didn't take her eyes off them as she moved in close and took Tate's cock firmly in hand. He filled her palm, and she could barely close her fingers around him. With a firm stroke of his dick, she leaned in and took Eric back into her mouth. Multitasking. Someone had told her she was a brilliant multitasker, though she rather thought they'd been discussing her secretarial skills. It came in handy when sexually satisfying three gorgeous men.

She sucked Eric while she stroked Tate. After five lingering, agonizing passes over Eric's cock, she turned slightly and took Tate's dick past her lips, licking and sucking and loving. She moved back and forth, lavishing one with the affection of her kiss while she palmed the other, enjoying the strength of the cock in her hand, the taste in her mouth.

It seemed so odd that she'd once been a little wary of this act, hesitant. They'd taught her not to be afraid, not to hold back. There wasn't any shame in making love, not when emotion and promise flowed between them. This was simply another way to show she cared. Her submission was her gift to them, a sign of her love, a demonstration that she trusted them with her heart, her body, and her pleasure. She gave them everything she had, down to her soul. They rewarded her with thankful groans and tender touches.

Kellan's fingers moved to the cleft of her backside, splitting her cheeks apart and making her shudder. "Don't move, love. Stay still. You've taken the plug before, but you still need to be carefully prepped. I don't want to hurt you. You can stop me at any time, but I want you to keep your hips as still as possible."

She didn't want to stop him, hadn't come close to thinking about her safe word. The command to stay still was a different matter. It was so hard because she could already feel the lube he'd been warming against his skin touch her.

He slid the lube along her flesh, making her shiver ever so slightly and awakening nerve endings that still stunned her. As she tried to concentrate on her task, she felt a hard finger pressed against her back entrance. Kell massaged her with his touch, circling the rim of her ass before dipping briefly in only to start the process over again. She couldn't help clenching. He corrected her with a hard smack.

"Don't you dare try to keep me out," Kellan smacked her again.

She didn't bother to mention that it was sort of an involuntary response. Why bother? She liked the spanking too much. It sent sparks skittering over her skin and waves of sensation rolling down her spine.

Kellan delved between her cheeks again, his finger searching her out once more. She focused on relaxing and letting him in.

Heat and a jangly pressure lit her up. The sensation started where his finger massaged, but it quickly sparked outward, sending heat spiraling throughout her body.

She had to force herself to focus on the task at hand. No matter what Kellan was doing to her, she had to remember her other husbands had needs as well.

Belle ran her tongue along the underside of Eric's cock before letting it go and sucking Tate's head deep inside her mouth. When she released him, she could see the way his balls had drawn up, the angry purple hue of his cock. Tate's eyes looked sleepy with arousal as he stared down at her.

With an urgent grip, Eric found her hair and directed her

back to lick him again. She ran her tongue along the underside, licking until she give his balls a kiss.

"Fuck, that feels good," Eric said with a gasp.

All the while Kellan probed her. He was patient, taking his time and letting her get used to the feeling. He seemed to understand when she was ready to move on.

Belle stayed as still as she could, but it was becoming even more difficult as the sensation turned sharply pleasurable. The instinct was there to press back against him, but she held off.

He delved deeper and deeper with his fingers until she finally felt him breach her, the tension giving way to fullness. She nearly sighed at the exquisite feeling.

Kellan continued to work lube around her flesh. That strong finger massaged her, making it slick and slippery and ready for something bigger. She was opening for him, preparing for him to take her in a way she'd never been taken before.

"Can she handle it?" She heard Tate groan the question.

Kellan added a second finger, stretching her gently. "She's tight, but she can take it."

She better be able to. She'd worn anal plugs for a few hours nearly every day preparing herself for her men. It had been an intimate little ritual—one she'd oddly enjoyed—but she didn't want a plug tonight. They were plastic and cold. Unreal. She needed heat and flesh and their love.

"That's right, love. You like this. You're going to like my cock even more. I knew you would love this." Kellan's words vibrated along her flesh. "Do you know how full you're going to be, Belle? When all three of us are deep inside you, you'll finally know what it means to be our woman. You'll be surrounded and taken and so fucking loved. You won't believe how filled you'll be with our cocks."

"But first, I want a taste." Tate pulled away.

As if this was something they had rehearsed, Eric took a

step back with Tate, and Kellan slid his fingers from her backside, leaving her feeling lonely and empty and aching.

"I'm going to clean up and get ready," Kellan said, giving her a wink. "You two make her scream a couple of times because I doubt any of us are going to last long once we get inside her. I wouldn't want to be accused of not satisfying our woman."

That wasn't possible, but before she could voice her opinion, Tate lifted her into his arms. He cradled her to his chest before setting her down on the bed. She loved it when he carried her. She felt petite and delicate and treasured. The softness of the comforter cradled her back. Her skin was alive and singing. Even the air caressed her.

Tate stood at the end of the bed, his stare all over her body. He wore a predatory smile. "I'm hungry, baby."

Her body tightened in anticipation. "You're always hungry, Tate."

"Damn straight," Tate shot back. "I'm always starving for you. Now spread your legs for me."

Eric joined him, looming over her like sex on two legs. "Spread them wide, baby. We want to look at our pussy. You've got the prettiest pussy in the whole fucking world. I want to look at it all the time."

Belle spread her legs wide. Eric wasn't joking. He really did want to look at her pussy all the time. It was yet another kink they somehow made loving and affectionate. At the oddest times, Eric commanded her to spread her legs just so he could look at her. Sometimes that's all he'd do. He would simply look, sigh contentedly, and leave with promises to come back later. She would shake her head at him, but for hours afterward, she felt as if she was glowing.

But sometimes he would look for a few moments. Then she'd find herself spread wide on her desk, screaming out her pleasure. Belle definitely liked those times best.

"You might be satisfied with looking, but I'm going to devour my dessert. The caterers didn't feed me anything I really wanted." Tate dropped to his knees in front of her. "Of course, nothing is sweeter than this."

Belle sighed because she was in for something sweet herself. Tate could eat her pussy for hours. He'd told her he was a true connoisseur of only one thing—her.

Eric climbed on the bed and palmed her breast, his big hand easily covering her. "Don't listen to a word he says. I watched him eat five of the mini éclairs and two of the tarts. He just likes to complain."

Tate's breath warmed her feminine flesh. "No, I just like to eat a lot. I'm a big guy. I need my sweets. And I intend to eat my fill of this because it's the sweetest piece I ever had."

He took her breath away with the first long swipe of his tongue. Pure pleasure made her toes curl. Tate lapped at her pussy in short, teasing swipes before settling in for a dizzying suck of her clitoris.

Eric played with her nipples, sucking and biting them playfully. He enveloped the buds in his mouth. Her whole body pinged with life, waiting for the ecstasy only they could bring her. The past fell away, and all that she was left with was a brilliant future with her men.

Belle clenched the sheets as she forced herself to stay still under their ministrations. They tortured her, bringing her to the edge again and again until she thought she might go mad. Her skin dampened. Her breathing shallowed.

"Please," she pleaded.

"Please what?" Eric lifted his head, staring down at her with dark eyes. "Kellan isn't the only one who tops you. He might have been the one to place that collar around your throat, but you belong to all of us, so you'll call us by our title or you won't get what you want."

"Please, Master." In their bedroom, she was content to submit to their every desire.

Tate's head snapped up. Her arousal glistened on his sensual lips. He licked them, obviously enjoying her taste. "I like hearing that. Since she begged so sweetly, I think we give her what she needs."

"Then do your worst, man. Make her scream. I'll help you out." Eric slid his hand down her torso until he found her clit, then placed his thumb right on top of the little nub.

"You always back me up." Tate lowered his head again.

Belle shouted out as he speared her with his tongue. Tate began to fuck deep inside her cunt with long strokes of his tongue while Eric pressed and rotated her clit. He varied the pressure, teasing and torturing her while Tate stroked her deep. She couldn't help but whimper and squirm as they held her down. Their grips were a sweet restraint she didn't want to escape. Eric licked at her nipple and finally settled in to suck. Long pulls on her tender buds had her eyes rolling to the back of her head.

They moved in perfect time. It wasn't long before they had Belle thrashing and crying out, a supernova of an orgasm exploding through her body.

She sagged onto the bed, her body heavy with pleasure as she floated back to earth. Eric kissed her lazily, cuddling her close, their tongues playing sweetly against one another. Tate moved up the bed on her other side, turning her to him as Eric eased back. She could taste herself on his tongue.

"You look like a satisfied woman." Kellan stood at the end of the bed. He stared down at her, his eyes hot.

"I'm a happy woman," she replied.

"And you're going to make us very happy men. You complete us, Belle. We love you. Let us show you just how much." He nodded toward his partners. "Tate, take her pussy. Eric try her mouth again. I'm going to work my way into that sweet virgin ass."

She found herself being twisted and turned gently, like she was a precious doll they wanted to share. Beneath her, Tate quickly donned a condom and thrust his cock deep before she was even settled.

Her arousal returned in that one long thrust, despite the orgasm she'd just experienced. Almost immediately, she pulsed around his cock. She would never get used to the way it felt when they thrust inside her. She closed her eyes, letting the sensation take over. Tate's hands eased her, soothing her even as he held her on his dick.

"God, you feel good." Tate's hips flexed up as though he could make his way deeper inside her body.

"She's going to feel even better when I'm done. You think she's tight now, just wait until I'm inside." Kellan put a hand between her shoulder blades, gently guiding her down. "Lie against Tate, love."

Eric took his place, kneeling close, directing his cock toward her. He teased her lips with it. "Come, baby. Take me inside. I can't wait to feel your mouth on me again."

She licked at the head while Tate held her still. Kellan moved in behind her once more. A spark zipped up her spine as he parted her cheeks and dribbled more lube.

Eric's cock invaded, filling her mouth as she felt something far larger than a finger at the rim of her ass. She couldn't stop from groaning as Kellan pressed against her opening. His cock was so much bigger than the plugs she'd taken. She knew she'd feel him even more keenly because Tate took up all the space in her pussy. Even the thought of having them both inside her made her moan.

"Fuck, baby. That feels so good." Eric pushed further into her mouth, obviously loving the vibrations stemming from the sounds she made.

"Stay still, love. Let me in. Don't fight it. I belong here. This body is fucking ours." Kellan pressed forward in little thrusts, gaining ground each time. Every move of his body was a mix of pleasure and pain and the anticipation of something to come.

Tate gripped her hips, stroking and calming her. "You're so gorgeous, Belle. Relax. This is how we were meant to be together."

He kissed her shoulder, giving her little love nips that countered the pressure in her ass.

She concentrated on pleasuring Eric, rolling her tongue over and over his cock. She laved the head and the underside with her affection, pouring her devotion into every pass of her tongue.

All the while, Tate held her still while Kellan thrust softly, opening her up more every time he inched forward until she finally felt him surge inside deep.

Belle gasped and held her breath. She'd never been so full. Kellan and Tate were deep inside her body, taking up all the space, impaling her on their cocks and holding her still for their pleasure. God, was there anything more perfect? She didn't think so.

Caught between the two of them, she drowned in pleasure as Eric slid his cock into her mouth, guiding her gently with his fingers tangled in her hair. All three of her men were inside her, and it was an intimacy unlike anything she'd ever known.

"You're so fucking tight, love." Kellan seemed to grind the words up in his chest before he spoke them.

She whimpered, and he petted her, holding himself still, allowing her to become accustomed to the feel of a cock invading her ass. She was stretched so tight, and for a moment she wasn't sure she could stand another second of it.

Then Kellan moved ever so slightly, dragging his cock back, suffusing her with pleasure. Nerves she'd barely imagined and never felt so alive sparked through her body.

"Are you all right?" Kellan asked, his voice guttural with arousal.

She didn't want to lose Eric, so she just hummed with satisfaction.

"I think she's fine, man. And you really better get to moving if you want us all to go off together because I don't know how long I'm going to last. She feels too good." Eric tightened his grip on her face as he thrust his cock further past her lips, forcing her to take more of him.

Tate thrust up while holding her hips against him. Her

clitoris ground on his pelvis, building the heat and fire inside her.

"Then we should show our woman exactly what we can do for her." Kellan dragged his cock almost all the way out, stopping just at the tight ring of muscle, then thrust ruthlessly back inside.

And they were off, setting a pace that took Belle's breath away. They worked in perfect harmony. Tate would thrust up while Kellan pulled back. Kellan's cock would plunge forward while Tate ground up, hitting her clitoris perfectly. Eric caught their rhythm, and his cock stiffened in her mouth. The musk rising up from his skin filled her nostrils.

Belle didn't fight the sensations. She gave over completely, submitting her body and heart to her men. She rode the wave they created for her, allowing her body to flow between them as the pleasure built and built.

Eric groaned in something close to agony, and she tasted the salt of his essence on her tongue. He pressed in again, his cock shooting off and filling her up. She drank him down, lapping at his cock, ensuring that he not only felt pleasure but her love too.

Tate's thrusts matched Kellan's as they picked up the pace. Each moved smoothly in and out of her body. Tate wedged a hand between their bodies, pushing up on her clit and sending her flying over the edge once again, tearing a scream from her body.

"Yes. That's it. Baby, fuck. Oh, Belle, come all over my cock." Then Tate shouted, stiffening and arching his back to bury himself even deeper inside her.

Belle's whole body convulsed in pleasure as the orgasm nearly ripped her from her body and tossed her into a storm of pleasure. She heard Kellan cry out her name, then he lost his perfect rhythm, slamming inside her over and over again, marking her as his. He stiffened behind her, shoving his cock deep until she could feel his balls rub against her. Warm satisfaction flooded her. Heat and pleasure became her world as Kellan shared her moment of release and her devotion to their forever.

They fell together in a pleasant heap on the bed. Belle sighed as she found herself in a happy tangle of arms and limbs. The light from the candles made the whole world soft and sweet. The moment had been nothing short of perfect.

Kellan settled in beside her, his head on her breast. "I missed you every minute I was gone."

She caressed his cheek. "I missed you, too. Don't leave again. Not for a long time."

"Hey, scoot over. I think I should be the one to sleep beside Belle." Eric stared down at Tate.

Tate merely wrapped an arm around her waist and cuddled close. He didn't even open his eyes. "You snooze, you lose, man."

"Come on. I'll arm wrestle you for it," Eric offered. "Hey, I'll walk Sir for the rest of the week. Come on, man."

Tate and Eric argued like big kids about who got to sleep next to the wife for the night.

Kellan chuckled. "They're going to be trouble, you know."

Belle just smiled. Yes, her men were trouble, but she'd realized she couldn't live without them.

She closed her eyes, sending a silent thanks to her grandmother for bequeathing her a home she and her men could share and eventually raise the children borne of their love in. She slept, her dreams untroubled because her house, like her life, was whole and at peace once more.

* * * *

Read on for excerpts from Shayla Black, Lexi Blake, and M.J. Rose.

Theirs To Cherish
Wicked Lovers, Book 8
By Shayla Black
Now Available!

The perfect place for a woman on the run to disappear…

Accused of a horrific murder she didn't commit, former heiress Callie Ward has been a fugitive since she was sixteen—until she found the perfect hideout, Club Dominion. The only problem is she's fallen for the club's Master, Mitchell Thorpe, who keeps her at arm's length. Little does she know that his reasons for not getting involved have everything to do with his wounded heart…and his consuming desire for her.

To live out her wildest fantasies…

Enter Sean Kirkpatrick, a Dom who's recently come to Dominion and taken a pointed interest in Callie. Hoping to make Thorpe jealous, she submits to Sean one shuddering sigh at a time. It isn't long before she realizes she's falling for him too. But the tender lover who's slowly seducing her body and earning her trust isn't who he claims…

And to fall in love.

When emotions collide and truths are exposed, Sean is willing to risk all to keep Callie from slipping through his fingers. But he's not the only man looking to stake a claim. Now Callie is torn between Sean and Thorpe, and though she's unsure whom she can trust, she'll have to surrender her body and soul to both—if she wants to elude a killer…

* * * *

Callie trembled as she lay back on the padded table and Sean Kirkpatrick's strong fingers wrapped around her cuffed wrist, guiding it back to the bindings above her head.

"I don't know if I can do this," she murmured.

He paused, then drew in a breath as if he sought patience. "Breathe, lovely."

That gentle, deep brogue of his native Scotland brought her peace. His voice both aroused and soothed her, and she tried to let those feelings wash through her. "Can you do that for me?" he asked.

His fingers uncurled from her wrist, and he grazed the inside of her outstretched arm with his knuckles. As always, his touch was full of quiet strength. He made her ache. She shivered again, this time for an entirely different reason.

"I'll try."

Sean shook his head, his deep blue eyes seeming to see everything she tried to hide inside. That penetrating stare scared the hell out of her. What did he see when he looked at her? How much about the real her had he pieced together?

The thought made her panic. No one could know her secret. No one. She'd kept it from everyone, even Thorpe, during her four years at Dominion. She'd finally found a place where she felt safe, comfortable. Of course she'd have to give it up someday, probably soon. She always did. But please, not yet.

Deep breath. Don't panic. Sean wants your submission, not your secrets.

"You'll need to do better than try. You've been 'trying' for over six months," he reminded her gently. "Do you think I'd truly hurt you?"

No. Sean didn't seem to have a violent bone in his body. He wasn't a sadist. He never gripped her harshly. He never even raised his voice. She'd jokingly thought of him as the sub whisperer because he pushed her boundaries with a gentleness she found both irresistible and insidious.

Certainly, he'd dragged far more out of her than any other man had. Tirelessly, he'd worked to earn her trust. Callie felt terrible that she could never give it, not when doing so could be fatal.

Guilt battered her. She should stop wasting his time.

"I know you wouldn't," she assured, blinking up at him, willing him to understand.

"Of course not." He pressed his chest over hers, leaning closer to delve into her eyes.

Callie couldn't resist lowering her lids, shutting out the rest of the world. Even knowing she shouldn't, she sank into the soft reassurance of his kiss. Each brush of his lips over hers soothed and aroused. Every time he touched her, her heart raced. Her skin grew tight. Her nipples hardened. Her pussy moistened and swelled. Her heart ached. Sean Kirkpatrick would be so easy to love.

As his fingers filtered into her hair, cradling her scalp, she exhaled and melted into his kiss—just for a sweet moment. It was the only one she could afford.

A fierce yearning filled her. She longed for him to peel off his clothes, kiss her with that determination she oft en saw stamped into his eyes, and take her with the single-minded fervor she knew he was capable of. But in the months since he'd collared her, he'd done nothing more than stroke her body, tease her, and grant her orgasms when he thought she'd earned them. She hadn't let him fully restrain her. And he hadn't yet taken her to bed.

Not knowing the feel of him deep inside her, of waiting and wanting until her body throbbed relentlessly, was making her buckets full of crazy.

After another skillful brush of his lips, Sean ended the kiss and lifted his head, breathing hard. She clung, not ready to let him go. How had he gotten under her skin so quickly? His tenderness filled her veins like a drug. The way he had addicted Callie terrified her.

"I want you. Sean, please . . ." She damn near wept.

With a broad hand, he swept the stray hair from her face. Regret softened his blue eyes before he ever said a word. "If you're not ready to trust me as your Dom, do you think you're ready for me as a lover? I want you completely open to me before we take that step. All you have to do is trust me, lovely."

Callie slammed her eyes shut. This was so fucking pointless. She wanted to trust Sean, yearned to give him everything—devotion, honesty, faith. Her past ensured that she'd never give any of those to anyone. But he had feelings for her. About that, she had no doubt. They'd grown just as hers had, unexpectedly, over time, a fledgling limb morphing into a sturdy vine that eventually created a bud just waiting to blossom . . . or die.

She knew which. They could never have more than this faltering Dom/sub relationship, destined to perish in a premature winter.

She should never have accepted his collar, not when she should be trying to keep her distance from everyone. The responsible choice now would be to call her safe word, walk out, quit him. Release them both from this hell. Never look back.

For the first time in nearly a decade, Callie worried that she might not have the strength to say good-bye.

What was wrong with her tonight? She was too emotional. She needed to pull up her big-girl panties and snap on her bratty attitude, pretend that nothing mattered. It was how she'd coped for years. But she couldn't seem to manage that with Sean.

"You're up in your head, instead of here with me," he gently rebuked her.

Another dose of guilt blistered her. "Sorry, Sir."

Sean sighed heavily, stood straight, then held out his hand to her. "Come with me."

Callie winced. If he intended to stop the scene, that could only mean he wanted to talk. These sessions where he tried to dig through her psyche became more painful than the sexless nights she spent in unfulfilled longing under his sensual torture.

Swallowing down her frustration, she dredged up her courage, then put her hand in his.

Holding her in a steady grip, Sean led her to the far side of Dominion's dungeon, to a bench in a shadowed corner. As soon as she could see the rest of the room, Callie felt eyes on her, searing her skin. With a nonchalant glance, she looked at the others scening around them, but they seemed lost in their own world of pleasure, pain, groans, sweat, and need. A lingering sweep of the room revealed another sight that had the power to drop her to her knees. Thorpe in the shadows. Staring. At her with Sean. His expression wasn't one of disapproval exactly . . . but he wasn't pleased.

For more information visit www.shaylablack.com.

Dungeon Games
Masters and Mercenaries, Book 6.5
By Lexi Blake
Coming May 13, 2014!

Obsessed

Derek Brighton has become one of Dallas's finest detectives through a combination of discipline and obsession. Once he has a target in his sights, nothing can stop him. When he isn't solving homicides, he applies the same intensity to his playtime at Sanctum, a secretive BDSM club. Unfortunately, no amount of beautiful submissives can fill the hole that one woman left in his heart.

Unhinged

Karina Mills has a reputation for being reckless, and her clients appreciate her results. As a private investigator, she pursues her cases with nothing holding her back. In her personal life, Karina yearns for something different. Playing at Sanctum has been a safe way to find peace, but the one Dom who could truly master her heart is out of reach.

Enflamed

On the hunt for a killer, Derek enters a shadowy underworld only to find the woman he aches for is working the same case. Karina is searching for a missing girl and won't stop until she finds her. To get close to their prime suspect, they need to pose as a couple. But as their operation goes under the covers, unlikely partners become passionate lovers while the killer prepares to strike.

* * * *

"I'm going to open the door now." She couldn't just sit there when he obviously needed affection.

She heard him shuffling, moving even as she opened the door. And then he was there, his muscular body seeming to shrink in on itself.

"You can't be around me when I'm like that, Karina. I could have hurt you."

She followed her instincts now and walked right up to him. He didn't move as she folded her arms around him, tucking her head under his chin. "I wasn't going to let you hurt me, Derek. I had a plan."

It took him a couple of seconds, but his arms wrapped around her, squeezing her tight. His big palm came over her head in a protective gesture that warmed her. "What was your plan?"

It felt so good to be in his arms. The man knew how to hug. He enveloped her, surrounded her. She couldn't help but cuddle closer. "I kissed you because I figured the dream was from your Army days. I'd tried to talk you awake, but I figured you probably hadn't kissed your Army buddy a whole lot."

He chuckled and she felt it all along her spine. "No. I hadn't even kissed Jones once. It was effective. You stayed calm, didn't you. I didn't really worry you at all."

She would bet he'd freaked the hell out of other women. "It takes a lot to panic me, Brighton. I know you don't like it, but I can handle myself. And I can handle you. You weren't going to hurt me."

"I almost killed Maia once. I thought I was trying to keep Jones quiet, but she was smaller than him. I covered her nose, too. She couldn't breathe. She hit me, but I didn't wake up. She finally managed to pick up a glass on the nightstand and broke it over my thick skull."

So he had his reasons to be worried. "I'm not Maia. I'm bigger and stronger than she is. I bet she hasn't had the same self-defense training I've had."

His hands softened, beginning to stroke her. One hand flowed over her hair, the other down her back. "Yeah, she wouldn't have thought to kiss me. Do you think you might want to kiss me in some situation other than trying to save your own life?"

Such a drama queen. She lifted her head and found him staring down at her. Heart-stoppingly sexy. That's what he was. With his sleepy eyes and that sexy beard of his, she couldn't quite look away from him. And his lips. Oh, they were plump and sensual and she wondered what it would feel like to have those lips on her body, worshiping her skin, kissing and licking and sucking.

She had a choice. She could step back and go to her widow's bed and be alone or she could make one small move and the night wouldn't be spent alone. She would spend it in his arms and she would finally know what it felt like to be Derek Brighton's woman—even if only for a little while.

With a shaky breath, she went on her toes and pressed her lips to his.

* * * *

Derek's whole body reacted to her. His heart pounded, his skin tingled, every available ounce of blood seemed to flow right to his dick. She was saying yes. She was offering herself, and he wasn't about to turn her down.

The need to burn off the dream was riding him hard. When he'd finally woken up and found Karina's body trapped under his, he'd damn near lost it. He could have hurt her, could have killed her. It was precisely why he didn't sleep with women. He fucked and pleasured and found his comfort in their bodies, but he went to his own bed so he couldn't hurt them.

Except Karina really did seem to have handled him.

He gave her a minute, allowed her to explore. Her mouth

was oddly tentative for an experienced woman, but then Karina seemed to be a study in contradictions. She was on her toes, her hands moving from around his chest to his jawline where she brushed against his beard, her light touches making him shiver slightly.

Fuck. He didn't shiver. He didn't get this weird tightness in his stomach. He fucked. He brought pleasure. He didn't get worried or nervous.

But he was kind of both because he wanted her so fucking bad, he couldn't see straight.

From the moment he'd woken up and found her underneath him, his cock had jumped and pleaded and twitched in his boxers. His brain might know that she wasn't his type but his cock had entirely different ideas about what was attractive.

She kissed him and he kept still, allowing her to explore, to be in charge for now because she wouldn't be later. What was attractive? She was. God, he loved the fact that she'd been willing to take off his balls if she'd had to. He also kind of loved that she'd come up with a way to save his balls.

He could still remember Maia crying. She'd sobbed for hours after the incident. Not Karina. Karina had that crazy sexy smile on her face that let him know she hadn't been bothered at all by his crazy fucking PTSD dreams. She'd handled it. She'd taken care of it and she hadn't needed to nearly kill him to do it.

Karina wasn't his forever sub, but damn he wanted her now.

She stopped, pulling slightly back. When she looked up at him, he nearly got to his knees.

She was fucking gorgeous with tears in her eyes. She bit her bottom lip, obviously nervous. "Do you want me to stop?"

He had zero plans to stop. He might never fucking stop. A dangerous thought played through his head. He didn't have to stop. He could fuck Karina until he didn't have an ounce of come in his body and then he'd just wait until he had more and he'd give that to her, too.

"Yes. I want you to stop." Because it was far past time for him to take over.

Her face fell, the sweetest pink flushing through her. He loved her skin when she was embarrassed or emotional. She couldn't hide from him. It all played out over that precious flesh of hers. "Okay."

She started to take a step away, but he wouldn't allow it. She might be able to handle him when he was asleep, but he was going to make it very plain that he was her Master when he was awake. He caught her, pulling her to his body, letting her feel every ounce of his will because it was all directed her way.

"I want you to stop because I'm the top, Karina."

For more information visit www.lexiblake.net.

The Collector of Dying Breaths:
A Novel of Suspense
By M.J. Rose
Coming April 8, 2014

From the internationally bestselling author, a lush and imaginative novel that crisscrosses time as passion and obsessions collide

Florence, Italy—1533:

An orphan named René le Florentin is plucked from poverty to become Catherine de Medici's perfumer. Traveling with the young duchessina from Italy to France, René brings with him a cache of secret documents from the monastery where he was trained: recipes for exotic fra-grances and potent medicines—and a formula for an alchemic process said to have the poten-tial to reanimate the dead.

In France, René becomes not only the greatest perfumer in the country, but also the most dangerous, creating deadly poisons for his Queen to use against her rivals. But while mixing herbs and essences under the light of flickering candles, René doesn't begin to imag-ine the tragic and personal consequences for which his lethal potions will be responsible.

Paris, France—The Present:

A renowned mythologist, Jac L'Etoile—trying to recover from personal heartache by throw-ing herself into her work—learns of the sixteenth-century perfumer who may have been working on an elixir that would unlock the secret to immortality. She becomes obsessed with René le

Florentin's work—particularly when she discovers the dying breaths he had collected during his lifetime.

Jac's efforts put her in the path of her estranged lover, Griffin North, a linguist who has already begun translating René le Flo-rentin's mysterious formula. Together they confront an eccentric heiress in possession of a world-class art collection, a woman who has her own dark purpose for the elixir . . . for which she believes the ends will justify her deadly means.

This mesmerizing gothic tale zigzags from the violent days of Catherine de Medici's court to twenty-first-century France. Fiery and lush, set against deep, wild forests and dimly lit cha-teaus, *The Collector of Dying Breaths* illuminates the true path to immortality: the legacies we leave behind.

"Rose masterfully combines romance, mystery, and dual timelines...The storyline and extensive historical details...are fascinating." *(Romantic Times (**** ½ STARS TOP PICK))*

"Mysterious, magical, and mythical...what a joy to read!" *(Sara Gruen, New York Times bestselling author of Water for Elephants)*

"History, mystery, ambition, lust, love, death and the timeless quest for immortality...a riveting tale of suspense." *(B.A.Shapiro, New York Times bestselling author of The Art Forger)*

"From the labyrinthine alleyways of 16th century Paris to the danger-infused woodlands of 21st century Fontainebleau, M. J. Rose has crafted a superb, mesmerizing tale of two people separated by centuries yet linked by a haunting secret. Poison, obsession and undying love have never been so enticing—or so lethal. I could not stop reading it!" *(C.W. Gortner, author of The Confessions of Catherine de Medici)*

"With an alchemist's skill, M.J. Rose mixes present and past with the dark scent of love and an intricate mystery, creating a blend that is splendidly, spookily magical." *(Susanna Kearsley, New York Times bestselling author)*

"M.J. Rose masterfully serves up suspense with generous sides of philosophy and intrigue. I devoured this fascinating tale about Catherine de Medici and her perfumer simmered with the compelling modern-day story of an intelligent woman in search of personal completion. Alchemy, mythology, and an exploration of reincarnation lace this tantalizing telling. A lavish and satisfying banquet of a book!" *(Lynn Cullen, bestselling author of Mrs. Poe)*

Chapter 1
March 1, 1573 BarBizon, France

Written for my son to read upon my death, from his father, René le Florentin, perfumer to catherine de Medici, Queen Mother.

It is with irony now, forty years later, to think that if I had not been called a murderer on the most frightening night of my life, there might not be any perfume in Paris today. And that scent—to which I gave my all and which gave me all the power and riches I could have hoped for—is at the heart of why now it is *I* who call myself a murderer.

It is one thing to fall in love with a rose and its deep rich scent. once the blood-red flower blooms, browns and decays and its smell has dissipated, you can pluck another rose about to bloom. But to fall in love with a woman after a lifetime of not knowing love? In the browning of your own days? Ah, that is to invite disaster. That is to invite heartbreak.

The château is cold tonight, but my skin burns. My blood flows hot. Who knew that yearning alone could heat a man so? That only memories could set him on fire? I feel this pen in my fingers, the feather's smoothness, and I imagine it is Isabeau's hair.

I close my eyes and see her standing before me.

Isabeau! exuberant, tender, dazzling. And mine. I see her sap- phire eyes twinkling. Her thick mane of hair like a blanket for me to hide in.

I whisper to her and ask her to undress for me slowly, in that way she had. And she does. In the dream she does. She strips bare, slowly, slowly, of everything but her gloves, cream kid gloves that stretch above her elbows. Her silken skin gleams in the candlelight, golden and smooth, smelling of exotic flowers. Gardenias and camellias and roses, scents that emanate from within. This is her secret and mine. Isabeau had a garden inside of her body. Flowers where other women had organs. Her own natural perfume richer and more luxurious than anything I ever could have created and bottled.

In this dream, Isabeau never takes off her gloves. Night after night, I beseech her to strip all the way for me, but she just smiles. *Not yet, René. Not yet.* And then she reaches out with one gloved finger and traces her name on my skin. *One day, René. Once you have found the elixir.*

I dream this asleep. And hear it, awake, in the wind. Her promise.

Once you have found the elixir.

I lie there, sweating into my nightshirt. Trembling from the memories.

There was something about the way the bell rang that first day she came to my shop. Its tone was different, almost tentative, as if it wasn't sure it should be ringing at all. Now, looking back, were the fates warning me? How cruel of those witches to give me love at that moment—after a lifetime of holding it back.

But I will have my revenge on them. I, Renato Bianco, known as René le Florentin, will figure out how to reanimate a dying breath and so wreak havoc for their folly. So help me God, this I will work at until I have no more of my own breath in my body.

Winter is upon us now, and it is quiet here in the woods and for- ests of Fontainebleau. The days stretch before me, an endless vista of foggy mornings and chilly evenings and dark nights devoted to one thing and one thing only: my experiments. If I cannot succeed with them, I cannot, I will not, go on with my life.

It was one man who heard the bell ring to the shop and opened the door, and another who closed it. That was how long it took for Isabeau to alter me. And it is the me who is altered who has this need for revenge on the crones who have done this to me.

Let me tell you first about the man who heard the bell.

About Shayla Black

Shayla Black (aka Shelley Bradley) is the New York Times and USA Today bestselling author of over 40 sizzling contemporary, erotic, paranormal, and historical romances produced via traditional, small press, independent, and audio publishing. She lives in Texas with her husband, munchkin, and one very spoiled cat. In her "free" time, she enjoys reality TV, reading and listening to an eclectic blend of music.

Shayla's books have been translated in about a dozen languages. RT Bookclub has nominated her for a Career Achievement award in erotic romance, twice nominated her for Best Erotic Romance of the year, as well as awarded her several Top Picks, and a KISS Hero Award. She has also received or been nominated for The Passionate Plume, The Holt Medallion, Colorado Romance Writers Award of Excellence, and the National Reader's Choice Awards.

A writing risk-taker, Shayla enjoys tackling writing challenges with every new book.

Connect with Shayla online:

Facebook: www.facebook.com/ShaylaBlackAuthor
Twitter: www.twitter.com/@shayla_black
Website: www.shaylablack.com

About Lexi Blake

Lexi Blake lives in North Texas with her husband, three kids, and the laziest rescue dog in the world. She began writing at a young age, concentrating on plays and journalism. It wasn't until she started writing romance that she found success. She likes to find humor in the strangest places. Lexi believes in happy endings no matter how odd the couple, threesome or foursome may seem. She also writes contemporary Western ménage as Sophie Oak.

Connect with Lexi online:

Facebook: Lexi Blake
Twitter: twitter.com/authorlexiblake
Website: www.LexiBlake.net

Sign up for Lexi's newsletter at www.lexiblake.net.

Also from Shayla Black and Lexi Blake

Masters Of Ménage
Their Virgin Captive
Their Virgin's Secret
Their Virgin Concubine
Their Virgin Princess
Their Virgin Hostage
Their Virgin Secretary

Also from Shayla Black/Shelley Bradley

EROTIC ROMANCE

THE WICKED LOVERS
Wicked Ties
Decadent
Delicious
Surrender To Me
Belong To Me
"Wicked to Love" (e-novella)
Mine To Hold
"Wicked All The Way" (e-novella)
Ours To Love
Wicked and Dangerous
Forever Wicked
Theirs To Cherish

SEXY CAPERS
Bound And Determined
Strip Search
"Arresting Desire" – Hot In Handcuffs Anthology

DOMS OF HER LIFE
One Dom To Love
The Young And The Submissive

STAND ALONE
Naughty Little Secret (as Shelley Bradley)
"Watch Me" – Sneak Peek Anthology (as Shelley Bradley)
Dangerous Boys And Their Toy
"Her Fantasy Men" – Four Play Anthology

PARANORMAL ROMANCE

THE DOOMSDAY BRETHREN
Tempt Me With Darkness
"Fated" (e-novella)
Seduce Me In Shadow
Possess Me At Midnight
"Mated" – Haunted By Your Touch Anthology
Entice Me At Twilight
Embrace Me At Dawn

HISTORICAL ROMANCE
(as Shelley Bradley)

The Lady And The Dragon
One Wicked Night
Strictly Seduction
Strictly Forbidden

CONTEMPORARY ROMANCE
(as Shelley Bradley)

A Perfect Match

Also from Lexi Blake

EROTIC ROMANCE

Masters And Mercenaries
The Dom Who Loved Me
The Men With The Golden Cuffs
A Dom Is Forever
On Her Master's Secret Service
Sanctum: A Masters and Mercenaries Novella
Love and Let Die
Unconditional: A Masters and Mercenaries Novella
Dungeon Royale
Dungeon Games: A Masters and Mercenaries Novella,
Coming May 13, 2014
A View to a Thrill, *Coming August 19, 2014*

CONTEMPORARY WESTERN ROMANCE

Wild Western Nights
Leaving Camelot, *Coming Soon*

URBAN FANTASY

Thieves
Steal the Light
Steal the Day
Steal the Moon
Steal the Sun
Steal the Night, Coming June 3, 2014

CPSIA information can be obtained at www.ICGtesting.com
Printed in the USA
BVOW07s0135080914

365721BV00001B/36/P